THE LOST MANILA FOLDER

DANIELA GLATTFELDER

First paperback edition December 2023
Cover by Lou Designs

ISBN 978-1-7384660-1-6 (paperback)
ISBN 978-1-7384660-0-9 (ebook)

Published by Daniela Glattfelder
www.danielaglattfelder.co.uk

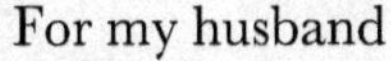

For my husband

Prologue

Madrid, Spain
1931

He threw the newspaper on the table, startling his wife and causing her to spill her coffee over the white tablecloth.

'Whatever has gotten into you?' she asked.

'This!' he said, pointing at the headline on the front page of the newspaper as he slumped into his chair. She glanced at the headline that had made her husband so furious on this fine morning.

'Why would he call for municipal elections?' his son asked confused. 'Surely he must know the Republicans and Socialists will win and oust him.'

'Exactly, son.' Despite the gravity of the situation a smile appeared across his face. At least his beloved boy took an interest in the political climate and understood the implications of an anti-monarchy government.

'Whoever wins, the King will protect us,' she said with a flick of her hand, closing the subject. Felipe opened his mouth but said nothing. There was no point in bursting her bubble, his dear wife was not aware of the state of their country and what it could mean for their family.

'Mother, when they win they will most likely request the king to abdicate and leave the country. We will be in danger too!'

'Xulián! That's enough!' Felipe reprimanded his son as he saw the worry on his wife's face.

'But father, you…'

'I said, enough!' He gave him a warning look that stopped Xulián in his tracks. It was rare that his father raised his voice but he understood. Scraping his chair back he left the parlour. The news had not shocked him – he knew the military would withdraw their support of the monarchy – but he was surprised at how fast everything was happening and it made him angry how politically unstable their country was. He wanted a second republic, he wanted the reforms the Republicans promised but the violence on the streets worried him. His mother didn't seem to understand the significance of the elections because her privileged upbringing prevented her from seeing the truth and what it would mean for the future of the monarchy. But Xulián knew this was the beginning of the end of the life they knew.

One

London, England
2014

Ava stood in front of her bedroom mirror trying on a series of outfits, hoping to find one that would suit the evening's event. A pile of discarded clothes deemed unsuitable lay on the floor next to her. She was invited to her best friend Lucy's company summer party as her plus one and, judging by last year's party, it would be such a glamorous affair that not even her finest dress would do. As always, she decided to settle for her trusted £50 black Ted Baker dress she had bought in last year's sale and worn to nearly every fancy party since. It wasn't that she didn't dress stylishly – if one considered slim-cut suits and a nice top stylish – but her clothes weren't fancy. Despite working in the events industry, her job mainly entailed off-site organising and being connected through walkie-talkies rather than being the actual hostess of the events. Therefore, comfort came above style. She wondered if she could still duck out of going and instead chill on the tiny couch she shared with her flatmates in a North London flat. As she reached for her phone to tell Lucy she wasn't feeling well (solely to protect her from having to spend the evening with a miserable friend), a message popped up. Speak of the devil, she thought. Lucy was letting her know that she wasn't allowed to drop out, that she was wearing a light blue wrap-around dress, and that they were meeting at 6.30 pm on the platform at Camden Town Station. Her friend had just proven her mind-reading skills again and Ava was left with no choice but to accept she would have to attend the party. She put on her only pair of high heels and touched up the make-up she had applied almost two hours ago. It was one of those rare days she was home on a Saturday and had ample time to mope around the flat, do some chores and agonise over her event attire predicament. None of her corporate clients had planned an event for today. Companies knew not to organise staff parties on Saturdays; who willingly gave up their weekend only to spend it with the same people they had to endure the rest of the week? No one was the answer! Clearly, Lucy's company didn't get the memo.

'Lucy, Lucy,' Ava shouted along the platform, having stood on the other side for almost ten minutes until she remembered that Camden had two platforms running south and they hadn't agreed exactly where to meet.

'You look gorgeous,' Lucy exclaimed as she hugged her friend and kissed her on the cheek. Ava knew she would say the same thing even if she had turned up in ripped jeans and a hoodie. Lucy, on the other hand, did indeed look stunning. The light blue dress complemented her blue eyes beautifully and hugged her figure in just the right places, highlighting her tiny waist. They had known each other since they were two years old and were inseparable from the beginning. Ava grew up in a small village close to Watford with her mum. Her grandparents lived nearby. Her father died when she was five and she had no siblings. They went to school together throughout their childhood and teenage years. When it was time to go to university, Lucy and Ava chose the same one in Leeds, where Lucy studied International Business and Finance and Ava did a degree in Business Management with Marketing. After years of partying and some studying on the side, they moved to London together to start their professional careers. Lucy was like the sister Ava never had.

The tube to Morden arrived and they got on, having to stand amongst myriad tourists returning to their hotels after a shopping trip to Camden Lock. 'Why do all tourists love going to Camden on a Saturday? I hate it,' Ava whispered to Lucy, who rolled her eyes at her.

'Cheer up, love. This party is going to be amazing. They pulled out all the stops and spent a fortune on the best catering and entertainment. I heard through the grapevine that Jim Morrison will be there!' Lucy said excitedly.

'Luce, Jim Morrison is dead, you do know that, don't you?'

'Oh, is he? What's his name then, the guy who sang "I'm yours"? Wasn't that Jim Morrison?'

Ava shook her head: 'No, he was in The Doors, died sometime in the seventies. You mean Jason Mraz.'

'That's the one! Anyway, he'll be there and I can't wait to see him!' Did anyone still listen to Jason Mraz in 2014, Ava wondered.

Lucy chatted about an ex-work colleague who threatened he was going to turn up at the party despite being unwelcome after a scandal that ended his career. 'He was a high-flying stockbroker with a promising career but couldn't keep his hands to himself. There was hardly a single woman in the company who hadn't seen his penis,' she informed Ava. 'Unfortunately, once only married women were left he had to find another hunting ground and went for the wife of one of his clients. It didn't take long for her husband to find out, and he threatened to sue the firm if they didn't fire him. No one knows what happened to him though someone mentioned he left for Manchester to try his luck there, whilst others are convinced he fled the country altogether.' Ava was only half-listening; Lucy's company was the kind she would never want to work for, where some people thought with higher pay and seniority came such power they were untouchable. Served that guy right that he got found out, Ava thought.

'Why did all those women sleep with him? Don't they have any self-respect?' Lucy rolled her eyes.

'I knew you'd say that, but not everyone is like you. Some women are attracted by power and wealth. Anyway, this hot guy started working in the European team. He's Spanish and only just moved to London, so I'm hooking you two up today,' Lucy winked.

'You know I don't have time for anyone in my life, Luce'. It was true, she really didn't have any time for romance anymore. With her working hours being as crazy as they were, especially at the moment during one of her company's busiest seasons apart from Christmas, she spent most of her spare time catching up on sleep.

'You always say that, but when was the last time you had a date? And I mean with an actual man, not one of your rom-coms and a tub of ice cream on your couch!' raising an eyebrow with a knowing smirk, Lucy was sure she had made her point.

'It's our stop,' Ava ignored Lucy, grabbing her arm to pull her off the train just as the annoyingly impatient people tried to push their way onto the tube without letting anyone off first. Making their way to the escalator, Ava hoped she had escaped Lucy's inquisition into her sex life, or lack thereof, but she was wrong.

'Back to my point, you need to get out there and have fun. You're only young once and could have date after date with your looks if you wanted to,' Lucy continued, not prepared to let Ava off the hook just yet. Lucy had always been a bit jealous of Ava's looks but, at the same time, annoyed Ava didn't make more out of herself. 'If I were you...' were the most uttered words in Lucy's vocabulary when it came to clothes, make-up, men and sex. She couldn't understand why Ava preferred wearing jeans and a plain t-shirt on her days off and tying her hair back in a bun.

'If I were you...' here we go, Ava rolled her eyes and sighed, 'I'd put on some make-up, wear a little black dress, and hit the clubs every weekend,' Lucy continued despite Ava's obvious annoyance.

'Luce, promise me you won't set me up with someone from your company tonight. Please. I don't even speak Spanish,' Ava said, looking at Lucy pleadingly.

'I'm going to introduce you to some colleagues, that's all. You can't stop me doing that but then it's over to you to decide what you want to do next,' Lucy said before she gave her name at the door to Sky Garden and they were ushered into a lift to take them to the top floor. The venue was stunning, beautifully decorated with a tropical summer vibe, sand, palm trees, little cabanas to relax in, and far too many inflatable beach balls. With a glass of champagne in hand, they headed to the windows of the far-right corner of the lower floor, which overlooked the River Thames, all the way to the London Eye. Ava smiled at the view, her favourite city at her feet. Clinking glasses with Lucy, Ava took a big sip of the golden liquid. It bubbled in her mouth and left a fuzzy feeling in her head. 'Let's find some food. I haven't eaten much today and don't want to end up drunk,' Ava said. As she did so, she noticed Lucy's glass was still full.

'That's an excellent idea since you'll be drinking my drinks too,' Lucy said, swapping her full glass with Ava's empty one.

'Why would I want to have your drinks?'

'Because…' Lucy quickly glanced at her belly and into Ava's widening eyes.

'Lucy, are you preggers?'

'Shhh, keep your voice down.'

'How, who, when and, most importantly, when did you find out and why are you only telling me now?'

'I don't think I have to explain the how, do I?' Lucy giggled whilst Ava was still recovering from the shock revelation. 'Do you remember Mike, the guy I went out with and who took me to Portugal on that romantic weekend?'

'Cheating Mike?' Ava felt like someone had slapped her. Surely her friend was not having a baby with the guy who seemed too good to be true, charming and romantic, and then turned out to be the most notorious cheater she had ever met. While he was away with Lucy in the Algarve, three other girls he'd been seeing bumped into each other in front of his flat. They all wanted to surprise him with chicken soup and movies because he felt poorly. Or so they thought. It didn't take them long to realise what was really going on.

'Yes, him,' Lucy sighed. 'I know, I know… you don't have to say it. I only found out a few days ago after having felt sick every morning for the last few weeks. But I didn't want to give you an excuse not to come tonight. So please just let me enjoy this party. I'll figure out what to do later.' Lucy looked at Ava with pleading eyes as if she was about to cry. Or maybe that was just the disco ball reflecting in her eyes.

'Okay, I'll have your drinks for you, but don't accept too many. You know I can't handle my drink!' Lucy nodded, relieved.

'When will you tell Mike?' Although it was not the right place to have such a conversation, Ava wanted to know and she had Lucy at a point where she was providing answers. She had to take this rare opportunity to get as much information out of her as possible. To be fair, it seemed like Lucy wanted to talk about it, so Ava was doing her a favour by asking.

'I'm not sure I will be telling him.' Ava gasped but was silenced by Lucy's hand before she could object. 'Ava, you know how important my career is to me. I'm not even sure if I want to keep this baby. Mike and I are over for obvious reasons and I am not prepared to be a single mum and give up everything I have worked for. I ought to think about my options first,' Lucy stated matter-of-factly before turning towards the window. Ava knew the conversation was finished and not to be revisited until Lucy wanted to.

The party was in full swing, everyone seemingly enjoying themselves, many taking full advantage of the free bar while others were still on their first pint discussing the latest football results as a musician took to the stage. Ava hid a giggle when she saw Lucy's face drop – it wasn't Jason Mraz, the guy was at least half a century older! But her amusement was short-lived when, moments later, Lucy swung around and announced, 'Ava, I'd like to introduce you to our newest recruit.' Lucy pulled her towards a tall, good-looking man with a mop of dark brown hair. 'Diego, this is my friend, Ava.'

'Hello, Ava, nice to meet you.' Lucy had got one thing right: he was handsome. And Ava sensed that he was well aware of it. She made up her mind to steer well clear of him but she thought she may as well at least enjoy looking at him tonight. Was there any harm in that? No, she decided.

'Can I get you ladies another drink?' Diego asked and, once in receipt of their order, pushed through to the bar.

'Urgh, I hate men who say "ladies"'! It sounds so disparaging. As if he needed to point out specifically that we are women!' Ava grumbled at Lucy, who seemed amused by her friend's little outburst.

'Give him a break! I think it's adorable and shows he has manners despite English not being his first language. I think you two would get on really well and you're not getting any younger!' Lucy reprimanded Ava.

'Thank you for reminding me,' Ava scowled as she gave her friend a slight slap on her arm.

Diego returned with two glasses of champagne and started talking to Lucy about work. 'Apologies, Ava, tell me something about yourself,' he said as he turned towards her and fixed his gaze on her with his deep brown eyes.

'There's not much to tell, really,' Ava started, 'I'm an event manager, live with three girls in a flatshare and I'm an only child.'

'I'm sure there's more.' Diego glanced at her empty glass and swiftly replaced it with a new one from the tray of a passing waiter. Ava could see an open bar and a friend who wasn't drinking wouldn't mix well for her. Looking at his expectant face, she told him about an embarrassing moment that had happened at work. Once she got her tongue stuck to an ice sculpture of Adonis at one of the events she had organised and had to text her colleague at the office to get them to call the caterer for help. Instead of saving Ava from her predicament as fast as possible, he decided to call over his colleagues who were setting up the buffet. As they were all having a jolly good laugh and took numerous photos that trended on Instagram with the hashtags #deliciousAdonis and #workfails, Ava was sure her career was over. Luckily, her client was more amused than angry and she was let off the hook. Diego had a deep, sexy laugh, and although Lucy had heard the story a million times before, it still cracked her up. While they were laughing about Ava, she stood there wondering what it was about this man that made her immediately share something embarrassing and personal. She realised she was either drunker than she thought and had lost her filter or something about the way he looked at her made her feel safe. Lucy handed Ava her glass and told her she was going to the toilet. Before Ava had registered what Lucy had said she had vanished among the growing crowd dancing around the stage. Ava downed both glasses in quick succession and then placed the empty flutes on the tray of a passing waiter. As she did so, Diego grabbed her hand and led her through to the middle of the dance floor.

Bobbing away to Las Ketchup's "Asereje", Ava was enjoying herself so much she didn't notice Lucy had returned until she had given Ava a quick peck on the cheek and said: 'I'll call you tomorrow'. Unsure if it was the deafening music or her alcohol-infused brain, Ava only half-registered Lucy's departure as she noticed how close Diego had come to her. She felt his breath on her neck and smelt his spicy aftershave. Their bodies moving in sync with the music, she felt free and sexy and wanted to stay in the moment forever.

Two

The distant ringing of "Call Me Maybe" woke Ava. She tried to grab her phone from her bedside table with her head still firmly on the pillow, eyes closed, but instead, her hand made contact with a glass and knocked it over. Opening her eyes slowly, she found the empty glass on the floor, wondering since when she had carpet in her room. Her head was throbbing and the bright sunshine was hurting her eyes. There was a knock on the door before it opened just a crack, enough for Diego's head to peek in. '*Buenos días*, I have coffee for you,' he said. Ava tried to sit up, but noticing she was only wearing her underwear, she quickly pulled the duvet cover up to her head. It was slowly dawning on her that this was not her room and, thus, not her bed either. If only her head wasn't hurting so badly, she could string a few words together to ask what happened last night. All she managed was a weak 'Thank you'. Diego put the coffee on the chest of drawers next to the door and told her he'd be back in five minutes to give her time to get sorted. 'As if five minutes will be enough to sort this mess out,' she mumbled to herself.

The smell of fresh coffee wafted towards her, making her stomach churn. She thought about taking a sip – maybe it was what her body needed. She crawled to the other side of the bed towards the chest of drawers and lifted the mug to her lips. The pungent aroma was too much for her, so she put it down again. No, it wasn't going to do, she wanted a proper cup of tea. Her phone pinged as a message came through. 'Oh god, what have I done?' she asked herself as she looked around to find it; her dress was in a heap at one end of the room, her shoes and purse at the other. Having successfully located her phone, she tried to read the message but the screen was too bright for her delicate eyes. Ava grabbed her dress and threw it on before the bedroom door opened again after a short knock as Diego returned. The five minutes to sort herself out were over. Diego spotted the coffee, raising an eyebrow. 'No?' was all he said. Ava apologised that she couldn't stomach the coffee right now but maybe a tea would be okay and so he took the mug, turned around and closed the door again. Telling herself to get her act together, she opened a door to what she hoped might be an ensuite bathroom – surely the flat of a wealthy banker would have an ensuite. Ava looked a state – her eyeliner was smudged under her eyes, her faded red lipstick was all over the place, and her long auburn hair was sticking out on all sides. Searching for some contact lens solution, she opened the bathroom mirror and tidied herself up, using toilet paper to remove the smudges around her eyes and lips, and running her wet hands through her hair. 'What have you done, Ava? This is not like you at all!' she thought to herself, addressing the woman with the green eyes staring back at her from within the mirror, shaking her head. Feeling a little more normal, Ava returned to the bedroom, opened the window and threw the duvet back to air. 'No need to lose my manners and knickers at the same time,' she said to herself before grabbing her shoes and purse. It was a chic and modern flat with colourful art hanging from the white walls that looked more expensive than Ava's rent, minimalist furniture and a couch that appeared to have never been used. Diego was sitting at an equally modern table with his phone, smiling up at Ava and passing her a cup of tea as she approached. The sun shone through the window behind him, brightening up the lofty space and providing Diego with a tiny halo. Ava looked at her companion of last night and tried to think of a way she could delicately ask him what had happened. No one liked to have sex and not remember, and even worse was having to admit to said one-night stand that they had no recollection of the night. Taking a sip of her tea, she looked up at Diego and said, 'So, last night was fun'.

He smiled again – the same smile that betrayed that he knew it was fun, he made sure it was fun, and he had seen her naked body. 'Yes, last night was entertaining. I enjoyed it,' he confirmed. Ava had a sinking feeling that her suspicions were correct. 'Until you passed out on my shoulder in the lift when we left the party and I had to hold you up,' he continued.

'Oh, I don't remember that part,' Ava admitted ashamedly, the heat rising to her cheeks.

'I'm not surprised,' Diego continued, 'you had so much to drink last night you didn't even realise Lucy had left.' She had of course noticed but didn't see the point in correcting him.

'So if I passed out, how did I end up here?' Confusion spread across Ava's face as she looked at him while going through everything in her mind.

'I called you a taxi but you were asleep when it arrived. I didn't know where you lived, so I took you home with me and let you sleep here,' he grinned. 'And no, nothing happened between us. I slept on the sofa.' Relief flooded her body.

'Thank you,' was all Ava could mutter, horrified that she had been so out of it that she couldn't remember. Anything could've happened had it not been for Diego and him taking care of her. It seemed Lucy was right and he did indeed have good manners, although she also suddenly realised that, had it not been for Lucy, she wouldn't have ended up in a stranger's bed in the first place.

After all, she was the one who made her drink more than she could handle and then left without taking her best friend with her.

'Do you want anything to eat? I don't have any food but there is a great breakfast place around the corner we could go to.' Diego cut into her thoughts. Ava looked at him, thinking all she wanted to do was go home and lie in her bed, pull the duvet right over her head and not resurface until Monday morning, or preferably never. But she also recognised what Diego had done for her last night. His back was probably killing him from his having to sleep on the couch, and he must be in a pretty bad state himself, she thought to herself. Though thinking about it, Ava couldn't recall a single moment last night when he was drinking. Did she just miss it because she was too drunk to realise or had he stayed sober? Either way, she owed him big time. The least she could do was take him up on his offer of breakfast.

'Sounds good to me,' she replied and with that they made their way to the little café Diego had recommended. He was dressed impeccably in brown chinos and a navy blue t-shirt that outlined his muscular body underneath. She was still in the same dress she wore last night, shoes that were killing her the moment she put them back on and last night's make-up. What a sight she must be, she thought.

They ordered two buttermilk chicken waffles with extra bacon and maple syrup that, according to Diego, would cure Ava's hangover. The food was delicious and Ava started to recover somewhat. After swallowing the last bite, she let out a satisfied sigh as she slumped back in her seat.

Diego grinned, having finished his waffles too. 'I said it was good.'

'Shame it's already over though,' Ava replied with a sad face. She caught the waitress' eye and paid the bill – in spite of vehement protestations from Diego. 'Seriously, after all you did for me last night, this is the least I can do,' Ava insisted.

'Well, maybe we should do this again sometime,' Diego replied as they walked to the exit.

Ava nodded distractedly. Her phone showed several missed calls from her mum and an unknown number, as well as a few messages. She remembered being woken up by her phone ringing and it dawned on her that she was supposed to meet her mum for brunch and some shopping. 'Shit,' she muttered under her breath while she started reading the first few messages.

'Is everything okay, Ava?' Diego asked, concerned.

'Yes, yes, everything is fine,' she said. She did not want to make him feel guilty for taking her for brunch, so she told him she needed to go and call her mum back. She gave him a quick hug and said 'Thank you' before turning in the opposite direction to his flat and hurriedly walking away. If only she had read those messages when she woke up or answered her phone she might've only been a bit late to meet her mum, but she was now so late it was inexcusable. Most messages contained the obvious question of where she was and if she forgot they were supposed to meet. Then there was a longer one, the last one, in which her mum quite accurately put two and two together, assuming she must've had a good night and was now either tidying up from the party or wiped out in bed. She said she would drive to the shopping centre and start looking for a dress, and as soon as her beloved daughter woke up they could meet for brunch. 'Shit, shit, shit,' Ava swore while clicking the star button on her phone for her favourites and dialling her mum's number. The phone went straight to voicemail. Ava left a message saying she was getting ready and she should let her know where she currently was. Ava looked at the time on her phone and realised her mum might've already gone home again since they were due to meet more than three hours ago. She decided to go home, get changed and go to her childhood home to apologise in person. She checked the fastest route home and then set off, but Ava kept wondering why she had so many missed calls from an unknown number. Did she give it to someone in her drunken state yesterday and couldn't remember, or was it one of those scam callers who try to convince people that they've been in a car accident and are entitled to compensation? Probably the latter or they'd call again if it was important, she decided. She messaged Lucy, hoping she knew more about everything that happened last night, including why she left her at the party alone. Maybe the early pregnancy hormones had made Lucy forget about her best friend, she pondered.

As she made her way back to her tiny flat in Camden, Ava hoped that no one else was home or at least that nobody was blocking the bathroom as was so often the case when she was in a rush. The three people she shared the flat on the third floor of a terraced house with she got on with but wasn't overly close to. It used to be different, though. Back in the early days after she finished university, she lived with Lucy and two other girls. They spent the best part of two years hanging out together, going on boozy nights out and then catching up over the latest episodes of their favourite television series while eating pizza from Domino's – Lucy had always insisted they were the best and wouldn't have any other – to cure their self-inflicted hangovers. But after Sara left to move in with her boyfriend, Lauren decided she preferred the North to the South and returned to Manchester, leaving only Lucy and Ava in the flat. They hoped they could find two new flatmates and continue in the same vein, living life to the fullest and not caring about any adult problems. But Hannah, one of the two new flatmates, was rarely home due to her boyfriend and her 'real friends'. And then there was Ian. He was nice enough when he viewed the room and the best option they had had after it turned out not many young people were prepared to pay the rent for the room that wasn't even big enough to swing a cat. But the moment Ian moved in, he changed. He went from a funny, talkative young man to constantly stoned, never tidying up after himself and leaving his belongings lying around. It wasn't a surprise when one Saturday Lucy tripped over his bike that he had dumped in the living room and broke her arm after Lucy and Ava returned from a drunken night out. They spent three hours together at the Accident and Emergency department, which gave Lucy ample time to complain about Ian and make it clear that if he didn't move out immediately, she would. Of course, Ava wanted her to stay so she promised to talk to Ian the next day. As if he had known what was coming, Ian wasn't to be seen all day on Sunday. Ava had sent him a message that they needed to talk when he was back. But he stayed away, and when Lucy got home from work the next day, she announced she was moving in with her boyfriend, Harry, as they had decided to take the next step in their relationship. He also lived closer to the City where she worked. And that was that. Lucy moved her belongings out during the week, and when Ava had returned home on Friday evening, not only was Lucy's room empty but also Ian's room had been cleared. Ava couldn't shake the feeling that Lucy had secretly looked for a reason to move out and had just used the incident with Ian's bike as the driving factor because had she waited just a few more days the whole situation with Ian resolved itself. Ava then came to realise that she had been holding on to the good times she had shared with Lucy, Sara and Hannah after uni. It started to sink in that those days were gone and, while her friends had moved on and got decent jobs, partners and a plan for the future, she was still trying to come to terms with the fact that she was stuck in an unhappy life and was the only one who wasn't moving on. She had vowed to herself that she wouldn't rely on others anymore and was the one who held the key to her happiness. She was determined to sort her life out.

The bus pulled up at her stop. Ava dragged herself off, hardly able to walk in her shoes any longer but as she urgently wanted to get back to meet her mum she almost ran home. Turning into her street, Ava noticed a police car next to her flatmate's battered Fiat Punto, another neighbour undoubtedly having called the police over a row with someone.

'Miss Brown?' a deep male voice behind her asked as she unlocked the door. Surprised, Ava spun round to see a police officer walking towards her while another officer was getting out of the car she had noticed before.

'Yes,' she answered, wearily. What has she done, Ava pondered? Why were the police waiting outside her house on a Sunday and why did they look at her as if they pitied her? Was her appearance that shocking? They must have seen worse on weekends on the streets of London.

'Miss Brown, we would like to talk to you. May we come in?' the officer continued. Usually, Ava wouldn't let strangers into her home but even fake police trying to scam you wouldn't turn up in a police car, would they?

Ava led the way up and into the flat, now praying there was no one home to witness her being accompanied by police officers. Luckily, the apartment was empty, and judging by the coats missing on the hooks by the door, her flatmates were either out again or hadn't even got home yet.

'Please take a seat, Miss Brown. I'm PC Boden and this is PC Stewart,' the other officer announced. Stepping forward and taking her hat off, the second officer said with a solemn expression on her face, 'Miss Brown, we have to inform you that there has been a fatal road accident involving your mother, Mrs Rose Brown. Unfortunately, there was nothing the paramedics could do. We are very sorry for your loss.' Out of nowhere, a glass of water was handed to Ava, who just stared at PC Stewart sitting beside her on the couch. Her face was as pale as a sheet of paper, her mind trying to make sense of the words coming out of the officer's mouth. 'We know this is a shock to you, and we have a specialist team who will help you through this difficult time.' In a trancelike state, Ava got up from the sofa and stumbled to the bathroom, where she threw up the dregs of last night's drinking and this morning's breakfast into the toilet. The cold bathroom floor was a welcome relief to her throbbing head as she lay down, hoping it was all a dream. The sound of traffic and beeping car horns from outside brought her back to the present as the enormity of what she had just been told slowly began to register.

A knock on the door reminded her of the police presence in her flat. A voice asked if she needed anything and whom they could contact for support. But Ava's mind was blank. The only person she needed was her mum. In disbelief, she took her phone out of her purse and pressed redial. The call went straight to voicemail. She tried again. And again. Maybe she had her phone on silent mode, or it was still in her handbag after returning from her shopping trip and she couldn't hear it. Or were the police correct? A cry emanated from deep within her, which alerted the officers. The door opened and she felt an arm around her. Ava couldn't remember how long she sat in the bathroom with the officer's arm around her, sobbing into her uniform. Eventually, they moved her to the sofa and put a steaming hot cup of tea in front of her. The specially trained officer held her hands and explained she was there to help Ava with the grieving process and all the legal formalities. Words like investigation, identifying the body, and police station floated into Ava's ear but didn't quite make it through to her brain to be processed. In the meantime, the officers managed to get a name from Ava and Lucy arrived shortly after, her soft voice muffled by the pillow Ava held over her ear, trying to block out everyone and everything. The officers left Ava in her care and left.

Lucy wrapped her friend in a tight embrace as the tears kept flowing uncontrollably after turning on the telly for some background noise. Ava insisted on showing Lucy the last few messages her mum had sent her, knowing she would now never be able to apologise for forgetting to meet her. Would her mum still be alive if they had spent the day together as planned and left the shopping centre later? The thought that her mum might still be alive if Ava had turned up as agreed suddenly hit her with such magnitude that for a moment she stopped breathing. Ava realised she was the reason her mum was dead.

After the initial shock had abated, anger slowly grew inside Ava. How was this fair, she kept asking herself. Her mum had only just survived breast cancer and was given the all-clear by her doctor a few weeks ago. The dress they were going to buy was to celebrate new beginnings, but without any warning she was so cruelly ripped out of her life. Worn out from the countless thoughts that had been running through her head and having shed every tear she had, Ava fell asleep to the sound of Paul Hollywood's voice telling a baker his tart had a soggy bottom.

***

On a beautiful day without a cloud in the sky, many people gathered to mourn Mary-Rose Brown. The doors to the village church, which was filled with white lilies, were left open during the service, and as friends and acquaintances continued to arrive, not everyone found a seat. Rose, as her mum preferred to be called, was buried next to her parents, Andrew and Elizabeth Brown, in the immaculate graveyard surrounded by a stone wall with a little water feature in the middle. Many of her parents' old friends attended the funeral, still in shock over the loss of such a pillar of the community. Her whole life, Rose worked in the nursing home up on the hill. She was loved and appreciated by everyone. Wherever she went, she carried a beautiful smile on her lips and her laugh that sounded like a squeaky mouse was so infectious it brightened everyone's day. The community was what kept her going when her husband died and she was left to take of a child by herself whilst also maintaining a full-time job looking after the elderly. The residents would give Rose sweets they usually kept for their visiting families to take home to Ava. They would ask Rose to bring her daughter to work every day and, although they promised to look after her, Rose never quite trusted them to keep her daughter from getting up to mischief. And after a long day's work, she didn't fancy a child bouncing up and down on her bed high on the sugar the residents would have given her. So it was her parents who mostly looked after Ava during the years when she wasn't at school. When at the age of 39 Rose had brought Ava into this world everyone instantly adored the little redhead with the cheeky grin.

Dressed in black at the front of the church, Ava was grateful for the same community that now helped her through the most challenging time of her life. She hadn't been to the house often since that fateful day and had still been a shadow of herself when her mum's neighbour Katherine had called to offer her help in organising the funeral and supporting Ava with all that needed to be done. Kate, as everyone called her, and Rose weren't only neighbours but became best friends over the years, hence Ava felt it only fitting to let Kate take charge as she knew just as well what her mum would've wanted.

Kate wrapped her hand around Ava's as the service began and she only let go when it was Ava's turn to pay respect to her mum and talk about her life. Barely able to keep it together, the only relative left was aware of all the eyes upon her as she spoke of the love her mum had given her throughout her life and how sorely everyone would miss her. Ava looked up from her notes, and as she scanned the congregation, looking into the sad eyes of so many people who held her mum dear, her eyes settled on an elderly lady who looked vaguely familiar but Ava couldn't place. Just as she tore her eyes away from the elderly lady to ask the congregation for donations to Rose's preferred cancer charity, a figure at the back of the church pushed through the people blocking the entrance and left.

'That was a beautiful speech. Your mother was always so proud of you and she would be today,' Kate said as Ava sat down again, squeezing her hand. But Ava's thoughts were with the man who left the church; who was he and why would he disappear before the service was over?

The service finished and many of the guests made their way to the wake at Rose's house. It was filled with friends who shared stories about Rose and how she had helped them in many ways despite not having the easiest life. Lucy's family were there to help and even Diego was in attendance. They hadn't spoken much since she woke up in his bed and Ava knew why. Although she knew her thoughts were irrational and she was mean for even thinking them, a part of her blamed Diego for her mum's death. Admittedly, Lucy was the one who left her alone at the party and was the main reason Ava had so much to drink. Still, Diego decided to take her home with him instead of calling Lucy to ask for her address or using Ava's finger to open her phone and check her saved addresses in her apps. Had he wanted to, he could've got her home, but he decided against it. And that was how Ava had felt about the situation – although she appreciated him being there, it left a bitter aftertaste.

Lucy was filling the dishwasher as Ava was saying goodbye to the last mourners at the door when the elderly lady from the church came up to Ava. She stared deep into Ava's eyes, her thick, long white hair done up beautifully in a bun at the nape of her neck and her head barely reaching Ava's shoulder. They just stood there for a moment, Ava unsure of who this lady was with her intense stare when a tiny voice with a tint of a foreign accent broke the silence. 'I am very sorry for your loss, my dear. Rose was very special to me. I have discovered that often life is unfair and tragedy hits unexpectedly. And often, we forget to watch our backs.' She squeezed Ava's arm. 'If there is one thing I learnt in life it's to be careful who you trust.' She shoved an envelope into Ava's hands, turned and slowly walked away, leaving Ava dumbfounded about what had just happened. Who was this woman, the one who had also stared at her from the pews, and why couldn't Ava shake the feeling that she had just been warned about something or someone?

Three

Despite having her own problems to deal with, Lucy had been a rock in those first few days. She had immediately driven to Ava's flat to support her best friend when the police had called her, and on the weekend of the funeral, Lucy refused to leave Ava on her own, even though she knew Kate was next door. Work had been a distraction for both Ava and Lucy after the initial shock. It had helped Ava to keep going instead of loafing around the flat, guilt eating away at her. But after bottling most of it up for a couple of weeks, the day of the funeral she let it all bubble over. Ava was glad for Lucy's company in the house her mum had filled with love, the smell of freshly baked cakes and flowers from the garden. 'A house is only a home when you fill it with flowers and cake,' her mum used to say, and she lived by it.

Those few times Ava had returned to her childhood home, she kept expecting her mum to come out of the kitchen and give her a big hug, ear to ear as they used to joke, given they were the same height. But emptiness greeted her. The sun shone through the French doors on the far side of the kitchen, bathing the kitchen and living room in a soft yellow hue, dust particles dancing in the air. It was eerily quiet; Ava felt a shudder run down her spine. Lucy had suggested tidying up the house and working through her mum's possessions after the funeral. This did not seem like a great idea to Ava initially but she trusted her friend knew what she was doing.

They dumped their shoes next to the front door after the last guests had left and went to put the kettle on. 'How are you feeling?' Lucy asked.

It still felt strange being in the house she grew up in, where she had enjoyed such a happy childhood and recalled fond memories of her mum and grandparents. Now it felt as if the house had lost its soul with her mum's passing. All those Christmases they had spent sitting around the dining room table eating the turkey granny had cooked and grandpa expertly carved, then sitting in front of the telly watching the Queen's Speech at 3 pm before going for a little walk so they could feel better about having eaten so much, knowing full well that was exactly how they were going to continue on Boxing Day.

'I remember when granny and grandpa used to stay with us for several days during the holiday to help when mum had to work. We would eat biscuits and chocolate for breakfast and play games all day,' Ava smiled at the memory. She was known as a cheater – although her granny never said anything, she always knew but would let Ava win anyway. It was just what grannies did she used to say. Ava's smile faded, 'It was hard enough when they passed. I don't know what I'm going to do now.'

Lucy took Ava's hand, 'I know I'm no replacement but I'm always here for you.'

'I keep expecting mum to pop round the corner asking me about something I don't want to discuss. Strange isn't it, how one spends a lot of time getting annoyed at their parents at all the questions they ask about work and one's inexistent love life and then suddenly when they're gone, all you want to do is talk to them and tell them everything that's going on in your life,' she pondered.

'I can't imagine what it must feel like losing a parent. I know I'm fortunate as I still have my grandparents, but it seems unfair that I have them and you are alone. Although you know my

parents would happily adopt you,' Lucy said with a smile. Ava
tried to smile back but realised Lucy was right, she had no one
left. Her mum was an only child, so there were no aunts, uncles
or cousins.

'Maybe I should take one of those DNA tests to find long lost
relatives. Who knows, I might have a distant cousin in Australia I
could visit,' Ava mused. The thought of getting on a plane and
disappearing far away didn't seem too unpleasant.

'Obviously, you'd take your best friend with you to ensure
you don't get into trouble, right?'

'That goes without saying,' Ava grinned.

Having changed into something more comfortable, they
made their way to the study with a cup of tea. They decided to
work their way through some of the paperwork first. Her mum
wasn't the tidiest of people; although the house was always
spotless, Ava knew the papers wouldn't be filed away nicely and
instead just shoved into a box, out of sight, out of mind. Ava was
glad for Lucy's company; she didn't think she'd be able to do this
on her own and Lucy gave her the space she needed and didn't
talk as if nothing had happened. It wasn't easy for her either,
Lucy and Rose were very close from the day Lucy's first love
broke up with her. She had turned up at their house one
afternoon with big red eyes wanting to see Ava, but she hadn't
been home, so her mum immediately clocked and took her
through to the kitchen, sat her down with a cup of tea and made
Lucy tell her everything. That was the effect Rose had on other
people, they opened up to her, whether they were good friends or
acquaintances, and since that day they had had a bond that made
Ava wonder sometimes whose mum she was. Lucy was never that

close with her own mother. Rose's death must also have hurt her terribly, Ava thought.

'Right, you take this box, I'll take this one,' Lucy announced. 'I suggest we put everything into piles – house, bank, insurance, and miscellaneous.' Ava nodded her agreement.

'Maybe we'll find some letters or photos from your father,' Lucy remarked, 'wouldn't that be great?!'

'Yeah, maybe.' Ava wasn't sure she wanted to find anything relating to him. She needed to get to grips with her mum's death and couldn't start opening old wounds, despite her not remembering much about her father's death. There was a part of her that wanted to discover more but it felt like betraying her mum. After all, there must be a reason why she never spoke about him and why there weren't any photos of them all as a family before he died. It had never occurred to her how odd that was. One time, she overheard her mum on the phone to someone explaining that she didn't know where her husband's locker key was but would see if he had left it in the house. Ava didn't think much about it at that time other than that the key must be somewhere in the house. But thinking back now, the person on the phone must have been her father's boss from the biscuit factory he worked at. Her father had worked as an operations manager and oversaw all the processes required to produce the biscuits, Ava's favourite ones even now, especially when dunked into a nice cup of tea. Her father had loved what he did for a living and was one of those rare people who jumped out of bed in the morning looking forward to going to work. Ava's father was a tall and handsome man who always had a smile on his face. Everybody loved his charming personality, although her mum never established whether their love was purely because of him or because he kept promising everyone the latest secret creations at the biscuit factory. Not that there ever were any secret creations, so it must've been his easy-going charm and his laidback ways that won the hearts of mainly female acquaintances. Although he loved his job, he somehow just ended up there after his journalistic career ended before it even properly began.

'Earth to Ava? Are you still here?'

'Huh? Yes, sorry. I was thinking. You know, strangely, mum never spoke about my father. I mean, wouldn't she want to keep his memory alive?'

'I've often wondered that, as does my mum. She said the whole thing was strange when he died. There was no funeral to go to and no photos in the house. She always found it a bit harsh erasing him like that.'

'No funeral? I didn't know that.'

'Did Rose ever mention him?'

'All I know is how they met. He worked for a tiny independent magazine and was sent to the factory to report on a possible environmental cover-up by the factory. It was claimed they were using one of the fields around the factory as a dumping ground for toxic waste, killing flora and fauna and polluting the water of the surrounding villages. When he arrived at the factory to investigate and speak to the director, he was invited inside to see for himself how the factory worked. It became apparent that the toxic waste story wasn't true in the slightest and was a tale from one of the locals who didn't want her son eating the biscuits because of the sugar, so she had come up with the story to prevent him from trying them.'

'Could've been my mum,' Lucy laughed.

'Well, it was unclear whether it had worked, but the second my father had stepped into the factory and received a selection of biscuits to taste and take home, he had wanted to work there and eat biscuits all day. And who can blame him? That was the dream of a then 24-year-old. When he was offered a job as a factory worker he decided to end his career in journalism, much to the chagrin of his father. He was a successful investigative journalist himself, having uncovered some of the biggest stories in his day, I'm told. And he had hoped his son would follow in his footsteps.'

'And then he met your mum.' Ava nodded. Brian never regretted his decision, especially after meeting the beautiful Mary-Rose Brown. They met when she worked a summer job at the factory and he was sure she would one day be his wife. That was all Ava knew about her father but it wasn't her mum who had told her, it was her grandpa.

Something in the box she was going through, poking out from between the pages of an old book, caught Ava's eye. She grabbed the dusty edition of a Charles Dickens novel *Historia de dos Ciudades* and pulled at the paper with its rounded edges. It was a black and white photo of a man in a suit next to a beautiful young woman with a huge smile across her face looking straight at the camera. They were posing in front of a restaurant, *Casa España*. 'Who are they?' Lucy asked over Ava's shoulder.

'*Con cariño*, Henry, 1948,' Ava read on the back. 'What does that mean? Is Henry the man in the photograph?' she asked.

'It must be him. Let's Google what the words mean. I'm pretty sure that's Spanish. Or you could ask Diego,' Lucy teased.

'Haha, why bother with a man if you can have all the answers from the internet?!' Ava said while she grabbed her phone and started typing. 'It means *With Love*.'

'So, are you going to tell me how things are with Diego? You two looked head over heels when I left you on the dance floor.' Lucy broke into Ava's thoughts.

'Yeah, that was a lifetime ago now.'

'Yes, but he did come to the funeral.'

'I noticed, not that I wanted him there really. He didn't know mum.'

'He was there to support you!'

Ava reminded Lucy that it was unacceptable to leave your best friend in a stranger's hands when drunk.

'I apologised for that a million times. But you must admit he's handsome.'

'He is.'

'Will you see him again?'

'I don't know. Honestly, there's not much else I've been thinking about since my mum died.'

'I'm sorry, Ava, that was insensitive of me,' Lucy said while she leaned over and took Ava into a big bear hug.

But Ava's thoughts were back on the photo. Who were these people and why was their photograph in her mum's study in a Spanish book? Ava went through the rest of the pages of the Dickens book and found a folded-up piece of paper. It was a newspaper article from 1948, the year her mum was born. It showed the same Spanish restaurant but without the two people in front of it. Above the photo was the headline *Gas explosion at restaurant leaves 14 dead*. Ava gasped as she read on out loud.

Gas explosion at restaurant leaves 14 dead
By Edward Wilkinson

Yesterday morning there was a gas explosion in the Holland Park area where a new Spanish restaurant was due to open the next day. It is believed that the owners were inside at the time of the explosion and are two of the bodies that were recovered from the rubble. Further bodies from adjacent buildings impacted by the blast have been retrieved, many too charred by the subsequent fire to be fully identified. The police are investigating if any foul play was involved, and while no arrests have so far been made, witnesses claim to have spotted a
One of the
He
Civil

'I can't read all of it as the bottom right corner has been torn off. I wonder what the witnesses spotted,' Ava pondered out loud. 'Why did my mum have this?'

'Maybe she picked up the book from the library and these things were left in there by the previous owner,' Lucy suggested.

'Could be,' Ava mused 'but then why was it not in the bookshelf with the other books and instead in this box in her study?'

'That, I cannot answer,' she replied, shrugging. 'Does it matter?'

Ava looked at the two people in the photo again and something told her it did, she just didn't know why. She folded up the paper and put it with the photo back in the book to take home with her.

Four

Mieres, Spain
1934

'Got you, your turn,' Rosa tapped María on the shoulder and squealed in delight as she turned and ran away along the river towards home. María shouted after her that she was too tired to run. Her friend stopped skipping and returned to where she had left María standing, the sun beating down on them.

'What is wrong?' Rosa asked.

'I'm just tired.'

'Tired? We've been sitting in school all day. How can you be tired?'

'I don't know. It's so hot and my clothes are sticking to me.' María pulled at her dress, proving her point. 'I just want to sit and do nothing.'

Rosa looked at her friend irritated. 'How do you think I feel? You can go to school every day. I miss half of the year when I'm working on the farm and am always catching up when I return after the summer. You should be thankful for your easy life,' she spat, her eyes narrowing on María, who had never seen her friend so angry. She was left gobsmacked as her friend turned and ran along the river and out of sight.

María knew she was lucky, especially compared to her friend, who came from a farming family and was needed on the fields most days in the summer months. But in winter, when her father and brothers worked in the mines as *ambulantes* for the season before returning to the family farm, Rosa was allowed to attend school a few days a week. Grappling with what just happened,

María wasn't ready to go home yet. She needed a moment to herself and instead made her way up the hill to her favourite tree overlooking the valley towards the mine where most of her family was currently working underground. It was a hard job, but her grandfather had already been mining coal, and so did her father, her two older brothers, Pablo and Andrés, and many of her cousins. Her younger brother Juan Luis was soon to follow but had to finish school first. At 14, María was already beyond her official education, but her mother insisted on continuing to send her to school. Looking down at the little Spanish village below her feet, not for the first time, she wondered what else life had in store for her once she finished school. Since the proclamation of the Second Republic in 1931, women's rights had been improving and the way to higher education was being paved for girls. Despite her father not agreeing with the removal of the church from education and him not seeing the point of teaching girls, her mother was pushing for her only daughter to have a better life and not just be married off to an eligible young man.

'*Hola María.*' A shadow was thrown over María's face as she looked up, pretending to be surprised he was there. It was their tree, the place where they made plans to conquer the world. She grinned up at him.

'No one saw you?' she asked.

'No, I was careful.' He sat beside her crossed-legged, following her eyes towards the coal mine.

'Father would not be happy if he knew I was talking to you.' Sadness flickered across her eyes, thinking of her father and his strong opinion on intellectuals.

'One day, we will be free, and it won't matter what our parents do for a living and what they think. We will be able to decide for ourselves and live our own lives,' he read her mind.

'I don't think that will ever happen. My destiny is to stay with my parents and look after them until they die,' remorse creeping into her voice, immediately berating herself for even thinking like that.

'Not if the reforms of the Second Republic continue. We could go to Madrid together! My father said it will all get better now,' he said while nudging her, trying to bring back that beautiful smile she usually had reserved for him.

'You are too intelligent for your age.'

'You're not too bad either. Just a shame you don't always trust me,' he smirked. 'What do you dream of María?' It was a question to which she didn't have an answer no matter how often he asked her. Growing up in rural Spain as a girl didn't lend itself to big dreams. The course of her life was decided before she was even born. María was to help her mother with household chores, learn how to become a woman, marry, and have her own family while still looking after her elderly parents and attending church every Sunday.

'It is different for me. I'm a girl, and I have to help my mother. You are a boy, your parents want you to be successful.'

'Your mother wants the best for you, she's still sending you to school! Don't you know anyone who managed to escape from here to lead a better life?'

'No,' she said without looking at him, 'and anyway, our life isn't that bad.' As she said it, her mind was thinking of the one person who managed to leave, but Xulián already had his head in the clouds, there was no point in giving him hope.

'I hope that you find your dream and are able to follow it.'

'Thank you.' Brushing down her grey dress over her knees as she stood up, she gave him a quick peck on the cheek and ran down the hill back home, already late.

Her feet carried her directly to the kitchen where her mother was preparing the potatoes for dinner, nodding her head at the peeler on the table. The unbearably clammy and humid air made her dress stick to her skin again, and sweat started to drip from her forehead while the fire burned in the corner, ready for the pot of vegetables. Her day followed the same schedule every day, getting up and helping her mother prepare breakfast and lunchboxes for her father and brothers working in the mines, helping with the washing, then going to school and returning home to help her mother prepare dinner. After, she would help mend clothes, clean the house, and do other chores while the men sat around drinking, smoking and discussing politics. Sunday was the exception when the whole family attended mass in the morning, if they weren't working. Then she was often free to play outside with her younger brother, Juan Luis, before helping with dinner. She was brought up to respect her brothers and their hard work, and be grateful that she was allowed to attend school. But today, María wanted to be anywhere but here. Her argument with her eldest brother, Pablo, that morning still weighed heavily on her heart. She wondered why he was nasty to her and what she had done to anger him so much. She knew he disapproved of Rosa's family, one of many who only worked underground during the winter months and then enjoyed the summers outside in their fields. There was a big feud, and fights often broke out between the seasonal coal miners and those who went down the shaft daily. This had nothing to do with her friendship with Rosa though; she didn't understand why he told her to stay away from Rosa's family and defiantly told him so, receiving a slap across the face for disrespecting him. Rubbing her cheek, close to tears, he told her in no uncertain terms that she was too young to understand anything that happened outside of her little world. The feisty 14-year-old didn't let that bring her down though. Thanks to Xulián, she knew a lot more about what was happening around her than anyone gave her credit for. Pablo considered himself a leader and thought he knew everything. Having never seen eye to eye with Pablo, she knew that very morning the last shred of hope of ever building some form of relationship between them had vanished. And she knew she could never trust him.

Unbeknownst to María, Rosa had had the same discussion with her father that morning, warning Rosa not to go anywhere near the Calderín family, including María. Rosa was torn between obeying her father's request and spending time with her best friend, knowing it wouldn't be long before she had to leave school again to work on the family's fields for the summer.

'How's your cheek?' Her mother's voice tore her out of her reverie. She shrugged, not in the least surprised her mother had heard and most likely witnessed the altercation in the morning.

'You have to understand that your brother is only protecting you.'

'From what?' María retorted.

'There are things, my dear, you do not understand and don't need to. Leave it to the men.'

'Mamá, he is asking me to stay away from my only friend without giving me a reason. At least if he told me why I might accept it.' She knew that was a straight lie, and so did her mother, who raised her left eyebrow in response.

'How was school?'

'Good, I had to read a line of a poem.' It was a tricky line, and María didn't fully comprehend it, but her reading had invariably improved since she started reading parts of Xulián's books. He always carried one with him and after school, when they met underneath the tree, he would ask her to read to him. She loved the sensation it gave her when he moved closer to correct her and point to the word she mispronounced, his lips close to her ear.

'Mamá?'

'*Sí cariño?*'

'Did you ever want to leave here and follow Aunt Isabel to Madrid?' Her mother didn't say anything for a long time but stopped peeling the carrot she was holding. The oppressive air in the kitchen muddled María's brain, her mother seemingly was struggling with the heat too. Or her daughter's question had hit a nerve. She got up and started cutting the potatoes on the table more forcefully than necessary.

'I'm sorry, mamá.' María realised it wasn't a topic her mother wanted to discuss.

'When I was your age, maybe a year older, I wanted to do nothing more than run away from here. It was different in my time. I never went to school, couldn't read and write, and neither could my parents. No one ever questioned the path they were going to take in life, you just did what your parents said. But Isabel, she was different. Such a bright kid, and when she met a man on a trip to Oviedo while working at the local government, she knew she wanted to be with him. She saw the life before her that she could lead and did everything she could to get it.' She put the knife down, leaned on the table with both hands and looked at María. 'She was lucky, our Isabel. One day her man, Antonio, arrived at our front door out of the blue asking for Isabel's hand in marriage. Papá wasn't sure whether to give his blessing because he knew that after the wedding Antonio would take Isabel away from the family to settle in Madrid. But Isabel managed to convince our papá to let her go. It was hard for our parents, knowing they would never see her again, but they realised this was a chance for at least one of their daughters to escape poverty, so they accepted. In the months leading up to the wedding, she filled my head with everything she was going to experience, the beautiful dresses she would be wearing, the food she'd be eating, the visits to the theatre, and best of all, knowing her children would never have to know the poor conditions we grew up in.' María looked around the kitchen, thinking how fortunate they were that her father inherited his aunt's house, which was a decent size and close to the village centre. She knew most of the other miners' children didn't attend school and lived in far worse conditions.

Resuming the chopping, her mother continued answering María's simple question with her life story. 'Hearing about all those wonderful things, many of which I knew nothing about, made me yearn for them too. I was due to join my sister for a few months after she got married on their journey to Madrid and was counting down the days. But God had a different path for me, and when I met your father I understood what Isabel had meant when she talked about love at first sight. To this day, I haven't even made it as far as Oviedo,' her mother sighed.

'Do you regret staying?'

'No, never,' she said without having to think about it. 'I have a roof over my head, enough food on the table and four wonderful children. There's no one else I would rather spend my life with than your father.' It seemed to María her mother was happy with her decisions in life simply because she spent her days with her father. She felt the same when she was with Xulián – everything around them faded away and it was the only place she could be herself and voice her frustrations at life. He understood her in a way no one else did, didn't patronise her when she said something childish and supported her when she complained about the chores she, but not her brothers, had to do. Everyone always said it was a woman's job, it was what they were taught by the nuns when they ran the schools a few years ago. Alas, it was all changing, and if she were lucky, this would soon be a life of the past.

After a quiet dinner, María was relieved from her evening duties and allowed to go outside to play. The river was turning from its usual grey to black, María shivered at the thought of not knowing what was lurking below the surface. As she approached the bench she usually sat on to watch the world go by, she noticed Rosa was already there waiting for her. When Rosa's family came out of the valley for the winter, they stayed in town with her aunt and uncle and returned home for the summer. It was a warm evening when María left the house, but as she sat next to Rosa, she felt the cold breeze and wished she had brought a cardigan. Staring at the side of Rosa's profile, she noticed her hooked nose looked more prominent from the side than it did from the front, whilst her eyes, usually almond-shaped, were small slits, undoubtedly the eyes of someone angry.

'Are you okay, my friend?' María asked, unsure whether she was the cause of her anger. Rosa didn't answer. She kept staring across the river into the distance where workers were returning home after a long day and miners on the night shift started to emerge from their houses, waved off by their wives who yet again had to spend the night alone.

'So you were too exhausted to run after me but are out now?' came a small voice beside her. María was baffled for a moment, trying to think what had happened after school, before remembering they had been playing tag and Rosa had shouted at her.

'Sitting down while helping mamá and eating revived me. And I needed some fresh air.'

She could see her friend was not satisfied with her answer and wondered if there was something else Rosa wanted to say.

'How has your reading improved so much? You used to struggle, but now you're among the best.' María knew she had to tread carefully when explaining where her sudden improvement stemmed from. Those moments she spent underneath the tree reading to him were theirs alone, and no one could know about it.

'I often practise with mamá,' she lied. 'I would like to excel at school and find work earning a few pesetas.'

'You dream too much.' Rosa looked at María for the first time since she sat down. Her face was so much softer than in profile, and her almond-shaped eyes now looked almost cat-like. She wasn't particularly attractive and wasn't very popular with the other children, especially the boys in school, but she had a unique character and María appreciated her honesty. Though she spent much time on the family farm and they only saw each other for a few months a year, they built a strong friendship María knew she could rely on – although she sometimes wondered if staying away during winter prevented Rosa from growing up.

'Sometimes you must dream of a better future to endure the present.'

'And what kind of work are you interested in?'

'I would like to teach children or work for the government like my uncle in Madrid.'

'You want to move to Madrid?' Rosa looked crestfallen.

'Maybe. There is so much more to see outside of Mieres.' María's thoughts returned to Xulián, who told her about what the *Madrileños* wear and eat and how big the city was. 'Do you want to stay on your family's farm forever?'

'I don't have a choice.'

María felt for her friend, who seemed to have accepted a predestined life high in the mountains of Asturias in an area that extracted coal from the mines, produced dairy and grew apples. Where she was merely another cog in the wheel. 'A nurse,' she suddenly said. 'I would like to be a nurse, do something useful.'

'That's a very noble thing to do,' María agreed. She hadn't known Rosa had the desire to help others but could see the potential. Whilst María mainly lived her life for everyone to see, Rosa was an introvert who only interacted with those she trusted. She also had a calming presence, wasn't easily flustered, and would make a good nurse, María was sure. 'You should remember that dream.'

'What good would it do? I would only be disappointed. Mamá is getting older and has problems with her back. Esperanza is due to get married by the end of summer and will have her own family, and Cristina is entering the convent. There's no space for my dreams.'

'Your sisters are living their own lives, but you have to stay because you're the youngest? What about your brothers?'

'What about them? They are in the fields and the mines. They make sure the family can survive. I am here to help like you are for yours.' Rosa turned to face the river, now pitch-black, reminding María of Pablo and his deep anger towards Rosa's family and the world. It was time to get home before he returned from his shift.

Five

There was an electric atmosphere in the little town of Mieres in the build-up to spring. Everyone was outdoors enjoying the balmy evenings in the restaurants that spilt into the streets and the cider was poured from above the head into glasses below the knee in the typically Asturian way. The hope of new beginnings and a calmer life came with brighter and longer days, especially in the coal mines where the *ambulantes* would soon end their last shifts of the winter season and head back to their farms with their families. In the Calderín household the air was static though. Pablo hadn't spoken to María since their argument and, although she didn't care much about that, it bothered her that he was constantly there, ready to attack her. Whenever she started a conversation with her father or Andrés about the political climate he would interrupt her. He had made it very clear that he thought nothing of her, and although his feelings towards her didn't bother her, she cared about her father and Andrés and his influence on them. It often felt as if Pablo was the man of the house, and even her burly father answered to him. María had an uneasy feeling around him, never sure what he would do if she stepped out of line. Rumours amongst the villagers painted a vile picture of him. Mothers kept their daughters at home when Pablo was in a bar as his worst behaviour came out when he was drunk; he would start fights and do whatever he wanted to whomever was in his way. The fear was that it wouldn't be long before he killed someone with his bare hands, and María couldn't care less if they locked him away.

He was a week away from his 18th birthday, and her mother was preparing for the big party that took place each year in the town hall for families whose sons turned 18 that year. The women spent most days decorating, baking, cooking and sewing in preparation. Luckily, María wasn't asked to help as her mother had noticed the hostility between the siblings. It left María with more time on her hands than usual, and she spent every moment she could with Xulián under the tree, taking extra precautions and detours so as not to be spotted. They had moved on from reading, and he was now helping her with her maths, which also started to improve. After some time, and many sums, he switched to reading to her from Cervantes' *Don Quixote*, enrapturing her in a language she only dreamt of ever being able to understand. But it didn't matter how much she understood, she wanted to listen to his soft voice for the rest of her life. His accent was different to hers and sounded more sophisticated. The other children made fun of him in class, but María wished she spoke like him. While her mother was busy with the preparations and Pablo was on night shifts at the mine, she spent evenings with her father, Andrés and Juan Luis. They played games and teased each other, and not for the first time, María noticed a change in everyone when her eldest brother wasn't around, validating her own feelings. It became apparent to everyone that the dark shadow hanging over the family's happiness had a name, Pablo.

One warm afternoon, María found herself in her usual spot looking out over the valley. Catching a glimpse of the market square below next to the town hall, she saw her mother rushing about with flowers to decorate the venue while smiling to herself. The town was buzzy. Closing her eyes, she listened to market stall holders shouting for others to get out of their way, the hooves of horses clacking on the hard ground, children playing in the streets, and people greeting each other and asking how their families were. The smell of freshly cooked *fabada* was in the air, while in the background the low rumble of the machines digging coal from deep beneath the surface reminded the town's people of its heritage. She loved it when the village was as bustling as it was today. The thought of ever wanting to leave this piece of heaven seemed inconceivable. Her eyes flew open as she felt a presence beside her, almost entirely covered with a mop of brown curly hair and looking straight at her. He stroked her arm and moved his head towards her, planting the gentlest of kisses on her forehead. María's stomach did a somersault. Her breathing became harder and faster. She wanted more of him, to feel his hands around her waist, his body pressed against hers. Her whole body filled with the desire to touch him, feel his lips on hers and soak up his smell of sweet apples. A smile spread across his face just inches away, the tip of his nose circling hers, inhaling her scent. He stopped what he was doing and leant back onto his left arm. 'Don't stop,' she whispered without opening her eyes, trying to hold on to the sensations reverberating through her. She knew they had to stay apart even as she said the words. If anyone saw them, they would both be in trouble. But she didn't want it to end, she longed to keep this feeling for the rest of her life. Was this what love felt like? She knew then and there that this was the person she would marry, now understanding her mother when she decided to stay after meeting her father.

'One day, we will not have to worry about others. We can be free.'

'One day is a long time away,' she sighed, propping herself up on her arms, having been taken back to reality. 'Tell me about our life in Madrid.'

'We will take a stroll, arm in arm, in El Retiro Park, breathing in the scent of the roses in La Rosaleda, letting the sun warm our faces, greeting our neighbours and friends. I will treat you to an ice cream and row you to the middle of the great pond, showing you how strong I am,' he said, grinning.

'I'm scared of the water,' she said timidly.

'There's no need to be, I will be there to protect you. And if you fall in, I will jump after you.' He laughed, unaware of how uncomfortable she felt at the mere thought of falling into the water. A shiver ran down her back, the memory of being thrown into the depths of the Caudal river returning. The memory of trying desperately to stay afloat, the current pulling her deeper into the unknown, her swallowing gallons of water and treading like a dog, not knowing how to swim. Her arms and legs tiring out, and her will to survive dissipating more and more every time she was dragged back under the surface, finally accepting her fate and letting go. Feeling herself being caressed by the arms of the water enveloping her and leading her further into the depths. Her seeing the light at the end of the tunnel she was floating towards. Then finally coming to when hitting something hard with her back, opening her eyes and seeing Andrés, her saviour. Pablo, who threw her in, was nowhere to be seen.

Wrapping his arms around her, Xulián pulled her close, leaving her head resting on his chest, listening to his heartbeat. Only when María's breathing had steadied and she had stopped shivering, he loosened his grip.

María woke with a pounding headache from the exertion the evening before, her head still fuzzy with a mix of emotions from her resurfaced memory and the thoughts of Xulián. Dragging herself out of bed, trying not to wake Juan Luis, who was still asleep, she went downstairs to prepare breakfast and the lunch boxes. Her mother was already up and busy preparing the finishing touches for Pablo's birthday party the following day. He hadn't returned from his night shift yet, and María was happy she hadn't seen him for almost a week. Mother and daughter worked in silent companionship, both occupied with their thoughts. They hadn't spoken much since their conversation, but María knew her mother was preoccupied, and once this fiesta was over, she would have more time for her daughter again.

The day at school dragged on. María couldn't wait to get away and sit under her favourite tree despite knowing she would only have a few minutes as her mother was expecting her to get home immediately and get ready for the party. She had to accept that today she would only get to see Xulián from the row behind while trying to block out Rosa's constant chatter. Rosa had made it clear that she was not happy with María's improvement in school and demanded to know how she did it. María tried to explain in simple terms how she had been practising and that Rosa could do the same. Her friend took that as an invitation that María would help her and they decided they would start the next day, meeting on the bench by the river in the morning. María listened half-heartedly and nodded her agreement just as the bell rang for recreation, and everyone got up and left the room except Xulián, who was deep in concentration. Almost at the door, Rosa turned around, looking back at the boy scribbling in his notebook and the girl behind him staring at the back of his head, lost in her own world. In her eyes his head was the perfect shape, sitting on shoulders that, already at the age of fifteen, were broad and muscular. He was stronger than most other boys, although he was one of the few who didn't have to spend his summers on the fields doing physical work. María could've watched him all day, seeing the muscles move under his shirt when he was writing, his head tilted slightly to the left. Every now and then, he threw his head back, shaking his hair from his face without taking his eyes off his paper. She was captivated.

'María, María!' It wasn't his soft voice bringing her back from her daydreaming but rather her friend, standing next to her again. 'Come and play,' Rosa demanded, grabbing her arm and pulling her towards the door as her friend's eyes remained fixated on her object of interest. As she was dragged through the rows of desks and out of sight, he looked up from his paper and smiled at her, before dropping the pencil he was holding and sliding his right hand into the opening of his shirt above his heart, moving it up and down to imitate his heartbeat. It was the last María would see of Xulián for the rest of the day as Rosa commanded her full attention. Not wanting to anger her any more than she already had, María played the devoted friend on the outside, whilst on the inside the desire for him grew with every second they spent apart. Only a few more days and Rosa would be gone again, she thought, and she decided to accept her fate for the moment and concentrate on being a good friend.

The whole town gathered to celebrate several young men reaching adulthood, the gathering in the town hall growing bigger by the minute. María spent the morning running back and forth, bringing ever more food from neighbours to the venue before finally she was allowed into the bath as the last one for a quick soak in the now-murky water before the festivities started in earnest.

The hall was beautifully decorated, with blue and violet petunia hanging from the balustrade around the open space that was used as a dance floor. Tables were pushed against the walls along the far-left side with copious amounts of *fabada, bollos preñaos, tortos*, and many local cheeses, bread and desserts. Cases full of *sidra* stacked high in the corner were ready to be poured in true Asturian fashion, children watching in awe at the skill and hoping they might be able to sneak away with a glass themselves. Pablo and his friends were the centre of attention in front of the stage, where a band played uplifting music that got everyone on their feet. They were handed cider regularly, dancing with the pretty girls and passing cigarillos between them. The noise was almost deafening even before María entered. Listening to the music and laughter from outside, she took a moment to reposition the red ribbon she had tied around her hair in an attempt to look special for Xulián tonight. The thought of seeing him sent butterflies through her tummy, and the thought of them dancing arm in arm with everyone there to see and their parents promising them to each other filled her with anticipation. María took a deep breath and opened the door, stepping into a world she could only imagine would be even grander in Madrid. Scanning the room for Xulián, she made her way to the *sidra* table, hoping to calm her nerves with a small sip of the apple cider. The food smelt delicious, filling María with pride in what her mother had achieved. She walked straight past the decadent tables though, knowing she couldn't stomach anything. Felix was on *sidra* pouring duty. He was the town's butcher, a burly man with hands as large as María's face, and knew her family well. He always gave her a slice of chorizo when she was running errands in town for her mother and stopped by his shop. 'Aren't you a bit young for *sidra*, my dear?' He winked but poured her a little anyway, it was her brother's birthday party after all.

María smiled sweetly and thanked him. She took a timid sip of the crisp refreshment. She could feel someone standing behind her even before her shoulder was yanked backwards in an attempt to turn her around. She was staring at Rosa, whose face looked like thunder. None of the nice features of her face were visible now, she resembled a wicked witch. 'Where were you?'

'Where was I when?' María asked innocently.

'This morning, you promised me you were going to help me with my reading. I waited for you for an hour on the bench, but you didn't show,' she spat.

'This morning? I was helping mamá carrying all the food here for tonight and picking up more from our neighbours.' María wasn't sure what had happened, but she couldn't recall having agreed to meet her friend when she knew she was needed at home.

'You're lying!' Some people around them stared, wondering why the two girls were fighting. María took Rosa by the arm and led her away closer to the side of the hall, dropping her voice as they walked.

'Why would I lie? Do you think all this food here,' spreading her arms around her to make a point, 'walked here by itself?'

'Don't mock me!' Rosa's face was turning beetroot, her eyes wild.

'Rosa, I am sorry if I upset you,' she tried to soothe her friend, 'but I can't remember agreeing to meet you. Mamá needed me from the crack of dawn, and I only just finished getting ready myself. Can we catch up after church tomorrow?'

'No, María, it's not that you don't remember agreeing to meet. You didn't listen in the first place! You only had eyes for that teacher's pet, you should be ashamed of yourself! Your poor mother.'

Stunned about the accusations, María's mouth hung open, unable to say anything. Rosa wore a nasty and triumphant smile. Crossing her arms in front of her chest, she spun on her right foot like a ballerina and stormed off, knowing her words stung. Rooted to the spot, the dancing around her continued when she was swept off her feet and into the arms of Andrés. 'Have you seen a ghost, dearest sister?' He twirled her around the dance floor, making her head spin. Her brother stopped and led her away to a chair on the right-hand side of the hall, concern spreading across his face.

'Here.' Out of nowhere, he produced a glass of water. 'Are you feeling alright?'

'Yes, just a bit hot in here,' she tried to smile.

'Nothing to do with your argument with Rosa?'

'A bit, maybe, but nothing for you to worry about. Enjoy the party.'

'I will worry if it concerns you. It's not my birthday anyway. So tell me, why was Rosa so angry?'

María contemplated whether or not to tell her brother. He might be able to help and she knew she could trust him, she concluded. 'She told me I agreed yesterday to meet her today to practice reading. I can't remember when I agreed but I didn't turn up this morning because I was helping mamá, and now she's angry and got very nasty.'

'Ah, that sounds like she feels you have forgotten her. Have you been spending less time with her lately?' María's head shot up. How did he know? And more importantly, what did he know?

'I ...' she stammered.

'Don't worry, I know. Pablo saw you walking down from the hill behind the school a few times. He told me he was concerned you were becoming a hermit, being on your own all the time.'

'He saw me?' Fear spread across her face. Why did it have to be Pablo, out of all the people?

'It's okay. He worries about you, that's all. He says you should be playing with other girls your age, not hiding in the trees,' he said, grinning. 'Of course I told him you are fine and probably just want to be alone sometimes.'

María let out a sigh of relief. It seemed her brother hadn't seen her with Xulián, only her emerging from the forest.

'Yes,' she agreed, 'sometimes I just want to be alone and enjoy the valley's beauty from atop.'

'You and I are more similar than you think,' Andrés concluded. Enveloping her in a big hug, he kissed the top of her head and returned to his friends.

'If I didn't know he is your brother, I would have to be jealous that he got the first dance with you.' Xulián's soft lilt sounded from behind her, his finger brushing across her shoulders as he walked around her and took the seat Andrés had just vacated. A cold sensation ran through her body at his touch, mixed with fear of Pablo spotting them; she stiffened. 'No need to be tense, he's preoccupied with the butcher's daughter,' he said calmly, as if reading her mind.

'He saw me come down from the hill. What if anyone ever saw us?'

'No one will. People don't tend to be as interested in other people's lives as we think they are. To spot us, someone would have to climb up there and trust me, nobody will do that.'

'You're right, of course you are.' But María still had the niggling feeling that somebody would go to the trouble of denouncing them, an unchaperoned young woman with a young man was still a sin. 'We should keep our contact in public to a minimum though. Shall we meet at the tree later? The whole town is here, and no one will notice if we're missing.'

'Yes. I'll go first, and you will join later.' Was this a good idea though, María asked herself. Now that she knew her brother had discovered her hiding place, she didn't want to risk anything. But Xulián was right, tonight was the perfect evening to get away with everyone at the party.

The air was hot and sticky, and the trees offered a cool respite from the clamminess of the party. Xulián was already waiting for her on a small blanket with two bottles of *sidra* and a small plate of food. 'Where did this all come from?' María asked as she made herself comfortable, adjusting her dress and bow.

'I placed the blanket and bottles here this afternoon, hoping we might get away. The food is from the buffet. I thought you might be hungry.' Though she knew she hadn't eaten much yet, she only now realised how ravenous she was as Xulián indicated to her to eat and passed her one of the bottles.

'Thank you, this is exactly what I needed.' María tried to eat as elegantly as she could with the plate on her lap, but it was difficult and she dropped some food down her dress, staining it with a red blotch of sauce. Looking down, she decided she wouldn't bother cleaning it up, knowing it needed a proper scrub. Xulián smiled, watching her every move, placing a strand of hair that had come loose from her headband behind her ear while sipping from his bottle.

When she finished the food and washed it down with the drink, he set his bottle down, took her hand and started licking the sauce off her fingers. He moved along her arm, licking and kissing his way up towards her collarbone, the sensation of his rough tongue on her skin stirring something deep inside her, her knees going weak. He sucked her earlobe, making her giggle, while his lips moved along her jaw, fleetingly touching the corner of her lips. His breathing was hard as he moved closer, his hand finding its way up her waist. He hesitated before going further. 'Tell me if you want me to stop,' he whispered, their foreheads touching, his lips so close she could feel the heat of his cider-tinged breath.

'Don't stop,' she murmured, longing for him to kiss her. Their lips connected softly, teasingly. He forced her lips open with his tongue, and began exploring her mouth with it, the taste of cider on his breath. María couldn't control her body any longer and gave herself entirely to him. But as she did, suddenly a branch snapped. They jumped apart, scanning the surrounding bushes. María stood beside Xulián, startled and frightened, as they watched a figure run down the hill towards the village.

Six

It was almost pitch black now. A chilly breeze made María shiver, but she felt numb, a million thoughts running through her head. Who had seen them? The figure had long disappeared by the time María's feet finally started to carry her down the hill towards home. If it were Pablo, it wouldn't take long for her parents to find out, but she doubted it was him, he would've confronted her there and then, she thought. Leaving Xulián behind, she raced through the forest as fast as she could, trying not to fall finally reaching the bottom of the hill and deserted streets of the village. As she ran through the alley, her lungs burning, she thought she heard footsteps behind her. She ran even faster to escape her follower. Then she stumbled. The ground came closer at lightning speed, her nose feeling the impact first when it made contact with the hard dirt road and a crashing pain shot through her head. Then all went black.

María's head was pounding when she opened her eyes. The initial darkness made her believe she might be blind until her eyes adjusted. A tiny sliver of light illuminated the figurine of the Virgin Mary inside the little alcove in the wall. She breathed a sigh of relief she was in her bedroom. Her mouth felt dry dust mixed with the taste of blood. María felt a sharp edge where one of her teeth had broken off as she ran her tongue along her lips. She tried to sit up, her room slowly coming into focus. A glass of water on her nightstand indicated she didn't get inside by herself. She gulped it down, thankful she didn't have to get out of bed and stand on her throbbing foot. She tried to remember the events following her and Xulián's discovery when tiredness overcame her, and she fell into a deep restless sleep.

The sun shone through the window when María woke the next time. Unsure what time it was, she saw the glass had been refilled and a bread roll placed next to it. The rough blanket scratched her bare legs, a bandage had been put around her swollen ankle, and the dirt and blood on her body had been cleaned up. María sat up in bed and noticed her little brother had been and gone, his dirty clothes strewn over the floor while his Sunday trousers and shirt were gone. It was Sunday, María realised. Her family would, she thought, be at church, praying for her recovery and forgiveness for her sins. It slowly dawned on her that the whole village would speculate why she wasn't at church. Her family could say she wasn't feeling well after the party, but rumours would inevitably spread within hours, and the truth would come out, as was inevitable in such a small village. She'd be a disgrace to her parents, unless…

'Xulián!' María said and sat bolt upright, remembering she had abandoned him. The blood drained from her head, causing her to feel dizzy and lie down again. Voices alerted her that her family had returned from church for their Sunday lunch, and soon she would find out what her parents knew. Just as she tried to get out of bed and put weight on her foot, her mother entered the room and rushed to her side.

'No, *mi hija*, don't get out of bed.' She gently led her daughter back onto the mattress.

'I'm fine, mamá.' She grimaced as the pain shot through her leg. 'I need to prepare lunch.'

'The doctor said you need rest.'

'What happened?'

'I was hoping you could tell me.'

María looked into her mother's concerned eyes, realising that she didn't know. 'I…' she stuttered, 'I fell, and then it went black.'

Her mother took her hand. 'Señor Fernández found you lying in the alley. He carried you inside and came to find me. I rushed home with the doctor, who said you sprained your ankle and probably have a concussion. You were unconscious when we found you. María, the doctor said you must have been running very fast for the impact to be so severe.' She eyed her daughter cautiously. 'What were you running from?' María's mind was spinning; the footsteps she heard behind her were Xulián's, he followed her, and when she fell, he went to find his father to help. María's mother stroked her daughter's cheek. 'You are in shock. Have some bread and try and sleep some more.' Yes, María thought, she was in shock, maybe that was her excuse as to why she couldn't remember. But she did, every second of it. The gentle touch of his lips on her neck, his tongue exploring the inside of her mouth, the sensation deep within her when his hand slid up her waist, almost touching her breast, her letting herself go and prepared to do anything.

The next few days passed in a blur, and María was sure the days got longer the more time she had to spend in her room. Juan Luis was ordered to sleep on the couch so María could get enough rest, but she missed their usual chats before bed. Her only regular visitor was Rosa, their little altercation forgotten, it seemed. She spent most of her free time visiting and sitting next to María, practising her reading. María sensed her friend was happy that she couldn't move and was stuck in her room all day. Her other visitor was Andrés, who kept her company whenever he was home, telling her stories of the miners and even talking about the political climate, anything to get his sister show some emotion. Her last bit of hope that her actions had gone unnoticed started to fade away when even her mother's visits became more infrequent, and food and water were mostly replaced when she was asleep. Neither Pablo nor her father ever ventured into the room. Lying in her bed, she felt invisible to the world. All she wanted to do was go to school so she could see Xulián and apologise for running away that night. Every day María waited for him to visit. Every time there was a knock on the door her heart sank when it wasn't him. Aware he wasn't going to call on her and risk exposure made the whole ordeal even worse, and there was only one way she could end it. Her foot was still hurting, but she managed to put some pressure on it and hobbled around the room, which gave her the push she needed. María hopped downstairs in search of a stick she could use to get around, but instead she found her mother sitting at the table, a letter in her hand. The sound of sniffing alerted María to her mother's crying. Her mother hadn't noticed she had been joined. María put a hand on her shoulder and her mother screamed and jumped up from the table, knocking back the chair. Quickly wiping her eyes on her sleeve and folding the letter back into its envelope, she put the chair back and walked to the fire where dinner was cooking.

'Mamá, why are you upset?'

'Nothing for you to worry about.' Her voice had a forced jollity. María hobbled over to the stove and hugged her, which she reciprocated with such force that María thought she would choke.

'*Mi niña*, what have you done?'

'I do not understand, mamá.'

'We know why you left the party and what you did with that boy.' María felt the blood drain from her face. She felt unsteady and needed to sit down. Her mother handed her some water and sat beside her, taking her daughter's hands in hers. 'Papá is very angry and upset. You abused our trust. There must be consequences.' María's world came crashing down. Who betrayed her?

'W-w-what consequences?' María whispered, her eyes fixed on the table. She knew one consequence would inevitably be her being prohibited from meeting Xulián, but at least she could see him at school. No doubt there would also be more chores for her to help with, which she could deal with. But her mother didn't answer, her hands squeezed María's, nearly squashing them, tears falling from her eyes.

'Your father has decided to send you to Madrid to live with my sister.'

The shock momentarily froze María. The consequence was far worse than she could've ever imagined; they were throwing her out of the family home and sending her as far away as possible. Madrid – the city she was already in love with but not a place she imagined being so soon. It all started to fall into place why her father didn't visit her while she was poorly, why her mother stayed away too, and why they wouldn't allow her to go to school despite Andrés offering to carry her there.

'But what about school? I'm doing so well, and all my friends are here. I don't even know your sister.' Panic started to set in. Her life, as she knew it, was over; of that, she was sure.

'You will work as a nanny for your nieces. Going to Madrid is a new life, and you will learn so much. It's a punishment many would happily take.'

'I don't want a new life. I want to stay here with you, Andrés and Juan Luis,' she replied, shouting now.

'You should've thought of that before you met that boy at night! Your actions must have consequences. It's the only way your father can still be a respected man in this town.' She took a deep breath, moved a strand of hair behind María's ear and cupped her cheek with her hand: 'I'm sorry, *hija*, it's the only solution.'

'So this is more about his dignity than my life?'

'Don't say that!' Her mother snapped back in anger. She was losing her temper and was now shouting too. 'Your father and I did everything for you. He sent you to school because I begged him to. You hardly had to help in the house and you thank us by going behind our backs, doing filthy things with that boy, and expect us to accept your behaviour?'

'What filthy things? We had dinner together, and he kissed me. I'm 14!'

'Oh María.' She shook her head at her daughter's stupidity. 'This is what has been decided. Your aunt Isabel will pick you up at the train station when you arrive in Madrid. You are leaving on Saturday. I will prepare some food for you to take. Now I have to get on. Try and rest your foot for the journey.' Her mother got up abruptly and almost tripped over her feet, trying to reach the front door, leaving María shell-shocked at the table. She noticed her mother was trying to hold back tears, which María assumed was because she wanted to convey that she was united with her husband, but it was evident she wasn't convinced that sending her only daughter away was the right thing to do.

María had no recollection of how long she had sat at the table staring into space when Rosa arrived with a massive grin on her face. 'Oh, you can walk?'

'Only hop, but it's getting better.'

'Does that mean you will come back to school?' Rosa asked.

'No, I am leaving on Saturday.'

'Where are you going?'

'Madrid.' María answered without looking at her friend.

Rosa gasped, the grin wiped from her face. 'Why?'

'Because my parents decided to send me to my aunt.'

'But they can't do that!'

'Of course they can, they're my parents!' María stood up annoyed, and hobbled back towards her room, Rosa followed.

'María, why are they sending you away?'

'Because I did something shameful.'

'What did you do?' Rosa demanded. María sat on her bed and sighed.

'I sneaked away from the party and met Xulián. We kissed and someone saw us. They told papá and mamá, which is why I must now pack my few belongings and leave Mieres.'

Rosa looked as shocked as María felt, which made her wonder if it was, in fact, someone else who had seen them.

'Did you notice anyone leaving the party?' she probed.

'No, I didn't even notice you were gone.'

'Where did you go after you walked away from me?'

'Why are you questioning me? Are you suggesting it was me who followed you up the hill?' Rosa's nostrils flared with anger.

'No, of course not,' she said, more to herself than to her friend. 'I'm sorry, but I would like to be alone now.' Her friend slammed the door on her way out without another word. María's mind was racing. Talk of her leaving for Madrid meant she didn't get to ask Rosa why she was grinning when she entered the house. Had her friend already known of her fate? Was Rosa happy she was being sent away? And how did Rosa know María was on the hill with Xulián when they were spotted? She was sure she hadn't mentioned that. Did her best friend betray her?

The rest of the day went by in a blur as she lay the few possessions she owned on the bed, wondering what to put her clothes in for the journey. She questioned if her aunt would pay for some lovely dresses when she got to the city. Her grey one wouldn't do in a posh household. Andrés visited her that evening after work and immediately went to hug his sister. Through sobs, she voiced her biggest fear of never seeing her family again.

'Of course, you will come back. Mamá won't let you stay in Madrid, she wants you back here as soon as papá feels you've suffered enough.'

'Andrés, why is the punishment so harsh? I know what I've done, but I see him daily at school.'

'María, you have to understand that at school during the day there are other people around, but you were alone with him at night. He had other interests.'

'He's not like that, you don't know him.' María's anger grew. 'He loves me, and I love him!'

Andrés sighed. 'Maybe that's true, but you're young, you will fall in love many more times.'

'I don't want to, it's Xulián or no one. Can you deliver a letter to him?'

'But María, he's the reason why you are being sent away.'

'I'm just as much at fault here, and he doesn't yet know I have to leave. Please, Andrés, I have nothing to lose now. I just want to see him one last time.'

Andrés gave in, aware this was possibly the last thing he could do for his little sister for a long time. No one knew how long she would be gone, but something told Andrés she might never return.

It was midnight, and María was standing underneath the tree where the best day of her life had collided with the worst. She heard something rustle in the bushes and hid behind the trunk, but no one appeared. Deflated, María sat down, as she so often had, staring into the valley's darkness, a few lights below her in the town still on. She waited. 'María, wake up.' She opened her eyes and saw the sun was starting to rise. Andrés helped her up and carried her down the hill in a rush to get her home before anyone noticed she was out of bed. 'I'm sorry,' she muttered. He squeezed her hand. 'Thank you for finding me,' she mumbled as he set her down on her bed and fell asleep.

A few minutes later, her mother woke her up again. She insisted María must wash and put on her Sunday dress to make a respectable first impression in Madrid with a family she had never met. María sincerely hoped her aunt would be nice. Her parents were taking her in a horse and carriage to the train station in Oviedo, from where she was to be accompanied by the village priest to Léon. From there, one of the priest's friends would accompany her on the same train to Madrid, her final destination. Some part of María was actually looking forward to going to Oviedo, and even as far as Madrid; after all, she had never been further than the outskirts of Mieres before. But she was afraid of what was to come and the challenges ahead, and she was still haunted from never getting the chance to answer her most burning question: why didn't Xulián come last night?

She heard her father whistle to indicate the carriage was here, and they needed to leave. María hugged Juan Luis goodbye and promised him she would bring him back something nice from the city. Andrés forced himself out of bed after his night shift; he looked dishevelled and still had dirt on his face from the mine but María didn't care. He folded her into his arms, the warmth of his body comforting María while tears started to form in her eyes. Using his thumb to wipe away a tear, he told her to stay strong and that she would be fine but made her promise not to forget them. He planted a kiss on her head, sadness in his eyes. He gave her another tight hug, not wanting to let his little sister go. Her father whistled again, and still slightly hobbling, she made her way to the waiting carriage. Rosa had said goodbye to her the previous day, and her eldest brother Pablo had left for work early in the morning without so much as a glance backwards to bid his sister farewell. She waved to the brothers that did come to bid her farewell, not knowing when she would see them again, as the carriage set off on the bumpy road towards Oviedo. Saying goodbye to her mother was one of the most difficult things María had ever had to do. For as long as she could remember, it was them against the boys, and now they were both on their own. There was a feeling inside her that her mother would've wanted to join María to see her sister again after all these years, meet her nieces for the first time and experience the city she too, had once dreamt of. Instead, she was waiving her daughter goodbye, tears falling uncontrollably, hoping she wouldn't regret the decision.

The journey to Madrid was long and arduous, and although she tried to sleep on the train, by the time she arrived at

Chamartín station with her small bag of belongings, she was almost too exhausted to put one foot in front of the other. Her priest's friend dragged her to the meeting point, visibly glad to be rid of her, where an elegantly dressed lady hurried towards them. Aunt Isabel was not what María had expected. Compared to her petite mother, she was almost double her size, dressed in a dark green dress, matching hat, gloves and clutch, and smiling with beautiful straight teeth. María had been briefed on how to treat her affluent aunt, but Aunt Isabel seemed to care less about her social class when greeting her niece. She embraced María as fiercely as her mother had, which made her instantly warm to her, her sweet perfume reminding her of the fields of flowers back home.

'You are the spitting image of your mother when she was your age,' she said, stroking María's now matted hair. 'Let's get you home, and you can tell me all about my sister and yourself. My daughters are very excited to meet you.' Leading her out of the train station and onto the streets of Madrid, María stopped in her tracks, looking around her at the grandeur of the buildings and the masses of people. The streets were filled with horse-drawn carriages and what looked like an elongated train carriage, painted in yellow running on tracks. Attached to them overhead were sticks connected to wires running through the streets. Sensing her discomfort, Aunt Isabel took her hand to reassure her. 'That's a tram, and it will take us from one side of the city to the other. Would you like to take one home?' María was still in awe, and without taking her eyes off this modern mode of transport, she nodded and started walking towards it.

'Watch out!' A bicycle swerved around her, the man on it shouting expletives she hadn't heard before. She jumped back, shocked, and stood closer to her aunt.

'Don't worry, you'll get used to it. Always make sure to check left and right before you venture into the street.' Pulling her bag closer to her whilst walking behind her aunt, María wondered if she would ever get used to the chaos in this city, along with her aunt's strange accent and choice of words. She felt a pang in her heart as she thought of her mother and the very different life she could've led had she not met her father and stayed in Asturias. The noise in the streets was almost unbearable. She tried to listen for the sounds of nature – a bird tweeting, the river flowing, or the gentle hum of the machines in the mines – but instead what greeted her were the bells of the trams, and the whips on the horses' backs pulling the squeaky wooden wheels. And even these were nearly drowned out by the general throng of a big city. María already felt a deep fascination for this city that was so different to how she grew up, and even though it was a scary and daunting place to be, her heart started beating faster at the thought of Xulián having walked the very same streets she was now being taken through on a tram. Hoping he would make good on his promise of returning to Madrid, she smiled for the first time in a week.

Seven

London, England
2014

'This is a very spacious house. I like the layout, and it seems your mother has kept it modern.' Ava led the estate agent around the house. Everything about him annoyed her. He was an elderly man who stank of cigarettes and body odour, his food-stained shirt was too tight around his bulging belly, and his lack of sympathy for Ava's situation enraged her. He had contacted her soon after word got out in the small village where her mum died and caught her off-guard when offering to help put the house on the market. Not once did he ask if she even wanted to sell, and how he knew it wasn't a rented property was beyond her, although she assumed estate agents had systems to check these things. The agent was panting so heavily at the top of the stairs that Ava was afraid he'd have a heart attack, so she tried to guide him around the house and out of the front door as fast as possible. While he was commenting on the light, the size of the bedrooms and a few chipped floorboards, Ava zoned out, thinking of the newspaper article she had found the other day. She had started looking for the article online so she could read the last few lines that were missing from the cutting but hadn't been successful yet.

'I'll send my assistant around tomorrow to take pictures so we can put it online.' His loud voice brought Ava back to the present.

'I won't be here tomorrow. I'm heading back to London tonight.'

'When will you be back? Or if you give me a key, we can let ourselves in,' he said while going downstairs and into the beautiful garden full of her mum's favourite flowers. Ava hoped the person buying the house would keep the garden as it was and not rip out everything. It was more maintenance than a simple patio but looked stunning, especially when all the flowers in the pots were in full bloom. Her mum used to spend a lot of time in the garden, often at the same time as Kate, and they would chat for hours over the fence until one of them decided that they had better get on with what they came out to do. It wasn't Ava's cup of tea, though, as she didn't have a green finger and managed to kill every houseplant she had ever owned.

'Miss Brown, are you listening?'

'Huh? I'm sorry, I was miles away.'

'I asked if we could have a key to come and take photos tomorrow,' he repeated.

'I'll ask the neighbour if she can let you in. I'll call your office to confirm,' she answered, not prepared to hand over to a stranger she disliked a key to a house with such sentimental, let alone financial, value.

'Right, I'll see myself out then. Good day, Miss Brown.' Noticing he wasn't going to get anything else out of Ava, he walked back through the house and out the front door. Ava released a breath she didn't know she was holding and sank into the garden chair beside her.

Was this really it? Her home, where she had spent the happiest time of her life, would be sold to new owners who would hopefully make happy memories with their families. Ava turned her head towards the warming sun and closed her eyes, exhaustion washing over her. There was too much going on in her life right now, and she was struggling to understand the extent to which it had changed from one moment to the other. First, the whole story with Diego, who she actually quite liked but met at the wrong time. Then her mum's accident and the spooky old lady at the wake, plus the man who suddenly rushed out of the church. Then, whilst having to deal with putting the house up for sale, the human resources manager at work asked for a 'chat' on Wednesday at 10 am. Ava kept telling herself it was nothing, and Steph simply cared about her well-being, but she had a niggling feeling that there was something else. Especially after receiving a rather snotty email from her manager on Thursday that 'she could take Monday off for the house stuff, but she shouldn't get used to this special treatment.' She knew she was asking for a lot of time off, but surely it was understandable given the circumstances. Ava's eyes were threatening to fill with tears again. She opened them to the chirping of a bird and noticed a little robin sitting on the back of the other chair, looking straight at her. 'Hello little robin,' she whispered when it gave another tweet and flew off. They say robins are a sign that deceased loved ones are visiting, Ava thought to herself, and as she watched the little bird fly away, she felt her mum was there in spirit to let her know that everything would be alright.

Ava put the kettle on. As the water heated up, her phone rang. Grabbing it from the counter she made a mental note to call Kate and ask if she could let the estate agent in tomorrow. If Kate were in the house too she'd be okay with them taking photos, although it would mean tidying up a bit beforehand. Her mum's usually-spotless home hadn't seen a vacuum cleaner or a duster since Ava had returned.

'Hello.' Her tummy started doing somersaults when she registered who was calling.

'Hi Ava, how are you?' came Diego's deep voice. Ava took a calming breath to steady her trembling voice.

'I'm fine. You know, as good as can be. You?'

'Better now that I hear your voice.' She felt herself blush, and the butterflies competed vigorously in her tummy. 'I was wondering if you were free sometime this week? I'd like to take you to dinner to take your mind off things.'

'Ahem, sure, why not,' she stammered, kicking herself for being so nervous. It wasn't the first time someone had asked her out, but it was Diego who had let her sleep in his bed.

'You don't sound very enthusiastic. You don't have to if you don't want to,' he said, sounding hurt.

'No, I would love to go out for dinner! Sorry, there's just a lot on my mind right now. Would Wednesday work?'

'Of course, I understand. Wednesday is perfect. I'll pick you up at 8?' Ava grinned to herself, already mentally going through her wardrobe, deciding what she could wear for her date.

'Sure, bye'.

It was a date, wasn't it? Or was he just being nice? Why was dating so complicated? She moaned, picking up her phone again and typing a quick message to Lucy to ask for advice. Judging by the sounds Ava heard in the background, from closing lift doors to momentarily nothing while the lift was moving, to Lucy's high heels click-clacking on the marble floor in the lobby, to the sudden tooting of car horns of the traffic outside the building and general London noise, she knew Lucy had fled the office so she couldn't be overheard. 'Right, I'm all ears,' she panted.

'Okay, so I had just shown the estate agent around the house when I decided to sit outside in the garden and enjoy....'

'The short version, please,' Lucy demanded.

'Gotcha. Diego called and asked me out to dinner. He wants to "take my mind off things".'

'And you said yes?'

'Of course!'

'There's nothing 'of course' about that. When I gave him your number, you weren't even sure if you wanted him to call you because you were embarrassed about your little sleepover.'

'I wasn't embarrassed!'

'You were, you turned bright red when I mentioned his name!'

'Well, maybe a bit, but I'm over that now. He wants to see me again and treat me to a dinner.'

'He might take you to the golden arches for all you know.'

'You're nasty! He won't, he's got class, and I need to look the part.'

'When is this hot date going to be?' Lucy asked.

'Wednesday, he's picking me up at 8.'

'Okay, we'll go to yours straight after work. I'll do your hair and make-up. Please be prepared and put your clothes choices with matching shoes and a handbag on your bed. I can't waste time trying to find everything.'

'Understood.'

'Oh, and Ava, wash your hair on Tuesday evening and shave your legs,' she commanded.

'Why would I shave my legs? He won't get to see them anyway in my jeans.'

'Haha, you're so funny! I think I already know what you'll be wearing. Right, I need to head back before my manager notices I'm gone again. See ya.'

The restaurant was filled with flowers hanging from the ceiling in the conservatory, and fairy lights weaved through the branches of indoor trees giving the place a magical atmosphere. Ava had never been to 'Clos Maggiore' but knew it was one of those restaurants where several times during the course of an evening someone would get down on one knee and pop the question. She also knew that getting a table at such short notice was near impossible. Either Diego had got lucky or he had reserved a table a long time ago, probably with another woman in mind. Ava felt uncomfortable being here especially as she wasn't even sure if it was a date. After the waiter had shown them to their table, probably the most romantic one, next to the massive fireplace in the centre of the room, he left them with the menu. Ava tried not to gasp at the extortionate prices she was looking at, nor laugh out loud. Who would pay this much on a weekday dinner unless they were indeed going to make it a memorable evening?

While deciding what to order, she calculated the prices in her head, wondering if she could afford a starter, main and dessert or only a main and either starter or dessert. Probably the latter, she thought, and closed the menu.

'Would you like some wine?' Diego asked, already going through the wine list. Oh no, she forgot to add the wine. This would be a costly evening, not really something she could afford right now.

'How was your day?' Diego put the wine list down and straightened the collar of his light blue shirt that he matched to dark blue chinos and a beige jacket. Not the best colour combination he could've gone for but his smile and mop of dark brown, slightly curly hair made up for his lack of dress sense tonight.

Ava caught herself staring at his chest hair, just visible above the top button of his shirt, and realised he was still waiting for her answer. 'Fine. Busy. Yours?' This would be a long evening if she couldn't control herself and hold a normal conversation. *Stop it, Ava, concentrate!*

'You seem distracted. What's wrong, Ava?' he looked concerned.

'Oh, just…' the waiter interrupted to take their order. When he left, Diego unfolded his napkin across his lap and looked at Ava expectantly waiting for an answer.

'Well, you know, just a lot going on at the moment.' This was starting to become her preferred response, people usually knew better than to probe and she hoped he would too. She wasn't prepared to tell him what had happened at work today. There was only one person she wanted to speak to, her mum. When she had arrived at work that morning, the colleagues sitting closest to her suddenly halted their conversations, and Tasha's shrill laugh she had already heard from the lobby died away instantly. They all looked at her with pitying faces before Tasha broke the silence to ask how she was. How did Tasha think she was after having just buried her mum? Ava wanted to say but held back, unsure if Tasha cared or was just trying to distract from what the group had been talking about before she ruined the party. Ava mumbled she was fine and headed for the kitchen, knowing they'd restart the conversation the second she turned the corner. She then spent most of the next hour hiding in the ladies' toilets, or at the photocopier – anywhere to stay away from those chatting girls and take her mind off the impending 10 am HR chat.

10 am came and by 10:10 am she had been fired and the 'chat' was over. Apparently, her performance was lacking, she had no respect for her colleagues or manager, and she had taken too many liberties with her annual leave. It turned out that her manager had had a massive tantrum the previous Thursday when Ava emailed her asking about having Monday off for the estate agent's visit and went straight to HR to get them to 'do something about it'. That explained her colleagues' behaviour; they most likely heard her manager's heated debate with Tasha from HR. Ava now had one week to finish up and pack her things, which meant she could either ignore the 750 emails in her inbox or forward them to someone else in the team. Out of spite, she sent most of them to her manager as a parting gift and updated her CV. Knowing she would never find a new job in a week, Ava left early and walked home. Only the thought of seeing Diego that evening had somehow got her through the day.

Now she sat in a beautiful restaurant, a handsome man in front of her and her mind wandering elsewhere. She decided not to talk about her job – or soon-to-be lack thereof; instead, she wanted to tell someone about the discovery she and Lucy had made in her mum's house after the funeral. 'I found something intriguing in my mum's files when Lucy and I were going through her stuff.' Diego's eyes widened.

'What did you find?' he asked self-assuredly.

'I found an old black and white photo of a couple standing in front of a restaurant. On the back it says *Con cariño, Henry, 1948*. I don't know who those people are but 1948 is the year my mum was born.'

'That's very interesting. And you have no idea who Henry is?'

'Not a clue. There must be a reason why my mum had it and kept it in her study though.'

'Maybe she found it in the nursing home she was working at?' How did he know her mum had worked in the nursing home? Ava wondered. She was sure she had never told him. Maybe Lucy did. 'Can I see it?' Diego enquired.

'It's at home in my folder. I can show you one day.'

His face fell but immediately brightened again when he asked, 'Was there anything else with the photo?'

'Well, there was a newspaper article in a pretty bad state with one corner missing and a big tear.'

'What was the article about?'

'About a gas explosion in a Spanish restaurant the couple were just about to open. They both died, together with another twelve people from surrounding buildings.'

'Gas leaks often happened back then. Sounds like a tragic accident.'

'Yes, but why would my mum have the photo of a couple that died in that explosion in the same year she was born?'.

'She probably found it in one of the rooms in the nursing home after someone died and kept it.'

'Hmm…' Ava wasn't sure. Her mum would never take something that wasn't hers. She would have given it to the family of the deceased.

Ava's thoughts were interrupted by the arrival of their starters. Her niggling feeling returned that something was off; Diego had too many explanations despite having only just learnt about it and seemed a bit too interested. She changed the subject to Diego's job and then to current affairs, but became agitated when Diego voiced political views that she took issue with.

'How can you say people shouldn't be entitled to benefits?' Ava queried sternly, and with a raised voice, the wine definitely not helping her heated temper.

'All I'm saying is that some people choose not to work if they know they can be paid benefits and do nothing,' he said in a low voice, leaning closer towards her.

'Some people can't work because of chronic illnesses or mental health issues, not because they're lazy.'

'Ma'am, please keep your voice down,' the waiter said, hearing the duo's raised voices and seeing the diners around them starting to throw annoyed glances their way.

'Yes, of course, sorry,' Ava replied, noticing the stony glances pointing towards her.

'Can I bring you the dessert menu?' the waiter asked, also clearly annoyed.

Ava took the hint and asked for the bill. They sat in silence until the waiter returned with it, handing it directly to Diego. It seemed that in this restaurant the waiters expected the man to pay, and Ava was content to let Diego oblige after the way the evening had ended up – she felt mortified for having been told off by the staff and having people still intermittently look at them with furrowed brows, and now just wanted to leave and get back home to where she could shut the world and this arrogant man out.

'I'll walk you to the station,' Diego told her, making it clear this was the end of the evening.

Although Ava just wanted to get home, she still felt hurt, especially since he was the one who got her so angry and, consequently, almost kicked out of the restaurant. Him, and his black-and-white views on everything. There was no grey in between, and Ava couldn't just let it go; as much as she didn't want to make a scene in public, she had to tell him what she thought. 'You know, I really don't agree with you. I think it's extremely naïve to think people on benefits don't work because they're lazy. It's a generalisation, and just because you have never come into contact with someone who wants to work but can't due to mental or physical limitations doesn't give you the right to judge someone without knowing their story. You'd be surprised how many people on benefits hate relying on the system instead of being able to sort their lives out and get paid because they worked for it. Not everything in life is black and white.' There, she said it, and felt better that she did. He had no right to talk like that, and although she was now sure this was the last date they would ever have, she could at least go home with a clear conscience that she defended her grandpa who had to stop working as a baker due to a back injury from lifting a heavy bag of flour. He hated every second of being paid for sitting around the whole day.

'You're very passionate about this, aren't you? I apologise if I offended you, I'm not used to people – well, women – talking back at me. Especially such beautiful women like you.'

A somewhat backhanded compliment, Ava thought, but being called beautiful made her inclined to forgive Diego as they walked towards the tube station.

'I was thinking. With everything you've had to go through lately, maybe you should go away for a few days, clear your mind.'

'I keep going to my mum's house, why would I need to go anywhere?'

'Yes, but your mother's house has all those memories. Maybe you should ask Lucy to have a girls' trip somewhere this weekend, she looks like she needs a break too.'

Did he know about Lucy's situation? Ava wondered while she thought about his idea. They did plan on going to the Cotswolds for a weekend before her mum passed away, but then life got on top of them. Maybe that was a good idea after all, and she was sure it would be good for Lucy too. If anything, it at least gave them more time to discuss her situation and what she planned on doing.

'You know what, I'll suggest that to Lucy. You might be right, and we could both do with a break.' Ava smiled at Diego's thoughtfulness. Maybe he wasn't that bad after all, despite some of his views.

Diego took her hand at Covent Garden tube station and kissed it. 'I would like to see you again. Let me know when you are back from your girls' trip.'

'I… I have to check with Lucy,' Ava stammered, trying to hide her confusion about the kiss. If he enjoyed the evening as much as he was claiming and wanted to see her again, wouldn't he at least give her a kiss on the cheek? But, before she could even try and lean in for a hug, he dropped her hand, smiled and turned on his heels, disappearing into the crowd that had gathered around a busker next to the station.

Eight

Early on Saturday morning, they set off in Lucy's old light-blue Opel Corsa, which had surprisingly few issues despite its old age and Lucy's handling of it.

'Geez, I seriously wonder why you haven't been stopped from driving yet.'

'Do you want to drive? No? Thought so, so pipe down and turn the music up!'

Ava did as she was told as they made their way out of London listening to the radio in silence. It had been a long week, so when Ava messaged her about a trip to the Cotswolds after her date, Lucy immediately jumped at the idea and booked a room in a lovely bed and breakfast in Bourton-on-the-Water. Although Ava was open to taking the train, she was now glad they were driving; it gave them the freedom to crank up the music and pretend they were back in their student days when they regularly drove up and down the country just to get away from it all and meet boys in pubs. They had rarely bothered booking a room for the night, thinking they'd either go home with someone or just sleep in the car, and most of the time they found a place to crash. Several times they had ended up at other people's house parties when the pubs closed and stayed until they were either kicked out or woke up to a room full of sleeping bodies and tiptoed out as best they could without disturbing anyone. Ava looked back fondly at those times; everything seemed easier and more fun, not the 9-5 grind she was stuck in now – well, until next Tuesday. She was trying to tidy up her workplace and organise a handover, but she didn't have the energy to talk to her manager and was pretty sure that her manager was trying to avoid Ava as well. Everyone at work ignored her now, and those who didn't know what had happened weren't colleagues she spoke to anyway, so for the last three days she had felt more isolated than ever and couldn't wait to get out. The first thing she did after she arrived home from her date with Diego was to send out dozens of CVs to online job postings and sign up with various recruitment agencies. Three days later, though, she still hadn't heard from anyone, not even recruiters trying to throw any old job at her, which they usually did. Ava decided to sign up and paid for a professional CV writing service. Their turnaround time was five days, which was fine with Ava as she now had an excuse not to apply to jobs while she was on her weekend away with Lucy and waiting for the CV that would land her the job she wanted – not that she knew what job that was.

'How's the job hunt going?'

'What?'

'I asked how the job hunt was going. Where are you? Miles away with Diego in dreamland?' Lucy grinned.

'No, I was actually thinking about the job situation and how shit it is. I've got two more days to work and no new job to go to after. What will I do if I can't find a new job?' Ava was increasingly worried that she wouldn't find anything soon and would end up having to live off her savings and a potential inheritance. She made a mental note to contact her mum's solicitor and check up on the process, something she hadn't done so far.

'You will find something new. You're smart, and you can do anything you want. There's no need to stay in your current line of work.'

'I know, but event management is what I've always done.'

'Well, you'll just have to keep an open mind and apply to anything that might sound interesting,' Lucy said. 'I can check if there's anything going at my company. Imagine us working together!'

'Working with you would be fun. I'm not sure I'd want to see Diego every day at work though.'

'Unless you end up together and become one of those couples holding hands in the office.'

'That would be my absolute worst nightmare,' Ava said, a disgusted look taking over her face. 'And have you decided what to do yourself?'

'This conversation is about you and your job, not the baby. I need a glass of wine to talk about my situation. So don't change the topic.'

'You really shouldn't be drinking wine.'

'I know, I was joking,' she said, chuckling. 'You should've seen your face! Although sitting in a pub without a drink will be strange, I'll be a good girl and stick to lemonade.'

'Good, glad to hear. Now look what I found last night!'

Lucy squealed when she saw the CD case Ava was holding up, covered with printed photos of them and the giant letters *Lucy and Ava's road trip tunes.*

'I can't believe you still have it. And you waited until we hit the A40 to get it out!' Ava slid the CD into the player, and instantly loudspeakers blared out the Spice Girls' "Wannabe", a true nineties classic in their eyes and one of their all-time favourites.

As they cruised through the countryside, leaving the chaos of London behind, singing along to every song at the top of their lungs, Ava felt at peace for the first time since her world had come crumbling down around her. After two hours, they arrived at their dainty bed and breakfast in a tiny alleyway off the main road in the centre of the village. The village green looked picture-perfect surrounded by the yellow limestone houses that the Cotswolds is famous for, the many hanging baskets overflowing with flowers dangling from hooks on either side of the front doors, and all the cute little boutique shops and cafés lining the streets. 'No wonder so many tourists flock to this part of the country every summer. It's beautiful!' Ava, who had never been to the Cotswolds before, was absolutely delighted.

Upon arrival at the bed and breakfast, they were greeted by the lovely Becky, who showed them to their room. It had one double bed instead of two single beds as they had requested when booking, but it didn't bother them as they had had far worse sleeping arrangements over the years. They decided the first thing to do was to get a proper pub lunch and a cider for Ava. On their way out, they grabbed a map of the surrounding area and headed down the lane towards The Duke of Wellington.

'Oh, the joy of a proper country pub and fresh air was worth driving all the way here for,' Lucy remarked.

Ava agreed as they both tucked into a chicken burger and chips while enjoying the lively chatter of people around them who had returned from an early morning hike or, like them, were starting their own trip with lunch and planning on walking it off afterwards. 'Look Lucy, they have a live band playing tonight at 8,' Ava said between mouthfuls. 'Maybe we should come back later.'

'We should, if not for the music then at least for the bar staff,' Lucy replied while grinning at the barman in his tight-fitting black t-shirt, which showed off his arm muscles as he pulled a pint and gave them a glimpse of his flat stomach when he reached for a glass on the overhead shelves.

'Dishy!'

Lucy nearly choked, splattering her lemonade all over the table and Ava's arm. 'You didn't really just say *dishy*, did you? Which century do you live in?'

'Haha. Fit?' Ava looked at Lucy questioningly to see if she approved of her new choice of word. Lucy nodded, still wiping her face, and they both looked longingly in his direction.

'Oi, you have Diego. You better leave this one to me.'

'Maybe,' Ava said with a grin and absolutely no intention of doing so. After all, who was to say that Diego was still interested after what had happened on their date. Apart from that, Ava didn't think Lucy should be thinking of another man when the last one left her with a life-changing decision to make. She knew she should talk to Lucy about it, but somehow she felt she shouldn't broach the subject just yet. Maybe they both needed some fresh air and to walk off their burgers before they tackled any difficult conversations. Ava knew full well how it felt when others tried to help and offer advice but rarely considered that a different perspective was not wanted or needed, just a simple hug. Her ex, Adam, was one of those people who would look at everything in an extremely rational and, therefore, often-annoying way, not understanding when Ava just wanted to be held while she cried without someone jumping up and starting a pro and con list for her issue. But she was Lucy's best friend, and not only did she want to know what was going on in her friend's beautiful blonde head, but also what she could do to help. Ava had to admit that, secretly, she was a bit excited about having a friend with a baby and being able to do all the fun stuff a godmother got to do. Not that Lucy had asked her, but she knew once the decision was made to keep the baby, Ava was first in line for the job.

The countryside around the village was beautiful, and as they walked along one of the many paths, they fell into a pleasant silence. But Ava was desperate to know what was going through Lucy's head. Her friend had no idea what it felt like growing up without a father and always turning up to father/daughter day with either her mum, because she took care of both roles anyway, or her grandfather, who Ava begged to be by her side and tell the class about his baking. Whenever she managed to convince grandpa to attend, he would bring fairy cakes or blueberry muffins for everyone, which usually made her the most popular girl for the day. It was a rare experience for Ava to be liked by her classmates, not that anyone hated her as such, but she was always the quiet one, and no one really understood her. She had always preferred to sit in a corner reading a book or simply gaze out of the window dreaming of faraway places she had read about in her books instead of joining the games, so her classmates stayed out of her way most of the time. Apart from Lucy, who had always tried to drag her to join the fun but had also accepted when Ava wasn't in the mood for other people. Somehow, their friendship endured. Lucy had never dropped Ava as a friend, and Ava had made an effort when she felt she had to for Lucy's sake. It was still beyond Ava why Lucy ever bothered with her; she was the most popular girl at school with her curly blonde hair that bounced when she ran and later fell in luscious waves over her shoulders (which, unfortunately in Ava's eyes, she now straightened daily and dyed a platinum blonde like so many other people, as had become the fashion). But Ava wasn't complaining.

Being the best friend of everyone's sweetheart meant she wasn't picked on despite her red hair and fair skin. Instead, she got invited to all the parties because no one wanted to be in Lucy's bad books, so Ava was simply tolerated.

'What's going on in that little head of yours?'

'Oh, I was just thinking of when we were little,' Ava replied, as her thoughts returned to the real world.

'Why? Don't you have enough going on in your life as it is?' Lucy retorted. She had hated school and growing up.

'You know how it is. You think of something, and that thought leads to another and then another, and in the end you can't remember why or how you got there.'

'And what thought did you start with?'

'Well…' it was now or never, Ava thought. This might be the best and only opportunity to tell Lucy what she thought. 'Well, I was thinking of you and your baby and that I know what it feels like to grow up without a father and how hard it always was, having to justify why I only had a mum. I worry about you because you aren't that close to your family. My mum was lucky because she had her parents to help, and grandpa was like a father figure to me. It's hard enough to find your way in life, but sometimes I feel my life might've turned out differently if I had grown up with a father and maybe even siblings. And I'm scared that you will end up like my mum, just working and living for your child without having the help you need, and you'd be too proud to accept help anyway. But at the same time, I'm scared that you might decide not to go through with the pregnancy or might give it up for adoption and I'd be sad because I'm already excited about meeting your little one and I would never get to.'

For the first time, Ava stopped and took a breath. It all came tumbling out of her now. Every thought she had had since Lucy told her she was expecting and that the father wouldn't be sticking around for her flew out of her mouth before she could stop it. 'And I'm also scared that by telling you all of this you will hate me and never want to speak to me again, but I want you to know that whatever happens and whichever choice you make, I will be there for you and support you. Because you are all that I have left now.' Needing to sit down, Ava walked towards a bench on the side of the footpath when suddenly a massive dog came bolting down the path and jumped straight into her, making them both tumble to the ground. Ava hit her head and back on the gravel, momentarily taking her breath away. 'Ouch,' she croaked, touching the back of her sore head to check whether she was bleeding.

'Baxter, here!' she heard a man shout close to her while trying to pull the dog away. 'I'm so sorry, he's normally not like this. Baxter, sit! Let me help you up.' The stranger extended a hand to Ava and pulled her to her feet. 'He's never done this before. I have no idea what got into him. Is there bacon in your pocket?!' he continued, chuckling to himself. Still disoriented from the impact, Ava looked at him properly. The tall, handsome young man in front of her still held her hand. She pulled it away, irritated by the tiny dimples on his cheeks when he smiled, and dusted herself off.

'Ava, are you hurt?' came her friend's voice full of concern. 'You really need to keep this huge dog on a leash, he almost knocked her out!' she said, turning towards the man to reprimand him while putting her arm around Ava's shoulders.

'Like I said, he normally doesn't just jump at people like that, he's very well-behaved. And you can't expect me to put him on a leash out in the countryside. He must've smelt something that made him bolt.' Right on cue, Baxter started licking Ava's right hand.

'I guess I should've washed my hands after that burger,' she smiled, pulling a tissue out of her pocket to rid her fingers of the burger smell and dog slobber.

'Well, you better make sure he doesn't do that again.' Lucy steered Ava away from the man and started walking, her arm still around her shoulders.

'Can I at least invite you for a drink as a way of apology?' he shouted after them.

'We'll be at the pub tonight for the live music, you can buy her a drink then,' Lucy shouted back, making it clear that this conversation was over and they wanted to be left alone.

'He was cute. Why did you pull us away?' Ava looked at her with big eyes.

'Seriously, Ava, since I've known you, there was hardly a man you were interested in, and suddenly you start drooling whenever a guy comes your way,' she said sternly. Still, Ava could see the amusement on Lucy's face, who started grinning.

'Maybe I've been lying dormant and now want a prince to kiss me awake?'

'You read too many books, my dear. Princes don't exist, especially the ones to live happily ever after with. They will break your heart and leave you to pick up all the pieces yourself. Your best example standing right before you,' she said with a sad smile. Gone was the happy, laughing Lucy.

'I'm sorry,' Ava's said, her voice quieter now.

'Don't be. It was my decision to trust him despite you warning me, remember? But coming back to what you said before that dog attacked you, thank you, I appreciate your concern, and I am glad that you will stand by me because, quite frankly, I will need all the help I can get.' Lucy put a hand over her flat abs, and half smiled at Ava, who was grinning from ear to ear. 'So, if you've got nothing better to do next Thursday, would you come to my first scan? I haven't told my family yet, and I want to keep it that way for the moment. You're the only one who knows, and eventually, I will tell that good-for-nothing Mike. But, given that he has no place in my life, it'll have to wait. And I hope that you will respect that.' Ava hugged her friend tightly, barely able to contain her excitement.

'Of course I'll come with you! Even if I had a job, I'd be there for you. And I will respect your decision… at least for now.'

'Okay, I'll take that. But don't get annoying, alright?'

'Me? Annoying? Never! I'll be the best help ever and make sure you're safe, keeping all men away from you and drinking all your drinks at parties.' Ava felt more alive than she had in the last month. This was precisely what she needed, something else to focus on.

'Have you heard from Diego?'

'Yes, he messaged earlier today asking how I was and that he was on his way to visit a friend in Kent for the weekend,' Ava answered. She wasn't sure about Diego, he was nice, and she enjoyed their date to some extent, but she felt uneasy about him. He seemed to always want to know where she was and what she was up to, almost as if he was stalking her. But she dismissed that feeling immediately – he wasn't stalking her, he just cared. But why did he care? He hardly knew her, and she wasn't honest with him in any way, she didn't tell him about losing her job, and she found it difficult to talk to him about personal things like the photo she found and the newspaper article. Unfortunately, despite all of this, she also fancied the socks off him, and if the opportunity presented itself, she was sure all her reservations about him would go out the window. She'd happily give in to his charms.

'And?'

'Nothing and. I told him to have fun in Kent. He didn't ask to see me again, so I assume he has changed his mind.'

'I don't think so. He looked after you after the party, checked up on you after your mum's death and even drove all the way to attend the funeral. He really cares about you,' Lucy insisted, although she, like Ava, thought it was weird that he told Ava to have a weekend away with her and not a romantic getaway with him.

'We'll see. Honestly, after everything that has gone on, I currently don't need another variable in my life. If he's there, good; if not, I won't run after him. I have a house to sell, a job to find, a friend to support and a life to live. I let my flatmates know that I'm moving out, by the way.'

'What? When did that happen?' Lucy asked, astonished.

'I made the decision on Friday. I can't afford to live there without a job, and Hannah's sister will take my room, which is great because I can move my stuff out next Thursday without losing any rent. And moving into mum's house works out really well as it'll make viewings easier. I don't trust those estate agents and don't want them in the house when no one's there. Once a sale has been agreed, I can find a new place to live and hopefully, by that time, I will have found a new job too. Plus, I haven't been happy in the flat for a long time, to be honest, since you moved out, and it's time to put my big girl pants on and get my life together.' It felt good to tell someone her plans, to speak them out loud made them real. Ava realised that she had been keeping things to herself for too long. Still, this honest conversation with her best friend made her understand that, whatever decision she took, she'd have Lucy's support, which made such a difference. So, Ava continued laying down her plans, 'And I want to find out about this newspaper article mum kept. Something tells me there's a reason, and now that I have nothing else to do, it'll keep my mind off things.'

'Wow… just wow! And you decided all of this on Friday?'

'Yes, once I decided to move out of the flat, it all fell into place, and I knew what I had to do,' she said with a proud smile.

Lucy scrutinised her friend, her head slightly tipped to the left and her eyes narrowed. She noticed that Ava looked happy. For the first time in ages, her friend seemed content with herself and the world around her, which made Lucy happy.

With the sun on their faces, they grinned at each other and continued their walk, both feeling a weight come off their shoulders while Lucy put her arm through Ava's as they ambled down the path.

Later that evening, after they had returned to their bed and breakfast and popped the kettle on, they both showered and had a little nap before getting ready for dinner. Ava put on her trusted jeans and jumper combination and let Lucy do her hair and make-up. 'Keep it natural, please,' she pleaded while she felt more powder going onto her face.

Lucy knew what she was doing, though, and with precise strokes added enough colour to Ava's face to emphasise her huge eyes and full lips yet leave her looking natural. 'Just in case your dog man is there,' she teased.

Ava pouted. 'How can he? You told him 'at the pub', how will he know which one?'

'If he feels bad enough about his dog knocking you over, he will go to every pub in the area that has a live band playing tonight and he'll find you.' Good point, Ava thought.

Luckily, as they got to the pub early to have some food beforehand, they managed to grab a table before it got packed with people standing all around them and bobbing along to the music once the band started playing.

'Ah, there you are. I was wondering if I'd manage to find you!' Ava turned around to find the handsome man in front of her, holding a beer and two more glasses. 'May I?'

Ava moved to one side of the bench she was sitting on to make space for him as he set the drinks down on the table and sat beside her. He wore dark blue jeans, a white shirt with rolled-up sleeves and glasses. Was he wearing glasses when they first met, she wondered.

'I asked at the bar what you were drinking, but that douche didn't remember, so I took a stab in the dark and got you a cider,' he said, handing it to Ava, 'and a coke for you?' looking questioningly at Lucy.

'Thank you,' they both said. 'It's not very nice of you to call the barman a douche, though,' Lucy pointed out, clearly still a tad annoyed at their earlier encounter.

'Ah, but he is. He's my younger brother Tom. And I'm Luke, by the way.'

'She's Lucy, and I'm Ava. Nice to meet you, Luke. Cheers.'

'And again, I'm very sorry about Baxter. He got a proper telling off for his actions and now must spend the night outside.'

Ava looked at him, trying to figure out whether he was joking. 'I'm joking, he sleeps outside anyway, but he did get a telling-off from my mother. It's her dog. I only took him for a walk while I was visiting.'

'You don't live here?' Lucy enquired.

'No, I grew up here but moved to London for my career. As a journalist, there's only so far you can go in the Cotswolds, so after uni, I packed my bags and decided to try my luck in the big city.'

'You're a journalist? Which newspaper do you work for?' Ava wanted to know.

A smile played on Luke's lips. 'The Sun,' he answered with a glint in his eyes.

'I have a feeling you're winding us up again,' Lucy interjected.

'What gave me away?' he said with a grin while Lucy rolled her eyes, either annoyed by him already or enjoying the little banter. 'I work for the Telegraph, but my passion is investigative journalism. Unfortunately, people rarely want to read properly investigated articles and prefer celebrity gossip and sensationalist reporting. So, I'm currently stuck on the sports section while I wait for an opening to move into.' Ava felt a tingle when hearing he worked for the Telegraph; it was the newspaper that had printed the article her mum had kept. Maybe he could help her get access to the original in their archives so she could read the piece in full.

She was lost in her thoughts when Lucy suddenly kicked her underneath the table. 'Ouch.'

She rubbed the sore spot on her shin and looked at Lucy irritatingly, who raised her eyebrows and said, 'Luke wants to know what you do for a living. And since you're lost in your own world, I told him you work in the events industry.'

'Yes,' Ava said, unsure if Lucy was trying to save her from an awkward conversation admitting to a stranger that she had just lost her job or if Lucy was simply pushing her to talk to him. 'Until next Wednesday at least,' she finished.

'And what happens after Wednesday? Are you going to pack your bags and go on a gap year, leaving your friends and family behind, wondering what exotic places you will visit next?'

'Not quite, I lost my job, and I haven't found anything else yet,' she muttered, feeling hot and sweaty all of a sudden at the thought of this man so close to her who already knew about her job situation and just reminded her of all her "friends and family" that she didn't have to miss her if she went on a gap year. Not that anyone had the chance to just up and leave at her age – normally 30-year-olds were settling down, getting married and starting families and not travelling the world trying to find themselves while dancing the night away with 18-year-olds at beach parties. Ava got up and excused herself to get some fresh air; all of a sudden, the pub was too loud, and there was too much going on.

When she returned, the band was on a short break, and it seemed everyone was either pushing towards her to get out or milling around the bar, making it almost impossible to move either way. Finally, she reached their table, where Luke immediately got up and apologised for his remark. Lucy had filled him in about her mum's passing and family situation. 'I feel all I'm doing is apologising for either my dog's or my behaviour. You must think I'm a total melt.'

'No, not at all, you weren't to know. And sorry I dashed, but I just needed some fresh air.' It had helped her clear her mind, and she decided to see if he could help her. 'So, tell me, what kind of investigative journalism interests you?'

'Crimes. Imagine spending hours talking to witnesses, looking through records, and knocking on doors until you trod on someone's feet and then either had to publish what you learnt or move on to a different story. I'm not surprised they don't employ them anymore, they cost too much, and in the end you're never quite sure if the story will sell.' He was clearly in his element now, and Ava had a feeling if she told him her story, he'd immediately leap on it, but something was holding her back. Was it all too convenient that he turned up now and told her about his job and his true passion, and that out of all the women in this pub, most of them prettier than Ava, she thought, he chose her to talk to and spend the evening with her? Well, Lucy was there too, but Luke's object of interest was clearly Ava, which would typically flatter any woman if the most handsome guy in the pub picked you. But her gut told her something was off, and she couldn't put her finger on it. She contemplated why she suddenly mistrusted everyone. Diego had too many answers to her questions, and this random guy turned up out of the blue, supposedly with a hidden agenda. Ava was left wondering what tricks her mind would play with her the next time she met someone new and wondered when she had become so paranoid. *Always watch your back and trust no one,* floated into her mind. It's what the old lady at the funeral had said with her frail figure but steely eyes, and perhaps this warning – whatever it meant – had shaken Ava more than she had acknowledged, adding to the feeling that something had happened in the past that she needed to unravel.

Nine

Madrid, Spain
1934

The moment María stepped into the grand mansion on her first day in Madrid her jaw dropped at the sheer extravagance; white marble floors, crystal chandeliers, artwork on every wall, and an entrance hall larger than their whole house in Mieres. It took María a long time to understand the intricate design of the house and find her way around it without getting lost. She was shown to her room on the first floor next to her cousin Josefa's; it was the smallest of the bedrooms, but to María it nonetheless felt like a palace. It was fitted with a four-poster bed, crisp white sheets instead of just a scratchy blanket that she had been accustomed to in Mieres, fluffy pillows, and, best of all, it was hers alone. In the corner stood a chest of drawers with an enamel washbowl on top and a mirror hanging on the wall behind it, next to that was a writing desk and a chair, as well as a wardrobe in dark wood. She had been told her aunt was rich, but that alone didn't mean much to a young country girl. María only now started to realise just how much money her aunt must have. Although she expected to find a lovely home, this manor-like house seemed too much for a simple government worker. What exactly was it that her uncle did for a living?

On the back of the door hung a baby blue dress that was so delicate María wanted to touch it just to see if it was real but daren't with her mucky fingers. While taking in her new home, her aunt stood at the door observing her niece and the wonder in her eyes for a moment.

'It's much to take in, isn't it?' she said, and, without expecting an answer, continued by explaining all the practical details María would need to know. 'Your washbowl will be filled every morning and evening with fresh water, the soap and a towel are on the side. Our housekeeper and cook, Señora González, will wake you in the morning, giving you time to get ready before you wake the girls and help them wash and dress for the day. We have breakfast in the dining room, after which you will take the girls to school. On rainy and cold days, a driver will take you. On sunny days, the girls like to walk or take the tram. The day is yours until you pick them up in the afternoon, from when you shall help them with their homework until you are called for dinner in the dining room. The girls will be allowed to play before being prepared for bed, after which the evening is yours.' It all sounded very well organised to María, and she had a feeling that changing anything about the itinerary was not an option and being late would be regarded as disrespectful. Though her aunt's tone became slightly more serious as she detailed María's duties for the first time, she said everything with a smile. María was not going to disappoint her.

'Your uniform for the day is hanging in the wardrobe. And this,' she continued, lifting the dress from the door and holding it up, 'is for you. I had it made and hope it fits. We will get some more clothes made for you on Monday.' María's eyes lit up. Suddenly, she felt being sent here wasn't that bad after all. She wanted to wear the dress and show it to her mother. But then her heart sank as she remembered her family back in Mieres.

'I have asked Señora González to run you a bath; she will also help you with your hair and the dress. You are expected to join us in the drawing room, where I will introduce you to the girls.'

Sensing the change in María's mood, Isabel turned to leave to give the girl some space.

'Thank you for your kindness, Aunt Isabel.'

'Please call me Isabel and your uncle is Antonio.'

With one hand on the door handle, she turned around and smiled. And one more thing – try and behave,' she said with a wink. 'Welcome to Madrid, María.'

The first few months in Madrid flew by, and María started to settle into her new life. Gone were the days when she had to cook breakfast for her family before going to school and then find more chores waiting for her when she returned home It didn't take long for María to get used to the new routine with her nieces, who were delightful and eager to help whenever she was struggling with directions or instructions. At the tender age of eight, Josefa already cared for her younger sister Ana, who tried to copy Josefa in everything she did. They wore their long brown hair in plaits with ribbons and tiny bows that María tied for them every morning, reminding her of all the times she had wanted a sister to share these moments with. Despite their wealthy upbringing, they were both unpretentious, a trait María awarded to their mother, who seemed to have not forgotten where she had come from and her humble beginnings. Although rarely at home, Isabel's husband, Antonio, was pleasant to be around and interested in María's life in Asturias and her educational successes. Her interest in reading was soon a hot topic around the dinner table when Antonio joined them, and each time he would ask her opinion on a book he had lent her from his library. It became clear to María how much better her options were in the city compared to her rural home, where many older people were illiterate, and it was only slowly starting to change for the younger generations. She had sent her mother a letter a few weeks after her arrival in Madrid telling her about her new life and asking how the family was doing. In return, she had received a letter from Andrés, dictated by her mother, that nothing had changed apart from her absence and how she missed her daughter's company. To the sound of Tchaikovsky's Swan Lake playing from the musical box on her bedside table, María sat on her bed reading the lines her family had sent her while the white ballerina pirouetted inside the shiny wooden case so delicately and mesmerising María would wind it up again and again. A single tear rolled down her cheek, falling onto the paper, smudging the letters at the thought of her mother missing her whilst also having sent her away. As she put the letter back in its envelope, she noticed a slip of paper inside and her heart started to beat faster. One glance at the letters, though, and she knew instantly it wasn't Xulián's handwriting. The childish letters belonged to someone else. With a sinking heart, her eyes fell on the name at the bottom of the page. It was a letter from Rosa. Without reading it, she left the room and joined her aunt in the drawing room for some more reading. But her mind was elsewhere, thinking back to her excitement at the second letter –how she had hoped Xulián would explain why he hadn't joined her at midnight before she had left Mieres – and her subsequent disappointment. It dawned on her that this was what her father had intended, for her to forget all about him and grow up in a place far away. But could she just let go of the hopes and dreams they had shared, and the future they had planned together here in Madrid? Let go of the one person who had believed in her, had taught her so much and had given her the strength to believe in herself? She knew a day would come when she had no choice and had to move on, but she wasn't ready yet. She needed something to hold on to that would carry her through the lonely nights when she missed her family. She could focus on her future when she was ready instead of waiting for a letter that would undoubtedly never arrive.

'Are you listening to me?' The soft tones of her aunt's voice brought María back to the present.

'I apologise, Isabel. I was just thinking of mamá.' It was a lie, but she knew she would be forgiven if she mentioned her aunt's beloved sister.

'Do you miss them much?'

'Yes, I miss mamá, Andrés and Juan Luis. Papá sometimes. But it will get easier with time, I'm sure.'

'That is true, I remember when I left my family and Mieres behind, it took me a long time to adjust to my new life.' Looking intently at María, she asked whether she was enjoying Madrid. María nodded, explaining how much she enjoyed the buzz and the people but would like to have more nature around her.

'Then I suggest we go to Retiro tomorrow. The girls are going to their friend's after school and will stay there for the night. I was thinking of taking you to the theatre. Would that appeal to you?'

'I would like that very much, thank you!' María exclaimed enthusiastically.

'That's settled then.' Isabel smiled and continued with her correspondence whilst María returned to her book, excited for the following day.

After spending a few days with her aunt and friends, middle-class life began to feel more normal for María. She started looking forward to the luncheons she was often invited to, mainly as it gave her a chance to get out of the house in one of the beautiful dresses she now owned. Since Isabel's friends had children her age, she felt less isolated and alone. They were a group of four girls; herself, Concha, Esperanza and Dolores. She liked them and they all got on well with each other discussing art and literature as well as boys. No one was particularly bothered why María was a part of the group. Her aunt simply introduced her as 'my niece visiting from Asturias'. María was then asked to describe her part of the country. For the first time since Xulián, María could speak with like-minded people who were striving for a more significant influence of women in society and removing the obsolete patriarchal system. She still missed Xulián, but remembering what her mother had said to her about not being able to leave for Madrid when she met her husband, María started to understand that if Xulián had felt the same for her as she did for him, he would have set pen to paper by now. Her rational mind told her to start afresh and forget about him, but her heart told her to hang on, and there must have been a reason why he didn't meet her underneath the tree.

The educational talks María attended with her aunt enhanced her understanding of the forward-thinking high society she desperately wanted to be a part of. One day she expressed an interest to her aunt in private lessons for French and music, similar to her friends. Isabel was overjoyed at her niece's ambitions and the fine young woman she was growing to be. She told María to consider her wish granted and that she wouldn't have to pay. Her intellect reminded Isabel of herself when she was young, and firmly believed a woman had a right to learn and soak up all available knowledge. There was only one condition: María was asked to finish her school years and, with private tutoring, apply for further education, eventually attending university. Agreeing willingly, María knew having a purpose would help her study, succeed, and make her aunt and, hopefully, her mother proud. She must write to her to tell her the fantastic news.

Over the next few months, María was as busy as ever between her duties for the girls, her schooling and tutoring lessons, and meeting her new friends. The temperature during the height of summer reached 35 °C during midday and only cooled slightly towards the evening. At this time, people emerged from their homes and went for an evening stroll in the park. María was no different; she was not used to the city's stifling heat, and when she did have to leave the house during the heat of the day, she knew the fastest way to get to her destination and the streets to walk which would have the most shade. One of her favourite places to go to after dropping the kids off at school was the Mercado de San Miguel food market close to Plaza Mayor, where she found new and exotic foods she had never seen before. In the evenings, she would discuss her findings with her aunt, who had a wealth of knowledge about nutrition, and María would learn about the far-flung ex-colonies of the Spanish Empire and other countries where the produce came from. The more time María spent in Madrid, the less time she spent thinking about the past and her home. She hadn't heard from her family for several weeks nor bothered reading Rosa's letter. Perhaps she ought to now open it, María thought to herself. Although her friend was back at her family's farm in the mountains during this time of the year, sending a letter would take even longer to arrive than usual. Still, she was aware of how she had neglected her friend when Xulián had entered her life. Though she knew she should make amends, María kept wondering if it was worth it with her being so far away. She doubted she would ever see Rosa again, and whenever she thought back to that fateful night and the party, she couldn't shake the feeling her friend hadn't told her the truth.

But her life was about to change again as the biggest news story of the day was discussed during a luncheon with the girls on a sunny autumn day; a major strike was taking place in Asturias, led by the miners.

'They have already taken control of Oviedo,' Concha spoke in hushed tones. Ladies did not discuss politics, it was frowned upon, especially during lunch in a public place. 'And the workers are burning churches and killing clergy members in Mieres.'

'Why are they striking?' Esperanza asked, visibly shocked.

'Do you remember at the general election last year when the CEDA won the most votes but President Alcalá-Zamora didn't invite their leader Robles to form a government?' They all nodded, so Concha continued: 'Well, after fighting for their rightful seats, ministers of the CEDA were finally accepted into government, but the left is now blaming the president for letting the fascists run the republic. But it's not only happening there, in Barcelona they have declared a Catalan Republic, and papá said here in Madrid they are striking too. He said it's the culmination of all the strikes during the year, and this is now a revolution!' Audible gasps sounded around the table, and immediately their mothers reprimanded them for their outbursts. The girls continued with their lunch in silence. Whilst the others ate their soup, María's head was spinning. Feeling dizzy and sick, she pushed back her chair and started walking towards the exit. Almost out of the dining room, she suddenly broke into a jog. She ran down the stairs to the ladies' room, rushing into a cubicle as the contents of her lunch came straight back up and just made it into the toilet bowl. María sat in the cubicle on the floor, trying to make sense of what she had just been told. Her uncle hadn't mentioned anything about Asturias. Was there a reason for concern about her family? María needed to talk to her uncle.

'María, are you in here?' Isabel's voice sounded, followed by a knock on the cubicle door.

'Yes.'

'Are you feeling okay? I saw you run off.' María wiped her mouth with toilet paper and got off the floor. She opened the door and was greeted by her aunt's concerned face.

'You look very white,' she commented.

'I'm not feeling well. I will go home and have a lie-down,' she said while walking to the taps and rinsing her mouth. Sorting her hair, she turned around and apologised to Isabel.

'Don't apologise. Concha told me what you girls had talked about. It's not surprising the news hit you hard.'

'Do you know more about it? Is my family okay?' María panicked. What if she knew more but didn't tell her?

'I don't, my dear. Why don't we get you home and I will talk with Antonio when he's back tonight. He will know more.' María nodded as they exited the restaurant towards the waiting car, apologising profusely for her un-ladylike behaviour. Isabel shushed her, telling her Concha should not have discussed politics at the table and that she apologised to Isabel for having forgotten where María was originally from. When they arrived at the house, María went straight to her room, Isabel informing their housekeeper to keep an eye on her.

'I will ask Señora González to pick up the girls and let them play. You don't need to worry about them today.' She stroked

María's cheek and walked to the window to close the curtain. 'You rest now my dear. There's nothing you can do this very moment, so please do not worry until we know more.'

'Thank you, Isabel, you are too kind.' María lay on her bed and closed her eyes.

María woke up and noticed she must've slept for several hours as the sun was low in the sky, bathing it in a reddish hue as she put on her uniform and made her way to the kitchen, bringing her empty cup with her. The housekeeper must have checked on her at one point, and María was grateful for it, but now she needed something to eat. She was walking past her uncle's study when she heard voices from inside. Her aunt and uncle were having an animated discussion, and she held her ear against the door.

'We must tell her, Antonio, she's worried.'

'We don't know anything yet. If we tell her what's happening, she might worry for no reason.'

'I know, but she is my sister, and those are my nephews.'

'I can make some inquiries tomorrow, but I doubt I will find out anything useful. The rebels are focussing on Oviedo, they got hold of the city's arsenal and weapons and are prepared to use them. The government is sending troops under López Ochoa to minimise the bloodshed, but this revolution must be suppressed. We don't know if her brothers and father are participating and if they are in Mieres or joined the marches to Oviedo; hopefully, they were sensible and stayed at home.' He sighed. 'There are uprisings all over the country the government has to deal with, so I will be heading back to the office.' Isabel had gone quiet. 'I am very sorry, but until all this is over, we will just have to wait, and I might not be back until then.'

María dashed into the dining room next to the study just as the door opened. She heard heavy feet on the marble floor, and the front door fall back into its lock with a loud click. She waited for her aunt's footsteps to recede upstairs before emerging from behind the door and heading to the kitchen. The kitchen door was ajar, and the low humming of Señora González stopped when María pushed the door open fully and walked towards the big table in the middle of the room.

'I kept a plate for you in case you got hungry. How are you feeling?'

'I'm not sure,' María admitted. She had felt better when she had left her room, having accepted they didn't know enough about the situation. But having heard her uncle talk about sending in government troops had made her head spin again.

'Maybe just have a little bit of bread?' María nodded and started nibbling at a piece, her mind elsewhere. What was happening in that sleepy village in the mountains? Was Xulián still there? Was he safe? What about Andrés? Back in her room, she decided no one could tell her exactly what was happening apart from her family, so she sat down at her desk and penned a letter to her dear mother.

The next few days passed in a blur while every morning she anxiously sat on the house's front steps, eagerly waiting for the postman to arrive and deliver the letters. She skipped school and private tutoring and didn't attend the weekly luncheon. Josefa and Ana picked up on her mood and asked what was happening; they were lucky to be young enough not to worry about anything. Ensuring they didn't know what dangers were around them, María lied and, with a smile, said she was just very excited to hear back from her mamá as she had now waited for three weeks. One sunny morning, María was sitting in her usual spot in front of the house, her face tilted towards the sun, when footsteps approached.

'*Señorita,*' the postman greeted her and held out a pile of letters that María snatched out of his hand.

'*Gracias,*' she mumbled, distracted. Not even halfway back to the door, she spotted her name on one of the envelopes. Dropping the rest of the letters on the console table in the hallway, she ran upstairs, taking two steps at a time. She slammed her bedroom door shut behind her and sat on her bed, breathing heavily. Her hands were trembling while she wound up the musical box and set the ballerina to spin. The music instantly calmed her mind as she slid her finger underneath the flap and pulled out the letter in handwriting she did not recognise.

Her heart ceased to beat at the words she was reading, and the ballerina stood still as the tunes to Swan Lake died.

Ten

London, England
2014

When Ava woke on Sunday, the world was still turning, and her head felt like she was banging it against a wall. Lucy had already showered and was sitting on the bed with a book and a smile that told Ava something had happened that she couldn't remember.

'What's that grin for?' she mumbled, still half asleep.

'It's alive!' she exclaimed, followed by 'Tea?'

'Yes, please.'

'How did you sleep?'

'Should I be ashamed of something I did last night?'

'You don't remember?' Lucy looked shocked as Ava's face fell, trying to recall the events. Was there any embarrassing dancing, or was she nasty to anyone? All she could remember was a lovely evening over a few pints, talking to Luke and being introduced to his brother Tom, then strolling along the river through the village back to their bed and breakfast. What else was there?

'I don't remember anything bad happening.'

'Define bad,' Lucy teased. 'Don't worry, you had a few drinks, maybe one too many, but you were still civilised. And then you gave Luke your number and told him to call you as you want to show him something that might be of interest to him.' Lucy laughed so hard she nearly spilt the tea she was holding, clearly thinking it was hilarious, while Ava's brain was blank. What if Luke called, and she couldn't remember what she wanted to show him? Then again, she doubted he'd call; why would he?

He only spent the evening with them because he felt terrible his dog had knocked her over. Given the glances from the women last night, it was apparent that he could have anyone he wanted and most likely already had most of them hence why he had moved away to London to find new prey. The tea perked Ava up instantly, and after a quick shower she felt revived and ready to tackle the day. They decided to spend the day driving through different villages in the Cotswolds and have a history-filled Sunday visiting Sudeley Castle, hiking to Broadway Tower, stopping for some lunch in Moreton-in-Marsh and then driving back to London. The weather was glorious, and while they both weren't too interested in the castle itself, they felt proud to have gone there like proper adults without whining like they would have as teenagers.

'Do you remember when your parents used to drag me along to your family outings on Sundays?' Ava reminisced.

'You mean the ones you loved and my brother and I hated?' she laughed.

'They were fun. Well, some of them at least, and only if I wasn't stuck between you and your brother in the car.'

'And then wanting to have an ice cream or a burger, my mum always prepared a picnic and constantly complained about the extortionate prices at those sites. Fun times.'

'Yes, they were. Your parents always took care of me.' Ava never complained as, while she offered to pay for her entrance fee, Lucy's parents always declined firmly, reminding her that she was part of the family. Often it made Ava feel odd, as it wasn't as if she didn't have a family of her own and needed rescuing by adoptive parents, but likewise, she also enjoyed being part of this family construct. She never voiced all of this to her mum, fearing she would feel bad for not being able to take her to all those places. Thinking back now, Ava would've been happy going around castles and visiting museums and art galleries if it meant spending more time with her mum.

On their drive back to London, a message came through on Ava's phone, and somewhere inside of her, she hoped it was from Luke. Her heart sank when she saw it wasn't from Luke but rather from Diego: 'Hey, how was your weekend? I'm just on the train back to London from Kent.' So he hadn't forgotten about her. She had been wondering though, given she hadn't heard from him since Friday when he had said he was on his way to his friend's house. Was she his personal assistant, who always needed to know exactly where he was? She sighed and threw the phone back into her bag, irritated that it annoyed her so much that she hadn't heard from him, but now that she did she wished he hadn't. With her hormones all over the place, sometimes she wondered if she was the one who was pregnant rather than Lucy, who seemed to radiate pure calmness. When Ava got dropped off at her flat, she was not only drained from the long day but also too exhausted from trying to figure out her feelings that she made herself a cup of tea and decided to ignore everyone until Thursday, when she had all the time in the world to organise her life. After catching up on her favourite television series she had recorded, she went to bed early, hoping she'd be out like a light. But instead she lay awake for several hours, tossing and turning, wondering how her life had ended up in such a mess with so many new people in it and why, despite all these people, she felt incredibly lonely without the one person she cared most about.

The three days leading up to her last day at work passed in a blur. She made a point of getting to the office before everyone else and staying longer than most, with only a half-hour lunch break. It was her way of sticking up her finger at her manager for getting rid of her when all she needed was a bit more time to get used to the new situation instead of getting the sack. Ava ensured her handover was second to none, with an empty inbox, all her contacts informed and no open issues or projects. When she was called into a meeting for her exit interview with HR, she was so drained that she wasn't sure if she cared enough about being honest. However, when Steph remarked that things wouldn't have ended this way had she shown the same effort in the last few weeks as she was doing now, Ava's anger at her treatment bubbled over and she threw caution to the wind and told Steph exactly how she felt. She returned to her desk, shut down her laptop, double-checked her pedestal was empty, put her access card on top of her laptop, grabbed the little Body Shop bag she was given as a goodbye present from the team, and left the building for the last time. Only when she stepped out onto the pavement did she finally take a deep breath as the weight of the previous few weeks fell off her shoulders. She and her flatmates had planned a night in with pizza and wine while she finished packing. Lucy was to pick her up the next day for her first scan and then drive to Ava's mum's house with all her belongings. Although she thought she didn't have a lot of things, Ava still managed to fill two suitcases and three enormous blue Ikea bags, mostly with clothes and shoes, of which a few belonged to Lucy and probably some to other friends. Having cleared away all the remnants of their evening, Ava went to bed before the new chapter in her life began.

Ava's nostalgia was almost too much for her to cope with on the morning of her move, especially after her disruptive sleep.

Last night it finally started to sink in how much her life had changed in the last couple of months and how it would never be the same again. It felt as if she suddenly, at the age of 28, had to grow up and deal with all the adult things she had quite happily ignored previously. Since she left university, all she had to worry about was finding a job and a place to live, and both had been sorted out relatively quickly. Once that was out of the way, all she did was live, go out and meet new people, experience all that London had to offer, spend the money she earned on nights out, shopping sprees, and take away meals, and rarely think about the future. Like so many young professionals, Ava just enjoyed her freedom and had bobbed along nicely until it all came crashing down, one drama after another. Ava took a deep breath and got out of bed. There was no point in thinking about everything now, she couldn't change things anyway. At least she had a place to go that was more her home than anywhere else she had ever lived, and it filled her with comfort to return to where she had spent the happiest times of her life and push the reset button. She felt being back home would give her the break she needed. With that thought and a smile, she got moving, showered, packed up her remaining belongings, and quickly cleaned her room. Her flatmates had already left for work, so when Lucy arrived Ava insisted her friend sit on the sofa while she carried all her bags to the car and somehow managed to get everything in. 'This is goodbye then. How do you feel?' Lucy asked. Ava recounted all her thoughts from the previous night all through to the morning.

'We had some pretty good times in this flat,' Lucy agreed. Leaving her keys on the kitchen table, Ava grabbed her handbag and, with one last look closed the door behind her and her old life.

'Do you want to know the sex of your baby?' the sonographer asked Lucy, who looked inquiringly at Ava.

'It's your baby, not mine. You decide if you want to know,' she answered, shrugging.

The sonographer turned to Ava and said, 'It's also your baby. Just because Lucy here is carrying it doesn't mean you're not a part of it. Many couples feel the same where one feels more connected, but you need to ensure you get involved as much as possible.'

Ava caught Lucy over the sonographer's shoulder and saw she was trying not to laugh, but when the little speech was over, she couldn't control herself anymore and burst out laughing, setting off Ava.

'I'm sorry,' Lucy said to a slightly confused, if not hurt, woman who looked at them in turn, trying to understand why they were laughing so hard. 'You're right, of course, everything you said. The thing is, Ava is not my partner, the baby's father is just such a lowlife that he got replaced with my best friend here.'

'Ah, well, then your reaction makes a lot more sense. Now do you want to know?' the visibly relieved sonographer asked again.

'No, not now. I might change my mind later, though.'

For the rest of the time the two were there, Lucy got to ask all the questions she had, and she got a full briefing on what to expect prior to her next scan.

Leaving the doctor's practice, Ava felt she needed to nudge her friend to come clean to her parents. They needed to know, especially as she was now ending her first trimester when usually people announced the happy news to the world. But it seemed nothing was usual in this situation, and Ava was fully aware that

Lucy was taking her time with everything, from making her first appointment with the gynaecologist to telling her employer.

'Are you going to tell anyone soon?' she asked tentatively.

'And with *anyone*, you mean my parents?'

'Yes.'

'Maybe. Mum might notice anyway. She has a knack for these things. Remember when my cousin was pregnant at 17, and mum asked her when she was due in front of everyone? Poor Stacey didn't even know herself yet!'

Ava did indeed remember. She was mortified for the poor girl who got kicked out of her home by her own mum when it turned out to be true. Lucy's mum, Pat Hinds, was inconsolable for having caused all of it despite Dave reminding her that the girl's pregnancy was not her fault, and she just said what would eventually be out in the open anyway. Pat offered to take Stacey in to make amends, hoping it would all blow over in a matter of weeks and her sister would take her daughter back. Unfortunately, that wasn't the case, and after a month with the Hinds, Stacey packed her bags and left for good. She kept in touch with Pat occasionally, sending postcards from all over the world, never mentioning a daughter or son though, so no one knew exactly what had happened after she had left, and to this day, she had never spoken to her mum again.

'Do you think they will be happy?'

'Definitely not in the beginning, unless it turned out to be Harry's baby, then they'd be over the moon,' she said with an annoyed tone while rolling her eyes. Harry was Lucy's ex, the one she had moved in with and therefore abandoned Ava for, and the Hinds adored him. He was handsome, well-educated, had excellent manners and was always respectful towards the elderly.

What they didn't know, or didn't care to know, was how boring and lazy he was when no one was watching. While he could talk for hours about the weather and politics, making him the star of every family gathering, he preferred staying at home every evening, skipping work drinks so he could be back in time for *Pointless*, never going out for meals to save money, and generally not doing anything.

'I always wondered why you fell for him. He was so boring.'

'He was different in the beginning, the complete opposite. He was rarely at home and always experiencing something different, trying a new restaurant, partying until the early morning hours, hopping on a plane with his best mate to Ibiza, and living life. But it all changed when I moved in, and he realised I was there to stay. He turned his life around and settled into the role of domesticated husband-to-be.'

It hadn't taken Lucy long to pack her bags and move into her work colleague's spare room. Sometimes it felt like her parents hadn't quite forgiven her for leaving him, and now they would soon have to find out that the baby Lucy was carrying was from a man who had cheated on her with three other women, and whom she had no intention of raising the child with, at least not full-time.

'Welcome home,' Lucy announced as she parked in front of Ava's old and new home. 'Did you check if you are legally even allowed to live in the house?'

'Why wouldn't I be? I'd inherit it anyway, and then I can do with it what I want. Although I still haven't looked into the mortgage situation or mum's finances, so I could be in for a shock.'

'I'm sure your mum didn't have any debt.'

'I know, but I guess that's what my weekend will be, sorting through more of her things,' Ava said with a sad smile. 'Why don't you go through and put the kettle on, and I'll bring my stuff in?'

'Sounds good.' Lucy made her way to the kitchen. 'Ava, why is there milk in the fridge? How long has this been here?' she asked as she unscrewed the top, preparing to sniff before noticing it was a new bottle.

'Kate must've left it. I messaged her earlier this week to tell her I'd be staying.'

Ava joined her in the kitchen with her bag of pots and pans and found a note on the counter:

Welcome home, Ava. I have put some milk in the fridge and some biscuits in the tin. Let me know if there is anything you need or just want to chat. Kate x

'How lovely! And here are the biscuits! She must've known that I'd be here too,' Lucy said, grabbing the pack of Jaffa Cakes, her favourites, and grinning to herself. The colourful flowers in her mum's pots in the garden were bathed in beautiful sunlight, ideal for enjoying while they drank their tea outside. Ava grabbed the mugs and biscuits and set everything on a tray. Lucy dutifully opened the patio doors.

'I think you forgot to lock the door,' she commented as the door slid open without her using a key, 'or maybe it was Kate when she was here earlier in the week.'

'She wouldn't forget to lock up after herself. She's meticulous and double-checks everything. There was also no reason for her to go into the garden,' Ava pointed out as she set the tray down on the table, sat down, and sipped her tea. Something wasn't right, she thought, before standing up again to inspect the door and lock.

'This is really strange. I'm sure I locked the door after showing the estate agent the garden. I remember I went around the house twice before I set off for London to lock all the windows and switch off all the plugs. I'll ask Kate.'

Sitting down again, Ava took her phone out of her pocket and messaged Kate, thanking her for the milk and biscuits and asking whether she went into the garden when she was in the house. While they waited for a reply, Ava's eyes looked around the beautiful garden, which was still in full bloom. Kate must have tended to it, opening the doors to water the plants and tidy up, and then forgetting to lock up, Ava concluded. Probably the foxes were also having a field day in the garden while no one was there permanently to look after it, which would explain the broken flowerpot at the far end next to the gate. Relieved, they sat in silence, soaking up the sun.

After a short while, Lucy declared she should probably be getting back to London before there was too much traffic on the roads. As Ava walked her to the door, her phone beeped, announcing a message from Kate.

You're welcome. Glad you arrived safely. And no, I didn't go into the garden at the house on Saturday. I entered the garden through the side gate like I always do so I don't have to bother removing my shoes. But I left first thing Sunday morning to go to Liverpool to stay with my sister for the week, she had a hip operation and needed some help. Why? Is there something wrong? x

'Are you alright, Ava? You've gone rather pale,' Lucy looked at Ava with concern. When Ava didn't reply, she took her shoes back off, steered her towards the sofa to sit down before she collapsed, and grabbed a glass of water.

'What's up? Who was that message from?' she asked her again.

Ava didn't respond but instead handed her phone to Lucy to read for herself while she took a few sips of water. What does this mean? Ava was sure she locked the patio doors, and Kate confirmed it wasn't her, which she had a feeling was the case anyway. Kate also would have tidied up the broken flowerpot when she watered the plants, but she was last in the garden on Saturday. Ava wished for the umpteenth time her mum had had security cameras installed around the house, then she could just check and be sure it was just a fox who knocked over the pot.

'Ava, this doesn't mean anything. Clearly, you just forgot to lock it last time. There's no other explanation.'

'What if someone broke in while no one was here?'

'Why would anyone go to the trouble of breaking into a house and not take anything? Look, the telly and all other appliances are still here. Your imagination is just running wild. You were in a difficult place when you showed the estate agent around while knowing you had to see HR the next day, and then you saw that robin in the garden. Your mind was all over the place.'

'I just have an uneasy feeling. When I entered the house today, I thought something wasn't right.

'Yes, unfortunately, your mum isn't here. That's what's not right. Now please stop making yourself mad. I'll tell you what; I'll stay longer and help you unpack, then we'll cook something for dinner, and I'll leave later when traffic has died down again. Okay?'

'No, don't worry. You don't have to babysit me.'

'You would actually do me a favour. I really don't want to go home and risk running into one of my flatmates, especially Charlie, who I've been trying to stay away from as much as possible. If she found out I was pregnant, the whole office would know, and I'm just not ready for that yet. So far, I've managed to dodge her most of the time, and at work, I started wearing baggier clothes, mainly jumpers, which isn't easy in this heat,' she sighed.

Ava smiled and put her hand on Lucy's, 'Thank you. I'd appreciate that.'

They put on the radio and started unpacking the bags with the kitchen utensils and food, before moving on to the shoes bag and coats bag. When everything downstairs was put away, Ava carried the suitcases upstairs and dumped them on the bed in the spare room, which used to be her bedroom. 'Don't you want the bigger room?' Lucy asked.

'No, that's mum's room, it still has all her things in it. I'll stay in my room for the moment.'

Together they unpacked Ava's clothes, hanging them up in the wardrobe or putting them away in the chest of drawers, her make-up bag on top of the chest where a mirror hung on the wall, and the rest into the bathroom.

'Right, that was easier than I had imagined,' Ava said as she sat on the bed.

'And faster too. How do you feel?'

'I wonder how mum could live here alone for so long. It feels way too big for just one person. Think of all the money she could've saved by moving to a smaller place!'

'Yes, but this was her home, and she had her parents and friends nearby. And it is lovely, I'm not surprised she never wanted to leave.'

'Even with all the memories of my father attached to this house?' Ava had never previously considered this and now wished she had asked her mum why she had stayed.

'So, what next?'

'Nothing. I only have my handbag left with my laptop and the book we found after the funeral. I should start looking into things, Kate is such a sweetheart and did what she could to help, but there's still a lot to do to sort out finances, insurance, etc. She will have more information on what I need to do.' Too many things were piling up on Ava's to-do list that she hadn't tackled yet, and she knew she was running out of time before there were serious repercussions, if not repossessions.

'I think I saw some pasta sauce in one of the cupboards when I was looking for the biscuit tin, and I noticed you had some penne. So how about we get cooking? I'm starving.' Without waiting for an answer, Lucy got up from the bed and headed back downstairs to the kitchen. While they were sitting down to eat, Ava's phone beeped again. It was a message from Diego.

Hey, how are you? Do you fancy a drink tonight?

Oops, she thought, 'I haven't told Diego about losing my job nor that I've moved back home,' she said to Lucy through a mouthful of pasta.

'Do you want me to tell him at work tomorrow?'

'Don't worry, I'll message him back later.'

'How are things going with him?'

'Things have gone a little bit cold. I haven't really been in touch lately. I just wanted to finish everything at work, pack my bags and leave. It's not a great feeling having to admit that you're unemployed. All I wanted was to draw a line under everything and start afresh.'

'Which is your right. It won't matter if you tell him now or in a few weeks. Unless he asks you straight out if you lost your job, then yes, you should tell him, but if he doesn't ask you, there's no need to point it out until you're ready.

Ava raised her eyebrows at Lucy. 'Are we still talking about me telling Diego or you telling HR about being up the duff?'

'Both,' she answered with a grin.

After dinner, Lucy decided it was time for her to get back home before she became too tired and risked falling asleep at the wheel. 'You're welcome to come and stay here if you want to get away from your flatmates, by the way,' Ava mentioned as they hugged goodbye at the door.

'Thank you, I might take you up on that offer. I'll let you know,' she called as she walked towards her car, blowing a kiss at Ava.

'Drive safely,' she shouted back.

Ava sat down on the couch and got her laptop and folder out. She decided she might as well start looking at the documents so she was ready to call the relevant people first thing in the morning. It became apparent that her mum was more organised than she had realised and even took out life insurance a few weeks after Ava's father passed away. Ava opened a spreadsheet on her laptop and started adding information from the documents she would need, like account numbers, account managers, telephone numbers and anything else salient she could find.

When she went to pick up the next piece of paper, she noticed several were stapled together. The first of these was a mortgage agreement taken out in 1981, the year her parents married, and the next was a deed of trust with a big red stamp on it reading PAID. Ava looked at the deed trying to understand what that meant. From what she could see and thought she understood, it seemed the house's mortgage was fully repaid back in 1992. This could not be true. Her mum definitely did not have the means to pay off the mortgage in one go, especially in the year her husband died. She noted this in her sheet, knowing she would probably only find out the truth when she called the bank the next day. As she picked up the documents again, she noticed the stack was thicker at the top and turned the pages until she found what it was. A letter was wedged in between the papers with her name on it. She released it from the staples and eyed it suspiciously, unsure how she felt about opening it. A last message from mum, she thought, as she put the letter on the coffee table and got up to make herself a cup of tea. While pouring the water into the kettle, she noticed her hands were shaking. Taking her mug to the couch, she sat down, tucked her feet underneath her and slowly opened the letter.

My dearest Ava,
If you are reading this letter, I lost my battle against cancer and am no longer with you, and it breaks my heart to know that my darling girl is now on her own in this world. Please remember that you are never truly alone, and I will always

watch over and guide you. You are the most special person in the world, and you cannot fathom the sheer joy you have brought me since the day I knew you existed. What you are going through is the most challenging thing you will ever have to do in life. Grieving for a loved one will sometimes test your loyalty towards them and make you wonder if all the happy memories were as magical as you remembered them.

Ava, your father didn't die, but you need to understand that it was easier to tell you a lie to protect you. I know I never spoke to you about him, and you had a right to know who your father was, but it was too painful for me to talk about his disappearance. I never stopped loving Brian. He always was my true love. I knew him like the back of my hand and know that whatever made him leave his beloved baby girl behind must have been so devastating that he saw no other way. And trust me when I say that during all those nights when I cried myself to sleep and wondered if the nightmare would ever be over and he would come back home, you were the only reason I kept going and didn't give up. And I hope that one day you might meet him again.

I took out life insurance when your dad left, and his parents paid off the mortgage in full. Please take the money from the insurance and do something you have always dreamt of. Go travelling and see the world, sip cocktails on a white sandy beach, and dance the night away. I will always be there to guide you.

Take care, my beautiful daughter, and celebrate life. It can
be over so soon.
Love always,
Mum

The room started spinning as Ava sat there shocked, her
mind racing, a million thoughts coming and going. Her head felt
like a train station where questions entered and rushed through
before she could grasp and answer them. Her father was alive.
Closing her eyes, she took a few deep breaths to steady her
heartbeat and sat on her hands to stop them from shaking.
Looking around the living room, she took in the fireplace where
they used to hang their stockings for Father Christmas, the old
rocking chair that stood to the side next to the bookcase filled
with the novels her mum loved to read, and grandpa used to
claim for himself every time he visited because he had the best
view from it and could see everything that was happening around
him. The old battered cushions that her mum didn't get rid of
despite the fraying ends, the colourful plates they had found at
antiques markets up and down the country. Everything she saw
was hers now. Their family home, where they were so happy, no
one could take it away from her, and she didn't need to pay a
penny for it. Slowly she started to calm down, and her breathing
returned to something resembling normal as she felt her eyes fill
with tears at the enormity of her mum's words. Not just about the
house but also the undying love she still felt for her husband. The
magnitude of the situation started to sink in. Her father was
alive.

Ava couldn't recall how long she was sobbing for when she woke to her phone ringing; she must have fallen asleep. Groggily, she reached for it. It was an unknown number, and as she slid the toggle to the right to answer, she hoped against all odds that it might be her father.

'Hello?'

'Hi, it's Luke. Do you remember me?'

'Eh, hi. Yeah, I remember you,' she stammered while her heart sank that it wasn't her father.

'Sorry for not calling sooner, but work has been crazy. How are you?'

'I'm fine,' Ava said sleepily, kicking herself for her short answers, but her brain was still muddled.

'Is this a bad time?'

'No. Sorry, I just woke up. I must've dozed off on the couch.'

'I apologise for my intrusion. I can call back at a more convenient time.'

'It's fine, I just need a second.'

'Long day?' he asked.

Ava laughed involuntarily at the fact that long didn't even come close to the kind of day she'd had as she tried to remember if she had told Luke about everything that had been going on. Something about his voice made her open up, and maybe it wasn't necessarily him but just the need to talk to someone. While rambling on, she realised that Lucy's pregnancy was one thing he didn't know about.

'Oh no, I shouldn't have told you! Please promise me that you won't tell anyone. She hasn't even told her parents yet.'

'Wow, I feel honoured to be among the first to know. But don't worry, who would I tell anyway?'

'Thank you.' Ava was mortified that she managed to break the one promise she had given Lucy within just a few days.

'So, do you really think someone has broken into the house?'

'I'm not sure. Maybe I didn't lock the door last time I was here.'

'Have you checked all the rooms, just to make sure?' When Ava told him about the back door being unlocked, Luke sounded concerned.

'No, I didn't go into my mum's room, the study or the loft,' she admitted, feeling a cold shudder run down her spine while she looked around nervously. Ava got up from the sofa and ensured all the windows and doors on the ground floor were locked and the lights were on. She took a deep breath and sat in the rocking chair in the corner, her eyes scanning the living room and kitchen from left to right and back.

'I'm sure it's nothing. You had a lot going on and probably just forgot,' he suggested, but Ava wasn't listening. Her eyes stared at a black shadow outside the patio doors, her heart beating uncontrollably when the shadow abruptly moved. She screamed and jumped out of the rocking chair, dashing to the other side of the living room.

'What happened? Are you okay, Ava? What's going on?' came Luke's voice down the phone.

'Cat,' was all Ava could say when she realised the shadow was just a black cat that had jumped out of the garden onto the fence and was gone.

'A cat what? Ava, talk to me!'

Still clutching her phone and trying to calm her breath, Ava slid to the floor and started crying. Through sobs, she tried to explain.

'Text me your address and stay on the phone until I arrive.'

'I'm fine,' she lied.

'I can hear you're not fine. Is there a neighbour who could come over or a friend?'

'No, my neighbour is in Liverpool, and I have no friends here.'

'Right, I'm not leaving you alone tonight. Tell me your postcode and pour yourself a drink, something to steady your nerves,' he instructed her. Ava said nothing. Why would she give a stranger her address? 'Ava, please, I only want to help.' The concern in his soft voice made her crumble. She sighed with resignation and gave him her postcode. It didn't take long for Luke to arrive, and when she let him into the house, she fell into his arms, her tense body instantly starting to relax. For the first time in a very long time, she accepted that having a strong man by her side made her feel just that little bit safer, and as her thoughts wandered to her mum's letter, she wondered how her mum managed to keep going and stay strong, not once complaining, after everything life had thrown at her.

Eleven

The morning sunshine covered her bed in a warm light. Although she slept a solid nine hours, she felt exhausted. She wasn't sure if it was because of last night's events or not being used to the bed anymore. She remembered how well she used to sleep and loved being woken up by the sun instead of one of her flatmates banging on the bathroom door to hurry up the person who was blocking it. As so often when Ava thought back to those times, she felt a little tug in her chest, and a melancholy overwhelmed her, but today, she was determined to start her new life in her own house. She roused from the bed and quickly checked her phone when she saw she had several unread messages. The one from Lucy asked her how she felt, so she quickly replied that she was okay. The next was from Kate, saying she was relieved that it was a false alarm about the back door, she wouldn't have been able to forgive herself, and that she was returning on Sunday and would pop over. The third text was the one she dreaded most because her reply the evening before was pretty curt, and she was sure she had now blown all chances of a happy ending with Diego. All it said was 'okay, maybe next time', but she noticed no characteristic 'x', signifying a kiss, at the end. Ava sighed, knowing she might never hear from him again. She threw the phone back on the bed and quickly showered while mentally noting everything she had to do. Firstly, she had to call the bank to confirm the mortgage situation. The thought of telling the estate agent she wasn't going to sell made her smile. He had been calling her non-stop since their first contact, and while packing up her old life, she had ignored him. After that, she had to check the situation on the life insurance to find out how to receive the money. Lastly, she needed to find a new job. Her mum didn't spend years paying insurance for her to use it all on utility bills, so the sooner she was employed again, the calmer her mind would be. She just hoped it wouldn't all come crashing down soon and that it was all just a dream.

Luke handed her a cup of tea when she got to the kitchen before returning to the hob and his cooking. 'It smells delicious, what are you making?' Ava had to admit she had almost forgotten Luke was in the house.

'Pancakes. I hope you're hungry, I might've gone overboard with the batter.'

'I'm starving,' she answered as her tummy started rumbling.

'I guessed you're a tea drinker as I couldn't find any coffee, and I hope you don't mind that I went through the cupboards to see what there was in terms of food.'

'Yeah, not much, I'm sorry. My neighbour took most things as it was easier than me taking everything back to London. And tea is perfect. Where did you get the food from in the end?'

'So there's this thing called a corner shop, and they had everything I needed,' he said sarcastically, grinning.

She couldn't help but smile too. How considerate of him to make her breakfast, although she was sure it was mainly for himself after a very rough night. Ava did offer that he could have her mum's bedroom, or she'd take it, and he could have hers, but he decided that it didn't feel right anyone sleeping in her mum's room, so he spent the night on the couch. At least it was comfortable, and he assured her he had spent the night in much worse places. Ava set the table, put the maple syrup and whipped cream on the table, washed the blueberries and strawberries and added them to the delectable spread.

The morning felt rather perfect, and the thought of Luke leaving after breakfast wasn't something Ava wanted to entertain despite all the things she should get on with. She told him how safe she felt when he arrived last night and how much she appreciated what he had done for her. They had talked for a few hours about everything, and by the time Ava started yawning, she had almost forgotten why he was there in the first place. She had told him about the house situation. While she was talking to him, he looked at her with such genuine interest that she kept on talking, and in the end, she even told him about her mum's letter, her request to find her father and about the photo of Henry and María and the newspaper article. Being in his company, Ava felt extremely at ease and wondered if this was how it felt to be in a happy relationship. She wasn't sure, but she knew she didn't want it to end and would happily have kept him there for the whole weekend if she could.

'I'm sorry that you had to come all this way for me and now have to head back to get to work.'

'I didn't have to come, I wanted to. You needed someone, and I am glad it was me. Our conversation last night was fascinating, especially the photo you mentioned. Maybe you can show it to me today?'

'Sure.'

'Great! As for getting back to work, I can work from anywhere if I have my laptop with me, and I do, so I'm in no rush to leave. Unless, of course, you want to get rid of me?' he asked, looking at her, hoping she'd say no.

'Of course not, it's lovely to have you around, and it's not as if I need to be anywhere myself. So, if you'd like to stay longer, I can get you a towel if you want to shower?'

'That would be great, thanks,' he said, as they locked eyes and smiled. Ava went to grab a towel for Luke and showed him where everything was, leaving him to start on her to-do list. The faster she could work through it, the more time she could spend with Luke, and at the moment that felt like the perfect day. Sitting on the couch, she noticed all the documents were still lying where she had left them the night before. Luke, therefore, had the chance to look at everything. Though she had told him most of what she had learnt, even the letter's contents, she hadn't told him about the life insurance. Taking a deep breath, she put that thought aside and called the bank. After a long wait, she finally got through to someone and Ava explained why she was calling. After ten minutes discussing the matters, she barely managed to thank the lady and hang up the phone. *How life could be so cruel?* Losing her father, then her mum and job, and finally being told that the house she thought was hers wasn't. The news that technically Ava shouldn't be living there was gut-wrenching. The gravity of the situation hadn't fully sunk in when Luke returned to the living room. He saw Ava muttering to herself with her head in her hands, sat beside her and put his arms around her shoulders for comfort.

'Bad news?' he asked while still holding her. She breathed in the scent of his clean body.

'It turns out it isn't as straightforward as I thought.'

'How come? Is the mortgage not paid off in full after all?'

'Oh, it is. But it's not my mum's house. Well, only partly.'

'What?'

'My parents owned it together, so I only inherited my mum's share, the other part is still my father's. After his death, mum didn't get his share, and now I obviously know why.'

'What does that mean?' Luke pulled away slightly to look at her directly.

'It means theoretically I'm not allowed to live here and need to apply for something called probate for which I need to find a solicitor, and I need to check if my mum left a will. Because if she didn't, the house would pass to my father and not me.'

'And you were told this by the bank?'

'The lady I spoke to told me she had just inherited a property herself, so she knew quite a bit about it. She advised me to get a solicitor as soon as possible to investigate, although she also mentioned that all of this would normally be done sooner after a person's death.'

'Better late than never. And your mum didn't leave a will?'

'I don't know. I couldn't find anything, and no one has contacted me about one.'

Luke didn't seem to fully believe what Ava was telling him, especially about her mum not leaving a will, particularly after having been diagnosed with cancer.

'I assume mum thought it would all come to me anyway, so she didn't think a will would be necessary.'

'What are you going to do now?'

'Well, I suppose I'll call the estate agent and tell him I won't be selling. He doesn't need to know the truth, and I should probably find a solicitor. But to be honest, I think I might wait with that. Because right now, apart from that woman at the bank, Kate and Lucy, no one knows I'm here and that I'm in a house that isn't mine,' Ava said as she sat up straight with determination in her eyes. 'If I get a solicitor involved, I might get kicked out, so the longer I wait, the more time I can buy myself to do the most important thing: find my father.'

Luke smiled and slowly nodded in agreement, affirming that she might be breaking the law, but he liked the energy Ava had regained and wasn't going to spoil it. Before she could change her mind, she grabbed her phone and called the estate agent, telling him she wasn't ready to sell yet. He tried to convince her unsuccessfully that now was a great time to sell and her property could reach a higher price than in a few months when demand might not be as strong, but she politely promised he'd be her first call when she decided to put it on the market, already knowing he wouldn't.

Both needing some fresh air, Ava and Luke stepped outside and went for a walk in the woods, past the pond and back towards the village, where they decided to drop in at the pub. For the umpteenth time, Ava wondered why Luke was prepared to go to such lengths for her, and although they had spent a lot of time together and spoken about many things, they didn't know each other yet.

Nevertheless, her heart started falling for this young man while her head reminded her of Diego and everything he had done for her after her mum passed. She had her heart closed for so long, but the moment she opened it just a tiny bit, two men came along at the same time. She wished she could speak to her mum about it, she always had good advice when it came to matters of the heart. Ava was sure she would've loved Luke, and with a sudden pang, she remembered that her mum would never meet the family Ava hoped to have one day and her heart was filled with sadness at the realisation.

'A cider and a pint of lager, please.' Luke's voice brought her back to the present. 'Are you okay?' he asked, pushing his way through to an empty table in the corner.

'I must be great company if that's the only question you ask me,' she said, laughing. 'I'm fine, just thinking.'

'Care to share?' looking at her inquiringly. Ava blushed remembering her last thoughts on Luke, and she certainly wasn't going to tell him. Thinking on her feet, she explained how unsure she was about finding her father, given that she thought he had died long ago.

Luke mentioned how a DNA test could help find him or even relatives she had on his side of the family. It seemed he didn't want to be found if her father was still alive. What if he had forgotten all about her and started a new family? The thought that half-siblings might be out there both scared and exhilarated her.

'Wouldn't it be better to find out than never knowing?'

'What? Knowing that he didn't want my mum and I, and instead found someone else to be happy with? I don't see how that would be better,' Ava said boldly.

'From what you told me, he was happy, maybe something happened that made him go away, and he didn't leave you because he didn't love you anymore.'

'And what if he was happy because he knew he could leave us soon and jet off with his new wife.'

'Your mother said something must have happened, as did his parents. From where I am standing, it looks like unless you find him, you will never know the truth,' he concluded, sitting back in his chair and taking a swig of his beer.

'Thanks, Sherlock.' She rolled her eyes at him despite being aware he was right, but because of the glint in his eyes, she didn't want to admit that just yet.

Establishing that they were both pretty hungry, they ordered food and more drinks, but having done so, Luke mentioned he had to head back to London soon for an awards night from his newspaper. Ava found herself disappointed that he had to leave again. After returning to the house, Luke grabbed his rucksack and headed back towards the front door. Desperate to give him a reason to see her again, Ava went to her bag and got the photo and the old newspaper article out. He eyed them with curiosity, pointed out the swirl of the letters in the article and that his newspaper used to print their papers in that font. He offered to check the newspaper's archives to see who originally wrote it. Maybe that would be a lead. Ava did a little internal dance that Luke took the bait and jumped at the opportunity to do some digging for her and, of course, would meet her again to present the results. Ava stood at the door and smiled awkwardly, unsure how to say goodbye. Luke bent down and kissed her on the cheek. He'd be in touch, and she should call him if she needed him, day or night. With a wink, he got in his car and drove off.

Ava closed the door behind her with a big grin and got her phone out. She messaged Lucy that she had news and asked if she fancied coming to the house on Saturday. Lucy immediately replied, saying she'd be there in the morning and bring an overnight bag as she needed to get out of the house. Ava read the message and felt relief that she wouldn't be alone over the weekend, and tonight, she would just have to stay up late and keep the lights on. Sitting on the couch, she grabbed her laptop and searched the internet for DNA kits, after all she didn't have anything to lose but might, in fact, gain a whole new family. After she had ordered one, she found the insurer's online form to claim her mum's life insurance but decided to hold back until she had spoken to a solicitor. Instead, she made herself a cup of tea, grabbed one of the books from the shelf, sat in the rocking chair and started to read. Almost immediately, Ava was interrupted by a message on her phone. She jumped out of the chair and dived for it on the sofa, hoping it was Luke.

'Free for a drink tonight? x.' Her heart sank slightly at Diego's message. In the space of a few days, she managed to almost push him out of her mind and find someone new to concentrate on. Was she so desperate for love that she would jump from one guy to another within a matter of days? How did women deal with dating someone new every other week? She felt bad enough as it was, and she had only been on one date with Diego and none with Luke, unless the walk and pub lunch today counted. Ava noticed the kiss was back at the end of his message. Did he forgive her for not being in touch? Agonising over what she should answer, she wondered why she hadn't been honest in the first place about losing her job and moving out of her flat in London. What was holding her back from telling him? Surely it wouldn't change anything between them? But somehow, she wasn't entirely sure that was true, she had the feeling if he knew she had been fired from her job, it would change his opinion of her. She didn't have that feeling with Luke, he just took her the way she was, but Diego had an expectation around him like a father had for his child, which made Ava uncomfortable. That was it, she thought to herself, she felt uncomfortable around Diego, uneasy, and although she couldn't yet pinpoint why, she knew it made her hold back from being honest and open. Before she could change her mind, she replied that she was on a small break and not in London. Maybe they could catch up when she was back. She deliberately left it open to interpretation and didn't give him a date when she would return to the city, hoping that she'd have figured things out by the time he asked again.

Ava slept deeply that night and felt refreshed when she woke the next morning. Luke had been messaging her, making sure she was okay and felt safe, as well as sending her photos of the evening. These included a selfie of him in a suit and numerous pictures of the extravagant ballroom decorated like a winter wonderland with white balloons, fairy lights, and artificial snow. A mix between chic and tacky, Ava scoffed, thinking she could've done a better job. There was no sign of another woman on his arm in any of the photos, she noticed. Empty champagne bottles on their table explained the photos getting blurrier the longer the evening went on. She decided to call it a night when she couldn't make anything out anymore. She had gone to bed on such a high that she slept soundly without another thought of the previous night's scary incident. Grabbing her phone, she saw even more messages from Luke, most with more blurry photos as well as a few saying he was bored, he wished she was there with him, he assumed she had gone to bed so he wished her goodnight, and the last one sent this morning apologising for all the texts he had sent and stating the obvious that he was pretty drunk towards the end. Ava smiled to herself and then read a message from Lucy that she was on her way with breakfast and would be there in fifteen minutes, so she jumped out of bed to get ready, ignoring the message from Diego. When Lucy arrived, Ava filled her in on everything that had happened after she had left on Thursday evening, not leaving out any details, as they sat outside in the garden with their breakfast, enjoying the early morning sunshine. Ava could see Lucy was trying to decide on her next question, deliberating if the situation with Luke or finding her father was more important.

'Diego was fired yesterday,' she blurted out instead.

'Why?' Ava didn't see that curveball coming, and there she was, worried whether he'd think less of her if she told him she'd lost her job.

'Turns out he bluffed his way into the company with fake university degrees, previous work experience and references. No one noticed, and the companies he worked for had a website and all, and the references of his previous managers seemed legit too. And because it was all in Spain, he had no P45s. No one knows how he pulled it off.'

Ava couldn't believe what she was hearing, but somehow, it wasn't too surprising, it confirmed the uneasy feeling she had about him. But why go to such lengths?

'Are they going to investigate him?'

'I don't know. If they did report him, it could be extremely damaging to the company, and clients would think twice about future investments. It's a serious security breach, though, so I assume it'll come out sooner or later. Stuff like this spreads like wildfire.'

'Wow, and I thought he was such a successful man when he's just a fraud.' Ava told Lucy how uncomfortable he made her feel, and this proved her uneasy feeling about him was justified. At that moment, Ava remembered he had messaged her again and she grabbed her phone to read it: 'Are you avoiding me, Ava? If you don't want to see me, please be honest.'

'He's got nerves telling me to be honest. He's the one who's been lying to everyone!' she huffed, angrily.

'Calm down, love, just ignore him. He's at rock bottom now and might even be sued by the company. I'm almost certain he has already packed his bags and returned to Spain, so chances are pretty low you'll never see him again. Just block his number,' Lucy said calmly.

Ava didn't want to block his number yet, even though cutting all ties was probably for the best. 'Men!' was all Ava said.

Lucy laughed out loud. 'Tell me about it!'

They finished their teas and decided today was the day to sort out the master bedroom, so Ava could move in there while Lucy stayed in the guest bedroom. Having stripped the bed, Ava put everything in the washing machine, and they used the empty mattress to make piles of her mum's clothes, those that were still in good condition and her mum had worn frequently, those that were still in good condition but her mum had rarely worn, and those that needed to be binned. Ava decided that was the best way, then she and Kate could decide if they wanted to keep anything, and the rest could go to charity. Lucy suggested she could sell some of it, but Ava felt weird making a profit from her mum's demise and selling on a dead woman's clothes. After a few hours, they had finished, and just one last garment was hanging in the wardrobe, her mum's wedding dress.

'Wow, this is beautiful and so modern! Have you ever seen it, Ava?'

Ava looked at the beautiful cream dress with two wide shoulder straps made of tulle, a tight corsage with a heart shape cleavage and where the fabric twisted from the right to the left side, flowing into the puffy lower part with a five-foot-long trail. It was stunning.

'No, not even a photo,' she answered, stunned that she had never seen it before.

'You should try it on, see if it fits.'

Ava wasn't sure if she should, but like Lucy, she wanted to know what it looked like when someone wore it, so she did. Her friend took a photo as Ava looked at herself in the big bedroom mirror. It fit perfectly. Her mum must have been exactly her size when she got married to her father. The thought gave her comfort as, for the second time in the last couple of days, she remembered her mum would never see her daughter get married.

'Maybe one day I can wear this dress and have mum walk down the aisle with me.' Ava said. Lucy stood up from the bed from where she was marvelling at Ava and gave her a big hug, tears starting to roll down her face.

'Don't ruin the dress,' Ava scolded, when she felt a tear drop on her bare shoulder, bringing tears to her own eyes. They hugged each other for a long time, and when they pulled apart, they both felt slightly lighter. Taking the dress off and hanging it back in its bag, they packed the clothes that needed to be recycled and set off to the closest charity clothes collection bin. Ava was silent on the drive but was glad she wasn't alone; throwing away her mum's clothes felt like getting rid of a part of her mum's memory. However, she also knew if she kept everything the way it was, she wouldn't be able to move on and find closure. Instead, she would keep expecting her mum to turn up. She needed to focus on the future, and just because she had cleared out her wardrobe, it didn't mean she had in any way come to terms with the situation. Back at home, they decided to research her father and see if anything would give them a clue as to where he might be. Leading the way up the stairs and into the study, Ava immediately felt something was off. She couldn't put her finger on it, but standing in the doorway, she scanned the room and tried to recall what it looked like the last time she was there. She looked around the room, checking the wall to her left with the low bookcase where her mum kept boxes of sewing kits, loose buttons, rags of fabric, a folder full of patterns and her sewing machine. Everything was there. Above the bookcase hung one of Ava's many drawings and paintings she produced as a child, the one with the blue flowers that her mum had put in a gold frame which used to hang in the living room. On the far wall adjacent to her mum's room was a fold-out sofa that had been Ava's before she got a proper double bed. Another of Ava's paintings, a colourful display of their garden in full bloom with three people in the middle, hung above the sofa. She had forgotten all about that painting. It showed her parents and her, so she must've painted it before her father died, or disappeared, as she now knew. Lucy bumped into her, having not noticed that Ava had stopped, and looked over Ava's shoulder, before asking what was wrong. 'I'm not sure yet,' Ava replied, slowly moving into the room and trying to get a grip, 'do you remember how we left it last time?'

'You're scaring me. What's wrong?' Lucy was breathing hard, and Ava felt a shudder down her spine, having moved her eyes from the sofa to the opposite wall where the desk was located.

'The hatch.' They both looked up and saw the trapdoor to the loft was open and dangling down with the ladder attached to it but drawn in.

'Maybe it fell open after we went up there last time and didn't close it properly.'

'No,' Ava said, she was sure she had closed it properly. Had she not, it would've opened while they were still in the room looking through the papers. Slowly, as she moved back towards the door, she spotted the box on the desk, the one they got down from the loft and within which they had found the newspaper article and the book with the photo. It had been moved. 'Someone was in here, and they were looking for something specific.' Ava's heart beat faster, as her mind went into overdrive. She knew she hadn't imagined it all, someone did break in through the back door and made their way to the study and the loft, not disturbing the downstairs and making sure not to leave any traces. And it would have worked had the hatch to the attic not been left open. Ava closed the door and called the police.

The officer who attended the crime scene couldn't have been any nicer and made Ava feel like a responsible adult again, having initially felt so stupid for allowing someone to break in to her mum's house. She told him everything in exact detail, from the moment she noticed the back door was unlocked to her checking with her neighbour about it, the plant pot that had been knocked over in the garden, her uneasy feeling that something was wrong, her fright when she saw the cat and thought it was a man, to discovering that someone had been in the study and the loft. He wrote it all down, making sure he knew which surfaces they had touched and which ones they hadn't since they'd arrived, who else had been there, when the last time she had been in the house was, where the owner of the house was, and so on. It all got so overwhelming that the officer got up and left to room to give Ava a moment to gather her thoughts. While she sipped the tea Lucy had handed her, Ava asked whether she should tell the police her mum had died or that she'd just gone away for a bit. Lucy looked at her with an expression of disbelief, before telling her not to lie to the police as they would surely find out anyway. 'But what if they tell me I can't stay here?' Ava asked.

'Ava, do you really *want* to stay in this house knowing someone has broken in without leaving any traces? That must've been a professional, what if they come back?' Them coming back hadn't crossed Ava's mind yet and it scared her even more.

'What's going on here?' A voice came from the front door. 'Ava darling, are you okay?' Kate entered the house. Ava fell into her arms, crying, and explained what had happened. Kate confirmed to the officer she hadn't noticed anything untoward when she had been in the week before. As the officer continued with his questioning of Ava, she patiently answered in full, admitting her mum had passed and that she was looking after the house. The officer confirmed the patio door lock had been tampered with as he took a photo of a dark mark on the carpet, a muddy shoe print.

'Miss Brown, has anything been taken?' the officer asked.

'I don't know. I would have to check the loft and the boxes, but I don't know what was in them.'

'Jewellery, maybe?'

'No, nothing was missing. My mum didn't have a lot of jewellery anyway, and I went through her possessions this morning. Nothing seemed to be missing.'

'Has anything been removed from the house since your mother's passing?' Kate squeezed Ava's hand, before asking the officer if all these questions were necessary.

'Unfortunately, yes, we're trying to find out why this house was broken into, but if we don't know what was taken or what the burglar was looking for, it makes it very difficult,' the officer replied.

'The only things I took were some insurance and mortgage papers. And just this morning, we removed some of my mum's clothes.'

'Right, well, the team will need some time to dust for fingerprints. Let us know if you notice anything missing that might help us. And I suggest you have security cameras installed when you can.' And with that, the officer left the house, leaving the team to finish. The three women sat there in silence, lost in their own thoughts. After a couple of minutes, Kate announced she was going over to hers to put the kettle on and suggested the girls should grab a few things and join her for the rest of the day and the night. Ava and Lucy did as instructed and went to Kate's once the police had left. Before they entered Kate's house, Lucy grabbed Ava's arm and asked her in a low voice why she hadn't told the officer about the photo and newspaper article she had taken. Ava responded that she was scared those things would be taken away from her for inspection as she felt they might be connected. Lucy understood and nodded. Secrets buried in the past needed unravelling without the police's prying eyes.

Twelve

Madrid, Spain
1936

Tensions in the country and minor conflicts between the left and the right had been mounting since the Asturias uprising in October 1934, those fateful days when María's world was torn apart by a few sentences in a letter from her family. The memory still haunted her; the bedroom felt small and claustrophobic, her chest tightened, and she struggled to breathe, her whole body shook with anger at the world that it was always the good ones that had to suffer. Her dear brother Andrés was killed by the government troops, having taken part in an uprising he was dragged into by Pablo. The pain she felt over the loss of Andrés, mixed with the hate for Pablo, had spread to every fibre in her body. She couldn't deal with the sensations, she had needed to get out and release her emotions. It had taken the police more than two hours to locate her after her uncle had reported her missing. Isabel had found the letter on the floor after María had failed to pick up the girls from school, she had known there were only two options for where a 14-year-old girl could have gone – either try and run home to Asturias, which was unlikely, or go somewhere that reminded her of home. The Guardia Civil had already searched El Retiro Park and moved on to Casa de Campo, even though María had only been gone for a few hours. Still, Antonio had made sure they immediately started the search. They had finally found her curled up underneath a tree in a grass-stained dress, her hands covered in blood, her eyes red and sore from crying, and her body shivering in the cold evening air.

The doctor had been called, and for the next two weeks, María had been a shell of herself, rarely leaving her bed, and answering only by nodding and shaking her head. Every effort by Isabel to get her out of the house had been unsuccessful, every book Antonio had brought her from his library went unread, and every drawing the girls had shown her was acknowledged with a nod but had failed to put a smile on her face.

A few days before Christmas, Ana had slipped on the steps in front of the house, letting out a cry of pain so loud it had travelled through the house to María's room, who, against her own will, had rushed to the little girl she had become so fond of. Señora González had tried to comfort her, but the moment María had arrived, Ana had wanted only her. If the housekeeper had been shocked to see María, she hadn't shown it. Instead, she simply explained Ana had to see a doctor while Josefa had to be taken to school, and had given her the choice of what she wanted to do. The little girl bawling her eyes out in María's arms had stirred her out of her state of shock and into action. Watching a doctor take X-rays and a nurse fit a cast onto Ana's tiny arm had given María the push she needed to pick herself up and re-enter the real world outside her bedroom.

María was in awe of their work, and felt the urge that she wanted to help others in the same way. She knew she would have to attend university to study medicine and that she needed top marks to be considered. So over the next few months María committed to studying as much as she could and excelled at her school, and her private French and music lessons. When the time came to prove what she had learnt, she passed her final exams with flying colours and she was ready to go to university.

María enrolled at the Faculty of Medicine in Madrid close to home, but after just two weeks of attending lectures in a class filled with boys and just one other girl besides her, María knocked on her uncle's study door one evening. 'María, how is university?' he greeted her, delight in his voice.

'Antonio, I would like to discuss something with you.' Sensing a major announcement, he removed his glasses and folded his hands.

'What can I do for you, my child?'

María swallowed, before speaking. 'Uncle, I am not happy at university. All I do is sit there listening to someone talk. I want to do something practical, not theoretical.'

Antonio took his time before he answered. 'There was one condition when we paid for your French and music lessons. That you would go to university.'

'Yes,' María mumbled, looking down at her hands in her lap, remembering what she had promised her aunt years ago. 'Apologies for having disturbed you, uncle.' She got up to leave the room.

'What do you want to do instead?' Antonio asked. María turned around.

'Nursing. I want to help the sick now, not in five years when I finish university.'

'Hmm. I see.'

A few weeks later, María entered the nursing school as one of the youngest students ever, thanks to her uncle who had managed to get her into the school with a letter of recommendation and a substantial donation. Since she had arrived at her aunt and uncle's house, María had been treated like one of their own daughters, but since that fateful night, she often wondered if Antonio felt guilty that his government had killed her brother.

Whilst the tensions in the country rose following the general election won by the left-wing Popular Front, María followed her newfound purpose. Still, the fear of what was to come became palpable in the violence-filled streets of Madrid. Though she tried to persuade herself otherwise, she started preparing for worse times and an influx of work. She was proven right on a sunny day in July when she was working her shift in the hospital, bandaging the ankle of an elderly man who had taken a tumble at home, when news broke of a military uprising that had started in Spanish Morocco and was quickly spreading to the rest of the country. As the nurses debated the implications it could have for them and the hospital, María realised the nightmare of two years ago had only been the beginning; she could feel worse was yet to come.

To clear her mind, she headed to one of her favourite places – browsing the produce at her favourite *mercado* – when she spotted a mop of brown hair walking towards the Plaza de San Miguel exit. 'Xulián!' she shouted. The man continued pushing through the throngs of people, and María tried to follow, shoving elderly ladies out of the way. When she got to the plaza, she ran towards Calle Mayor, looking left and right, but he was gone. She turned right and continued running along the street, hoping she had chosen the right direction and would catch up with him. Only when she got to the Puerta del Sol did she stop, finally accepting that she had lost him. Trying to catch her breath, she looked up at the clock tower and, noticing the time, ran straight to the girls' school to pick them up. As she ran, she debated over and over in her head if it really was him or someone else. Was he in Madrid?

María didn't see Antonio for several months while she was busy with her nursing school and he worked increasingly long hours in the office, trying to help the government where he could. The country was entering a civil war, and Madrid would be an essential target for the rebels. While everyone was banned from speaking about the on-goings at home, especially with the children present, they tried to continue to live as normal a life as possible. After dinner, María went to Antonio's study, where he informed her about the issues their country was facing. Luckily, her uncle didn't object to women talking about politics. He knew all María cared about was her family in Mieres. She hadn't heard from her mother for a long time. The last letter she had received was a few months ago. The letter revealed that her father had been released from prison, a changed man, thin and sick. Juan Luis, who had written the letter, had finished school and entered the mine. Pablo was still missing. María's heart broke all over again at the thought of her burly father reduced to nothing.

After Andrés' death, Pablo's disappearance and her father's imprisonment, Aunt Isabel had suggested that her sister join them in Madrid. But María's mother had firmly refused, not wanting to leave for as long as her husband was still alive and could return home any moment and Juan Luis was still at school. Aunt Isabel had understood and instead arranged for money to be sent to her sister to enable her and Juan Luis to buy food. At least with the return of her father her mother wasn't alone. Several times María had thought about going back to see her mother but she decided she would only do so when she had finished nursing school, which would make her mother so proud of her. But her plans fell apart when war broke out, and Antonio told her the rebels had taken Oviedo. María was cut off and could no longer visit Mieres. Was she ever going to see her family again?

Nursing helped María focus on the good in the world. While everyone around her was starting to join unions and deciding which side to support, she felt strength in what she was doing. The friendships she had formed over the last year helped her through difficult times, missing her family, wondering where Xulián was, and being concerned for Josefa and Ana. As the children of a government minister, they had to be extra vigilant and weren't allowed outside on their own anymore. The other nurses often took María to places she usually wouldn't be allowed as she was too young, but even with the war going on around them, the group of six were determined to carry on as usual. They still went to the cinema or for strolls whenever their work allowed. One night, a few of them had just come out of a bar when they heard rumours on the streets that Madrid would be attacked. Immediately, they dispersed and either went back to the hospital to wait or home to catch a few hours of sleep before they were needed.

María arrived home to a hallway filled with suitcases. Aunt Isabel called for her children to prepare to leave before turning to María to explain the chaos. The government, including Antonio, was moving to Valencia, and they were going with him. María was part of the family as well and could join if she wanted. She declined, knowing she was needed at the hospital if the rumours were true.

'I didn't expect you to abandon your work when you're needed most.' Isabel hugged her tightly. 'I'm very proud of you,

María, you have done your family proud. Please take care and look after yourself.'

'Thank you, I will.' Isabel gave her a piece of paper, 'This is our address in Valencia. Join us when it gets too dangerous here.' The women wiped their tears away and then the girls hugged María fiercely, making her promise she would visit them soon. The thought of these young girls having to leave their home reminded María of when she was sent to Madrid. She took comfort in knowing the girls weren't alone but had their mother with them. They got in the car that would take them out of Madrid. María waved goodbye, not knowing if she would ever see them again. That night, as she lay in her bed in the empty house, María played her musical box and watched the ballerina dance. Her eyes fell on the pile of letters from her family and Rosa's from two years ago that she had never opened. Not knowing what else to do with herself, she opened it and started reading.

Dear María,
I hope you arrived well in Madrid. Here in Mieres, everything is still the same. Oh, I have happy news, I have found someone. Do you remember Xulián? We became close after you left and have fallen in love. We are delighted, and he has promised to make an honest woman of me and ask papá for my hand in marriage when I turn 16! I am so excited. I hope you will find someone in Madrid to make you happy.
Your friend, Rosa

María felt like she had been kicked in the stomach, the two-year-old letter sailing to the floor as the truth hit her. Suddenly it made sense why Xulián had never written to her, Andrés had been right. While she had waited patiently to hear from him for two years, he had married her best friend. He never loved her, he had only wanted her for one night. María cried herself to sleep that night, relieved no one was in the house to hear her howls.

The next day María was woken by gunshots in the distance. She jumped out of bed, packed her belongings and ran to work, knowing she would be needed. The days passed in a haze; no one who worked in the hospital slept, and when they did manage to lie down for a few minutes, the constant rattle of guns was their companion. The front was now in the Casa de Campo, a mere five kilometres from the hospital. María and a few other nurses were asked to work in the military hospitals set up in the Ritz Hotel and the Palace Hotel. The days were long, and the constant flow of soldiers being taken to the hospital from the front was so demoralising. María sometimes wondered why she hadn't joined her aunt. But María kept going. It was the only thing she could do. She started to stay at the hospital instead of going home, and one day, a new arrival caused much stir amongst the doctors and nurses. Rumours spread as she was changing the bandage of one of her patients that the leader of the anarchist movement, Buenaventura Durruti, was the man dying in one of the beds, shot during a battle in the university complex. She wondered how many of the young men she had started studying medicine with had already been lost to this war. María could hardly keep herself on her feet when she heard the humming of planes overhead; she, like many others, ran to the window just as there was a big explosion and a cloud of smoke and dust rose close by. The nurses and doctors looked at each other, preparing for the worst.

Thirteen

London, England
2014

It was a lovely evening at Kate's notwithstanding the unhappy circumstances that had led them to be there in the first place. Kate told Ava and Lucy about her week up in Liverpool and that her sister was doing well, which was why she had left a day early – because she was doing so well that she started bossing Kate around the house. She admitted that ever since she had received Ava's message about the back door, she hadn't felt quite as jolly and had arranged for a security company to visit on Monday to install an alarm system and security cameras, and suggested Ava request a quote at the same time. But Ava wasn't sure if she was allowed to do it. Kate threw her hands in the air, asking who would care anyway, no one would know, and the house would go to her anyway, so it really didn't matter.

'Kate, can I ask you something?' Ava stared at her hands, forming the next words in her mind.

Sensing the severity of Ava's question, Kate arched her left eyebrow and asked: 'Is it about your father?' Ava's look of surprise confirmed Kate was right. 'I was wondering when you would start asking questions.'

'I never had a reason to. Until yesterday, I thought my father was dead, but it seems he might still be alive, and mum wants me to find him.'

'He might as well be dead after what he did,' she said disapprovingly.

'What did he do?'

'He left your mother and his 5-year-old daughter, never to be seen again. Even his parents never heard from him again. Who knows, maybe he really isn't among the living anymore.'

'Why was I told he died?'

'It was easier, darling. You were still so young, you wouldn't have understood, and Rose didn't want you to think your father didn't love you anymore. By telling everyone he had died, she didn't have to be known as the woman who was walked out on. Her parents were against it, mind you, but there was not much they could do. They understood.' Kate was grappling with how much she should say. She knew Rose wanted to protect her daughter but felt it was probably time for Ava to know the whole truth. She gathered her strength and started telling her all she knew.

'It was a Thursday morning, I remember it vividly,' Kate began, closing her eyes. 'Your father went to work early in the morning with a smile on his face, as he always did. I was outside getting the newspaper and wished him a good morning. He looked happy and had a spring in his step. Later, your mother took you to nursery and went to work herself. A few hours later, I heard their front door slam. I was out in my back garden weeding, and I thought it rather odd for one of them to return early. Curiosity got the better of me, and I peeked over the fence, through the French doors. I saw your father. He looked distressed, his hands in his hair, and muttering to himself. Then he went upstairs. I didn't think much of it, although I do recall thinking it was out of character for him to be so on edge. He was a very easy-going and relaxed person; there wasn't much that could fluster him. I went back to my weeding but couldn't get his distraught look out of my head, so I headed for my front door to go and check on him. But by the time I got there, I heard a car door slam and wheels screeching, he was gone.' Lucy took Ava's hand to comfort her. Kate took a sip of her tea. 'It wasn't until your mum called later in the evening asking if I could mind you for a couple of hours and if she could use my car that I realised something was wrong. I told her what I had witnessed. She went looking for him everywhere and your mother knew something must have happened. He didn't come home that night. The next day his company confirmed how he had grabbed his coat and just walked out, leaving his boss a note that he wouldn't be back. Your mum called his parents, but they hadn't heard anything either. He had just disappeared.' Shaking her head, visibly affected by the memory, Kate sighed deeply.

'Your mum never reported him missing. She said it was obvious he left of his own free will and that there must have been a very good reason. Your father was a smart cookie, and Rose never believed that he left because he didn't love you two anymore. She hoped that one day the reason for his disappearance would become clear. She never gave up hope.' Kate's eyes glistened with unshed tears as she continued, 'I had never seen your mother at such a loss. She struggled to keep it together for the first couple of months and had to take sick leave.'

'I didn't know that.' Ava was surprised and sad at what she was hearing. Her mum, who always held herself together so well, never complained and just got on with things, had been struggling so much.

'How would you? You were five, and your grandparents tried to keep you away from it all as best as possible. You went to stay with them, and when you returned, Rose was back to her old self. From somewhere, she got summoned the strength to continue and decided to tell you your father had died. The worst for her was lying to you because you never got the chance to meet him again, but it did save her a lot of heartbreak, knowing she wouldn't have to answer any questions. When people in the street asked where he was, she told everyone that he was in a car accident and died. It's quite the coincidence that this is how she ultimately met her own fate. The only ones who knew the truth were your four grandparents, his boss, and I. And now you two.'

Gobsmacked, Ava sat back in her chair, her mouth hanging open, so many questions going through her head that she didn't know where to start. Too stunned to talk, Lucy poured some more wine. She took a tiny sip herself and then put the glass down in front of Ava.

All three were silent. Ava tried to process everything she had just heard, Lucy looked anxiously at Ava, ready to support her friend, and Kate, who had kept this secret for over twenty years, finally allowed herself to cry.

'Did mum ever try again to find him?' Ava's voice was little more than a whisper. She was scared of asking the question and hearing something she didn't want to.

'No, she accepted it and moved on. Don't forget, the internet was in its infancy and without the help of the police, it would've been hard, especially with a little one. Though she never stopped loving your father and every day hoped he would return. That's why she stayed in the house, in case he ever returned. His parents knew that Rose didn't earn enough to pay the full mortgage, she wasn't working full-time back then and had only gone back when you started nursery. As they were getting older, they decided to sell their house and use the money to pay off the mortgage, I think they were ashamed that their son abandoned his family, so this was their way of trying to make amends. They died shortly after, but Brian wasn't at their funeral.'

Kate looked at Ava, who decided to take a sip of the wine Lucy had put in front of her while trying to work out which question to ask next. The one thing Ava wanted to know was if her mum thought that her father would return, but something was holding her back.

'I'm sorry, love. I know it's a shock for you to find out like this,' Kate said softly, putting her hand on top of Ava's.

'I wish I had known sooner, when mum was still here,' she replied. 'Do you think he's still alive?'

'I think so, yes. He wasn't a man to end his own life, and after I saw him so distraught, my feeling is that something happened, and he couldn't find another way out without dragging your mother and you into it. I'm convinced he did what he thought was best for you both and left.'

'What do you think happened?'

'That, my dear, I don't know. Maybe he got mixed up with the wrong people? I don't know. But I agree with your mum, you should try to find him. He's the only one who has those answers.' Kate got up and went to the living room to pour herself a glass of brandy, and left the girls alone at the kitchen table.

Lucy hadn't said much while Kate was going back in time to help Ava piece together her childhood, but the more she learnt about Ava's parents, the more suspicious she grew. Who broke into the house, and what were they looking for? And why only now, more than twenty years after Brian had disappeared? Unless the break-in had nothing to do with the past, why were no jewellery, money, or other valuables taken? 'I think this is affecting Kate more than she's letting on,' she mused.

'Do you think she knows more than she's telling me?' Ava replied, surprising herself in the process by thinking Kate could be holding something back from her.

'No, she would never do that. You could see how upset she was.'

Ava agreed and threw her head back, huffing at the information's sheer impact. 'I'm going to install cameras too, and an alarm system. Someone is out there looking for something that might be in the house, which means whoever they are they will most likely come back.' It seemed logical, and Ava knew she would feel more secure if she had those systems in place. She was determined not to be scared in her own home. Ava and Lucy stayed in Kate's guest bedroom, and when they got ready for bed, Ava noticed she hadn't looked at her phone since she had called the police. Locating it in her overnight bag, she scanned the missed messages and calls and spotted that most were from Luke. Her heart skipped a beat and she grinned from ear to ear, fully aware of Lucy's raised eyebrows demanding to know what had brought the smile to her face.

13:23
How is your day going? x

14:17
Feeling bored without me around? x

15:54
missed call from Luke

15:56
Seems like you're either not near your phone or ignoring me. But I have news. Call me when you can. x

17:11
missed call from Luke

17:24
I'm leaning towards you ignoring me.
19:45
Okay, definitely ignoring me. Or you've been attacked by someone else's dog and knocked unconscious?

19:46
Alright, I'm bursting to tell you. I've done some digging in the newspaper archive and found something very interesting. Can I show you tomorrow?

22:03
I'll just wait for you to answer…

'Shit,' Ava muttered.

'Someone's keen!' Lucy replied smirking, having read the messages over Ava's shoulder. 'Tell him to come tomorrow, I want to know what he found.'

Ava felt Lucy was more interested in seeing Luke than knowing what he had found. She typed out a message to Luke, starting with a barrage of apologies and letting him know they were at Kate's. Luke replied, seemingly relieved that he wasn't just being ignored, and said he was happy to meet them the next day. Before Ava put her phone on the bedside table, she saw Diego's message was still waiting to be answered. After what Lucy had told her, she knew she had to stay away from him and decided to be honest, hoping he would take the hint and leave her alone.

Hi Diego. I heard about your job, so I think it's best if we don't stay in touch.

His response was instant as if he was waiting for Ava to reply.

You could ask me what really happened instead of believing others. But you clearly don't care about the truth, no one ever cares.

Was he right, though? Should she have asked him what had happened instead of just believing what she was told and accepting it? Ava deliberated while turning onto her right side, facing the window and watching the moon light up the night sky. Not long ago, she had butterflies in her stomach at the thought of going on a date with Diego, and suddenly, she wished she was a million miles away from him. What had changed between them? When did she recoil at the thought of touching, even kissing him? But that night at Clos Maggiore changed their dynamic, and while she had felt uncomfortable during their date, their disagreement shed new light on him; instead of respecting him for his achievements and charm, she now felt rather disgusted by him. Feeling sleepy, she recognised that since Luke had come onto the scene her feelings for Diego had changed more pointedly. With Luke, she felt safe; he was easy-going and genuine. With a smile on her face, she fell asleep.

The next day, Ava and Lucy ventured back into the house, feeling uncomfortable knowing someone else had previously gained entry without them noticing. Luke arrived at 10 am, and they agreed to get all the boxes down from the loft and into the living room. They added the folders from the study and any other loose papers they could find. While Lucy and Luke went through the kitchen and living room drawers to see if there was anything else hidden, Ava searched her mum's room for boxes she might have kept old photographs in. She joined the others in the living room, where they had made themselves comfortable on the couch with a cup of tea, sharpies and sticky notes, and a paper pad to take notes. Being very methodical, she advised the others on how this would work, starting in the eighties when her parents met and Ava was born, through to her mum's death and the circumstances of her father's rediscovery. She wrote down the key dates she knew next to the year, hoping it would make it easier to place whatever they found correctly. Instead of each working on a separate box, Ava wanted to work together as a team to make it more enjoyable, and so they wouldn't miss anything. They set to work with the first box, which contained several of Ava's old toys and teddy bears. On each item, they searched for clues as to who had given it to her, if it had belonged to anyone beforehand, and if there was anything that hinted at how old it was. They deduced that many things were explicitly bought for Ava, and quick searches on the internet often confirmed if it was the trending toy of that year. They continued with the same method, working their way through the boxes and finding more of Ava's old things, including drawings and many school arts projects, some of which were rather embarrassing. Ava felt herself blush when they found something that looked very inappropriate for a young girl.

'Care to explain this?' Lucy held a clay figure in her palm with a four-inch-long pointy middle stick and two connected pink spheres at the bottom. Ava felt her cheeks grow redder as she looked at the figure, trying hard to think when and why she had made it. Lucy and Luke burst out laughing while Ava just stared at it.

'Oh, come on, Ava, it's pretty funny, don't look so mortified.' Lucy laughed with tears in her eyes.

Sensing Ava's discomfort, Luke continued rummaging in the box on his lap and it wasn't long before he produced another clay figure. 'Maybe this belongs to it?' he suggested, handing Ava the upper body of a ballerina.

'Of course!' she exclaimed, turning the first piece around to form two legs touching in the middle, covered with a bulging pink tutu and ending in pointe shoes. She put the upper body with the ballerina on top and turned it towards Lucy, whose laughing had now reduced to grinning.

'I didn't think you'd make something so naughty, but I think I still prefer just the bottom part upside down,' Lucy said, laughing hysterically again.

'Of course, you do, your mind is always in the gutter.' Ava grinned back, relieved that it was an innocent ballerina. 'I always wanted to be a ballerina. There was a time when I wanted to wear my tutu everywhere. Once, I put it on over my school uniform and mum had to ask me several times to take it off. I went into a meltdown. She explained that I had to keep it safe and clean otherwise the other ballerinas would have nice ones, while mine would be dirty and torn. After that, I only wore it to my ballet classes, but it never saw the light of day again when I gave up dancing.' Ava reminisced about those happy days when all her presents were ballet-themed – ballet-dancing dolls, picture books about ballerinas, and even a pink ballerina birthday cake made by grandpa.

She wondered if her musical box with the pop-up ballerina was in one of the boxes too when Luke broke into her thoughts. 'I can mend that for you and add a little platform so it can stand if you'd like?'

'That would be amazing', Ava replied, still stroking the figure in her hand as she looked up and smiled affectionately at Luke. 'Thank you.'

'Shall I leave you two alone?' Lucy looked at Ava and Luke in turn, amused.

'Let's continue,' Ava said, stealing another glance at Luke, who continued getting things out of the box.

After a couple of hours, they had got through five full boxes and rearranged them into piles separating objects Ava definitely wanted to keep and others that needed to go to charity. Unfortunately, they hadn't found any photographs or other helpful documents yet, and Ava was starting to get tired of going through all the memories and taking notes. If only they could find something that would help them know where to start looking instead of ploughing through endless boxes and papers, reading more into them than they revealed. Luke got the next box and opened the lid that was covered in a thick layer of dust. There wasn't much inside apart from a crème muslin cloth, a blue towel, a white babygrow with blue, red, and green cars on it, a green dinosaur soft toy, and a wooden train with three separate carriages. He took everything out and carefully laid them on the table. They seemed very old and delicate, and the fabric was going yellow from years of storage in the loft.

'Whose are these?' Lucy was the first to break the silence whilst they all stared at the items. Ava picked up the still-soft towel that smelt musty and opened it up to reveal the letter T stitched onto it in the bottom right corner.

'Who's T?' she asked.

'Look,' Luke said while rearranging the train carriages in a row and hooking them together, the locomotive at the front followed by the three carriages. 'Tim.'

'Okay, I'll rephrase, who's Tim?'

'Might be your father's name, but he changed it to Brian?' Lucy suggested.

'I don't think so,' Luke said as he lifted the last carriage with the M on it and pointed to a date in the bottom right corner. 'It says 30.04.1982. Do you know a Tim with that date of birth, Ava?'

'No. That was four years before I was born, and I don't know a Tim.'

'I don't remember a Tim either, not even at school,' Lucy added.

Ava blew out her cheeks and leant back in the armchair, feeling even more confused. 'This is getting mysterious, and we're nowhere nearer to finding my father. Where are you?' Ava said to the ceiling.

'Of course, I nearly forgot,' Luke said before jumping up from the sofa, almost running to the front door, and disappearing outside. Ava and Lucy followed him with their eyes, then turned to look at each other.

'What's up with him?' Lucy asked just as Luke returned with his rucksack, sitting back on the sofa.

'Remember I messaged and called you yesterday because I found something interesting?' he asked, slightly out of breath as he looked at Ava. He grabbed a folder from his bag, producing a rolled-up paper that he slowly spread out. He continued: 'After the meeting yesterday, I went down to the archives to see if I could find anything on the article that you found about the restaurant that went up in flames. We keep a copy of each printed newspaper in the archives, so as you can imagine, it's extensive. Once I found the year 1948, it took me a good half hour before I came across the June 4th edition, and there we have it, black on white, the full article I copied. And the interesting thing is, look who wrote the piece!'

He passed the paper to Ava with a smile on his face, Ava scanned it and spotted the name, which was also on the one she was carrying around with her, but she had never made the connection. 'Edward Wilkinson,' she read aloud and continued reading the article she was already so familiar with, but for which she could read the last sentences in full for the first time.

Gas explosion at restaurant leaves 14 dead
By Edward Wilkinson

Yesterday morning there was a gas explosion in the Holland Park area where a new Spanish restaurant was due to open the next day. It is believed that the owners were inside at the time of the explosion and are two of the bodies that were recovered from the rubble. Further bodies from adjacent buildings impacted by the blast have been retrieved, many too charred by the subsequent fire to be fully identified. The police are investigating if any foul play was involved, and while no arrests have so far been made, witnesses claim to have spotted a man fleeing the scene.

One of the unidentified bodies is believed to be the owner Henry Jones, a public servant who fought in the Spanish Civil War with the International Brigades, where he met his Spanish wife María, presumed to be one of the other victims.

'How sad. At least we now know Henry and María from the photo were the restaurant owners and died in the explosion.' Ava started feeling a connection to them, having looked at their photo so often, wondering who they were, and now she knew they weren't just two lovers who happened to have their picture taken in front of the restaurant but were the owners – they had plans. Lucy took the paper from Ava before her tears had a chance to make it illegible and squeezed her hand.

'So, do we think this Eddie is connected to Ava's father?' Lucy asked Luke, who'd stayed quiet throughout. Not taking his concerned eyes off Ava, he nodded and handed Lucy another piece of paper. She took it with one hand, not letting go of Ava's as they put their heads together to look at it. Luke summarised it for them: 'There's a record of everyone who ever worked at the newspaper with their biography, and it's accessible to all employees. The idea behind it is that if you needed someone to cover a story or investigate, you could easily find a competent journalist. Edward Wilkinson had a son born in 1948 called Brian but stopped working for the newspaper when he said he and his family were being threatened while he was investigating the gas explosion. It seemed he didn't believe the police's theory that the company hadn't connected the gas pipe properly, as records showed it had already been inspected before the grand opening. He alleged the pipes had been tampered with and the explosion wasn't an accident, and the police never found the man who fled the scene. One day, his wife was threatened by a police officer to stop her husband from digging into the story. They then knew it wasn't safe to stay, so he halted the investigation and moved with his family to Hertfordshire, where he found work for a local newspaper.'

'It doesn't say any of what you just said on here,' Lucy said, waving the paper before him.

'No, well, at the awards night the previous evening, I met an elderly guy and got talking to him. It turns out he was a young journalist who had just started out at the newspaper with another guy when all this happened, and his friend had been shadowing Edward to learn from him. When I found his friend's name and biography, I called him and asked what he remembered after explaining how I was looking into the story. He mentioned Edward had carried around a manila folder with him that included all the evidence he had gathered, but he wouldn't share it with anyone, not even him. They had stayed in touch for a long time after Eddie moved away, so he knows your grandfather personally. I'm sure he'd be delighted to meet his granddaughter if you're up for it.' Ava was struggling to process all the information Luke was throwing her way.

'Okay, so let's get this straight: My grandfather, who I never met, wrote about a gas explosion that he thought wasn't an accident. He then started investigating the story and a police officer threatened him and his wife. They moved away and started a new life as a family. His son, my father, suddenly disappeared when I was five. Then, twenty-three years later, when my mum dies, I find the very same newspaper article in her possessions, along with a photo of the restaurant's owners, who it seems were killed in the explosion. Then someone breaks into this house looking for something specific, and we have no idea what that might be and who is behind all this.' Looking at Luke, Ava realised her heart was hammering against her chest; she was sure this time it wasn't because of him and rather because it seemed everything was connected, and if she solved one mystery, she might solve all of them and find her father.

Luke nodded his agreement. 'It seems like it, yes.'

'That is too much for me to deal with. How about we head to the pub for some lunch? I'm ravenous,' Lucy said, raising her eyebrows at Ava questioningly, before getting up and walking towards the door without waiting for an answer. Ava was torn between wanting to find out more after they just had a breakthrough and agreeing with Lucy. Hunger won, and they headed down the road towards the pub, breathing in the fresh air and enjoying the midday sun. Having secured a table in the garden, Luke went to the bar to order their food and drinks while

Lucy took the chance to interrogate Ava. 'Tell me what's going on between you two!' she demanded.

'I already told you everything.'

'You told me how he had slept on the sofa and made breakfast for you, yes. And now I can see how you two are undressing each other with your eyes! There must be more.'

'There really isn't. But maybe there soon will be,' Ava said, grinning. 'There's just too much going on right now, and I just wish I could focus on one thing at a time. How can it be that either nothing interesting happens in life or everything happens at the same time? It's exhausting!' Lucy gave her a sympathetic smile.

'But Ava,' Lucy whispered, 'did you know your father was called Wilkinson? I assumed it would've been Brown, like you and your mum.'

'Yes, I thought so too, but then as I went through my mum's documents and came across the mortgage papers, I noticed that it seemed mum had kept her maiden name and given hers to me.'

'Hang on, if you only just found out, how did Luke know that Edward Wilkinson was your grandfather?' Ava hadn't thought about that and shrugged.

'Are you two talking about me again?' Luke joined them with the drinks and a smile.

'Of course! Getting the juicy details from Ava.'

'Good to hear.' It seemed like Luke didn't mind that Lucy was talking about them as he just smirked and took a sip of his beer.

'I was thinking,' he started after setting his drink down, 'that manila folder with all the information must be in one of those boxes. So, if we can find it, we might be closer to the truth.'

'Why would it be in one of the boxes?' Ava asked.

'Well, Edward spent much of his time investigating and talking to witnesses, according to Paul, the old guy I spoke to. Even though he stopped, I doubt he would've thrown anything out. Most likely, he buried it deep inside a box in the loft. And Brian was his only child, so when both his parents died, he would've been the one to go through everything, and unless he threw it away, it's likely to have ended up in his own loft,' he concluded, looking pleased with himself.

'You're missing a tiny detail, though. My father left in 1992, his father died in 1993, and his mother in 1994. Their possessions never made it to him.'

'We can't be sure about that. We just assume he didn't stay in touch with them. Who sorted out their flat when they passed?' Lucy pointed out.

'Maybe they were still in touch with your father, and he returned when your grandmother passed away, or one of their friends organised everything in his absence,' Luke suggested.

'Kate told us he wasn't at his parents' funerals, though,' Ava replied. 'I guess it's a mystery that won't be solved until I find my father.'

Fourteen

Back at the house, the three of them continued working through the boxes, this time with a clear goal to find the manila folder and find out more about Edward Wilkinson. 'We should Google Eddie and see if anything comes up,' Lucy suggested. 'I'll get my laptop.'

'Thanks!' Ava smiled sweetly at her knowing fully why her friend was leaving the living room. Since leaving the pub, Luke's body had kept moving closer to Ava's. Walking down the lane, their hands brushed. When she opened the front door, he had been there to push it open for her. Now sat on the sofa, his thigh was touching hers, and he made no attempt to move away. When Lucy left the room, he turned towards her and put his right arm around her waist while his left cupped her face, stroking her cheek with this thumb. He looked deep into her eyes. The air in the room felt charged. Ava waited with anticipation, longing for him to move even closer. Slowly she raised her hand to his face and pulled him in for a deep kiss, their tongues circling around each other's. It took all of Ava's strength not to push him back and move on top of him, so strong was her desire to wrap her body around his. When Luke finally broke the kiss, he was breathing hard, his face only inches away from Ava's. 'I have wanted to do that since the day my dog knocked you over,' he said smiling. Abruptly, he sat back and picked up a battered teddy bear from the box by his feet as if nothing had happened. Ava was too lost in the moment to register that Lucy had returned. She announced that with a name like Edward Wilkinson and him having been a journalist, she produced too many hits, and she needed more details to narrow down the search. She doubted they would find much more information, though, as the majority of the contents of the boxes seemed to comprise old articles he had written for the local newspaper later in his career.

While Lucy was reading some of his articles aloud, Luke whispered in Ava's ear: 'I haven't finished yet.' His words sent shivers down her spine. Ava knew how lucky she was that both Lucy and Luke were there for her and kept her company when she didn't feel safe. Going through the boxes together felt like opening wounds that had only started to heal a little. She wouldn't have been able to face the memories alone. Ava went to grab her laptop, and as she wedged it out of her bag, a small envelope fell onto the floor.

'What's that?' asked Lucy. Ava picked it up and looked at it momentarily, trying to remember where it came from. Turning it around, she slid her finger under the flap and pulled out a note. *Always watch your back and trust no one*, it read in tiny, scrawny handwriting. It dawned on Ava where the letter had come from. 'It's from that old lady at the funeral! She said the exact same words when she left after the wake, and it freaked me out a little.'

'Why would an elderly person write something like that and then just leave and not explain herself?' Lucy asked whilst taking the envelope from Ava to see if another letter was in there. She looked inside and turned it upside down, a small golden key fell out that looked like it belonged to a tiny lock. She held it up to show the others. They all stared at it. 'This is seriously getting weirder by the second,' she said, voicing what everyone was thinking.

'What could it belong to?' Luke asked. 'A wind-up puppet maybe?'

'A doll's house?' Ava added. 'Or maybe one of those heart-shaped pendants?'

'I think it's too big for that,' Lucy interjected. 'Let's see what the internet suggests.'

'If only you can Google something, you're happy, right?' Ava teased her friend and smirked.

'Haha, it'll save us loads of time, you'll see,' she announced happily and started typing. But nothing she entered gave her the desired results, and she quickly grew frustrated. 'It can't find anything,' she exclaimed after a while. 'Whatever I type in, it either shows me examples of tiny keys, videos of how to open something without a key, or devices to find a missing key.'

'I guess the machine is only as intelligent as the person behind it,' Ava joked, grinning at her friend. Lucy threw one of the cushions at her in retaliation.

'Could belong to this?' Luke held up a box. Ava stared at it in awe, it was a musical box with a pop-up ballerina.

'Oh, aren't you clever,' Lucy remarked, somewhat annoyed he got there first.

Ava took the box from him, beaming. 'It was mum's,' she said. The once-polished dark wood had lost its sheen from endless rubbing with her mum's grubby fingers. Her mum used to pop it open before bedtime, the ballerina twirling around to the sound of Tchaikovsky's "Swan Lake" as Ava lay in her bed spellbound and instantly calmed. 'I used to get out of bed and dance around the room like the ballerina. Mum chided me repeatedly and explained how special and old the box was and how they didn't want it to break.' The memory brought a smile to her face. It was their usual bedtime routine and what had started her ballet frenzy. 'It was granny's previously and must now be at least a hundred years old.' Carefully she opened it, expecting the mechanics to be broken after all the years of neglect in the damp and cold attic. It was a huge musical box, the lid heavy, and the hinges almost too weak for the weight. Having wound up the box a few times, she slowly lifted the top and placed the ballerina onto the pin. The once-smooth tunes sounded distorted, and the ballerina stood still. Even though Ava had anticipated it, the disappointment that her favourite toy no longer worked made her sad. It didn't matter that she had forgotten about its existence for so long, but looking at the intricate carving on the outside brought back memories of her mum as she felt a deep desire to make it work again.

'I take it the key is not for the box?' Lucy said, pointing out that it was unlocked and already had a key in its lock.

'No, it's not. I never realised it had a key as otherwise I'm sure my mum would've locked it after playing it at bedtime so I couldn't open it again.' Ava smiled at the thought. 'Thank you for finding it, Luke. I might take it to an expert. Hopefully, it can be fixed.'

'Have you found anything else in the boxes for which a key might be needed, Luke?' Lucy asked, walking over to the boxes before peering into each one.

'No, I put all my money on the musical box,' he said, deflated.

Ava placed the music box on the coffee table, noticing again how heavy it was as she moved it. She used to think its weight was normal, given it was made of solid wood, and as a child, everything seemed big and heavy, but even amongst the numerous musical boxes Ava had subsequently held since growing up this was by far the heaviest.

'Okay, so let me recap for a moment,' Luke said, having written down everything they had learnt so far in an effort to bring some clarity to proceedings. 'We're now looking for the manila folder containing the information your grandfather Edward collected and because of which he was threatened and had to drop his investigation. The folder might be with your father, whom we now assume is still alive, or it could be in one of these boxes. And now we have a tiny key we don't know its use for yet and a note from an old lady to either warn or scare you.' Luke looked at Ava to confirm the details so far were correct. She nodded. 'The only thing we know for sure is that the old lady lives in the care home where your mother worked, so I'd say your best bet to get some answers is to visit her.'

Ava half-berated herself for not realising she could go and speak to the lady sooner. She stood and grabbed her bag, then put it down again and walked to the kitchen to put the kettle on. There was no point going today, it was Sunday and most likely her family would be visiting. Everyone visited on a Sunday, she knew. The busy sons usually arrived around 12 pm to take their mothers to the best local restaurant for lunch before returning them to the home by 4 pm in order that they could rush home to the city. The more fragile residents only got a ninety minute visit from their families, during which they would sit at one of the white plastic tables with a cup of tea, being updated about their grandchildren who were running around in the garden. Once the families had left, the residents returned to their rooms or the common area to wait for the next visit the following Sunday. Ava had always felt sad for them, and often when her mum was working at weekends Ava was asked to accompany her and keep the elderly company. She had never minded and had enjoyed the attention she got. Looking back now, she could see how much joy she brought to residents who had no one else left. Was that old lady there too, and why couldn't Ava remember her? She re-entered the living room with three teas, announcing she'd visit the lady the next day.

'Pass me the tiny key we found, please,' Lucy said as she held the musical box and peered at the lid from the inside. Luke grabbed the key and handed it to her. 'It fits,' Lucy squealed excitedly.

Ava moved to her side. 'Careful now,' she urged Lucy. Slowly, Lucy turned it, careful not to break the key or lock. They all held their breath while she gently pulled to release the lid, but it wouldn't budge.

Luke, who had been oddly quiet, got up and left the room, a few seconds later, he returned with a sharp knife. 'Don't break it, please!' Ava implored. Luke instructed Lucy to hold the box upside down while he tried to wedge the knife into the slit and ease the lid out. The old wood creaked but finally gave way. Lucy passed the box to Ava, who exhaled as she fumbled inside the newly-discovered secret compartment in the lid and pulled out a bundle of envelopes and letters. A few of the envelopes were addressed to a Señorita María Calderín at a location in Madrid. The rest simply read the name Andrés, but it appeared they had never been sent. Rooted to the spot, Ava gingerly opened the first one, a letter from someone called Rosa to María, written in Spanish. 'How good is your Spanish?' Ava asked, turning to Luke.

'Basic, but I think the handwriting would cause more issues,' he replied, glancing over her shoulder. Ava opened the other envelopes carefully, making sure not to tear them. The oldest was dated June 1934. 'If I remember rightly, that was the beginning of the Spanish Civil War. Do we think this María is the same woman as in the newspaper article?' Luke asked.

'The one who died in the explosion along with her husband? Possibly.' Lucy agreed. 'It wasn't the beginning of the war, by the way, it's two years prior. But more importantly, if the letters were sent to María, it means this box belonged to her.'

Ava racked her brain to try and recall anyone with that name. 'Then how did my mum end up with it?'

'If we translated the letters, we might gain some insight?' Lucy suggested.

Luke scratched his chin. 'Another thing we know is that the old lady was the one who gave you the key, so she knew your mother and now you had the box. But if she knew your mother had the box, why didn't she give your mum the key at the care home. Why wait until the funeral to hand it to you, and what's with that note?'

'I'll go and see her now. She can clear up so many things before we go mad trying to figure them out.' Ava got up, grabbed her bag again, and went to the door.

'I'll drive you,' Luke said, following her to the door.

'And while you're gone, I'll type up the first letter so we can run it through Google Translate, if that's okay with you?' Lucy proposed. Ava nodded to Lucy and gave her a quick wave.

'Do you know what you're going to say?' Luke asked once they were in the car and had set off towards the care home on the hill.

'I'll ask her why she gave me the key and what she meant with her note.'

'Keep in mind that she might not remember anything she did or said.'

'Fair point, I guess we'll just have to see how it pans out.'

When they arrived at the home, Ava made her way to the reception with an uneasy feeling. She hadn't been there since her mum's death and hadn't spoken to any of her mum's friends and former work colleagues. Whenever she had popped by or picked up her mum, she was always greeted like family. Ava had basically grown up in that home that now felt empty. At least that was how it felt for Ava, although she recognised she was biased.

'Ava!' Margaret beamed at her from behind the desk. 'What a lovely surprise to see you! How are you doing, dear?'

'Hi Maggie, I'm okay. How are you?'

Maggie had worked at the care home for as long as Ava could remember and was one of her mum's closest friends. She always had a smile and a sweet ready for Ava. 'Oh, you know, getting on. It's so lonely here without Rose, and many residents miss her.' Maggie shook her head sadly before recovering her smile. 'What brings you and your friend here?' she asked, eyeing Luke, clearly pleased with what she was looking at.

'This is Luke, and we're here to see one of the residents. But honestly, I don't know her name.' Ava realised she had no idea who she was looking for. 'She was at mum's funeral and handed me an envelope before she left. She was elderly with grey hair, probably about five feet tall and wearing a black two-piece.' Even as she described her, she realised how her description could have referred to a significant number of the care home residents. Judging by the look on Maggie's face, she clearly thought the same.

'That doesn't necessarily narrow it down. Let's go to the common room and look around to see if you can spot her. Was she close to your mum?' Maggie led the way down the sterile corridor that smelt of cleaning products and that familiar old people smell.

'I've been trying to place her, but I'm struggling to remember. Maybe she's a new resident?'

'Maybe, but the last resident who joined us was Alan, and before him there were a few men but no woman. It could be that she's from another home, but that wouldn't explain how she had known your mother.'

The common room was alive with activity – the television was on in one corner showing Andy Murray playing at Wimbledon, a group of ladies were playing bridge in another corner, and some residents still had family visiting and were chatting away at the tables in the middle. Ava scanned the room but couldn't spot the lady she was looking for. Instead, she saw many other familiar faces smiling back at her. Some residents had lived in the home for the last twenty years and seen Ava grow from a girl into the woman she was now. She smiled back and gave a little wave before turning around to leave.

'Hi Ava, lovely to see you. How are you?' a nurse said as she approached her from the right.

'Oh, hi Patty, sorry I didn't see you there. I'm doing fine. How are you?'

Patty always turned up out of nowhere and often made Ava jump. 'Thank you, we're just about coping without Rose. Walter especially misses your mum, they always had some banter going between them.' she said with a sad smile. It hit Ava that she wasn't the only one grieving her mum's loss; all these people here had known her for just as long, and although it wasn't their mum, she was their friend. Ava hadn't given it any thought previously, but she now recognised that she hadn't had the chance to grieve properly with everything that had been happening. She promised herself she'd pop by more often to chat with these ladies who had spent more time with her mum than anyone else.

'Ava and Luke are looking for an elderly lady who attended the funeral and the wake. The lady gave Ava an envelope, but we don't know who it was,' Maggie summarised for Patty. 'Do you remember which residents were there that day?'

'Sure,' Patty replied, 'Sue and I went to the funeral with a group of residents. We had Annie and Walter, Elisabeth and Patrick, Desmond, Patricia, and Tom with us. But we returned after the service and didn't go to the wake.'

'Are residents allowed to leave without telling anyone?' Luke asked.

'Yes, if they're in the independent living quarters, they can come and go as they please. Not in this part though,' Patty answered.

'Can we assume, then, that this lady lives in the independent part of the home?' Luke continued.

'Probably, yes, otherwise we would've known,' Maggie agreed.

Ava said goodbye to Patty and promised to visit again as the four of them walked back to the reception desk, aware Ava hadn't got any closer to finding what she had been looking for.

'Just because it was an elderly lady doesn't necessarily mean she lives here,' Ava said, shrugging, ready to go home.

'Maggie, does a lady called Rosa live here? Or María, perhaps?' Luke asked, turning to Maggie.

'You know I'm not supposed to give you any details, so if we keep this between us, I'll have a quick look.'

'Thank you.' Luke turned to Ava with an expectant smile. 'Have you noticed that the two ladies in the letters are Rosa and María, and your mother's official name was Mary-Rose? That can't be a coincidence, can it?'

'My brain is currently not processing everything that's going on, so no, I haven't. But that's where you come in, you can connect all the points for me and make them make sense,' Ava replied, grinning up at him.

'Okay, I've found someone,' Maggie announced, 'Rosa Humphries-García, 94 years old. Still lives in the independent living quarters.'

'Great, can we visit her?' Luke asked, already making his way towards the door.

'Not so fast young man, she's not there at the moment.'

'When will she be back? We can wait,' Luke continued.

'She's in hospital. Fell over in her flat and couldn't get up anymore. One of our nurses found her when she didn't attend the art class.' Luke's face fell. 'I can give you the hospital's address, but I can't guarantee they will let you see her.'

'We appreciate that. Thank you, Maggie. We'll have a think about what to do,' Ava said as she took the piece of paper with the address and squeezed Maggie's hand. 'You're welcome to pop by for a coffee whenever you feel like it, I'm currently living in mum's house.'

'That would be lovely, thank you, Ava. You take care now.'

In the car, Luke put the car in gear and asked for the hospital's address. It didn't feel right to turn up at the hospital, though, asking questions that might be distressing for an old lady,

Ava felt. She put her hand on Luke's and told him to take them home and they could visit her the next day. Luke was dismayed – he was scared of losing momentum, and with a 94-year-old in hospital, every minute counted. He looked across at Ava to explain how precious time was right now, but when he saw her downcast eyes and sad smile, he acquiesced and started driving back to the house.

'Going back to your mother's old workplace was harder than you thought it would be, wasn't it?' he observed.

'Yes, it was. And seeing Maggie and Patty, they clearly miss mum too – I've been so self-absorbed that I never thought of them and their grief.'

'Don't think like that. They know you care but that you need to work through this yourself. No one expects you to look out for others who are grieving.'

'I hope you're right. I wouldn't want them to think I'm cutting all ties. They're like family. When I was young, I used to think they were my aunts because they were so close to mum, they were like her sisters.'

'That's a lovely thought. Maybe that's how you should see them, as your aunts, people you can rely on.'

'It certainly would be nice to have some "family" around.'

'There you go. And tomorrow, we'll find out what role Rosa plays.'

'That was an excellent idea to ask about the names. I just hope we'll be able to see her.' Ava understood that time was against them, and if they wanted answers, they needed to act fast. 'Are you staying for the night?' she asked, glancing at Luke.

'If you don't mind?' They arrived back at the house, and Luke parked the car in the driveway. 'Ava,' he said, turning towards her and putting his hand on her arm, 'I just wanted to say that this is all very mysterious, and if you feel that it's getting too much, please let me know. I'm happy to help where I can.' Ava could have melted right there and then – this man was kind and thoughtful, and the touch of his hand on her arm sent tingles through her body.

'I'm happy you are here. Without you and Lucy, I wouldn't know what to do with myself, and diving into the past is keeping my mind busy. And I like having you around,' she said, blushing.

'Good, because I like being around.' He moved in closer and gave her a long kiss.

Lucy was asleep, lying on the sofa underneath a blanket with her laptop open next to her and one of the letters still in her hand. Luke made himself comfortable in the armchair, Ava sat on his lap with the laptop, and they began reading the translation of the first letter from June 1934 together.

Dear María,
I hope you arrived well in Madrid. Here in Mieres, everything is still the same. Oh, I have happy news, I have found someone. Do you remember Xulián? We became close after you left and have fallen in love. We are delighted, and he has promised to make an honest woman of me and ask papá for my hand in marriage when I turn 16! I am so excited. I hope you will find someone in Madrid to make you happy.
Your friend, Rosa

Ava closed the laptop and got down from Luke's lap. She indicated to him to follow her to the kitchen, where she got her phone out to order pizza for dinner. Keeping her voice down so as not to wake Lucy, she summarised the new information for her own benefit.

'Okay,' Ava started. 'So Rosa is María's friend from Spain. This confirms the lady from the care home is indeed the Rosa we are looking for, as her name was Humphries-García. Which means she left Spain and moved to England. The letter is dated 1934, which is pre-Spanish Civil War, and it looks like María left the village they grew up in and went to Madrid. If we assume María is the one from the article, we know she also left Spain and married an English man, Henry, and died in the explosion.'

'Maybe we should read more letters to see what happens to them,' he wondered.

'Well, we know what happens to María eventually,' Ava reminded him.

'Imagine you survive a civil war and think you're safe only to be killed in a gas explosion in a foreign country.' Luke said.

'It sounds horrible when you say it like that,' Ava wasn't sure she wanted to know what happened.

'Have you guys read the letter?' Lucy turned up in the kitchen. 'And are we planning on having dinner?' The doorbell rang.

'Yes, we have, and that's our dinner,' Ava answered.

As they sat down to eat, they discussed the letters and Rosa and what they would do if they weren't allowed to visit her at the hospital the next day. Although they didn't want to lie to gain entry, it was clear that Rosa could answer many of Ava's questions, so they agreed to play the granddaughter card. In the meantime, they would continue with the letters and see what else they could learn from them. Who were these women and Andrés, and why did Ava feel they would turn out to be very important?

Fifteen

Ava woke to the sound of men's voices downstairs and needed a moment to understand where she was. After they had cleared out her mum's room the previous day, she and Lucy moved in there so Luke could have the guest bedroom instead of spending another night on the couch. Slowly she sat up and realised that Lucy had already left the bed and her clothes were gone too. Through her sleepy haze, she was sure one of those men's voices she had heard belonged to Luke. She threw her trusted battered jeans and t-shirt combination on and went downstairs to see what the commotion was. On route she spotted a van parked outside the house with a security company logo. While Luke showed the security man around, Ava made tea and checked her phone. She had a message from Kate asking her if she could pop over to her house when she had a moment to discuss the costs, as it was cheaper to do both houses in one go. Ava concluded she had a moment and went out and knocked on Kate's door.

'Good morning,' Kate said, smiling as she opened the door, 'I see we're at the point where you bring your own tea – mine not good enough for you anymore?!'

'Yes, the water is different in your house, you see!' Ava answered, grinning back. 'I just read your message. The security guy is with Luke, so I probably shouldn't stay too long.'

'Ah, don't worry, I won't keep you. I wanted to let you know that I will proceed with the quote he gave me. It's not cheap – £2,000 for cameras and alarms – but I will sleep better at night knowing I'm safe. And it's all connected to their centre, so if a camera detects something or an alarm goes off, someone can immediately react and alert the police if needed, making going away on holiday easier too. If they do my house and yours simultaneously we can save ourselves a £250 call-out fee. That's what I wanted to tell you.'

'Yes, I guess it would make sense to do it all together. I'll see what quote he comes up with and message you my decision. Thank you for arranging this.'

'You're welcome. Speak soon.'

Ava made her way back to her mum's house to talk business. She was grateful to have Luke there by her side during the negotiations – after the initial quote of £2,000, the same as Kate's, Luke managed to push the security man down to £1,500 for both Ava and Kate's installations. With the deal agreed, the security man explained how the system would work before Ava messaged Kate to let her know and set a date for the installation. Once the security man left, she turned to Luke: 'Have you seen Lucy?'

'Yes, she went for a run and said she'd be back with croissants from the bakery.'

'Oh lovely. In that case, I will quickly go and shower. I feel shattered.'

'How long did you stay up reading the letters?'

'It was definitely past midnight, but I only got through a couple. My Spanish isn't what it used to be, and the handwriting was making my eyes sore.'

'I see. By the way, I haven't showered yet either.' He put his arm around Ava's hips and pulled her into him, kissing her neck and making his way down her collarbone towards her breasts. He picked her up and carried her upstairs towards the shower.

When Lucy returned with the croissants, the shower was running, and clothes were strewn in a trail leading upstairs. *You naughty girl*! Lucy thought to herself, smiling. Lucy wandered through the house, looking at photos on the walls of Ava and herself in the back garden or building sandcastles on the beach. The day at the beach occurred during the first trip Ava had been allowed to join Lucy's family for. Lucy's brother was at a scouts camp, so Lucy's parents suggested that Ava join them for a week in Devon. Ava had never been to the seaside and was blown away by the waves crashing against the harbour wall of the little fishing village, wondering how it still stood. Ava and Lucy spent most of the time either in or next to the water, and only the promise of an ice cream could temporarily lure them away. They were already best friends but that trip had made them inseparable. Lucy smiled at the memory, hoping that one day her own child would find a friendship that was so strong it could endure anything. From what she had deciphered so far from reading the letters, she imagined something a bit like Rosa and María's friendship. If their story was connected to the present, then their friendship endured a civil war as well as the Second World War, a new country to call home, and possibly way more than Lucy would ever know. With this thought, Lucy was eager to learn more about the two women and not only wanted to keep translating the letters but hoped Ava might take her to the hospital instead of Luke. She went upstairs, picked a lovely summer dress, and sat on the bed to wait for Ava to come out of the bathroom. Ava entered the room and the hope of her little escapade going unnoticed immediately vanished when she saw Lucy sitting on the bed, grinning up at her, arms folded across her chest while the fingers of her right hand tapped against her bare arm.

'Back from your run, I see. Was it good?'

'I could ask you the same question!'

'I didn't go for a run.'

'You know exactly what I mean. You left a trail of clothes up the stairs.'

Ava blushed a deep red.

'Oh,' was all she could say.

Lucy burst out laughing, 'You should see your face.'

'Alright, pack it in.' Ava threw her wet hair towel at Lucy in an effort to shut her up and glanced towards the door, conscious of Luke being in the next room. 'Yes, we showered together. His body is amazing.' Ava gave in to Lucy's stare, knowing full well that she wouldn't be able to leave the room before her friend heard the words she wanted to hear.

'Not that you care about his body, obviously,' Lucy grinned.

'No, but it doesn't hurt. Luce, I think I'm falling for him.'

'No shit, Sherlock! I could've told you that the day you two met! But I'm happy for you. He's nice and been able to make you smile lately, and that's all I care about.'

'Are you sure? I don't want you to feel I'm rubbing salt into the wound after what's happened to you and what's-his-face.'

'You dafty, of course, I don't mind. Just because I fell for the wrong guy doesn't mean you have to put your love life on hold for me. I'm genuinely happy for you, I hope you know that!' Lucy tugged at Ava's arm to pull her in for a hug.

'Thank you, Lucy.' The friends hugged for a long time while Ava's wet hair dripped onto Lucy and the bed. 'Why don't you shower and get ready to go to the hospital with me?' Ava suggested.

'Really? I'd love to meet Rosa! I'll be ready in a jiffy,' she said and made her way to the shower with a spring in her step.

In the car, the girls decided they'd say as they were working, they've only now been able to make the journey to visit. Over breakfast, they had calculated that Rosa must have been born in 1920, and they knew her married name was Humphries and that she was originally from Spain. They hoped this extra information would be sufficient to gain them access to her room. They planned on asking her if she knew how María's musical box ended up at her mum's house and what she meant with the note saying: *Always watch your back and trust no one* . To their surprise, they were directed to Rosa's room with no questions asked and made their way inside. Rosa was lying in the bed with tubes and machines hanging off her. She looked even smaller than Ava remembered. The hospital room was rather bare; there were no flowers or 'get well soon' cards, the chairs for visitors stood next to the other bed in the room, and there was no smell of perfume or aftershave. Only the hum of machines brought life to the room. The second bed was empty so Ava grabbed two of the chairs that were stood next to it. She sat in one next to Rosa, taking her hand.

'Lucy, I think there aren't any flowers and cards because no one has visited her so far,' Ava said, looking up at her.

'That's so sad.'

A nurse entered the room and stalled when she saw the women. 'Oh, I didn't realise there were visitors. Are you a friend of Mrs Humphries?' she asked Ava, who was still holding the lady's hand. 'Yes, a close family friend, as no one else could make it.' Ava thought on her feet. It was clear the nurse knew she wasn't her granddaughter, but it seemed she didn't really care.

'We've been advised there are no next-of-kin, so it's nice that someone is here to visit. Unfortunately, she's not very talkative, as you can see. You're welcome to tell her about your day, though. She has normal brainstem auditory evoked responses.' Ava looked at the poor woman lying in a hospital on her own, squeezing her hand, feeling her only chance of getting some answers was drifting away from her the moment she had found it. A tear started to form involuntarily about the lost opportunity. The nurse put the flipchart back in its case and gave Ava a sympathetic smile. 'Take as long as you need.'

Later when they left Rosa's room, they made their way to reception and stepped outside into the glorious sunshine before heading home. When they arrived back at the house, Luke was pacing up and down the living room. He told them he translated more letters and confirmed what they already suspected: María is the woman from the newspaper article and she wrote to Andrés about meeting an Englishman named Henry in Madrid.

Sixteen

Madrid, Spain
1937

María's days and nights were spent at the hospital, leaving only to go home to her shared room for a few hours of sleep before returning. The siege of Madrid started in November 1936, and with the government having fled to Valencia, the city was left to defend itself. Led by General José Miaja and the Madrid Defence Council, the fascist troops were held back around the university campus and the Casa de Campo, where much of the fighting happened. María was glad her family left when they did, and while the city was still trying to evacuate its children to safer places on the east coast and further south, the shelling increased during November and December. But with the republic having finally organised itself, they managed to keep the attackers at bay, and it became evident that Madrid wouldn't be captured anytime soon. The *Madrileños* stayed put and were joined by many evacuees from other parts of the country, together with those who had left and were slowly returning home. María was on her way to the hospital, feeling a strange pride in being part of it all, when she stopped before a poster plastered to a wall reading: *¡No pasarán!* The early morning streets were bustling with people going about their business. María smiled to herself with renewed energy, determined to put the past behind her and do her bit to prevent the fascists take the city she had fallen in love with, *no pasarán* – they shall not pass!

One day, as she was busy changing the bandages on one of her patients, she spotted a new arrival in the opposite bed. The doctor on duty called her over to clean the patient's wounds and dress them before her lunch break. María did as she was told and set about her work in silence. She noticed his eyes watching her as she worked, but he said nothing. After she had finished, he touched her hand and attempted a nod. María smiled and walked to one of the rooms that had been converted to a makeshift staff room to eat her *bocadillo*. She continued smiling as she ate. This new arrival was intriguing; his blue eyes had followed her every move while she had delicately tried to tidy up his injuries without causing him too much pain. Judging by his injuries, he would be with them for some time to fully recover. She wondered what had happened to him. Most likely he was caught by a blast down in the Casa de Campo, she thought to herself; the fighting there was so fierce with the Nationalists trying to cross the Manzanares River but being pushed back by the Republicans. While Madrid stood firm against the attackers, María feared what was happening in Mieres and what her family was going through. Since her uncle had left for Valencia, she relied on the pieces of information about the situation on the front that the injured fighters gave the staff at the hospitals when they were brought in to be treated for their injuries. The last she had heard from Antonio was that Oviedo had fallen to the Nationalists in October, and with that, she assumed her hometown too. While she was sure her father would do what it took to survive, Pablo's continued disappearance meant he could be anywhere, fighting on either side.

'What's wrong, *guapa*?' María heard Victoria's voice ask her.

'Nothing,' she replied.

'And does that nothing have a name?' María looked up from her sandwich, confused. 'I haven't seen you smile like that for a long time, just before your face clouded over.' Victoria pointed out.

'Just thinking of my family back at home.' María answered.

'Ah yes, and before that, which soldier has caught your eye?'

'I…' María knew she was not going to get away with it, Victoria knew her too well. 'I don't know. He's new, got here today.'

'Is he cute?' Victoria asked.

'Probably not, his head is in a bandage. I only saw his blue eyes, and the hair on his leg was blond.'

'Oh, interesting. He might be one of the foreigners.'

'Why?'

'Well, we don't get many blond-haired and blue-eyed men around here. Unless he has come from another part of Spain.'

'Just because he might be from another part of this country doesn't mean he's a foreigner?'

'No,' Victoria said, rolling her eyes. 'Haven't you heard? Carmela told me about it yesterday. There are men from all over Europe who are coming to Spain to fight for the republic. They are called the International Brigade. Many arrived by ship in Valencia and now lie in the trenches to defend our city.'

'Why would they do that?'

'That, you have to ask one of them.' Victoria winked at her friend and left. María realised she had to get back to work too, hoping this stranger would stay on her ward long enough for her to have the courage to ask him who he was.

From then on, whenever she did her rounds, she couldn't resist glancing at his bed, her heart beating faster when she changed his dressings. But he was in and out of sleep, so she never said anything. One night when she was on duty, one of her patients cried out in pain in the middle of the night and she rushed to stabilise him. She was making her way back to the nurse's room, all patients now soundly asleep, when her curiosity got the better of her. She grabbed the clipboard at the end of his bed and checked for his name. Henry Jones, born 1916, British. María's heart fluttered. 'So you are a foreigner,' she whispered to him. Glancing around to check no one was watching her, she took a closer look at him. She noticed the muscular arms and broad shoulders, a blond strand of hair peaking out from underneath the bandage around his head. Footsteps alerted her to a nurse in the corridor. María put the clipboard back in place and left the room. She started living for the moments when he was awake. He smiled at her when their eyes met and she lowered her eyes bashfully. Even the bombing raids over the city couldn't dampen her spirits, and she found copious excuses to enter the room to check on patients while secretly hoping he would do what she was too scared to do and speak to her. Her change in mood didn't go unnoticed by the doctors and other nurses, and soon, her constant smile became infectious, and people started to beam whenever they saw her.

'I'm thrilled you have found your spark again, María. Whoever broke your heart has not deserved that smile.'

'Thank you, Carmela.'

The heavy battles surrounding Madrid started to cease in December, a new arrival had told María; both sides were tired, and Franco hadn't expected such resistance. The new patient lifted his arm in salute at Henry to say *gracias* for supporting them, then turned to María and told her to finally go and talk to Henry.

'It's unbearable watching you dance around each other, stealing glances. Go and say hello.' He winked and shooed her away in Henry's direction. María's eyes settled on his as she slowly moved towards his bed. He smiled at her, his teeth whiter than she'd ever seen. Tenderly lifting his ankle, she started unravelling the dressing on his lower leg where a piece of shrapnel had lodged in him. She took a breath and looked up at him.

'*Hola*,' she said, smiling, before immediately focussing on the bandage again.

'*Hola guapa. Cómo estás?*' he replied. María dropped his ankle, shocked at hearing Spanish coming out of his mouth. He cried out in pain and sat up, reaching for his leg.

'I'm sorry!' María cried. 'I wasn't expecting you to speak my language.' Laughter sounded from the beds around them, and María's cheeks grew hot. She wanted to run out of the room but knew she would get into trouble if she didn't finish her job. She looked at Henry, who was chuckling to himself while she finished the task as quickly as possible while he grinned at her.

'Maybe next time, don't try to kill me!' he joked. Although María was mortified when she dropped Henry's leg, it broke the ice between them. His Spanish wasn't perfect, but he spoke enough to ask her how her day was and when he would see her again. By mid-January, his injuries were mostly healed, and the doctor discharged him to free up the bed. He waited for María to do her rounds but was left disappointed when another nurse he hadn't seen before entered the room. Watching her for a moment whilst deciding whether to ask her about María, he noticed she was roughly the same height as her, her hair was a dark brown, and had it not been for her hooked nose she could have been mistaken for María. Henry decided he preferred to talk to María directly, and he would return the next day. He got up and walked out of the room under the scrutiny of the new nurse.

After a day in the park with Victoria, she returned to work the next day only to find Henry had been discharged. Her heart broke knowing it would be impossible to ever find him in this big city. She dragged herself around the makeshift ward with a heavy heart, and even the men's jokes couldn't lift her mood. As she stood in front of the shift board checking when her next day off was due, a tap on her shoulder made her jump. She turned around. Standing in front of her, he was taller than she imagined but and just as handsome she had imagined, his blond hair now combed to one side and his smile so sweet it melted her heart.

'Henry.'

'Hola María.'

'How are you?'

'I'm almost whole again, thanks to you.' María smiled, hardly able to contain her joy over seeing him again.

'I thought I would never see you again.'

'Well, they kicked me out of my bed, but you weren't here. Would you like to go for a drink with me this evening?'

'Yes, I'd like that.'

'Good. Meet me at 9 in La Venencia.'

The bar was dimly lit with basic wooden tables. Posters decorated the walls and smoke filled the air inside. It was not a place the girls would have chosen themselves, but they were there for María. It was 9.10 pm, and María, Victoria and Carmela scanned the room for Henry, all the while being looked up and down by the bar full of men. María felt uncomfortable and was unsure whether women were even allowed to be there. Certainly, she couldn't see another woman in what seemed to be a drinking den for Republican fighters.

'You made it,' Henry announced as he approached them. He led them to a table he'd secured with enough chairs for the three girls; he'd anticipated that María wouldn't turn up alone. He ordered some sherries and introduced them to one of his comrades. Henry passed around his Celtas, but María declined.

'You don't smoke?' Henry asked while holding a cigarette to his mouth, ready to be lit.

'No, but I don't mind, so please go ahead.'

'Thank you for coming, María. You look beautiful.' She blushed at the compliment, realising that he had only previously seen her in her nurse's uniform, whereas tonight she was wearing one of her lovely dresses and a little bit of red lipstick she had borrowed from Victoria.

'Tell me, Henry, why did you come to Spain to fight?' It was a question María had been dying to ask him from the moment she realised he was British.

'Straight to the point!' he said, a smile appearing across his face. 'Because I don't want my children to grow up in a fascist world.'

'That's it?'

'Isn't that reason enough?'

'So you have children?'

'No, not yet. But one day I hopefully will.'

'You're risking your life in a foreign country, fighting for a cause you believe in for children you don't have?' María was incredulous.

'Yes,' he replied, shrugging, 'I am fighting because if no one stops this, I only have myself to blame if I have to live the rest of my life at the hands of the fascists.'

'Even in your country?'

'You never know what will happen in Europe. Hitler can't be trusted either, so it's better to stop this nonsense before it spreads.'

'Is it your first time in Spain?'

'A few years ago, I went to Málaga with my father.'

'Did you like it?'

'I loved it. That's why I had to volunteer, your country is too beautiful to have it destroyed by a few men. When I arrived in Spain, there were only a handful of us, and I fought with the Franco-Belge battalion here in Madrid, securing the Casa de Campo. Then I got hit – as you know,' he said, winking. 'But now things are changing, there are more and more volunteers arriving each day from all over the world, everyone ready to take up arms against the Blues (the Nationalists) and fight for what they believe in. Now I will be joining the British Battalion.' Henry's eyes shone as he revealed his justification for being here and optimistic outlook. María was mesmerised, ignoring the occasional English word that Henry used when he didn't know the Spanish equivalent. 'Enough about me, though, I want to know more about you, María. Are you from Madrid?' His finger stroked her bare arm, sending shivers of excitement through her body.

'No, I'm from Mieres in Asturias, in the north of Spain.' María tried to concentrate, focussing on his lips and cheeky grin instead of his hand still stroking her bare arm. She told him about her upbringing and how moving to Madrid differed from everything she had turned her life upside down – although she deliberately omitted the real reason why she was sent here. If her parents saw her now, at the age of 16 sitting in a bar filled with men, one of whom was inching closer with each passing minute, she would most likely be expelled from the country entirely and sent to Spanish Morocco to live in sin. To María's relief, her two chaperones tonight were both similarly enjoying the attention of some soldiers. Several sherries later, when the bar announced it was closing for the night, Victoria indicated they had to take their leave too.

'Will I see you again?' María asked.

'If you would like to. I will be joining my new battalion in a few weeks. Thank you for a wonderful evening.' Henry lifted her hand and softly placed his lips against her skin. 'Good night, María.'

'Good night, Henry.' High on sherry and hormones, she swayed out of the bar and into the cold winter night.

From that night onwards, María and Henry spent every moment they could together, going for walks in the park or sitting in the restaurant below María's flat talking until the early hours. One cold afternoon, Henry arrived at the hospital with a flower he picked from El Retiro Park on his way. The usual glint in his eyes was gone. His marching orders had arrived, and he was due to report in the evening, ready to be sent to the front. He didn't know when or if he would return. The British Battalion was not stationed in Madrid, but he promised María that he would write to her as often as possible and make it back alive for her. Whilst Henry was gone, María worked harder than ever, spending every free minute looking after the wounded to keep her mind off worrying about him. As the weeks went by, reports started to trickle through about the Battle of Jarama where Henry was fighting, and the heavy losses they were suffering. She was expecting the news she feared the most any day, but it never came and that filled her with hope. Her infectious smile once again greeted her patients.

A month after Henry returned to the front line, she felt a tap on her shoulder. María's heart somersaulted as she rejoiced that he was back. She turned around, ready to jump into his arms. But it wasn't Henry that had tapped her on the shoulder and she was instead greeted by Rosa's eyes staring at her.

'Hello María, remember me?' María was stunned to see her old friend in front of her. After everything that had happened in Mieres, their argument at her brother's birthday party, and Rosa's betrayal, María had become glad that she had left. She remembered Rosa's letter that had broken her heart into a million pieces. The heart that was only now starting to mend. She couldn't let Rosa get to her anymore, she didn't have the energy for another fight.

'Rosa,' she frowned, 'what are you doing here?' Rosa's face was stony.

'I told you I wanted to become a nurse, unlike you.' She smiled, but it didn't quite reach her eyes, and María detected bitterness in her voice.

'Well, things have changed since then, we're at war, and I wanted to do my bit to help. Are you working in this hospital?'

'No, across the road in the Palace.' María's heart sank as she realised how close they were now working to each other. All she wanted was to cut all ties with her past. Seeing Rosa brought back all the painful memories she had so desperately tried to suppress. 'When does your shift end? We should go for a drink and catch up on old times.'

'Yes, we should,' she answered unenthusiastically, ready to head back to work.

'I finish at 6. I will pick you up at 6.30.'

'I'm not sure when I will be able to get away today.'

'That's okay, I will come here and wait for you.' Rosa was not giving up, María knew the only way out was to say no. But a part of her wanted to know what Rosa could tell her about Xulián and if they really were a couple.

'Fine,' she said. Rosa smiled triumphantly and dashed back across the road to the Palace Hotel whilst María stood rooted to the spot trying not to cry.

The rumble of guns in the distance shook María into action again as yet more fighters needing clean wounds and dressings, morphine injections, and someone to reassure them that it would be fine, as more injured fighters were carried into the Base Hospital No. 1. By the time her shift was over, María had been run off her feet and was covered in blood; she had tried to stem the blood flow from a man's stomach but, screaming with pain, he twisted and turned, rendering María powerless to keep pressure on the wound. By the time he had passed out and they could finally help him unencumbered, he had already lost too much blood. They lost him after a few minutes. Leaving the Palm Court used for the surgeries, María was glad to be in a safe space on her ward where the chances of losing patients were lower, and most were just in recovery, waiting to get back out there and beat the Nationalists. There was only one place María felt safer than in the hospital, her old home in the Goya district, now eerily empty without the laughter of its former inhabitants. Señora González still visited the house, keeping it clean for when the owners were ready to return and ensuring it wasn't subjected to burglaries.

Whenever she was in the area, she would call on María at the hospital with letters sent to the home or bring food she managed to source. As a portly lady, she was concerned María didn't have enough meat on her bones and had always tried to feed her more than she could eat at mealtimes.

Today María felt the need to visit the house after having stayed away for more than a year. It was a short walk from the hospital, and she knew which streets to take to stay undercover. Despite her nurse's uniform, she could never be sure someone wasn't following her, and entering the home of a government worker was always a risk. It was a mild day after the cold of the winter. Putting on her brown coat, she stepped outside through the back door of the hospital and dashed into the closest side street, heading towards the Puerta de Alcalá and into Goya, avoiding El Retiro Park. Having passed a few buildings that were hit in the area, María was relieved to see that the house still stood in all its glory. She let herself in with the key and stood stock still as she listened for any movement. She had heard empty many houses had been seized by fighters as hiding places or used by squatters. She felt for the scalpel inside her coat pocket though she knew she wouldn't stand a chance if she came across someone with a gun. María waited several minutes but didn't hear anything. The house was tidy and clean, an indication to María that no one apart from the housekeeper had been there. She made her way upstairs to her old room. As if she had stepped back in time, the room looked and smelled exactly the same as it did when she had arrived three years ago as a young, disgraced girl, humbled by her aunt's generosity in taking her in and willingness to help her succeed. She opened the bottom drawer of her old bedside table, and underneath the jute bag Andrés had given her she found the unopened letters Rosa had sent her. There must have been at least five. Holding the bag tight, she breathed in the musky smell of burnt wood and the faint smell of Andrés. In the distance, she heard the roar of guns as she ran downstairs to the library and grabbed a few books Antonio would most likely prefer her to have than lose if the house got hit. In a rush to get back to the hospital, she hurried through the same backstreets towards her flat, where she thrust the bag underneath her bed and quickly changed into a simple dress. She made her way back to the hospital to meet Rosa.

They walked the short distance to the same bar where she had had her first rendezvous outside the hospital with Henry, the tall wooden doors inconspicuous in the narrow street. Inside, it was packed with Republican fighters and journalists enjoying one of the Sherries on offer whilst exchanging stories from the battlefield. Rosa made her way to the bar, leaving María propped up against the wall, trying not to attract too much attention. But it seemed most of the men had better things to do than observe a young lady and returned to their conversations after a quick glance at the new arrival. The noise of the chatter was almost unbearable; María struggled to hear herself think when a young man caught her attention, explaining to his friends how his battalion had got trapped in Jarama. Her ears pricked up and she moved closer, hearing him explain that the Reds and the XV International Brigade were experiencing substantial losses and casualties – especially the British Battalion. María's knees buckled. Leaning on the back of someone's chair and steadying herself, she gazed through the open bar doors. Knowing that somewhere out there on the battlefields along the Jarama was Henry.

'Are you okay, Miss?' The gentle touch of a hand on her arm drew her eyes towards a concerned-looking young man sitting on the chair she was leaning on. His companion offered her his chair and a sip of his sherry, which she both gratefully accepted.

'Do you know anyone fighting that battle?' he asked. She saw his lips moving but hardly registered his words. 'I'm sure he will come back,' he added, seeing the shock still sinking in.

'How do you know?'

'How do I know what? That he will come back or about the battle?'

'The battle.'

'I received the news from one of my officers there.'

'If that's your division, then why are you here?' The men laughed, his mate slapping him on the back. María didn't quite understand what was supposed to be so funny about her question, raising her eyebrows accusingly at him.

'I have only just been discharged from the hospital after an injury and am confined to menial work behind a desk while I fully recover.' María nodded sympathetically.

'What is so funny?' Rosa interrupted from beside María, having returned from the bar with two glasses of sherry.

María nodded at the men and got up, leading Rosa by the arm towards a quieter corner of the bar. 'Let's sit over here so we can hear each other.'

'What were you talking about?'

'Oh, I felt faint, and they offered me a chair. I haven't eaten much today.' Rosa looked sceptical but didn't say anything. 'How have you been?' María steered the conversation away from any possibility of talking about Henry.

Rosa sighed: 'You would know if you had answered any of my letters.'

'Letters? I don't have any letters from you,' she lied.

'I sent about five over the last three years but never heard back. I wondered if something had happened, but your mother told me you were well.'

'I apologise, but I never received anything. Maybe the housekeeper threw my correspondence away.' It wasn't right to blame Señora González, but she justified her white lie by knowing Rosa would never meet her and no one would ever know.

'You have a housekeeper?'

'Had, yes. My aunt and uncle are rather affluent and live in a lovely house. I moved out to be closer to the hospital. When did you arrive in Madrid?'

'I started training in June last year in Oviedo, and in February I visited your mother to see how she was doing. She worried about you a lot, so I told her I would come to Madrid to ensure you were well. I asked for a transfer and got on the train a few weeks later.' María frowned – why would she get on a train to check on her if she was married? Maybe Xulián joined her in Madrid as he had always intended. But she couldn't ask Rosa or else she would give away that she had read one of her letters. Something felt wrong.

'Are you here alone?' she ventured.

'Of course, my family is still working the land – someone has to feed the nation.'

'Have you met a suitor yet in Madrid?' María tried again. Rosa looked at her with raised eyebrows.

'Have you?' Rosa asked, without giving an answer herself. María blushed. 'You have! Who is he? One of those men you were talking to at that table?'

'No.'

'I see, you are not going to tell me. Well, I hope you are happy and can let go of the past.'

'What do you mean by that?'

'Nothing. Just that it is good you are moving on.' For the first time since reconnecting with her old friend, Rosa smiled and swiftly changed the subject, telling her what had happened the day of the Asturias uprising and during the following two weeks when the revolt was brutally dismantled – participants were either imprisoned, shot, or lost their employment. The bar became even noisier. María didn't want to hear this, and with the laughter in the bar deafening to her ears, she begged Rosa to stop. Rosa insisted on continuing, however, claiming María had to know the truth. They were her people, fathers and brothers of families she knew, torn apart by what the miners did.

'Your father and brothers were miners too!' María reminded her.

'They were only *ambulantes* and there for the winter. We are farmers.'

'You're saying the revolt was my family's fault?' she almost shouted.

'And others', yes.' María was gobsmacked at the audacity. Rosa blamed the Calderín family for something hundreds of men had started, and thousands more joined. Wasn't she the one who had suffered the most, losing two of her brothers?

Rosa lent across the table and whispered: 'Be careful what you say around here, you never know who's listening.' The smoke of the Celtas filled the room making it difficult to breathe. The crowd was getting louder the more they drank. Her eyes stinging, María looked at Rosa and told her it was time to leave. On the street outside, María breathed in the fresh air, pulled her coat tighter, and made sure her scalpel was still in there. Rosa offered to walk her home. María was desperate for her not to know where she lived, though, and another lie quickly left her lips when she explained she needed to get back to the hospital. Rosa was not convinced: 'I'm sure whatever you need to do can wait until you're back at work tomorrow.'

'I promised one of the nurses I would keep her company tonight. The beds are all occupied and she is alone. I wouldn't forgive myself if something happened and she had no one to help her.' María realised that Rosa knew she was lying and walked with her to the hospital. At the entrance, they said goodbye and embraced awkwardly before María went inside. She made her way to one of the back doors and ran home as fast as she could. Unbeknownst to her, Rosa was hiding next to the front entrance waiting for María to come out and admit her lie. She waited more than thirty minutes before giving up.

Since that evening in the bar with her old friend, María hadn't seen or heard from Rosa, although she had a suspicious feeling that Rosa was watching her. She started taking detours home from the hospital via the restaurant next door, exiting through its back door and climbing up the fire ladder to her flat. It was Victoria's suggestion when María had told her about her concerns at work. The restaurant was Victoria's family's, and María often stopped for a chat with Victoria's mother on the way through.

The days dragged by and still there was no word from Henry. The longer she didn't hear from him, the more she lost hope. The worst casualties from the Jarama started arriving at Madrid's hospitals and were operated on in the former Palm Court of the Ritz. Every evening after her shift she visited a few to see if he was among them. But he never was. They had now been at war for almost a year, and even the arrival of spring couldn't lift her mood.

One morning, when María had just arrived at work, she and Victoria were asked to bring medical supplies to the front of the university campus. Carrying a bag each, they made their way up the *Avenida de Rusia* passing collapsed buildings and bombed-out shops where children climbed over the rubble to see what they could salvage from the shops and take home. The street was often subjected to shellings, and gunshots were a constant companion to everyday life as the *Edificio de Telefónica* was located there. The tall building served the Nationalists as a reference point as it could be seen from a distance. As the women walked along the street, the humming of aircraft above came closer. Looking up at the sky, barely able to see because of the sun, they immediately started running towards the closest metro sign to shelter from the impending bombs. In the dark, damp tunnel below the city, sitting amongst them on the platform where often trains would stop were children with their mothers, who tried to calm their offspring down by singing. No one ever knew how long they would have to stay down there – once, María had spent almost the whole night in a metro station. The stench of unwashed bodies mixed with urine made many of the inhabitants feel nauseous and the relief when they could finally resurface for fresh air was always palpable. This time they were lucky as they emerged from the metro station onto the streets to see what damage had been done after less than thirty minutes. Clouds of dust from collapsed houses filled the air as María and Victoria continued on their mission to bring supplies to the front line, leaving the bodies of those who didn't make the shelter on time behind. The echo of the falling bombs still rang in their ears and was accompanied by the rumble of even more gunshots as they made their way towards the front.

Seventeen

Footsteps followed María as she ran as fast as she could down the street, turned the corner and immediately hid in a doorway to her left. She listened to the sound of the steps slowing down, feeling for the scalpel in her coat pocket, when a figure appeared in front of her. She thrust her weapon at the boy's throat. He stepped back, when his foot caught on a loose stone, causing him to fall backwards onto the cobbled street. The moon lit up his face. He was no more than 15 years old.

'Why are you following me?' she demanded, towering over him.

'I…' he stuttered, 'was told to.'

'By whom?'

'A lady.'

'Do you know her name?' María had a suspicion who it might be.

'No.'

'What did she look like?'

'Like you.' The boy was terrified. He kept looking at María's right hand with the scalpel. 'She was wearing a nurse's uniform.'

'Rosa.' She knew it. He just shrugged. 'What did she offer you?'

'Food.' María could see how thin the boy was.

'And what does she want to know?'

'Where you go, who you meet.'

'What's your name?' An idea formed in her head.

'José.'

'Listen José, come to the Hotel Ritz at 8 in the morning. I will give you food if you stop following me and reporting to her.'

'How can I trust you?'

'I would've killed you already if that's what I wanted.' She moved back, put the scalpel in her coat pocket and raised her finger in warning. 'Now go home.'

María went to her room and got the letters out from the bag. Why was Rosa spying on her? She hadn't heard from her since that evening at the bar, which, although she was pleased about it, unsettled her. She was practically waiting for Rosa to pounce on her when she least expected it. María knew someone was following her but was surprised to see to what lengths Rosa had gone to. She started reading the first letter, a short one asking her how she was settling in in Madrid, what she was up to and if she missed Mieres. The second letter started with Rosa asking María why she hadn't written yet and assuming the reason was that María was overwhelmed with her new life. It went on to explain how Rosa wished she could be in Madrid too, how they'd have so much fun. In the third letter, dated four months after the first, Rosa was starting to get more desperate asking why María hadn't written yet – maybe the postman had lost her letters or she couldn't remember her address so she wrote it at the bottom of the letter, just in case. The last letter was the most acrimonious, Rosa demanding to know why María was ignoring her, accusing her of hurting her feelings deliberately, and asking her why she hated her. María's head was spinning; the words on the paper started to swim in front of her eyes. She couldn't take it anymore and shoved them all back into the bag and placed the bag underneath the mattress out of sight. The allegations in the letters sounded so familiar; María recalled that fateful night at her brother's party when Rosa spat venom about casting her aside whenever Xulián was near. Her mind drifted to Xulián and everything that had happened. But did it still matter? She had a new life, friends, and Henry if he made it out alive.

María woke to Victoria's squeal. Victoria jumped onto her bed and presented her with a letter, clearly expecting it to be opened. Rubbing the sleep from her eyes, María obliged and tore the envelope open. She scanned it and sighed deeply, letting herself fall back onto the pillow with a smile. 'Is it from Henry? Please read it to me,' Victoria begged.

My dearest María,
I am sending you these words to let you know I am still alive and to apologise for not sending word sooner. I will not bore you with the details, but it was a brutal battle, and I am glad I made it out alive. So many did not. However, I am to be transferred directly to Brunete for a new offensive. I will see you when I return and take you to dinner.
Yours,
Henry

'We should go out and celebrate!'

'It's eleven at night, and I was already asleep.'

'So? He's alive!'

'Yes, he is, and he's going straight from one battle to the next.'

'You should be proud of him, of what he is doing for our country.'

'I am, but I also don't want to lose him so soon after meeting.'

Victoria pushed María to the side of the bed so she could lie beside her. Draping her arm around her friend, she held her tight, fantasising about everything María and Henry could do once it was over.

Mail was delivered rarely, but when it did arrive there was always a letter from Henry. The letters revealed that fierce fighting at the Battle of Brunete had caused injury, but nothing life-threatening. María was amazed at his resolve to stand firm against the invasion despite his battalion having been decimated substantially, leaving only a handful of men fit for service. The heavy losses forced the battalion to withdraw from the front to a reserve position which offered the surviving men welcome respite and a chance to recharge. He wrote about the conditions they had to endure and that the men's morale only slightly wavered despite the heavy losses incurred. Reading his letters gave María an insight into the war she and the other nurses hadn't known about, so she took it upon herself to tell others what she learnt. Everyone had family fighting all over the country, and whilst María knew about Henry's whereabouts, the high illiteracy of the poor, especially women, meant they had no means to get in touch with their loved ones. Whether the letters María sent on their behalf were answered often depended on whether someone in the group could read and write for them. She became the lifeline between her friends and their husbands, sons, and brothers. It spurred María to reach as many fighters as possible and gave her another purpose while waiting for word from Henry, her family, or maybe even Xulián.

María was sitting on a bench in the hotel garden enjoying the evening sun when Victoria hovered behind her, clutching a letter. 'Do you want to join me?' Handing María the letter, she sat down. Looking down at the brown envelope, María's heart skipped a beat, although she was relieved to see it wasn't for her but rather for Victoria.

'Can you read it to me please?' Victoria said softly, fearing the worst. María slid the brown paper out of the envelope. There was just a tiny note:

Mrs Gómez Santos, José Antonio was killed in action near Belchite. My condolences.

Pulling Victoria close, María tried to comfort her friend over the loss of her beloved brother, only too aware of what she was going through and the grief that was yet to engulf her. The sun had started to set by the time Victoria's tears had stopped falling, the wet patch on María's uniform damp against her skin, the white salt stains clearly visible. Against María's advice, her friend insisted on working her entire shift into the night; it would take her mind off things she had said. Accepting that everyone had different ways of dealing with pain and grief, María informed the doctor on duty and offered her help.

Victoria losing her little brother made María think of her own family, wondering what Juan Luis was up to, if he was still working in the mines or had been drafted into the war efforts on the fascist side. She had no means of knowing since Mieres was firmly in Nationalist hands and mail couldn't get through enemy lines. In any case, if anyone sent her a letter, she most likely wouldn't receive it. Instead of heading back to the flat that night, she made her way towards her former home under the cover of darkness. The big wooden door creaked as she pushed it open and entered the dark hallway, which was covered in a film of dust and confirmed that even the tough Señora González had left the city. On the floor in front of her were several posters, one showing the emblematic bear of Madrid and the strawberry tree from the *Frente Popular* telling its readers the party was the salvation of Madrid and Spain. María picked up a folded poster depicting children playing in the streets of Madrid, German planes overhead, and a mother running towards her children while a bomb was falling from the sky. María stared at it, thinking of Josefa and Ana. They were taken to safety by their parents before a bomb could destroy their young lives in contrast to one young boy whose demise María and Victoria had witnessed. He had been running around the Puerta del Sol with a paper aeroplane, oblivious to the real plane above his head, when a bomb dropped centimetres from his body. His mother rushed out of the shop and shrieked at the crater where her boy now lay face down. The Madrileños sitting in the packed café on the other side of the square didn't bat an eyelid and continued with their morning coffee or a *sol y sombra* a mix of sweet anise (sol) and dark brandy (sombra), whichever was needed more. There was nothing the two nurses could do and, like everyone else, they waited for the bodies to be picked up and taken away.

María's eyes fell on a small brown envelope hidden amongst the posters on the floor. There was no address or stamp on it, just her name. She instantly recognised the writing and ripped it open:

María, I am in Madrid. Xulián.

A knock on the door terrified her. She spun around and tip-toed behind the door, holding her breath. There was another knock followed by a whisper. She thought she heard her name.

'María, it's me, open up, I know you're here. Quick.' Against her own will and better judgement, her hand reached for the door handle, unlocking it. The door pushed open just a crack but enough for a tall, thin man to squeeze through. Immediately she stepped backwards, but he was faster and wrapped her in his arms, holding her tight. His familiar smell, dark brown curly hair, and the warmth of his body made María's resolve crumble; she leaned into him and soaked up a piece of the past.

'Oh María.'

'How did you find me?' she asked.

'Shhh,' Xulián whispered, putting his finger to his lips before leading her away from the front door towards the library at the back. 'I waited for you in the house across the street. Your mother gave me the address.'

'How long have you been in Madrid?'

'A few months.' María pushed him away. She couldn't be seen with him again. He was a married man.

'I thought you would be happy to see me?' he said, looking hurt.

'It's been almost four years, Xulián!' She thought of her new life and Henry, fighting for her country. 'Why did you never write?'

'I didn't have your address!'

'That's because you didn't meet me under our tree the night before I had to leave!' They were both shouting now, angry at each other at the broken promises and how the world that was to be their future was abruptly taken away from them.

'I was in a hospital!'

'Why?' María instantly calmed down, concern in her eyes.

'After you tripped, I ran to the party to get José. But while he went to you and alarmed the doctor, I was stopped by your brother and his friends.' María gasped.

Four years earlier

'Why are you running?' Pablo stood in Xulián's way.

'My father told me to be home by eleven, and I'm late. So if you don't mind…'

Xulián tried to push past Pablo but was shoved to the ground. 'I hear you were trying to have fun with my sister.'

'You must be hearing voices in your head then.'

'Are you calling me a liar, *coñu*?' Xulián tried to get up, but Pablo was faster, pushing him down, his knee on his chest, his hand around his throat.

'Pablo, don't sink to his level.' Andrés interjected, trying to get Pablo off the boy.

Pablo stood up and turned to his brother. 'Why are you defending him? She is your sister too! Do you want him to get away with what he did?' He pointed his finger at the boy, who tried to get up and escape while he could but was held back by others.

'All I'm saying is we don't know exactly what happened. We only have Rosa's word.'

'Always the rational one of the family, aren't you.' Pablo scoffed. 'I don't have time to find out if she's lying. If it is true, then this entitled bastard has to pay!' Pablo started to pummel Xulián with blows against the stomach and head while his friends held on to his arms, holding him up when he began buckling over.

'That's enough. He has learnt his lesson!' Andrés said.

Pablo swiftly dealt a blow to Andrés' stomach. 'Do you want more of that, dear brother?' They locked eyes, Pablo standing triumphantly over him. 'Thought not,' he continued before returning to beat Xulián.

'Xulián, Xulián, are you okay?' Rosa leant over him, feeling for a pulse. His eyes flicked open momentarily before he slid into unconsciousness.

*

María had to sit down. 'I was in hospital for a very long time. The doctors didn't think I would make it, but the thought of seeing you again kept me going. I knew it was Rosa who saw us, and she told Pablo.'

'If you knew, why did you want to marry her?'

'What, why would I do that?' Seeing the hurt in his eyes, María realised it was just another of Rosa's many lies. 'Did she tell you that? And you believed her?' Xulián concluded, the anger audible in his voice.

'I waited three years for a letter from you – for anything that proved you hadn't forgotten me. Then I found her letter and suddenly it made sense why you didn't write.'

'I couldn't. I was beaten so badly that it took months to recover. And don't forget that I didn't know you were sent away! By the time I was ready to leave the hospital and come to you, the Asturias uprising had started, and it wasn't safe to return.' María was shaking from all the betrayals and hurt caused by Rosa. Was that why Rosa followed her, hoping María would lead her to Xulián?

'Is this really what happened or did Rosa get you to say all this? I'm not sure I know who you are anymore.'

'I'm the one who loves you, María, that's all that matters.'

María pushed him away. He wasn't answering her question. Was she so blind to see? She started putting the pieces together. When he arrived in Mieres with his father the story was that they had moved there to look after his grandmother. But now María wondered who his grandmother was, she couldn't recall an elderly woman who lived alone and needed help. Was that story just a cover-up? María shoved at him, causing him to lose his footing. She ran towards the main staircase, taking two steps at a time, reaching her old bedroom out of breath before locking the bedroom door from the inside. She heard his footsteps on the stairs and ran to the window, but being on the second floor of the house she was too high up to climb out. She was trapped. The doorknob rattled as he tried to get in. María stood in the corner furthest away from the door, clutching at the scalpel in her coat pocket. 'Let me in, María, let me explain.' She didn't answer. How long could she stay there before he tried to enter the door? Her heart was beating fast as she tried to understand why she was running away from him. This was her Xulián. She heard him slump against the door. 'You are right, I am not who I said I was. But I had to protect myself.'

'Who are you?'

'I will only tell you if you let me in. I have waited too long to see you again.'

Timidly she walked towards the door. 'Why should I trust you?'

'Because I am still the same person.'

'No, you lied to me. You are the reason I was sent away to Madrid. Because I trusted you, I haven't seen my family for four years.' Tears started to fall from her eyes. 'Now Andrés is dead, and my father and Juan Luis are somewhere fighting this stupid war or already dead too. I never got the chance to tell them how much I love them. You have no idea how this feels for me!'

Sobbing, she slid down the wall, pulling her knees tightly towards her chest. 'I know how you feel, María, and I am sorry for what has happened, but I didn't lie to you,' Xulián said, himself sounding close to tears. 'My father is a scholar – or was. When the Second Republic was declared and the royals had to flee the country my father didn't leave. He thought he was safe, just a minor royal, a distant cousin of King Alfonso XIII. He stayed and kept on teaching, which proved to be a fatal misjudgement – one of his students shot him. My mother sent my brother and I away to save us. The last thing I said to my father was that I hated him because he made me rewrite my homework. He died thinking his child hated him.'

'Where are your mother and brother now?' María asked, her voice almost a whisper.

'My brother was sent to France. I tried looking for my mother, but it's not safe for me in Madrid. This is Republican territory; any wrong move could get me killed.'

'Then why are you risking your life?'

'I needed to see you one last time.'

It was a tranquil night, the gunfire merely a faint rumble in the distance, scarcely audible over the sound of María's heartbeat. Slowly her hand reached for the key; she knew that if she unlocked the door there was no way back.

The tenderness with which he had made love to her transported her back to the fateful summer of four years earlier when she had still been an innocent young girl.

The blistering summer heat took its toll on everyone in the hospital, adding dehydration to the list of ailments to treat. Food shortages were fast becoming one of the biggest threats, and María often skipped breakfast to bring what little food she had to the hospital. She told herself that she could survive without the tiny morsel of dry bread in the mornings. She was drawing her strength from the hope of seeing Xulián again but struggled with not knowing where and how he was. Desperately hoping for a word from him, she snuck back to the house every night and waited for him. But he never showed. Sitting in her old bedroom, waiting for him to come home to her, stirred feelings deep inside her of that fateful night when she waited underneath their tree. Would she have to wait another four years to see him again?

Summer turned to winter, conditions in the hospital became even more brutal and the morale of those defending the city sank. When María received a letter from Henry she learnt that he had been sent to fight for the town of Teruel, an important strategic offensive in the mountainous Aragon region of eastern Spain. Would he return from the battle? And would María have the courage to tell him about Xulián? Her feet ached, and her body felt heavy from her 14-hour shifts at the hospital, yet her heart was even heavier. The prospect of Henry returning to find her yearning for another man riddled her with guilt. She was on an emotional rollercoaster, jolting between happy for having found Xulián and spending a magical night together and devastated that she had no idea where he and her family were and the only person she had heard from was Henry. María leant against the window frame and looked up into the sky, checking for planes, dreaming of a future with Xulián when the war would be over and they could sit under a tree in their garden while he read to her. She felt a tap on her shoulder and her smile vanished the second she turned around as she saw Rosa, the last person she wanted to see at that moment.

'What do you want?' María scowled, barely containing her anger over the lies and subsequent devastation "her friend" had caused her and her family. Had it not been for Rosa, María would have never had to leave Mieres and her family. Rosa instinctively took a step back, sensing a change in María's feelings from unfriendliness the last time they had met to pure hatred.

'I… I wanted to check on you,' Rosa stammered, not having expected such a spiteful tone from María, which had thrown her off-guard.

'Why do you care?' María snapped, squaring up to her. María was a few inches shorter but Rosa looked intimidated and shrank back. Taking full advantage of her momentary superiority, María shoved Rosa, pushing her further back against the wall. María felt blood rush through her body, and by now she had forgotten about her body's aches and pains. 'You ruined my life!'

Rosa found her equilibrium again. Standing taller, pushing herself away from her position against the wall, she shouted back, 'I ruined yours? And what do you think you did to me?' María's confused look encouraged Rosa and a disturbing smirk spread across her face. 'Look at me, I'm beautiful,' Rosa mocked, 'my brothers will protect me, and I can do whatever I want.' She flicked her hair as she twirled in front of María, who was standing with her mouth agape. 'I'm so intelligent, I sneak off every day to sit under a tree with my lover, and nobody knows, *jajaja*. Even if my friend is waiting on the bench by the river, I don't care.'

'That was four years ago. How can you still be mad about that?' María was incredulous.

'Oh, you think that's why I am angry? Are you so narrow-minded that you don't see the bigger picture? That day was just the tip of the iceberg. You have no idea what it feels like to live on a farm, working day and night, waiting for the moment you can go back into town and attend school, only to turn up after a long winter and realise your best friend has no interest in you anymore and has replaced you with a boy and his books. Like I'm some broken toy you can just throw away when you get bored of it.'

Hearing these words shoot out of Rosa's mouth felt like bullets out of a machine gun. The way Rosa almost stumbled over them it seemed like years of wrath was being unleashed on María. The sky outside darkened and the heavens broke, releasing torrential rain over Madrid. They turned their eyes to the window, through which they saw people down in the streets below running for cover while the water washed away the dust from the roads and gave the *Madrileños* a much-needed break from the stifling heat. María listened to the rain pellets hit the glass while the distant rumble of gunshots ceased – no doubt the soldiers were hiding from the rain like everyone else. The lights in the hallway above them were switched on, and it brought them back to their conflict.

'I didn't throw our friendship away, but things changed while you were gone. I grew up,' María said in a small voice, 'I started thinking about other things than hide and seek.' After Rosa's outburst, the silence that had followed was beautiful, allowing her to hear the beeping of the machines and the low hum of the hospital noises, which reminded her of how far she had come since leaving Mieres and the person she had become. On the other hand, Rosa appeared to still be the young girl she had been back then in Mieres.

'You were only thinking of one thing,' she said through gritted teeth.

'And what would that have been?' María asked, her deadpan tone giving nothing away.

'How to sneak off and meet Xulián.'

María tried to remain calm at hearing his name. 'I don't see how that had anything to do with you.'

'Of course you don't. You are so self-centred that you never once thought about your family, who didn't suspect anything.' Rosa was shouting again. María flinched. 'All those hours you should've been at home helping, and not once did I hear a thank you for covering for you when they came looking for you.' It felt like a blow to the stomach. Not only did Rosa know about her secret rendezvous, but she also lied to her family about her friend's whereabouts until that night.

'Then explain why you ran straight to Pablo on the night of the fiesta? You're the reason I was sent to Madrid and Xulián ended up in hospital!'

'How…?' Rosa's shocked expression pleased María, but her eyes instantly clouded again. 'So Xulián is in Madrid after all.' María gasped, she hadn't intended to give this precious detail away by enabling Rosa to make the connection. 'And I bet you couldn't wait to get your hands on him again. I bet you jumped at the opportunity to steal him away from me.'

'Steal from you? When was he ever interested in you?'

'Who do you think cared for him after your brother beat him up?' A satisfied smile played on Rosa's lips. It dawned on María why the boy had followed her – Rosa didn't care where María was going, but she might lead her to Xulián. María felt the urge to run and warn him. This girl was crazy; she thought she had some right over him. The rain had stopped again, and the sun was trying to push through the clouds. It wouldn't be long before the heat would dry up all the rain, leaving no reminder that there had been any at all. She could feel Rosa's eyes following her, waiting for a reaction, and realised at that moment that she could not risk being followed by Rosa. She needed to find an escape.

'María,' came a man's voice from behind Rosa. 'I'm glad you are still here. We need an extra pair of hands for a complicated operation. Please follow me.'

'Of course, doctor.' María pulled back her shoulders and stuck her chin up high. She walked past Rosa without glancing at her and followed him to the makeshift operating room, only letting out the breath she was holding once safely behind the closed doors and thanking the doctor when she registered the room was empty and the complicated operation was just a ruse to save her from Rosa.

As winter turned to spring, food shortages became an even bigger issue than before, as did the lack of blood to enable much-needed blood transfusions in the hospital. The nurses were working night and day trying to source food and material for the injured soldiers, more and more of whom were dying each day. The mood was deteriorating as news of more battles being lost and major cities falling into the hands of the enemy filtered through. Victoria was on the brink of collapsing, having never quite recovered from her brother's death. She spent most of her days in bed, staring into space, and even María couldn't get her to go for a walk for some fresh air. Their once-close group of friends rarely met outside of work these days, and on the rare occasion that they did go to a bar, they were too tired to say much to each other. Everyone was preoccupied with their thoughts, wondering when the war would end and give them their lives and loved ones back. On a bright sunny day, after an incredibly long and draining week cleaning open wounds, stabilising broken bones and watching even more men slip away, María dragged her feet home through the restaurant downstairs. Behind the counter Victoria's mother looked at her tired face as she passed, still scarcely able to contain her suffering after losing her son. Her soft voice asked María to tell Victoria to come downstairs for some food. María nodded, slowly shuffling down the hallway and up the two flights of stairs to her shared room. Victoria was lying on the bed, her arm hanging off the side, her wrist slit open with a scalpel. The blood had already dried in a pool on the floor, her eyes were glazed over, staring ahead. In her left hand she was holding the letter close to her heart. Standing in the doorway, stunned, María slid her hand into the pocket of her coat, which was hanging on the back of the door. It was empty. She slid to the floor, staring at her friend whose pain must have been so deep that she had seen no other way. María sat there for a long time before she managed to rouse herself again to go downstairs and break Victoria's mother's heart again.

The shock of Victoria's suicide stirred something deep inside María; she blamed herself for not looking after her friend enough. A thought ran through her head, accompanied by a cold sensation down her spine: Was Rosa right? Was she a self-centred person? She knew she had hurt Rosa, yet she left the party to meet him instead of sorting things out with her. And when Victoria needed her most, María's thoughts were with Henry until he wasn't good enough anymore when Xulián returned, and she abandoned both Victoria and Henry. For the umpteenth time in her still-young life, she felt her world crumble around her. She felt culpable for her friend's death with her thoughtlessness. Guilt ate away at her insides for all the people she had hurt over the past few years. She needed to get away from it all, María decided – Madrid was no place for her anymore, and after weeks of noticing changes in her body, she realised she now had to think of someone else too. María sent Isabel a letter asking to join them in Barcelona, knowing it was the safest place to bring Xulián's child into the world.

The transfer to Barcelona was straightforward as her uncle sent the hospital a letter requesting her presence in the city the government had resettled to in October 1937. She toyed for a long time with the idea of sending a letter to Henry, unsure what to say and not wanting to build up his hope before she had to tell him the truth. In the end, she relented and notified him of her move. If the thought of seeing her again kept him alive, then who was she to go and crush his hopes. The farewell from her colleagues was as emotional as she had expected, with more than one asking who would read and write their letters to and from the front without her. She looked at one of the doctors, who shrugged. After the women had dispersed, he approached her, embraced her, and pushed a gun into her hand. 'You might need this to protect you two. Take care,' he said and walked out of the lobby. His warmth surprised her and more so the gesture; María suspected that he had heard more of her fight with Rosa than she had first realised, and therefore knew she needed help. She shoved the gun into her pocket and vowed to herself to keep her and her unborn child safe. She stood outside gazing across the *Fuente de Neptuno* towards the Palace Hotel and pondered what game Rosa was playing and whose side in this relentless war she was on.

María was due to join a convoy heading out of Madrid at 1 am. But before she said goodbye to the city she had come to love with its beautiful buildings, green spaces, and entertainment, she decided to visit the house one last time and leave a letter for Xulián. Walking one final time through El Retiro, she sat on a bench in front of the lake, recalling sitting underneath the tree with Xulián, talking about their life together in Madrid, and wondering where he was now. The roar of guns brought María back to the present as she hurried out of the open space and into Goya's streets; it was getting dark now, and she didn't have much time.

She entered the house as quietly as she could and put the letter on the sideboard. She had enough time to grab a book from the library and ram it into her already-full bag. As she did so, she heard the floorboards above her creak. María looked up and held her breath. Slowly she made her way to the front door, feeling for the gun in her pocket, realising she had no idea if it was loaded nor how to use it. Almost at the front door, she glanced towards the staircase where two feet appeared on the top step. She aimed the gun at the dark figure while she tried to open the latch on the front door behind her with her left hand. The footsteps came closer and stopped where the moon threw light through the window. María aligned the gun with both hands, ready to shoot when she recognised the face.

'Pablo,' she whispered, shocked. He didn't move. María wanted to embrace him and run away at the same time. He was the brother she loathed, but her feelings had changed somewhat when she learned that he had done what he did to protect her honour. Was he responsible for Xulián's injuries and Andrés' death, or was that a lie too? She didn't know what to believe anymore. Could he be trusted after all that had happened? Maybe not but he was the last link to her family. There were so many questions María wanted answers to, but none would form as Pablo slowly walked towards her.

'How's mamá?' He stopped. Only now did María see he was also holding a gun, but his was not aimed at her.

'I don't know.' He sounded choked. 'I fled after the uprising, never saw them again.' María gave a tiny wail. How awful it must be for her mother to lose three of her children at once. She remembered Victoria's mother, appreciating how many parents in this country were going through the same pain and suffering.

'Why are you in Madrid?'

'It was the easiest and safest place to hide.' He pointed his gun at her bag. 'Where are you going?'

'Barcelona.'

'Good, you'll be safe there.'

'Since when do you care about my safety?'

'Oh, María,' he said, shaking his head and taking another few steps towards her. 'You always thought I didn't care about you when all I was trying to do was protect you.'

'From whom?'

'From your "friend" Rosa for one,' he replied. 'Did you know that she was the one who denounced you?' María nodded. 'Did you also know that her father gave up our hiding positions during the uprising, which led to twenty-four of our men being killed, among them Andrés?' Her hands flew to her mouth, a gasp escaping from within her – her poor dear brother. 'I always tried to warn you to stay away from her. Her family is no good and never has been. But I let you off in the beginning – how much damage could a young girl do? Well, quite a lot, it turns out.'

What else didn't she know, María wondered? 'Why did you beat up Xulián?'

'To protect your honour after what he did to you.'

'He didn't do anything. We had a picnic.' María understood how Rosa betrayed her whenever she could, but to gain what?

'I was told he was on top of you with his trousers down when Rosa found you. I'm not surprised that was a lie too.' Every emotion, from hate, to fear, to what resembled love for her eldest brother, ran through María's body. A tear escaped the corner of her eye. She felt his body move in closer, his arm pulling her into an embrace. Instantly her body relaxed. This was the brother she had always wanted him to be. His smell reminded her of home and everything she had lost. 'Pablo,' she murmured, 'I'm scared.'

'I know. We all are.'

'And I am pregnant.' His body tensed slightly.

'Who's the father?'

'Xulián.' He pulled her in closer and kissed the top of her head. The floorboards on the gallery above them creaked; they sprang apart and held their breath. Pablo's hand grabbed his pistol, pointing it at the dark, waiting for another sound.

'Well, well, well, look at you two. Brother and sister making amends just before death, how lovely.'

'You!' Pablo shouted and pulled the trigger.

Eighteen

María was shoved and hit the floor with a thump, the gunshots ringing in her ears. Pablo was lying on the floor, holding his chest, breathing hard. María crawled slowly to him, listening for a sound from upstairs. Nothing.

'Run, María,' Pablo insisted, breathlessly.

'You need help,' she said, inspecting his chest, feeling for an exit wound on his back. She pressed a piece of clothing from her bag onto the wound, making him flinch. Blood was seeping through her fingers as she tried to stop the bleeding.

'Go, I can take care of myself. She wants you, not me.' María's head spun towards the gallery. Rosa's arm was dangling through the balustrade, her body laid on the floor, motionless. But had Pablo fatally wounded her? 'Please, María, go. I would never forgive myself if something happened to you or the baby. Promise me you'll stay safe.'

After all the years of hatred between them, they had made amends, feeling the love that had faded but never entirely left them. She kissed his forehead. 'Take care, Pablo.' She grabbed her bag and ran as fast as she could to the meeting point, tears streaking down her face, her legs shaking.

The journey to Barcelona was long and arduous, and María's strength and resolve slowly left her. Still only 17 she was exhausted from life and the constant struggle to survive and protect herself, never knowing who she could trust. Maybe she should have stayed in Madrid and waited for Xulián, or perhaps even followed in Victoria's footsteps. She put a protective hand around her bump, knowing she had made the right decision to leave; she now had someone else to think about. They might be some of the last ones to make it to Barcelona before the Blues broke through to the Mediterranean Sea and cut Madrid off. María's gaze fell on the lorries behind them, all following the same route towards Valencia. They were all trying to make it to safety before daylight revealed their position. Once in Valencia, they would spend the day there before continuing at night up the coast to Barcelona. She shared the battered lorry with an injured major who was spread out on the floor and looked like he wouldn't survive long enough to reach his destination. Also there was a doctor, most likely there to keep the major alive María had surmised, and the wife of a government minister with her children, who were fast asleep leaning against their mother. Even the tiny baby in her arms was in dreamland despite being shaken about on the battered road. Exhaustion was written all over their faces. María's knee kept banging against the woman's leg opposite her. She tried to rearrange herself, the gun in her pocket digging into her thigh, and whenever she closed her eyes, all she could see was Pablo's eyes pleading for her to leave. She should have stayed, María admonished herself. She should have helped her brother and tried to save him. But she knew what danger she was in. He was right, after all; Rosa wasn't interested in him, she was baying for María's blood. How the tables had turned after Rosa found out that Xulián and María had rekindled their relationship. Instead of finding Xulián and professing her undying love for him, she wanted revenge; yet again María was in the way of her happiness. The pieces started to fit together. Rosa hadn't been lying to María's family to protect her friend, Rosa was ensuring no one found out about them so that Xulián wouldn't be sent away. But something had changed that night when she spotted them and saw their love for each other – Rosa knew she had to get rid of María to make Xulián her own. And it would have been her lucky day when María was sent far away from Xulián had it not been for Pablo beating him up so badly that he had to stay in hospital for almost two years. No wonder Rosa wrote that they were to marry, it was the only way she could think of to keep them apart when he got discharged from hospital. She needed to prevent María from harbouring any hope of ever seeing him again. And then war broke out.

María gasped, recognising her fatal mistake when she gave Xulián away at the hospital. She had been so careful that Rosa hadn't followed her during the preceding months, but ultimately María had led her straight to the house. The bullet that hit Pablo was intended for María, who would forever have to live with the guilt of her brother's death.

'It is good to see you.' Antonio greeted her at the drop-off point in Barcelona the following night. 'I know it was a long journey, so let's get you home where you can rest.'

'Thank you very much for getting me here and picking me up, I appreciate your help, Antonio.' María was glad to have made it safely; the last part of the journey had been excruciating, with bombs falling close to the slow-moving convoy and the drivers unable to see much in the dark without their headlights on. Exhausted, María slumped into her bed and instantly fell asleep. She was so tired she slept all the way through until the following evening, only awoken by the sound of her cousins Josefa and Ana, running towards her bed and jumping on it, oblivious to her pale skin and puffy eyes. María still felt drained from the previous night, during which she had alternated between being sick and crying herself back to sleep. The girls told her how excited they were that she was back and that they had missed her terribly. María's heart burst with love as she hugged them, kissing the top of their heads.

'We told everyone at school today that you made it safe from Madrid!' Ana told her enthusiastically, still jumping up and down on the bed.

'Shhh Ana, mamá said not to be loud, sit down.' Ana did as her older sister said, disappointed. Josefa was sitting on the side of the bed, looking at María through glasses.

'Oh, when did you start wearing glasses?' María asked.

'Do you like them? Papá got them for me a month ago because I couldn't see the blackboard at school.'

'They suit you, you look very intelligent,' she smiled. 'Are you getting ready to go to school?'

Josefa looked at her, irritated. 'No, we just got back from school! We wanted to say hello this morning, but mamá said we should let you sleep.'

'Oh,' María responded, turning to look at the drawn curtains through which no light was coming in.

'And that you should get dressed and join us for dinner. Mamá says you have to eat.' Ana nodded vigorously, skipping after her sister out of the room. The house was in darkness when María went downstairs. The dining room was almost as big as the one in the old house but decorated more plainly. Isabel got up to hug her niece, welcoming her back to the family. When the plates with the food were brought in, she realised how for her family life was still the same as it had been – they had enough food, they still had a cook and a servant, Antonio was still working, and the girls were still going to school. The ordinary family dinner felt like she had travelled back in time to a moment in life when all was still normal, the main dinner topic was squabbles between siblings, and there was enough food to feed the hungry mouths.

She eyed the massive portion on her plate, looking up questioningly at Isabel. 'You must be hungry,' Isabel said, her eyes settling on María's bump. María put a hand on it, aware it was showing – with her slender frame, it wasn't hard to miss – although she was trying to do her best to cover it up. Carmen had been the first to notice when María had repeatedly headed for the bathroom and subsequently asked her to cover the night shifts in the hospital so as to afford her much-needed rest in the mornings. She could see the suffering in María's eyes when she returned from throwing up what little bit of food she had managed to eat the previous day. Seeing all of the food in front of her now almost made María nauseous. She had known what it was like to go without a decent meal for a few days since the beginning of the siege of Madrid. When the fascists had managed to capture some of the most important food producing regions in the country and cutting of the capital from receiving food deliveries. Chronic hunger was a daily companion for every Madrileño who had no contacts in the government or unions or enough possessions to exchange for food at the *Torrijos* market. More often than not, a bowl of lentils had to keep a family going for several days, and it was only when María could hardly keep herself on her feet at work that she went to exchange some of her aunt's possessions for some bread which in turn she shared with her friends. The guilt of taking what wasn't hers still gnawed at her, though seeing the state of the country, she doubted her aunt would ever make it back to her former home, which had probably already been stripped bare of anything valuable anyway. María started to understand what privilege meant and how lucky she was to have been welcomed back into her family's fold, where she and her baby would be safe.

The next few months were a world away from what María was used to in Madrid. Though she helped at the hospital initially, her pregnancy soon got in the way of her getting out of bed and doing something worthwhile. During this period, she witnessed Antonio becoming a shadow of himself; the once-strong man almost diminished to nothing, the circles under his eyes became more prominent, and his upright walk succumbed to a stoop. The Republican government had lost the strategic town of Teruel. Countless lives were lost in the battle during one of the coldest winters Spain had experienced for decades. Shortly after, Franco and his troops cut through to the Mediterranean. María and her family knew it was only a matter of time until they would march into Barcelona. María did her best to stay positive and reminded her uncle the International Brigadiers were here to help and that they would ensure Barcelona would not be taken.

'I wouldn't be too sure about that, my dear.'

'France has reopened the frontier and supplied our fighters with more material. You'll see, we will win this war!' She spread her arms as if speaking in front of a crowd. Her only spectator wasn't convinced.

'With the border open again, getting their nationals out of Spain will be easier. So I ask you, will they fight until the end and risk being on the losing side, or will they leave and go back to safety in their own countries?' He shook his head and took a deep breath. 'I know we need to stay positive and believe in our win but look at this country – our children are starving, the battlefields are stained with their fathers' blood, and we rely on foreign governments to help us fight our own people.' Antonio threw his hands in the air, despondent. 'We knew what was building up after the uprising in Asturias, we knew it was only the beginning and foolishly thought if we showed our power and suppressed their anger it would all go away eventually. But we were wrong, so wrong. You know what the worst thing about this was, María?' María stood stock-still. Antonio hadn't said anything about what happened in October 1934 apart from confirming there was a revolt by the miners. Did he know more about Andrés' death than he had told her? 'The worst thing was when it started, our war minister Hidalgo wanted to send General Franco to lead the 25,000 troops against Asturias, but Alcalá-Zamora decided to send López Ochoa to limit bloodshed. We knew we had to suppress the rebellion, or it would turn into a civil war, but what if Franco had been sent and later killed instead of Ochoa?'

'It wouldn't have changed anything,' María sighed, 'López Ochoa got killed because of his beliefs and because both the left and right didn't trust him. This war was always going to happen with whichever general was available to lead the Blues.'

'I suppose you are right.' For the first time during this conversation, Antonio looked up at her from his glass of sherry. 'When did you grow up? You were still a child when you joined our family.'

'Uncle, do you know anything about Andrés?'

His smile disappeared instantly. After a long pause, he asked, 'Do you really want to know?'

'Yes.'

'You'd better sit down then.' He took a large sip of his sherry, put the glass on his desk and looked straight into María's eyes. 'The miner's strike was, in actual fact, a much larger strike that took place all over the country. But for various reasons it didn't go to plan. It all started when the right-wing CEDA won the majority of votes in 1933, but instead of inviting their leader José María Gil-Robles to form a government, our president Alcalá-Zamora invited Alejandro Lerroux from the Partido Republicano Radical to do so. Of course, the CEDA wasn't happy with that, and after a year of political pressure, they were finally allowed to send three ministers to Madrid. That's when it all started. No one wanted them there and other parties tried to force them out again, whilst the CEDA made it clear they wanted to seize full power. The Republicans were alarmed that their strength could lead to a return to the monarchy or another dictatorship, and that's when many decided a revolution was needed to put a stop to it. Workers' strikes were called in many parts of the country for the fourth of October, and the rebels armed themselves with rifles, pistols and dynamite. But the strike didn't go as planned. In Asturias, though, it was a different story, and once the uprising began, the government had to react.'

Antonio stopped and took another sip of his sherry, ready to continue when María interrupted him: 'You knew it was wrong not to invite the CEDA. Why didn't ministers like you fight for democracy? Maybe the CEDA wouldn't have been such a threat?'

'Well, I wasn't a minister then and therefore had no power. But yes, you are right; many of us knew what was happening, but we were all scared of the threat the CEDA posed and thought if we didn't invite them into the government, we would be stronger without alienating our alliances. Like you said, this war was always going to happen.'

'Maybe not if the government hadn't angered the CEDA. I didn't know about this.'

'The CEDA was already angry before they won the majority of votes, as was much of the population of Spain. They wanted to change the course of this country, and now are close to achieving it.' María sat back in her chair as she processed it all. Maybe this was what Pablo had meant when he had told her to keep out of things she didn't understand. He knew what was bubbling under the surface and wanted to protect his then-14-year-old sister.

'As I mentioned, our president sent López Ochoa to Asturias along with the Guardia Civil, Spanish Legion and the highly skilled Moorish troops. The miners who had made their way to Oviedo took the city and its arsenal, which provided them with some 24,000 rifles and machine guns. Both Pablo and Andrés were part of the revolutionaries. After Gijon and Oviedo had fallen, Ochoa demanded surrender from the revolutionaries. The committees were only prepared to agree to his terms if he kept the Spanish Legion and Moorish troops away from the mining towns; the committees knew what bloodshed they were capable of. I believe, during the repressions in the towns, the police arrested your father in Mieres and threw him into prison along with thousands of others. Andrés was wounded in the fighting at the barracks that followed the march to Oviedo and was left bleeding to death in the streets. Pablo found him in agony and spent his last moments with him. I'm very sorry.'

'How do you know this?'

'Pablo sent me a letter accusing me of being directly responsible for your brother's death as I work for the government. According to him, I tore your family apart, first by taking you away to Madrid and then by having my men kill your brother.' This came as a shock to María, who had blamed Pablo for dragging Andrés into the revolution. She was now starting to see that Andrés was just another cog in the wheel of something much bigger, and he would have inevitably been a part of it with or without Pablo. She hadn't realised just how big the revolt was and how many miners and workers had participated. After processing this new information from Antonio, she was almost glad she hadn't previously known the full extent of the bloodshed. She looked up at the ceiling and silently thanked Pablo for being there for Andrés in his final minutes. Imagining her brother lying wounded in the streets fighting for his life shattered her heart. 'I don't know what happened to Pablo.' Antonio broke into her thoughts.

'I do,' María whispered. When she had arrived in Barcelona, she had buried what happened during her final night at the house in Madrid deep within her, determined to never re-live it. 'He's dead, killed by Rosa in the house in Madrid.' She proceeded to tell Antonio all of what had happened.

'I am so sorry for everything you had to go through on your own. We never should have left you there alone.' Antonio got up and gave her a tight fatherly hug. María fell into his arms and sobbed for everyone she had lost.

The bombing raids over Barcelona were taking their toll on the inhabitants, though nothing compared to what they had had to endure in March when for two full days bombs were dropped every fifteen minutes. It had been chaos at the hospital during those turbulent days; the nurses and doctors had tried to save the injured during the brief window before the next bomb fell, resulting in more casualties. The Italian bombers had sailed over Barcelona, only turning on their engines when they had dropped their bombs and hit their targets. Not once did María hear the alert sound before she felt the explosion which had made the alert system redundant and had caused terror amongst the population. The Blues had been relentless and bombed military targets, arms factories and trains filled with soldiers, but what had caused greatest concern was the bombarding of theatres, civil buildings and cinemas. Everyone lived on edge, fearing that the two days terror of March 1938 could happen again.

After those struggles, María was told to take it easier so as to not risk her baby's life. It meant she was housebound for most of her time. One afternoon she found Isabel in the living room and joined her with her favourite book.

'What are you reading?' her aunt asked.

'It's a book by an English author called Charles Dickens.'

'Did you find that in Antonio's library?' María stroked the cover, remembering the day she had found the book in the jute bag Andrés had given her.

'No, it was a present from my brother.'

'It's a difficult book to read,' Isabel remarked. María was unsure whether she meant the language was the reason for the difficulty or the emotions attached to it and the person who gave it to her.

'I'm still not sure how Andrés got hold of it. I don't recall him ever looking at a book in his life.' Isabel smiled but said nothing. Opening the book at the piece of paper she used as a bookmark, María re-read the words on the snippet for the hundredth time. *Always watch your back and trust no one.* If only she had heeded her brother's advice.

After a while spent turning pages without taking in anything she read, María turned to her aunt and started telling her about Xulián, the father of her child, and Henry, the man she knew she had feelings for but was now confused about what those feelings were. Isabel listened with interest, only nodding occasionally to indicate for María to go on. If her aunt was shocked at the revelations, she didn't show it, which made María tell her more than she had intended, including Henry's promise that if she made it to England, he would take care of her. When María was finished, she felt exhausted and looked up questioningly at Isabel, hoping her aunt was as good at giving advice as her mother was.

'I wish I could tell you what to do, but only you can decide what's best for you and your baby. I'll be honest, though, if this Xulián is really who he says he is, I'm not sure if his family would accept a child out of wedlock and a miner's daughter as his wife.'

'I hadn't considered that,' she huffed.

'When was the last time you heard from Henry?'

'A long time ago,' María admitted. 'He left Madrid to fight in the Battle of Jarama in February 1937, then Brunete. I sent a letter before I left Madrid in case he wrote to me, but I haven't heard anything.' Isabel looked at her niece's bump and spoke softly.

'My advice would be to focus on your pregnancy. You're a month away, and all we can do is live from day to day. Everything can change in the blink of an eye.' María knew what her aunt meant – perhaps neither Xulián and Henry would come back to her. She closed her book and got up to leave the room. 'Thank you, Isabel.'

María wandered down the hallway mulling over Isabel's words. She couldn't go to England without knowing where the father of her child was, and would Henry still take care of her and a child that wasn't his after all this time? Antonio's study door was open as she passed it. She spotted a pile of books on the floor and walked over to see if there was one she could read. Isabel had been right about her current one being too difficult. She selected the second of the pile *Romancero Gitano* by Federico García Lorca when something on the desk caught her eye. She picked up the week-old newspaper. The front page showed a photo of a young man shot in Madrid. She let out a shrill scream. Isabel reached the room just as María's knees gave away, and she collapsed into her arms.

The housekeeper rang for a doctor, who ordered them to the hospital straight away as he wouldn't be able to get to them on time. At the hospital, María came around again to the pain of contractions and was taken to the maternity ward. She spent several hours in labour, her aunt not leaving her side until her baby boy was born. María was drained after the ordeal, and though she was tired, she wanted to hold him. But the midwife had immediately taken him with her for checks as he was premature, and the new mother fell into an exhausted sleep. When she woke, Isabel had just returned from the cafeteria with a coffee, eager to meet the newest addition to the family. María was anxious that she hadn't held her little one yet, wondering why the checks were taking so long. She had a knot in her stomach that something wasn't right. One of the doctors looked familiar, but she couldn't place him. Isabel tried to calm her down, explaining that she recognised the doctor from when she was working in this hospital, and that her baby was most certainly in an incubator as was standard procedure and she could ask to be taken to him. When she called for the doctor, a nurse approached her with a nervous smile, rubbing her hands together like she used to do herself when she had to recite in front of the whole class and was nervous. The knot in her stomach grew tighter, she felt the ward go quiet, and all she could hear was her heartbeat. The nurse told her there was bad news. As she did so, María noticed a doctor had appeared next to her. The nurse turned and almost ran away. The young man with a subdued expression wouldn't look her in the eyes when he spoke: 'Your baby didn't make it; there was nothing we could do. I'm sorry for your loss.' He immediately turned to leave. Isabel asked if María could hold him just once, but the doctor said no and didn't return.

Nineteen

London, England
2014

The sun set and bathed the living room in a warm glow when Luke finished reading María's letters. They sat in silence while processing the story they had just read and tried to comprehend what these young people had had to endure. Ava checked her phone for the time and saw several missed calls from Diego and a message asking her to call back. It felt strange seeing his name come up, not only because she thought she had made it clear she didn't want any contact with him but also because something inside her still stirred when she thought of him. Had she been too harsh when she had cut him off? After all, she blindly trusted what Lucy had said, and she had only heard it on the grapevine herself. Ava didn't know why Diego had lied and bluffed his way into a job he wasn't qualified for, but she remembered how he had taken her home after the party and let her sleep in his bed while he took the uncomfortable couch. Surely if he was such a bad person he wouldn't have taken pity on her that night. She recalled the discussion they'd had on their failed date and her reluctance to accept his point of view while she stuck with hers, and she had to admit that although she disagreed with him, he had accepted her explanation and their different opinions on the topic. Now she realised she was so quick to judge him because Luke had turned up and claimed her full attention. He was the one who had driven to the house when she was scared, but was it simply a coincidence that Luke had called? She was certain that, had she answered the phone to Diego, he would have done the same for her. After all, he had supported her at her mum's funeral without having ever met her and having only known Ava for a few days. It dawned on Ava that since Luke had turned up she had been engrossed in the mystery of her past, and things with Luke were moving very fast, but it also meant she had less capacity to grieve her mum's death. Luke was somewhat invested in her search for her father and solving the mystery of Henry and María and finding answers to why they turned up in her life along with Rosa. Not for the first time, she questioned his motives – was he genuinely interested in Ava or was the story he might unravel as an aspiring investigative journalist driving him?

Although she knew how lucky she was to have both Lucy and Luke supporting her during this difficult time, not for the first time she wondered how it had all happened so fast and how both had managed to move into a house that legally wasn't hers and dive into her family's secrets and possessions. Ava felt a pang in her chest when she realised that the musical box she had owned throughout her life held such cherished letters that may or may not be connected to her, but she wasn't the one who had found them or the first to read them. Both Lucy and Luke decided to translate them, and although she gave them permission, she wished she didn't have to share the information and could work through everything on her own. Luke even tried to pressure her into visiting Rosa in the hospital on the same day they found the key again, and Lucy was desperate to join her the next day. Ava knew then what the right thing to do was – she needed time and space on her own. She put the letters in a safe place only she knew of. Most of her life she had been on her own, and apart from her mum, she had never really needed anyone, and it suited her well. Ava suddenly felt claustrophobic and felt the urge to get some fresh air to clear her head and think things through. Getting up from the table she took her phone and told the others she was going for a walk. When Luke offered to accompany her, she declined, saying she needed time on her own. He looked surprised and hurt, but she didn't have the strength to care at that moment.

The streetlamps illuminated the quiet street as she ambled towards the village centre, feeling safer with houses and people around her. The shock of the break-in was still playing tricks with her mind whenever she was alone. She took her phone out of her pocket and pressed dial.

'Ava, I'm glad you called.'

'Hi Diego. It seemed important.'

'Yes, thank you. How are you doing?'

'Fine. You?' She couldn't prevent herself from sounding annoyed – why did she call him? What could possibly be so important?

'I'm doing okay. I visited you in your office today, but they said you don't work there anymore, and that's why I wanted to make sure you are okay.'

Ava thought she heard concern in his voice and remembered she hadn't told him she was fired, she had lied to him on their date, saying work was going okay but stopped talking to him when she found out he had been lying.

'Are you still there?'

'I am. Thank you for checking. Yes, I was fired.'

'I am very sorry to hear that. Where are you now?'

'Home,' she almost whispered. It was her home, but did it really feel like that without her mum?

'You could have called me, I know how it feels.'

'Tell me, Diego, why did you lie your way into the job?'
There was a long pause on the line. Ava heard him breathing and
imagined him sitting at the kitchen table in his modern
minimalistic flat that he most likely wouldn't be able to afford
much longer, the flat she should have never been at that night.
She felt her heart beat faster, her chest tightening, and she
struggled to breathe. The same thought she had had a million
times before flooded her memory. Had she not got so plastered
drinking all of Lucy's drinks and ended up at Diego's flat, she
would have met her mum as planned, and maybe this whole
nightmare would never have happened. And it was Diego who
told her to go away to the Cotswolds to forget her worries on her
girlie weekend trip as he had called it, but why? They had a good
time, and it brought Luke into her life, but the guilt that engulfed
her from having fun so soon after having laid her mum to rest still
overwhelmed her. She took some deep breaths to steady herself,
to prevent the anger at Lucy for abandoning her at the party and
at Diego for bringing her home from bubbling over.

'I lost my father a few months ago.' His words cut through
her thoughts, almost making her jump. She looked at her phone,
confused, forgetting she was still connected to him. The sound of
his voice brought her back to the present, where she was standing
in front of the pub. 'After his death, we realised his finances were
in an appalling state, and while I had a job in Spain, I knew to
make big money London would be the best place. I changed my
CV and set up some false email addresses as references, and it
worked, two companies offered me a job.'

'And no one noticed that you didn't have the skills?'

'I'm not stupid, I learnt all I needed to before my first day. I already understood financial markets, and YouTube helped fill the gaps.'

Ava was shocked at his easy admittance of a criminal act but couldn't help but also be slightly impressed that he managed to pull it off, especially with a wealth management company in London. One could say it served them right for not doing their due diligence before they employed him.

'What will happen now?'

'They won't pay me my last salary, but they aren't going to sue me.'

'Why?'

'It would ruin their reputation with clients and potential investors. They know someone didn't check my background properly, which would also reflect badly on them. It's easier for them to just let me go and never talk about it again.'

'They're just letting you off the hook, and you're a free man?'

'Yes.' Ava could hear the happiness in his voice and couldn't blame him. 'I'm sorry I lied to you.'

'Theoretically, you didn't lie to me. You never told me any of your background, you only said where you worked and what you did for a living, which wasn't a lie.' While she knew this to be true, the question remained as to whether he would have told her the truth had she asked. Through the pub window, Ava spotted Maggie sitting at a small table looking forlorn, a half-empty glass sat in front of her. 'Look, I have to go. Thank you for explaining, we'll catch up another time.' Ava hung up before he could ask when that would be, deliberately leaving it vague, not wanting to commit to anything at the moment.

The pub was almost empty despite a big sign promoting 50% off a beer and a burger combination on Mondays. Maggie was staring into space, oblivious to Ava approaching until she touched Maggie's shoulder, giving her a fright.

'Oh, I was gone there for a moment.' she said, justifying her reaction.

'Sorry, I didn't mean to startle you. Long day?'

'Yes, very. We're understaffed and it's taking its toll.'

'I suppose losing mum didn't make it any easier.'

Maggie took a sip of her drink and sighed, before setting it down again. 'No,' she answered after a few seconds, 'losing Rose is one of the worst things that has ever happened to the care home and the staff. You expect residents to pass away, but when the person who holds it all together, makes everyone smile with her presence and is genuinely loved by everyone is suddenly gone, it's like the soul has been sucked out of the place. Everyone can feel it, no one can understand why it had to be her.' Ava was moved by Maggie's words. She knew her mum was appreciated, but she hadn't realised just how important she seemed to be for the place and to its residents. A small tear rolled down her cheek when she thought of her mum's infectious smile that she would never see again. It felt good to talk to someone who cared so much about her.

'I'm sorry, love, that was insensitive of me,' Maggie said, putting her hand on Ava's.

'No, please don't be. It's lovely to hear how much she meant to everyone.' Not knowing how much she should confide in Maggie, Ava took a moment to gather her thoughts. She knew she could trust her, and maybe that's exactly what she needed, someone who knew her mum. 'May I ask you something?'

'Of course, sweetheart.'

'Did mum ever mention my father after he left or that she had discovered something from the past?' Ava tried to stay vague in case Maggie knew nothing, not wanting to burden her any more than was necessary.

'How much do you know?'

'I know he didn't die but left.' Maggie nodded.

'She didn't say much. Most people were told he had passed away so there were no questions she had to deal with.' This confirmed Ava's suspicion that Maggie knew the truth as well as Kate. 'But one thing she did mention was that he didn't leave without a reason. Your mum assumed something had happened, giving him no choice, but she never went into it. I think it was just her way of coping instead of having to admit that he didn't want to be with her anymore.' Maggie played with the stem of her glass, and Ava waited for her to continue.

'I remember she once came into work shaking, saying she felt someone was following her. That was about one week before Brian disappeared. The day after he didn't go home she found a note in the study saying: "I've left. Don't report me missing." It didn't make sense, but I had to swear not to tell anyone. I kept an eye on her, but she seemed okay and didn't mention being followed again. After a couple of weeks, she was back to her usual self, burying the experience deep inside her and focusing on you and her job.' Maggie shrugged as if that answered everything.

'How close was she to Rosa?'

'Not close as such, I think. She never mentioned her, but Rosa was also in good health, which would normally mean their visits would've only lasted a few minutes.'

'Do you know if Rosa has any family? I noticed no one had visited her in hospital.'

'Not that I know of. I didn't see her that often, and I'm sure no one ever visited her in the care home. Her husband passed away in the nineties, and they had no children. That's what I also told Luke.'

'Luke? When?'

'Oh, he came to the care home today. He said you asked him to pick up some of Rosa's personal things that she had asked for.' Maggie looked just as confused as Ava. Ava's surprised reaction betrayed to Maggie that Ava hadn't asked him to pick up Rosa's belongings and it dawned on them both that Luke had lied to gain access to Rosa's room. But why? Ava's mouth hung open. She was incredulous that Luke went behind her back and used Ava as an excuse to snoop around Rosa's personal things. She was just about to set the record straight when Maggie told her that she didn't let him through as it would've been against the rules, and she had said she couldn't let a man go through a woman's underwear. 'I offered to pack a bag to be brought to her, but he declined and walked out in a huff. It's probably not what you want to hear, but I don't trust that one. Be careful.' Ava was drawing the same conclusion.

'Rosa is in a coma,' Ava said in a quiet voice. 'She didn't ask me for anything. Luke was lying,' she continued, angrily and a bit too loudly. Maggie put her hand on Ava's shoulder and took a deep breath, indicating her to do the same. Ava took some deep breaths and remembered Rosa's note, *Always watch your back and trust no one.* What did Rosa know about Luke that she didn't, Ava wondered. 'Please pop by the next time you're off, there are some plants I'd like to give you,' she said with a smile, thinking of her mum's beautiful potted Azaleas that she knew Maggie would love in her own garden and Ava was most likely to kill soon anyway. Maggie smiled and gave Ava a comforting hug that only mothers knew how to do. By the time she reached the pub door, she had already decided that Luke needed to leave for deceiving her, but before that she needed to make sure she had all the letters.

Ava was still fuming when she got back to the house and walked through the door. She took some deep breaths before gathering the letters on the coffee table and counting them, knowing that one was still in her bedroom. She hid them behind some of the books in the bookcase and went to look for her friends. She found them in the garden sitting at the table. Luke immediately closed his laptop, hiding what he had been doing. Ava couldn't see clearly but was sure she had glimpsed an open Word document and knew he was writing his article. Her mind went into overdrive again. Why would he close the laptop? She knew he was investigating the story unless he was writing something he didn't want her to know about. Lucy was sitting with her back to the door and seemingly hadn't heard Ava return. She jumped when Ava put her hand on her shoulder. Lucy spun around in her chair, putting her phone into her back pocket, and blushed as if she was caught red-handed.

What were these two hiding? Ava checked her phone for the time; it was 8.10 in the evening, and she wondered if it was too late to ask them both to leave. Not Luke, she concluded, but Lucy? After all, she hadn't lied to her, just acted weird, and she was pregnant and her best friend – it would be wrong to kick her out, wouldn't it? She was still debating this when Luke stood up and kissed her cheek. 'Feel better? You were gone for quite some time.' Ava looked up at him, his hand still on her arm, and for the first time saw him through different eyes. He was still good-looking, there was no denying that, but now she noticed the bags under his eyes and the stubble on his face and wondered why he looked so tired when they hadn't had a busy schedule for the last few days. She looked from Luke to Lucy, giving her one last chance to give her a reason not to kick her out, but Lucy was miles away with her own thoughts and didn't register Ava's imploring eyes.

That was it, she'd had enough. 'I want you both to leave, I need space and time to process the last few days.' They stared at her, waiting for more, but Ava was spent, she had nothing left to say or give. Luke turned to Lucy, raised his eyebrows as if to say 'What was that all about?' before turning back to Ava.

'Oh, okay. I'm sorry, I didn't realise I was treading on your feet.' He took a step back, looking hurt and, at the same time, annoyed, which he had no right to after lying. The last thing she wanted, though, was to confront him. At the moment, she didn't know who she could trust; for all she knew, he could be dangerous. Ava folded her arms in front of her and didn't say anything while Luke mumbled that he'd better go and get his stuff. Ava followed him through the house; she'd read enough online to know some people didn't handle rejection well, and their behaviour could turn from caring and nice to angry and destructive. Luke's eyes fell on the coffee table. He noticed the letters were missing. For a split second, Ava could sense he was about to turn towards her, his muscles tensing. Ava took a step back out of reach in case he swung around at her. He continued walking up the stairs, and Ava let out the breath she was holding. Why was she scared of him? She was being irrational again, almost paranoid, and wondered where her sudden trust issues came from.

'Are you okay? You seem off.' Lucy stood behind her.

Ava at least knew she could trust Lucy despite her odd behaviour, which could be down to her hormones. 'I'm fine, just realised I haven't had much time to be here and think about mum. And I want to do that now.' She didn't mention the niggling feeling she had that something was wrong.

'I understand. I need to return to work tomorrow anyway, so I should probably get going.' In a quiet whisper she added, 'Glad that he won't be here though – not sure what he's up to, but be careful,' before heading upstairs. This was the second time Ava was warned to be careful. Was she missing something? She had thought Lucy liked him. Did he say anything to her while she was out? The sooner she understood what had happened, the sooner she could move on with her life. She let her eyes wander around the living room, where all the boxes were still stacked to one side.

Luke returned with his holdall and gave Ava another peck on the cheek, telling her to get in touch if she needed him, and he hoped she could mourn her mother properly. Lucy followed shortly afterwards and gave Ava a hug on the way out. 'Message when you get home,' Ava told her out of habit. Lucy smiled and told her to take care. Once the car had left the driveway, Ava closed the front door and listened to the silence that descended on the house. She walked over to the bookcase where she had hidden the letters. She looked at a photo of her mum and herself, picked it up and took it over to the armchair. Staring at her mum's face for a long time, she finally let the previously-unshed tears come.

It was almost ten o'clock by the time Ava put the picture frame back in its place and went to pour herself a glass of water. Walking back to the living room, she looked at the boxes in the corner. She decided to put them back into the loft the next day and went upstairs. She stopped when she walked past the study, wondering if any documents had her father's address on them. Not that she expected to find anything, but after everything she had already found out, she wouldn't be surprised if her mum had been in touch with her father. She went through every folder that contained bills from twenty years ago all the way through to the latest offer of having the walls repainted. But there was nothing with her father's name on it after he had left. As Ava sat there wondering what she hoped she'd find, her gaze fell on a quote from the decorator from a few months back. Each room in the house was listed, together with details of the square footage of each of the walls and how many windows each room had. One room had an additional note. The study mentioned a wall safe. Ava looked at the walls around her but didn't see a safe. She moved the desk away from the wall, but nothing was behind it. Turning on the torch on her phone, she tried to see behind the bookcases, where she believed she only saw the wall. She established that she would have to empty the bookcase to move it and check properly, so instead, she turned around and grabbed the edges of the smaller cupboard with her mum's sewing accessories and moved it away from the wall. But alas that wall was empty. She sat down again and swirled in her chair, hoping it might just jump out at her, when her eyes caught sight of a drawing she made as a girl. She removed the frame from the wall and stared straight at a safe with a combination lock. Ava ran her fingers along the numbers and pulled at the handle. She just stared at it for a moment, perplexed and unsure what to do. Would a locksmith be able to gain access to it, or was that against the law? If in doubt, Google it, she said to herself. And there she had it, yes they could, which meant she could also try and open it herself. Looking for a brand name on the safe, she again resorted to the internet, checking how many attempts she may have to try and unlock it. Unable to locate a brand name, her internet search didn't help, offering answers varying from only one attempt to any other number of attempts. She grabbed a pen and paper and thought of important dates in her family but realised she didn't know her father's date of birth or their wedding date. She hoped it might be similar to a hotel safe with four numbers and a hash. So Ava took a breath and started with her mum's date of birth, typing in 0406#. A red light lit up to confirm her attempt had been unsuccessful. Next, she tried her own date of birth, 1610#. but the red light lit up again. Her eyes scanned the safe, willing it to open. Chances were, she surmised, the most important documents, like her parent's marriage certificate, would be in that very place she couldn't get to, and she had already run out of dates. Unless... Ava ran downstairs to search the boxes. She grabbed Tim's wristband which contained his date of birth, and returned to the safe. 3004#. She heard the sound of the locking mechanism, and the safe sprung open. Ava held her breath, pausing for a moment before reaching inside to see what secrets it held. Her fingers touched paper. The manila folder! Sitting back down, she put it on the desk and stared at it. This was it, the answer to all her questions. Why her father left, and where he was now. She felt a flood of relief that she was on her own.

On top of the folder, she noticed a beige envelope addressed to Rose. It was sealed and clearly had never been opened. Her heart sank as she realised that her mum never read a letter her father had left for her. Opening it felt wrong, but she knew no one would tell her off, so she carefully pulled out the piece of paper. Its date told her it had been left the year he disappeared, 1992.

Dearest Rose,

Writing this letter is the hardest thing I have ever had to do. Please know that I didn't go because I don't love you and Ava, I left because I do, but I am scared you're not safe around me anymore.
You reading this letter means you found the safe I had put in a few months ago. Sorry for not telling you but I knew you would find it.

Well, she didn't, Ava growled, close to tears. He did love them. She read on.

Remember the story my dad used to work on, the one that took over his life and was why he had to leave London and move to the countryside? I fell into the same trap and thought I could continue what he had started. I was under the impression that I could find the missing pieces, publish the truth of what had happened, and continue with my life. But I was wrong.
Darling, the story my dad and I were investigating concerns your family. Everything you need to know is in the folder. A word of caution, though, don't share this with anyone.
My dad left London because he received death threats against him and mum, and now I had to leave because I

received death threats against you and Ava. They've been following me, and they've been to Ava's school. I'm sure they also followed you. I could never forgive myself if something happened to the two of you, and it is with a heavy heart that I must entertain the possibility that our little Timmy was no accident. The day the truth comes out, I will return. It won't be long until we're reunited. Until then, I will hide in our special place.
I love you and always will. I need you to know that.

Forever yours,
Brian

Twenty

Ava's world began to spin, swirling around her in a dizzying haze. The weight of the newfound information bore down upon her, threatening to crush her. It was not only the shocking revelations that shook her to the core but also the realisation that the story woven within those pages was entwined with her mum's family and, consequently, her own. But her true anguish stemmed from a different source altogether. The letter, once unfolded, revealed a truth that Ava's mum had never beheld. Her thoughts turned to her dearly departed mum, who had harboured suspicions but never held the concrete proof she so desperately craved. The knowledge that her mum had departed this world without ever tasting the bittersweetness of enlightenment struck Ava to the very core of her being. How was it just or righteous that her father had departed, leaving her mum behind, ignorant of the reasons and his enduring love for them both? For over two decades, her mum had been clueless.

Ava wanted to talk to someone, but whom? Luke had lied to her, Lucy was too pushy, and she had kicked them both out a little earlier. It was difficult to trust Diego after what he had done. That just left her mum's friends, Kate, Maggie and Patty, but she felt it was too late to call one of them, and they might be just as devastated knowing how much their friend suffered for no reason. A thought occurred to Ava – was her father still at their special place like he said he would be? Ava doubted it – after all, it had been twenty years and surely no one would wait that long – but if she could find out where this place was, it might lead her to him. Without a second thought, she wrote down all the places she could remember her mum mentioning. After a few minutes, she looked at her list and crossed out the places that only meant something to her and her mum. Then again, maybe her mum took her there because she had been to the place with her father? Ava decided to keep them and added a few more for which she needed more information, like the place they got married. She was sure that this was something Kate or Maggie could help her with, so she parked it for the moment to go downstairs to the boxes, somewhere there would be photographs, postcards, receipts from holidays, anything that could help her. Determined to find answers to the mystery, Ava went through box after box, discarding everything she didn't need to her left while anything potentially useful was put in a pile to her right. She knew herself too well – if she started looking at all the things her mum had accumulated over the years, she would never finish. She felt like she was now racing against time, and the sooner Ava could end all this, the sooner she could get back to her life – what was left of it.

Luke might be out of the picture for now, maybe even forever, but with the manila folder, Ava was convinced this was one problem she ought to be able to solve. After emptying the last box, she returned everything that now sat on her left back into the boxes from which they had come. She ran upstairs to grab the manila folder to add to the pile on her right when her eyes fell on the trapdoor in the office's ceiling. She stalled. The burglar didn't take anything valuable but was looking for something specific and even went into the loft to search for it. With a sinking heart, Ava knew what he was looking for, and now that she had it, he might come back. At that moment, she knew it was wise to send the others away; right now, she couldn't trust anyone, and as long as that was the case, she needed to keep everything secret. Her father wrote in his letter not to share it with anyone, and that's precisely what Ava told herself she would do.

Back downstairs, Ava started to go through the pile of potentially useful items and found several photos in an album of her parents in various locations. In most of them, they looked happy and in love – be it on a beach, in someone's house, in the car, in the countryside – but none of them had a location written on the back, only the year the photo was printed. Taking a picture of each one and putting a Post-it note on the page, she kept going until she found a photo of her parents and a newborn baby with black hair. In an instant, Ava knew the baby wasn't her; she was often told she was born with blonde hair, and no one could understand how she became a redhead at the age of three. Inspecting the photo closely, she saw a tiny armband on the baby's wrist. She grabbed one of the boxes that contained the items she had just discarded for being of no use. She knew she had held an armband in her hand a few moments earlier. Pulling it out, she turned it around to read 'Tim Wilkinson, DOB: 30.04.1982, St. Mary's Hospital, London'. The wooden train with the same name and date and all the blue baby clothes they had found sprang to mind. The world stood still as it dawned on her – she had a brother. What had happened to him? Having just discovered that she wasn't her parents' first child, Ava drew a deep breath and sat back. For a moment, she contemplated burning everything, packing her bags and never returning. A month ago, she had lost her mum, only to then learn her father was still alive. Now she had discovered that she also had an older brother. Looking at the armband in her hand, she noticed it was shaking. All these secrets she was uncovering were hard to grasp. Before continuing with the photos, she decided she needed to steady her hands so she poured herself a large gin and tonic. As she did so, she noticed it was already past midnight. Ava grabbed her drink and the manila folder, locked all the doors and windows, and went to her room.

'Ava, Ava, are you here, darling?' There was a knock on the bedroom door as Ava slowly woke up from a terrible night's sleep. Her head was hurting, her mouth was as dry as sandpaper, and her teeth felt hairy. It took her a moment to fully wake up and open her eyes to Kate standing in the doorway.

'So you *are* here. Good, I was worried for a moment.'

'What time is it?' Ava mumbled while wondering how people could be so chirpy early in the morning.

'It's eleven o'clock. The security guy is here to install the cameras. He came to mine when you didn't answer the door, so I let him get started on my place. I hope you don't mind,' Kate said.

'Shit, I forgot.'

'Don't worry, love. Now why don't I go downstairs and make you a nice cup of tea while you get dressed?' Without waiting for a reply, Kate turned around to go and put the kettle on. This was Ava's cue to shower and get out of yesterday's clothes. She must have fallen asleep with the contents of the folder strewn across the bed, as she had with the letters previously. Reading the copies of the two witness statements while she was already half asleep wasn't the best idea and this morning she couldn't remember much of the contents. She put the two statements on her bedside table and rearranged the other papers in the folder, then returned the folder to desk in the study.

When Ava arrived downstairs, Kate handed her a cup of tea and raised her eyebrows. 'Feeling better?'

'Thank you, yes. I have never slept until eleven in my life.'

'You probably needed it. Are Luke and Lucy not here?'

'No, I kicked them out yesterday,' Ava mumbled into her tea, not really wanting to get into it, while she watched Kate looking at the contents of the boxes strewn across the living room. She knew Kate was too polite to ask, but Ava needed her on her side, so she sat on the couch and told her not only why she got rid of her two friends but also why so many photos and memories were lying around. Kate didn't say much, just nodded and 'uhmed' and 'ahed'.

'Kate,' Ava started, unsure how to ask but feeling this was as good as any moment, 'what happened to Tim?'

There was a long silence, Kate gathered her thoughts on how best to tell Ava about her deceased brother. Her eyes were raw with pain; it took all of Kate's strength to start talking about it.

'It was a beautiful summer's day. Your father had already gone to work. Your mother was getting him ready for nursery. Rose opened the door to leave but, as she did so, noticed she had left a letter she was meant to post in the kitchen, so she quickly went to get it. Tim made use of the open door and ran out into the front garden, where he said good morning to the flowers and to me. He was such a cute boy with his black hair and olive skin. I expected your mother to follow, so I returned to my roses when I suddenly heard tyres screeching.' Kate took a deep breath and wiped a tear from the corner of her eye. 'This is the first time I have spoken about it.' She sipped her tea. 'I ran towards Tim, but I was too late. The impact against his tiny head killed him instantly. Rose never forgave herself. Nor have I forgiven myself.'

'It was an accident, there was nothing you could've done.' Ava was now at Kate's side with her arm around her shoulders, hugging her tightly. The pair sat there in silence for a long time, both holding on to each other.

'You will now understand why your mother was so protective of you.' A lot of Ava's childhood started to make sense, especially when roads were involved, and little Ava decided it was a good idea to let go of her mum's hand the moment they got to the crossing so she could skip across the road. She would never forget how her mum had pulled her back and carried her across the street, making her promise never to skip ahead and let go of her hand.

'Thank you for telling me, I didn't realise you were there too, I should've asked someone else.' Ava felt guilty for bringing it up. But she was also glad that she knew now this boy was her older brother, having until yesterday not even known he existed.

'You said you were looking for special places that meant a lot to your parents?' Changing the subject, Kate brought Ava back to the present. She hadn't thought about the reason why she wanted to know, but either Kate didn't care or she knew it had something to do with her father and her previous questions that led her to start listing places she knew of.

'Whenever they were in London, they'd go to the Rivoli Bar at the Ritz, then there was the Red Lion they'd go to once a month on a Sunday for a roast. There's also a lighthouse down in Swanage, where your parents often went on holiday. You'll also find a few photos of the beaches around Swanage. They used to rent a caravan and absolutely loved it. They scattered Tim's ashes around there. And the hotel where they had their wedding reception, they went back every year for their anniversary.'

'Do you remember what the hotel was called?'

'I'll think of it and let you know. It just slipped my mind, somewhere around Guildford, though.'

'Don't worry.' It was very doubtful her father was hiding in a hotel in Guildford and definitely not at the Ritz. She knew the Red Lion and had been there several times, but that didn't seem logical either. The caravan in Swanage sounded more plausible and worth investigating.

They talked a little longer before the man from the security company announced he had finished with the CCTV installation and asked if he could walk them through how it worked. After all the drama and the sad story about her brother, Ava felt relief wash over her when she saw every angle of the house was now being monitored by cameras and all doors were alarm secured. Kate returned to her house and promised she'd be back tomorrow with some photos of the caravan from when she and her husband joined the Wilkinsons for a weekend break. Ava picked up from where she had left off last night and now specifically looked for photos with the caravan or a lighthouse. For every photo she came across with Tim, she looked closely to see any resemblance, but couldn't. Nevertheless, she photographed each one to keep them safe on her phone.

Many hours later, after having gone through all the boxes, she started putting the boxes she didn't need back into the loft and retrieved the manila folder from the study. Checking her phone for any missed calls or messages, she noticed quite a few people had tried to get in touch with her. Scrolling through them, she started with Lucy asking how she was. A similar question came from Luke, asking how she was coping. Ava moved on to the next message, having answered both with a simple 'I'm fine.'

A few were from Kate, sent in the morning reminding her about the security installation, which clearly hadn't helped. There were also a few missed calls from her. Diego had also been in touch a few hours ago, asking if she was free this evening as he was in the area for business. She wasn't sure why he would be in the area but decided she could do with a break from her wild goose chase and invited him over. The moment she pressed send she kicked herself – why did she invite him to the house? They should have met in a public place. But it was too late now, and at least the cameras were now installed.

Diego arrived later that evening, looking very dapper in his navy suit and white shirt. Ava was reminded why she had liked the look of him when they first met. He had had his hair cut and got rid of his long locks, which was a shame in Ava's eyes as his long hair had given him a mysterious look. She had liked how his fringe fell into his face covering his eyes, and during their dinner, whenever he looked up from his plate, he gave his head a little shake to remove hair from his eyes. Diego put his rucksack by the door and got a bottle of wine out from it. Ava noticed there was nothing else in the rucksack and wondered why he didn't have a laptop if he was in the area for business. They sat on the couch. Ava was glad that she had put away all the boxes either in the loft or the study; the last thing she needed now was Diego getting interested in the story again and demanding to see the article and photo. Pouring the wine into the glasses, she racked her brain for topics she could talk to him about that would avoid her needing to talk about what she had been through over the last week.

'So, how have you been?' she started.

'Good. It's nice to have a lot of time to enjoy London in summer,' he replied, grinning.

'Have you found a new job yet?'

'No, that's why I was in the area, for an interview.' That explained why he didn't have a laptop but was wearing a suit.

'Oh, how did that go?'

'I think it went well. It's a small company, very different to my old job.' Taking a sip of her wine, she enjoyed how close he was to her and the cologne he was wearing, and immediately thought she needed to be careful not to get too tipsy. The worst that could happen was her letting her hair down and babbling on about the past or getting too close to Diego. She had only just started to talk to him again and was not going to throw caution to the wind. After all, he had lied and fooled many people. But he did look handsome, she thought, despite her having felt disgusted at him just a few days ago. Her mind was playing tricks again, she noticed.

'Have you thought about going back to Spain seeing as what you set out to do didn't work?'

'I'm not sure. Maybe I will go home if I can't find a job.'

'How are you coping with the loss of your father?' It was common ground between them, and maybe he even had some advice on how to deal with her own grief. 'I mean, I don't think this will be a fast process, but I hope you can tell me that it does get easier over time?'

'Yes and no. Yes, it gets easier because you carry on with your life, but no, because when you start to feel better you become scared you will forget. And then you feel guilty when you start being happy again. You tell yourself you must be sad all the time.'

'I understand. Were you close with your father?'

Diego thought about this for a while as he took a sip of his wine and refilled Ava's glass before repositioning himself on the sofa, moving one leg underneath him and facing her, who also twisted slightly to face him.

'Yes, we were very close. He taught me everything I know. But it was my grandfather who was the head of the family, and even my father obeyed him. If anyone needed advice, they would ask my grandfather first. We are a very close family and stick together.' Ava realised Diego was very fond of his family the way he spoke, and it seemed it was safe ground to talk to him about it and get to know him better. She just hoped he wouldn't ask her too many questions about her own relatives.

'Do you have any siblings?' she asked, immediately thinking of Tim with his toothy grin.

'So many!' He threw up his hands as if to indicate that he couldn't even remember them all. A nice problem to have, Ava thought. 'I have three older brothers and a younger sister. We are a huge family. Family is vital.'

His words felt like a stab in the heart as if Ava didn't know how important family was, especially when having lost her own. Ava knew this was how it would be for the foreseeable future when people talked about their families, though; Ava would have to sit and listen to them complaining without realising that Ava would give anything to be able to complain about her family.

'I am the only one who left the family home. Everyone else is still there, living close by, meeting several times a week, all successful in their own right.' Diego seemed contemplative, as if he felt he didn't belong in that family. His goal to earn money must have given him a purpose and the hope he was also doing his part for the family, she thought. Ava wondered if they knew what he had done and had now been found out. She doubted it; if he had lied to everyone else, he had probably also lied to his siblings.

'I guess your mother is happy to have everyone so close?'

'Yes, it hit her very hard when my father took his own life. The family bond strengthened, and everyone looked out for each other.'

'She must be very proud.'

In total seriousness, he responded, 'I think she's proud of the others but not of me.'

'I'm sure that's not true. Sometimes we just don't realise it.' She tried to soothe him and put her hand on his arm, stroking it up and down, feeling the wine going to her head. She hadn't eaten a lot during the day, and the two glasses had already started to make her feel dizzy. Diego got up and said he was going to the bathroom and would return momentarily. Ava smiled and thought she should probably do the same, checking her reflection in the mirror at the same time, just in case he were to get closer when he returned. As Diego headed to the family bathroom upstairs, Ava went to the downstairs toilet and locked the door behind her. She looked at her red hair and thought to herself that she desperately needed a cut and a hair mask before deciding she looked okay apart from her mascara that needed a touch-up. Looking around, she noticed that all her makeup was in the bathroom upstairs. But she couldn't go there because that was the one Diego used, which suddenly struck her as odd – how did he know where to go? She brushed the thought aside and decided her mind could play tricks on her another day, and for now she would enjoy the evening and company. She ran her fingers through her hair and rinsed her red wine-stained mouth with water. After she had finished, she returned to the living room, where Diego was already sitting on the couch again. He handed Ava her glass.

'Now, where were we?' Ava moved her hand back to where it was beforehand and ran her finger along his arm, down to his hand, and up towards his neck. She moved closer, listening to his heavy breathing, while her hand moved further down towards his chest and her lips closer to his lips.

'What are you doing?' Diego jumped back, put his glass on the coffee table and got up while Ava sat in shock, unsure of what had just happened. Did she imagine his eyes undressing her and his tongue licking his lips with anticipation?

'What?' She looked at him perplexed. Diego walked away from the couch to his bag, throwing it over his shoulder and heading for the front door, stopping with his hand on the handle.

'I thought you just wanted to talk.' Slamming the door behind him, he left before Ava could utter another word, still too puzzled to react. It was ten o'clock by the time Ava managed to shake herself out of her trance-like state. As if on autopilot, she moved to the kitchen with her glass still in her hand, noticing it was empty. She was still trying to make sense of Diego's behaviour and what she had done to make him run away from her. Wasn't he the one who had asked to visit to make amends? And wasn't he the one who brought the wine and sat on the couch so he could look at her directly? It didn't make any sense and baffled Ava. She picked up her phone to call him and ask him straight up. Scrolling through her contacts, she stopped herself, her gaze falling on the empty glass in her hand. She concluded that it was better to sleep it off before she did something that she might regret the next day. Abandoning her plan for food, she went to the bedroom. As she did so, her phone pinged. Hoping it was Diego apologising for his behaviour, she opened the message.

Hey Ava, how are you? I hope you know you can call me if you need someone to talk to, and I will drive straight back. I'm unsure what happened, but I would love to repeat the moment we shared in the shower. Hope you're feeling better and to see you very soon! x

Ava reread the message incredulously: Luke hoped she was feeling better – what did he think she had, the flu? The way he worded it made Ava's blood boil even more after what had just happened with Diego. For most of her adult life she had stayed away from troublesome men, having learnt from her mum that a woman could live happily without one. Especially after her ex-boyfriend Adam, she had closed her heart, but the moment she opened it again, not only did two men arrive at the same time, but she learnt that both couldn't be trusted, which simply proved her point. Lucy was right when she had questioned whether Ava was so desperate for love, she would throw caution to the wind the second a handsome man turned up. Snuggled up in her pyjamas in bed, she decided she needed to distract herself from mulling over everything. She grabbed the two witness statements from her bedside table. The first one was from one of the workers from the gas network who stated: 'I connected their gas pipe to the mains yesterday, and my colleague checked everything. We smelled no gas when we left, so I know there was no leak.'

The second witness claimed she had seen a man in an overcoat and a hat run away from the scene after the explosion. She wondered how her grandfather had got hold of both, but they seemed to imply that the gas pipe was fiddled with after it was connected. Still, surely there would be more information on the police investigation if they thought it was murder rather than an accident. Getting out of bed, Ava went to the study to check if there was anything in the folder that she had missed the first time. It was gone. Diego! She instantly knew why he used the upstairs bathroom and suddenly left. Whilst she had been mulling over what she had done wrong to have caused his abrupt departure, he had found what he had wanted, and it dawned on her that it must have been Diego who broke into the house. He was the one who suggested she go to the Cotswolds with Lucy so as to make sure she wasn't in the house. He also knew where she lived and had probably planned this since the wake when Ava wouldn't have noticed him wandering around the house! Ava felt sick and rushed to the bathroom. Hanging over the toilet bowl, she berated herself for her stupidity leaving the folder on the desk instead of putting it back in the safe. He proved she couldn't trust him, yet she let him back in when he charmed her and got her tipsy so he could steal from her. But how did he know she had found the folder? No one knew apart from Kate. *Always watch your back and trust no one*, she remembered. Both Luke and Lucy acted very suspiciously around her, but Lucy was the one who obviously knew Diego and introduced them to each other. Was Lucy an accomplice? Ava wasn't sure what to think anymore when a knock on the front door made her jump out of her skin. Peeking through the spyhole, she saw two police officers. Ava thought for a moment – the officers would see her in her pyjamas if she opened the door, or she could go back to bed and pretend no one was home. Another knock followed. 'We know you're in there. Open up!' Ava took a deep breath, dishevelled her hair, and opened the door, closing her eyes slightly as if she had just been woken up.

'Hello?' she replied sleepily.

'Good evening, Miss. Is this your house?' asked the taller officer.

'Yes – well, my parents'. Why?'

'We've been informed that there's a squatter living in the house. Can we see your identification?' Ava looked at them, shocked; who called the police on her and said she was a squatter? But she didn't even need to think who – of course, it was Diego.

'I can assure you I am not a squatter.' She grabbed her wallet from her handbag on the floor and showed them her driver's licence. 'I can also show you the deeds to the house.'

'Are the deeds in your name?'

'No, in my parents' name.'

'And is one of them at home?' Ava felt like a teenager being asked for an adult to be present.

'No, my mum passed away a month ago.'

'My condolences, and where's your father?' Now that was a question she would have loved to be able to answer herself, and she was very tempted to ask them if they knew. But thought better of it and lied through her teeth, 'He's currently on a business trip. That's why I'm here, to look after the house while he's gone.'

'Thank you, we'll confirm that.' Good luck, she thought, and maybe it was the wine, but she couldn't resist asking them, 'Who told you I was a squatter?'

'That is something we can't reveal. If we can't confirm you have the right to be here, you'll be removed for trespassing. Good

night Miss.' The officers turned around and left, leaving Ava
again stunned at what had just happened. In all her years in this
world, she hadn't encountered the police. But since her mum had
passed away, various things had happened to her, and she had
already had the police around twice since she had moved in. She
started to believe the house was bad luck for her family and
everyone who lived in it was doomed to leave eventually. In her
case, someone wanted her to be removed forcefully. And when
the police did their checks, they may return to get rid of her.
Panic set in when she realised she might lose her home, having
just lost the folder with her father's last letter. She couldn't reread
it and see if she could find clues to his whereabouts or analyse his
writing, or anything. She had lost her last link to her family's past
because she fell for a thug who wanted her destroyed while her
best friend passed on information to him. She desperately wanted
to speak to Luke, but he was somebody else she had trusted
before he betrayed her. Ava was in bits and sank to the floor.
There must be something she could do before she lost even more,
the question was what.

Twenty-One

The sun was shining through the window of the train carriage. The teenager opposite was playing his music at such a high volume that, despite both of them wearing headphones, Ava could hear every word. Yawning from the lack of sleep, she closed her eyes again, hoping she might get a few hours before she reached her destination. After the police had arrived last night and told her she might be considered a trespasser, and the folder had been stolen, she decided there was only one thing for her to do. She had packed a bag in a rush, thrown on some clothes and got a taxi to the train station – only to discover when she got there that there were no more trains to her intended destination that night. Deliberating whether she should spend the night at the station or return early in the morning, she decided instead to take the next train to London, as trains to there were still running, and disappear amongst the masses until she could catch the first train further south towards the coast.

'Next stop Wareham.' Ava opened her eyes, having finally managed to doze off, and was greeted by a beautiful blue sky and the sea to her left. According to her internet search, there were several campsites in and around the town, so Ava would have to go to all of them and ask around. She caught the bus to the first caravan park, hoping luck was finally on her side.

The campsite was in the middle of nowhere, surrounded by lush green fields and accessible only via a dirt track. It didn't look like much, and without having to go into the site and find a reception, Ava could see there were no static caravans so she turned around. She followed the map for twenty minutes until she came across a road heading back into Swanage. Feeling deflated that she had taken a wrong turn somewhere, she decided to go back into town and get some breakfast before heading for another campsite. As Ava walked along country lanes, she took a lungful of fresh salty sea air and listened to the birds singing in the trees. Children screaming and shouting broke the sound of birdsong, and she knew she was close to her next stop. A young teenager sat in a booth at the entrance to the campsite, frantically typing something into her phone. Ava approached and cleared her throat.

'Yeah?'

'Hi, I am looking for my father's caravan and forgot the number where it's stationed.'

'What's his name?'

'Brian Wilkinson.' The girl swung her chair to the right and searched her computer.

'You sure he's here?'

'I thought this was the campsite he told me. Can't you find him?'

'No.'

'He might've booked it under his girlfriend's name, but I don't know her surname. I'll just look to see if I can find them.' Without waiting for a response in case the girl stopped her, Ava headed towards the caravans she could see in the distance. Luckily the sun was shining, which meant most residents were sitting in foldable chairs in front of their homes. The thought occurred to her that what she just lied about could, in fact, be true, and she might find her father sitting there with a girlfriend and kids. Ava stopped in her tracks but noticing people watching her, she took a deep breath and pretended she knew where she was going.

'Are you looking for someone, love?' An elderly lady in a blue swimsuit and a pink hat looked up from her crossword, inspecting Ava.

'Yes, my father told me to join him today. It seems he has forgotten.' She turned around and started walking back to the entrance.

'What's his name?' Turning around again, Ava answered. 'Never heard that name. Do you know a Brian?' The lady turned to her husband, who was lying next to her on a sun lounger with a hat and swimming trunks, turning an unhealthy shade of red.

'Nah, not here, but try the campsite down the road; I think there's a Brian there,' he said without opening his eyes to see who he was talking to.

Ava thanked them, hope rising that she might be close, and made her way back towards the road and onto the next campsite. There, she was met by curious campers, however none of them knew her father. And Brian, it turns out, was a golden retriever.

After three hours of walking around Swanage and its surrounding countryside, Ava had been to every campsite she could find and even went to a holiday park. She wasn't sure what to do next, knowing going home wasn't an option in case the police turned up again. Looking out over the hills, she saw a footpath leading to the sea and decided to head there. While on route, her phone vibrated in her pocket.

'Hello?' she virtually shouted into the receiver in consequence of the wind which had picked up the closer she got to the sea.

'Hello Ava, it's Maggie.'

'Oh, hello. How are you?'

'All good here, love. Just wanted to tell you that the hospital has updated us about Rosa Humphries-García.' Ava's heart sank, fearing the worst. 'She has awoken from her coma.' After everything she had gone through, tears started to fall from Ava's eyes at the news. She didn't know why she felt so emotional, but she knew she had been given another chance to discover the truth of Rosa's identity and why she ended up with María's letters.

'That's great news,' she managed to croak. 'Can I visit?'

'Yes, you can. She's responsive, and so far no major damage has been done. They'll keep her in for another few days to make sure, but then she can return to the care home. Strictly speaking, I probably shouldn't tell you, but it seemed important.'

'Thank you so much, Maggie. I really appreciate it. I'll be there as soon as I can.' Ava hung up and wanted to jump with joy – finally some good news. This gave her a reason to return home, but before she did so, she decided she wanted to see the sea properly. Walking further along a road that, for all Ava knew, might have been someone's private property, down a hill and up on the other side, the water came into view in the distance. To the left, Ava noticed a white building, which seemed almost lost sat atop the cliff. Speeding up to see more closely what the building was, Ava recalled a photo she had seen in the album at home; it was the lighthouse and a cottage. Now running towards the front door, she climbed over the wall surrounding the lighthouse and garden and knocked ferociously as suddenly she was sure this was where her father was. There was no answer. She knocked again. Still no answer. After another few knocks, her heart began to sink as she realised that no one was inside the building. The curtains blocked her from seeing inside to establish whether or not it was even an inhabited cottage, but she assumed somebody must live there if someone had made an effort to hang up the curtains. Once again, it felt like the whole world was against her as she searched to find answers. She jumped back over the wall and ambled towards the sea. Watching the waves crash against the cliffs some thirty feet beneath her, Ava closed her eyes and wondered what would happen if she took one more step forward. Who would care if she were gone? She burnt bridges with Lucy and Luke, her father was nowhere to be found, and no one was left apart from a few of her mum's friends. Hearing footsteps behind her, she retreated from the edge and turned around to see a couple walking past her. She was starting to get paranoid about everyone around her after what had happened with Diego and what he had done to her. Getting her phone out, she checked the fastest route to get back to Swanage and back home. She felt the urge to see Rosa and get some answers from her, and somewhere in her gut, she felt there was not much time left.

After an exhausting 4-hour journey back home, Ava was shown into Rosa's room. Rosa was sitting propped up in her bed, a food tray in front of her. 'You have a visitor,' the nurse announced. 'Maybe you can get her to eat something,' the nurse said and left the room. Unsure of what to do, Ava hovered at the bottom of the bed, looking around the room, noticing again there were no flowers and cards for the old lady.

'Come, sit down.' Rosa's voice was soft and heavily accented. She pointed to a chair beside the bed and smiled at Ava.

'I am so happy you came to visit me. It is lonely here.'

'I heard you are being discharged in a few days.' Rosa nodded. 'You don't have a family to visit?'

'You are family, and you're here now.'

'How am I family? I don't know you.'

'I was there in the background, looking out for your mother and you.'

'But why?'

Ava was on the edge of her seat; whoever this woman was and how she was linked to Ava brought her closer to the truth and maybe her father.

Rosa closed her eyes and said, 'When I was young, I made a terrible mistake. I disgraced my family. They sent me away to Madrid. Then war broke out, and everything changed. I fled with only a handful of letters.'

'The letters I found in the musical box?'

'Yes.' Rosa wiped a tear out of the corner of her eye, and Ava took her hand.

'Rosa, why was the box in our loft?'

'Because it was the only thing I passed on when I ran away.'

Ava felt she knew the answer before asking the question, but she had to hear it. 'Why?'

'*Mi niña*, your mother was adopted by who you believe were your grandparents, the Browns. You see, the explosion changed everything.' Ava felt everything falling into place – her mum was adopted and the reason the letters she found in the musical box were in the house was because they were connected to her. Which implied her mum must have received the musical box directly from her birth mother. It also explained her father's obsession with the newspaper article and the manila folder, as he must have seen what Ava saw in that photo of María and Henry. He concluded his wife was María's daughter. The fact that when Ava had looked at the photo of María and Henry she felt as if she was looking at an old picture of her mum suddenly made sense. The similarity between the two women was striking, and now Ava knew why she was drawn to it from the beginning. That was what her father had meant in his letter to his wife when he wrote, 'This is your family'. She realised all those letters were a precious insight into her grandmother's life that was ended prematurely and therefore meant Ava could never meet her. It was some consolation to meet her friend, but would it be that easy for Ava to just accept her grandparents weren't her real ones? She supposed it didn't really matter if they were related or not; her grandparents were the ones who were always there for her, who celebrated their granddaughter's achievements and loved her unconditionally. Did her mum know she was adopted and had Spanish heritage?

'Did mum know she was adopted?' Rosa looked at her with tired eyes, and Ava noticed she wouldn't get many more answers today.

'No, I don't think so. I gave her the photo and newspaper article to send her on her journey of discovery, but then that horrible accident happened.'

There was that feeling again like someone was pushing down on Ava's chest with full force. She struggled to breathe. It happened every time she was reminded of her mum's accident. Lucy had suggested seeing someone about it, a grief counsellor who could help, but Ava didn't see the point. What would a grief counsellor do anyway, say that it will get easier with time and suggest she hold on to the happy memories? How could she if her mum was her closest friend and last remaining relative – well, until now that was. She hadn't really given it much thought again after Lucy had mentioned that chances were high her father started a new family. Somewhere out there she might have half-siblings, and now knowing her mum was adopted, she might have distant relatives in Spain. Ava had always wanted a big family with relatives in other countries that she could visit, and maybe this was it. But it felt wrong without her mum, especially as Ava didn't even know if her mum had known. The thought of not knowing what her mum had learnt before she passed broke Ava's heart; it made her feel that she didn't spend enough time with her mum and talk about the important things in life. Had Ava ever bothered asking her mum about her life, she might have been told about Tim, and maybe her mum would have even told her that her father hadn't died. Their lives could have been different, but it seemed her mum had many secrets she carried with her, and Ava felt like a bad daughter for not sharing the load. Ava was still lost in thoughts when she felt a movement in her hand, realising that Rosa's hand, still in hers, was twitching and that Rosa had fallen asleep. Checking her watch, Ava saw that it was only 5 pm and visiting hours were until 8 pm, so she got up and went to the cafeteria to grab tea and a sandwich, hoping Rosa would only snooze for a bit. Her phone had a few messages from Kate asking if she was okay as she noticed she had stayed away for the night. Although this meant Kate kept a close eye on her, it also made Ava smile that her neighbour cared so much about her. She messaged back, saying she was in Swanage for the day and would be back later, to which Kate invited her over for some dinner, and Ava happily accepted. On her way back to Rosa's room, Ava passed the hospital gift shop and bought some flowers for Rosa. Thinking about María, and that her father and grandfather were both threatened when they investigated the story, Ava decided her next question for Rosa would be how the Browns adopted her mum and how Rosa stayed in touch. Ava sat in the plastic chair until she was told visiting hours were over and was asked to return the next day. Frightened to find police cars in front of the house, she was relieved when all was quiet in the street.

'Hello darling, come in, food is ready.'

'Hi Kate, it smells delicious!'

'Spag Bol, it used to be your favourite. I thought it was fitting as we're going down memory lane,' she said, smiling. She sat down and poured them a glass of wine from the bottle on the table.

'You've been watching me then?' Ava asked, enjoying seeing Kate go red in the face, and grinned.

'Sorry, I saw a police car last night, so I thought you might have got into trouble, and then later, when I heard your front door close, I knew you had left when you didn't answer the door today.'

'It's alright, no need to apologise. It's nice to know that you're looking out for me.'

Kate smiled and brought two bowls of food to the table. 'Cheers', she said, raising her glass.

'Cheers. Thank you for having me. This is exactly what I needed.'

'The food or company?' Kate asked.

'Both, to be honest,' Ava knew this was an invitation from Kate to talk about out how she had got on in her search on the south coast; she filled Kate in on her unsuccessful day by the coast and explained that no one knew her father.

'It was a long shot anyway, but ...' Ava suddenly realised that she previously hadn't revealed the real reason she had asked Kate about her parents' special places. It was too late to backtrack now, though. Instead, Ava went on and opened up about everything she hadn't told Kate yet, including Diego's deceit and theft and visiting Rosa in the hospital. Everything just came tumbling out, helped by the wine, and she wasn't even that surprised to see that Kate didn't seem too flustered by her revelations.

'Did you know mum was adopted?'

'No, I didn't, she never said anything.'

'I'm not sure she knew.'

'Me neither, I'm sure she would've mentioned it otherwise. That's the only part of your story that's truly shocking, although Rose never looked like Elizabeth.'

'No, and look at this,' Ava pulled out her phone to find the photo of her grandmother María to show Kate.

'I definitely see a resemblance there. These are your mum's parents, María and Henry, then?'

'Yes, it feels bizarre referring to them that way.'

'And we know we can trust this Rosa in the hospital that she's not confusing things given her age?'

'I hadn't thought about that,' Ava confessed. Could it really be that Rosa is just an old lady who got her memories mixed up, she then pondered?

'Sorry, I didn't mean to question it.' Kate was quick to reassure Ava, seeing her reaction.

'It's a valid point, though. Although I doubt it. I have the letters between them, and María does look like me. I'm going back to the hospital tomorrow to try and get some more answers. I would like to know how granny and grandpa were chosen and what she knows about the explosion.' Convinced that Rosa was telling the truth, she just needed to hear it to believe it.

'Let me know if you need me. After everything you've already had to go through, this is not something you should be dealing with on your own. Do you want to find out why Luke went behind your back?'

She hadn't thought about Luke for at least a few hours, but the mention of his name brought back the desire she had felt every time he was close. She wanted to kick herself for that thought the second it entered her mind. That's precisely what had happened with Diego, and he proved untrustworthy too.

'Not before I know the truth and have found my father. Maybe then I'll talk to him.' A further thought occurred to her. 'Do you think I should report the missing folder as stolen and mention that chances were high Diego was also the one who broke into the house a few weeks ago?' Ava asked.

Kate thought about it for a moment while finishing her glass of wine. 'I'd wait. From what I understand, you want answers. Many of those are in the folder or with Rosa and maybe your father. If you report Diego now, the police might keep the folder for a while as evidence. Have you contacted him saying you know he stole it, and if he doesn't want to get into trouble for theft, he should return it by tomorrow?'

'No, after the police turned up, I kind of forgot about it until we started to talk about it now. But yes, I should.'

'Why did he steal it in the first place?'

'No idea,' she shrugged.

'He's Spanish, isn't he? Maybe a relative?'

'That hadn't crossed my mind!' Ava sat bolt upright, realising that Kate might be right and they could be related. She needed to talk to him.

The bustle at the hospital the next day was making Ava uncomfortable. She needed peace and quiet to talk to Rosa, so it was a relief when she entered the room and the noise from the intensive care unit faded away behind the closing door. Rosa was perkier than the previous day, and judging by the half-eaten pudding on her tray, she was probably feeling better too. Ava kissed Rosa on the cheek without thinking about it, sat down in the same chair and held the lady's hand, who smiled at her lovingly.

'How are you feeling today?'

'Better but tired.'

'That's not surprising, take it easy, you've been through a lot.'

'It's nice to see you again.' Rosa smiled and squeezed Ava's hand.

'I guess you want to know more about what happened?'

'Yes, I do, but only if you're up for it.' Ava didn't want to tire Rosa out but was glad she didn't have to beg her to continue. Rosa asked to be propped up a bit more to enable her to sip a glass of water before she got ready to dive into the past again.

'If I remember correctly, the last I told you was that your mother was adopted.'

***

London, England
1938

María arrived in London, weakened by the journey, her body frail. She was still amazed at how Antonio had managed to get her onto one of the trains with the International Brigadiers as an accompanying nurse. She heard him mutter something about Major Smith owing him a favour for saving his life a few months earlier. Major Smith was a burly man who intimidated María, but she could see there was kindness in his eyes, and after what he had done for her country, she followed his orders to get her to safety. She felt guilty that she was on a train with soldiers heading back to their native England while her Spanish countrymen and women who fled to France were being held captive and interred in camps. As soon as the train arrived in London Victoria and waiting families rushed to their loved ones, María's orders from Antonio were to disappear into the crowds in her new nurse's uniform that she had sown from fabric Isabel had brought her and find her way to Henry's friend's house. It was only María's second train journey, and arriving in London reminded her of getting off the train for the first time in Madrid as a young girl. The emotions of having left her family behind came flooding back as she stood on the pavement, busses and cars whizzing past as she wished there was someone to pick her up and look after her. She looked around but all she saw was a sea of men of all ages rushing in and out of the station, women walking arm in arm, chatting and laughing, and mothers dragging their children by the hand. Much to her relief, she noticed that she didn't stick out like a sore thumb; with her chestnut-coloured hair and light complexion, her Asturian heritage was doing her a favour. She wrapped her grey overcoat closer around her body as the biting wind blew her hair across her face. Isabel had given her a suitcase to replace her jute bag so as to draw less attention to herself in this foreign city. The last thing Isabel wanted was for the police to stop her niece and request documentation before she could find Henry's friend. Major Smith had written a few sentences in

English on the back of Henry's letter to help her ask for directions but, knowing she wouldn't understand a response, she decided to start walking. Antonio had warned her about the rainy British weather and the size of the city. However, it seemed he had forgotten she originally hailed from Asturias, which was well known for its abundance of rain as well as the wet and harsh winters. María would have given anything to see the lush green hills of her home right now, although what she saw on her right surprised her: While on her left there were grand buildings almost as beautiful as the ones she saw in the Goya district, to her right an iron fence ran along the entire road, and behind it was a nicely manicured park. Searching for the entrance, she walked alongside the fence to the end, where it bent to the right. Across the road in front of her stood a grand monument. She looked along the road to her right but couldn't see any opening in the fence or any people inside the park and wondered what the barrier was keeping out or who it was protecting inside. Doubting she was going to get inside, she noticed another cluster of trees and a monument on the other side of the crossing. Trying to work out a way across the road, she saw there were no tramlines; instead, a red open deck bus with stairs at the back whizzed past her from the right. She remembered, having laughed at Antonio when he tried to explain what a big city London was, thinking she had already got used to Madrid, coming from a small village in the mountains. Now she wished she had listened to him. Following other pedestrians, María made it safely across the street. She entered Hyde Park, and quickly felt the tension melt away as she walked further into the park and sat on a bench, closing her eyes she imagined she was in El Retiro. After a few hours of wandering the streets of London, following directions from strangers, she arrived at the address she was given. As no one answered the door bell, María sat on the steps in front of the house and waited.

'Can I help you, Miss?' A tall, handsome man dressed in a brown overcoat and Fedora hat walked towards María, a briefcase in his left hand. A smile emerged across his lips as he approached, taking in her uniform and battered shoes.

'*Señor* Bron?' she asked questioningly, hoping she had been directed to the right place. 'Soy María,' she continued. His smile widened, and he nodded. María felt relief wash over her, and released a breath she hadn't realised she was holding. At last, after several hours of wandering through the park, pointing to the name 'Holland Park' on her letter, following people's arms pointing in a direction accompanied by words she did not understand, she had found the man who would help her.

'It's Brown, but please call me Andrew,' he said in fluent Spanish, showing his straight teeth. 'Let's get inside, it's freezing out here.'

Andrew was in his mid-twenties and worked for the government. He had read politics at university with Henry, and they bonded over their love for Spain, he explained. The conversation with Andrew about her experiences in Madrid was flowing when his wife Elizabeth arrived. She was a stunning woman with blonde hair set in waves, covered with a fashionable burgundy red hat to the side and a beautiful smile. María's mouth hung open as Elizabeth sauntered to the couch to greet the new arrival, a huge smile plastered across her face. Regaining her composure, María stood up and extended her hand, aware of her dirty clothes and the odour emanating from her. María was in desperate need of a shower, but Andrew's wife didn't shake her hand; instead, she went in for a hug and two kisses, one on each cheek, and said in dulcet tones, 'Welcome María, we are so happy you are here.' Seeing the confused look on María's face, Andrew explained how Henry had informed them about how he had met a remarkable woman in Madrid and how he hoped he could introduce them to her one day. It seemed ironic that their link was the only one not present in the room, and no one had heard from him for several months. María felt a stab of guilt at the mention of Henry's affection for her, so much so that he wrote home about her and was now being almost interrogated by his friend. Andrew switched fluently between Spanish and English to ensure both women understood, although she was sure Andrew was not translating everything María told him about the war their friend was still caught in and the true scale of what was happening. María stopped when she saw Andrew's face cloud over at the mention of Franco's name and the bloody battle they were fighting at the Ebro. If the Nationalists managed to cross the river and gain more territory in Catalonia, it wouldn't be long before Barcelona fell. And everyone knew if that happened, Valencia and Madrid would be next, and Franco's troops would soon enter the streets of Madrid in victory and begin to retaliate against their enemies. María shuddered at the thought of what would become of her home and everyone who tried to protect it.

Twenty-Two

London, England
2014

Rosa closed her eyes. A nurse came in to check the monitors and remove her tray while Ava paced around the room. She now knew how her grandmother had come to England and how she knew the Browns. After recounting what had happened Rosa looked exhausted, so Ava popped out for a cup of tea and some fresh air. Her phone found reception outside the building. A message from an unknown number popped up. 'Bring María's letters to the Kyoto Garden in Holland Park at 9 pm tonight. No police.' Ava's stomach turned, and she wanted to be sick. Was Diego threatening her? Despite the unknown number, she knew it was him. But why did he want the letters when he already had the manila folder? She sat on a bench in front of the Accident and Emergency unit and watched people rushing in and out of the hospital, wondering what she should do. Her tea had gone cold by the time she finally got up and wandered back inside. The doctor she had met the first time she visited was talking to Rosa as Ava entered. She apologised, turning around again to walk out so as not to disturb them. She heard Rosa call her name and waved Ava over to sit, explaining to the doctor that Ava should be informed about her health until she was released from hospital. Dr. Jamal nodded and continued with his examination, asking Rosa various questions and taking notes. He concluded that Rosa should be discharged the next day and that they will inform the care home to pick her up, then he left.

'That's great to hear,' Ava remarked.

'Will you join me for tea when I'm home?'

'I'd love to.' Ava realised she genuinely cared about Rosa. But still she needed answers. 'Can I ask you something?'

'Of course, my dear.'

'Who is Andrés?' Rosa's eyes misted over instantly. 'I'm sorry, I didn't mean to upset you. It's just that many of the letters I found in the musical box were written to Andrés, but it seems they were never sent off.'

'No, they weren't. Andrés died in 1934 in the Asturias strike. The letters to him were like writing in a diary, it's what he would've wanted to hear from Madrid. They were in the box because they were the last connection to him and private.'

'Are all the letters in the box?'

'Oh no, I still have a few,' Rosa said, looking sad, 'some are best kept secret.'

'Is there something important in them?' Ava wasn't sure how best to ask, but if Diego wanted the letters, then there was something he wanted to read.

'It all happened so long ago. Things were different then.'

'What happened?'

'I'll tell you next time.' The poor woman was caught in the past, and Ava's question about Andrés had upset her. After a while, Ava noticed that Rosa had dozed off again. She wrote a note on the back of a receipt telling her she would return tomorrow.

Arriving home, Ava went to the bookcase where she had hidden the letters. There were still two letters she hadn't read yet, and although Rosa told her she had kept a few, she wondered if any other secrets were buried within them. The first few letters from Rosa were about her life in Mieres, asking María how she was doing in Madrid, but it started to get weirder with each letter. Rosa had started demanding responses to her letters, and for almost three years it seemed she didn't receive any. Ava must have misunderstood them entirely, she concluded. She had thought Rosa and María were best friends, but from the sounds of it Rosa practically stalked María. Who was this Rosa? Maybe Kate was right that the old lady had lost her marbles and nothing was as it seemed. Reading about María's experiences in the letters to Andrés felt different, though; Ava got an insight into her grandmother's life during the war and how she had met Henry. The connection she had felt with the photo from the beginning was now even stronger, and she noticed things she hadn't before, such as the paper, the slight slant of the handwriting to the right, and addressing Andrés as "my beloved brother". What was Diego looking for in these personal letters that made him go to such lengths to break in and steal? It was difficult for Ava to understand while she didn't know the full story. She felt Diego would do anything to get what he wanted. She had to react fast, she decided. She called the hospital and the care home to report a potentially harmful man and to ensure no one had access to Rosa. She then got ready to head into London and meet her nemesis.

London was still bathed in beautiful sunshine by the time Ava got off the train. People were milling outside of pubs enjoying an after-work drink with colleagues and tourists were blocking station exits and pavements. She was nervous about meeting Diego after his recent behaviour – he was dangerous, and she was worried about how he would react when she told him she didn't have the letters. Thinking about it, she should have insisted on meeting somewhere else instead of a park, but it was too late now, she had to go through with it. At least this time she was prepared. She knew what he was capable of and not to trust him, and she wouldn't be led astray again. This was now personal and about her family and not just some old photo. Ava jumped on a bus in the direction of Holland Park station. From there, she planned to walk to where the restaurant would have stood. Rosa had remembered the exact location, although it now looked very different to what she had described, Ava noticed. The fifth house on the left was now a little tearoom with a grey façade and a glass front squashed between a hair salon and a luxury paint shop. Attached to it at the back stood residential houses, which Ava assumed would have looked similar all those years ago before the destruction. During her search, she had read about a few bombings during the war, and standing in front of the beautiful houses now in such an affluent area of the city made it hard for her to believe these streets were once covered in rubble. She looked on her phone at the photo she had taken of the original. Sadness washed over her when she thought of what her mum had to go through and that her mum never knew her true heritage. If it was true and the explosion wasn't an accident, then whoever murdered her grandparents was also responsible for not only killing residents of surrounding houses but also making more than ten families homeless during a time when the country was trying to get back onto its feet. Who had such hatred in them that they would go to such lengths? She wondered if it was because María was Spanish and no one wanted a foreigner in the area, or maybe someone in Henry's family was upset at him for marrying below his class. She might get a few more answers from Rosa, but she didn't want to overwhelm her; it was clear losing her friend and a close ally in a strange country was very painful for Rosa to remember. Ava snapped a few photos to show Rosa later and started walking towards the park, where she spotted the opening times displayed at the gate which made it clear the park would close thirty minutes before dusk. That didn't give them long if Diego only turned up at 9 pm. Contemplating back-up plans, Ava decided to check to see if she could climb over the gates in the event they were already locked. Taking the closest entrance to the Kyoto Garden, Ava memorised the route back to the gate in case anything happened and she had to escape. Walking around the garden, she noticed she didn't know where exactly they would meet. Therefore, she chose to position herself in an open area with several ways out. She tied her shoelaces on her trainers and opened a recording app on her phone, ready to press start. Her heart was beating at a hundred miles an hour. As she waited, there were a few people still in the Kyoto Garden taking selfies, and she hoped they would stay. She should have called the police, she suddenly thought. But would they bother waiting like she was to arrest someone who stole a folder? She was sure they wouldn't. They'd probably laugh at her. Ava heard footsteps behind her and attempted to turn around just when a hand grabbed her wrist and twisted her arm behind her back so she couldn't move.

'Where are the letters?' Diego said, emerging from the trees in front of her, anger in his eyes. Ava tried to turn around to see who was holding her but was forced to look at Diego. She stood there, motionless, when a hand started to search her around the waist and back. Ava wriggled to get away from the man, but he was too strong. She caught a whiff of his aftershave, a musky scent, the one she had so often smelt and that had filled her body with desire.

'Luke.' She said, perplexed as she managed to turn slightly and look into his eyes.

'She doesn't have them,' he said, ignoring her and letting go of her wrist.

'Oh Ava, why do you have to be so stupid?' Turning around again, Diego had moved closer to her, and she found herself sandwiched between the two men she had once both wanted and now felt nothing but hatred for. 'You had one job – to bring me the letters so you can walk.' Ignoring his threat, Ava was genuinely interested in what he had to say. Did he have the answers to her family's mystery?

'Why are an old woman's letters so important to you?'

'The old woman, as you call her, is responsible for causing extreme distress within the Spanish royal family, and as long as that letter exists, we will be haunted by it.'

'You are part of the Spanish royal family? Are you kidding me?' Ava laughed incredulously, trying to hide her fear.

Diego smiled like a Cheshire cat as if he couldn't quite believe it either. 'I'll tell you what we are going to do now. You and Luke will go to your house and you will give him the letter I want. Then we'll pretend this whole thing never happened, and you will never see me again.'

'So now it's just one letter? And which one would that be?'

An angry growl escaped Diego. 'You're really annoying me now. You know exactly which one, the one where she finds out who took her son!' Diego registered the shock on Ava's face and studied her. Ava shivered.

'I don't know what you're on about.'

'Don't lie to me.'

'Maybe Rosa has it,' Luke chimed in.

'Shut up, you idiot. This is all your fault!' Diego exclaimed.

'What does he have to do with it?' Ava enquired, interested.

'Do you really think it was a coincidence you met in the Cotswolds? And when you kicked Luke and Lucy out, I knew you had found the folder, all I had to do was come and get it.'

'And when you broke into my house, you couldn't find it?'

'So convenient for you to listen to me and leave for the weekend. But enough, get me the letter, and no one else will get hurt.'

'No one else?' Ava was trying to stay calm but instantly understood what Diego was implying.

'It was unfortunate. She wasn't supposed to die, only get a fright and stop investigating.'

'You monster, you killed my mum!' Ava shrieked and lunged at him. Luke grabbed her arms and held her back. 'Let me go!' Ava tried to get out of Luke's grasp, but he was too strong. It was getting dark, and even the last people who could have helped her had left the park. Diego slid his hands under Ava's jumper and searched her again. Ava tried to get away but realised she wouldn't get far anyway. Looking straight at Diego, she saw the hatred in his eyes. 'So you didn't come to London to work and help your family but to find my mum and take her from me because she found her real heritage.' It wasn't a question, Ava understood now how the past was connected and how Diego's family had ruined hers.

'Your family got what you deserved for threatening us for over eighty years, first María, then your grandfather, then your father and at the end your mother. You can end this now, Ava.' He stood back, looking her up and down, shaking his head. 'You disgust me!' he snarled, spitting the words like venom as he produced a small pocketknife.

She could feel Luke had loosened his grip, thinking she wouldn't lash out at Diego anymore. She had one chance to get away. She threw her head back, slamming it straight into Luke's nose. He howled while Ava grabbed Diego's right shoulder and rammed her knee into his crotch as hard as she could, pulling him towards her. She swung her foot backwards kicking Luke between the legs like a horse about to bolt. Ava turned and sprinted as fast as she could towards the gate, only turning around when she heard a thump and shouts. Looking back, she watched a figure smash a bottle over Diego's head, making him buckle and slump to the ground next to Luke. Ava knew the stranger saved her life, but she continued running and only stopped when she got to Holland Park station. A police car rushed past her. As calmly as she could, she made her way down the escalator to the Central Line eastbound platform. Breathing hard and fast, she slumped into the first free seat in the car to finally catch her breath.

'Ava, what happened? Come in.' Lucy led her friend to the living room, sat her down on the couch, gave her a blanket to cuddle into, and went to the kitchen to make a cup of camomile tea. Ava had no idea how she got to Lucy's place. Her legs just carried her there.

'Are you okay? Do I need to call the police?' It took Ava a moment to realise Lucy was talking to her; she was in a haze with thoughts running through her head.

'He killed her,' Ava mumbled.

'Who killed who?'

'Diego killed mum.'

Lucy took a sharp breath, not believing what she was hearing, but one look at Ava told her she was being serious. Once Ava had caught her breath on the tube and her thoughts had returned to everything Diego had thrown in her face about her family, her father's disappearance, and her mum's death, Ava started sobbing uncontrollably, attracting annoyed glances from the other passengers. When she heard Leyton was the next station, she got up and walked to Lucy's place, not knowing where else to go. The tears started falling again. Lucy held her close until her breathing returned to normal.

'Do you want to talk about it?' Knowing better than to push Ava, Lucy opted for a more subtle approach, still holding her and making calming noises. Ava opened her coat pocket to get her phone out and play the recording of the interaction with Diego and Luke. But her phone wasn't there. Ava started panicking, realising she must have dropped it while running for her life.

'It's not here. I lost my phone.' Ava checked all her pockets again.

'It's okay, we'll get you a new one.'

'No, it's not okay,' Ava said in a raised voice, getting up and thinking of returning to the park to retrieve it. She was sure Diego and Luke wouldn't be there anymore, but her phone probably was. Lucy got up, stopping Ava from leaving the house, knowing her friend was in no state to do anything rash.

'Ava,' Lucy said, shaking her, 'why is your phone so important?'

'Because it has Diego's confession on it that he killed mum. I need to get it, it's the only proof I have.'

'Where is it?'

'I must've dropped it when I ran away.'

'Where did you drop it?' Lucy asked.

'In the park.'

'Which park?'

'Holland Park.'

'That's across the city, and the park will be closed now.'

'But it's the only thing I have to prove it.' It dawned on Ava that Lucy was right, and even if she did make the journey back to the park, she probably wouldn't get it back. She knew she could jump over the gate, but she couldn't be sure Diego, Luke or that person she saw next to them when she had turned around hadn't grabbed it.

'We can go back first thing tomorrow morning when the park opens and look for it. Even if we go to the police now, I doubt they would do anything before tomorrow morning.' Lucy was right, Ava concluded, although she had a niggling feeling that if she told the police there was evidence on there, they might act faster.

'Why don't we call it from my phone and see if anyone answers?' Lucy suggested.

Ava thought about it. If Diego or Luke had it and they saw Lucy's name show up they would probably answer, assuming Ava was with her. She couldn't risk that, she had to keep her friend safe. 'No, let's not.' Lucy nodded and steered Ava back to the couch, asking if anyone might have seen her and Diego and taken the phone or overheard the conversation.

'Luke.'

'I knew it!' Lucy scoffed. 'I had a feeling he couldn't be trusted. I was glad you kicked him out, but why did you get rid of me too?' The question was clearly bugging Lucy, and Ava realised her actions had probably hurt her best friend.

'I'm sorry. I started to get suspicious of everyone. You started acting weird, too,' she admitted.

'I see,' Lucy said as she stroked Ava's arm. 'When we returned from the hospital, and you went for a walk, Luke went into the garden to make a personal call. I watched him through the kitchen window, and he looked agitated and angry, shouting into the phone. He didn't realise that the kitchen window was open, so I heard his side of the conversation saying that he couldn't get into the room, they wouldn't let him and that he would find a way. He was up to something, and I was going to warn you, but when you got back and kicked him out I knew you had doubts too. I did send you an email, though, with what I witnessed. Didn't you receive it?'

'No, I didn't. Why didn't you text?'

'I was scared he had bugged my phone. Ridiculous, I know, but I suddenly saw him with different eyes. I asked Kate to keep an eye on you in case he returned.'

Ava told Lucy why she had kicked them out, especially Luke, and as she started, everything that had happened came tumbling out. Lucy looked shocked, mainly at Diego's theft and what happened in the park, but she reprimanded Ava for not involving the police after learning that Diego was the one who broke into her house and came back later to retrieve what he couldn't get the first time.

'I know,' Ava admitted. 'I was a complete idiot that I trusted him again. Believe me, I feel foolish. But I never thought he would go this far. Breaking into a house is one thing, but killing someone?'

'May I ask how he did it?'

'I don't know, he didn't say anything about it other than that she wasn't supposed to have died, he had only wanted to scare her.'

'Hmm, if I remember rightly, your mum veered off the road and into the tree because a motorbike was blocking the road. The police concluded that she tried to bypass it as she was too late to break and unfortunately she lost control of the car. But that sounds very much like an accident to me.' Lucy shrugged and grabbed her phone and after a few minutes turned to Ava.

'Right, I suggest the following. You go and have a bath, then off to bed. The park opens at 7.30 am tomorrow, so we'll leave here at 6.45 am and look for your phone. Whether we find it or not, we will go to the closest police station and report the break-in, the theft, the assault, and the murder. Then we'll go to Kate's and keep an eye on your place, where we'll stay put until the police have arrested Diego. Okay?'

Ava nodded, loving her friend for being the rational one. 'I might skip the bath and go straight to sleep, though.'

Ava and Lucy arrived at the park just as a young ranger unlocked the same gate Ava had jumped across the previous night. They retraced Ava's steps to where the interaction had taken place and searched the ground for her phone, but they couldn't find it. After almost an hour, they gave up and headed for the police station. On route, Lucy called the park's lost and found service but was told nothing had been handed in. Entering the police station, Ava started growing nervous; not only was she about to tell the police that they hadn't done their job properly, but also that she didn't have the evidence to prove any of her allegations. Sensing her friend was nervous, Lucy took her hand

and the lead, navigating them to the front desk where a young female officer was filing papers. She looked up and smiled at the two women – a morning person, Ava thought.

'Hi, we would like to report several crimes. One should already be on record, but we now know who did it.' Lucy didn't beat around the bush like Ava, she wanted the police to take immediate action and to then leave the station as soon as possible. The officer looked genuinely interested in these young people who seemed to have solved a crime and merely needed the police to tie up the ends and make the arrests. Ava went through everything in meticulous detail, filing three separate reports and adding more information to the break-in report. When they had finished, Ava felt drained and dabbed her watery eyes with a tissue the officer had handed her. Talking about her mum had weakened her resolve not to get emotional, but she crumbled instantly, knowing that her mum would still be here had it not been for Diego. The officer looked sympathetic but made her aware that retrieving her phone was now very important because without it, as she didn't know how he killed her mum and it would be her word against his, it would make it very difficult for the police to investigate. But she also reassured Ava the police would do everything in their power to apprehend the offender. Ava appreciated the officer's compassion and she felt comforted that the nightmare of the last few weeks would soon end.

Twenty-Three

The journey in the taxi back to Kate's house felt surreal and scary. Ava didn't know what to expect when she got there. Would the police turn up to question her? Had they started investigating? Would her mum still be alive if Rosa hadn't given her the hints to find her family? It suddenly hit Ava that Rosa might be in danger now that Diego knew she didn't have the letter and Luke knew where she was. Lucy looked across from her seat and asked if everything was okay.

'We need to go to the hospital, I think Rosa might be in danger.'

'I thought you had called them to warn them?'

'Yes, but what if my warning wasn't passed on from one guard to the next?' Ava started to panic – she couldn't lose Rosa now.

'Okay, we'll go to the hospital first.'

Lucy instructed the driver to take a detour to the hospital and squeezed Ava's hand. 'It'll all be okay.' Ava hoped her friend was right. They arrived at the hospital and made their way to Rosa's room. But when they got there they saw her bed was empty. They ran back to the reception desk and asked where she was.

'She was discharged this morning and taken home,' the receptionist answered, looking less than amused at the inquisitive women before resuming dealing with the paperwork on her desk.

'Who picked her up? Was it a young man?' Ava continued.

Glancing over the top of her reading glasses and looking up at Ava from her seat, she said Rosa was picked up by two nurses from the care home, who took her in her wheelchair to the waiting minibus outside. Ava breathed a sigh of relief. Realising she had acted somewhat tersely towards the nurse because of her paranoia, Ava made a point of thanking her and giving her a beaming smile. Both were completely ignored.

Hailing another taxi, they went directly to the care home. Ava hoped either Maggie or Patty was working and could give her the reassurance she desperately needed. A young girl, who Ava had never seen, greeted them at the reception and told them she wasn't allowed to inform them about a resident's movements unless they were related or had a pre-arranged appointment with her. Ava asked if she could see someone she knew, but as she did so Maggie came around the corner smiling at her.

'Hello darling.' She gave both Ava and Lucy a kiss on the cheek. 'I thought I heard your voice. You sound agitated, is everything okay?'

'Hi Maggie. Yes, everything is fine. Has Rosa arrived safely?'

'Indeed she has, I picked her up personally since you sounded so worried the other day.'

'Thank you so much.'

'She's resting now, but she has already been asking for you, so you should be able to visit her soon. I'm going on my lunch break in fifteen minutes. Do you fancy having a quick catch-up then?'

'Yes, that would be great. We'll wait in the cafeteria.'

It didn't take Maggie long to join them at the table the furthest away from all the others. While Maggie got settled and unwrapped her ham and cheese sandwich, Ava started to tell her quietly what had happened. The only part she omitted was Diego telling her about her mum – she wasn't sure this was something to share just yet while the police were still investigating, and she still didn't know how he did it. Maggie was stunned at what she heard but, apart from a few gasps, she stayed silent while she waited for Ava to finish.

'And that's why we're here now. I just needed to make sure she was okay.'

Having eaten her sandwich and finished a packet of crisps she had produced out of nowhere, Maggie shook her head, slowly processing it all. She took Ava's hand but struggled to find the words to express her horror at what Ava had gone through alone.

'I'm sorry, and of course you know I'm happy to talk to the police about Luke trying to get into Rosa's room if necessary.'

'Thank you, although I'm still unsure how he ended up in cahoots with Diego. What was he going to gain from it?'

'That is probably something only he can answer, but it doesn't really matter, does it? He betrayed your trust and used you for his own gain. Good riddance, I'd say.'

'Yes, I agree. Shame though, he was rather handsome.' The three women giggled.

'Indeed he was,' Ava responded.

'But it's often the way, isn't it? Many handsome men turn out to be bad boys – just look at Daniel Cleaver in Bridget Jones' Diary,' Maggie threw in.

Lucy nodded her agreement and pointed at her now sizeable bump, for which she also had a good-looking man who betrayed her to thank. Maggie said she needed to head back to work and got up. The girls joined her to see if Rosa was ready to receive visitors.

Rosa was sitting in the common room in a high armchair with a cup of tea, some biscuits and a novel. She smiled from ear to ear and tried to push herself out of her chair when Ava rushed over. Ava insisted that Rosa stay seated. 'I was hoping you would visit me,' Rosa said, before instructing Lucy to grab more cups for the tea. Rosa joyfully clapped her hands when she spotted Lucy's bump. 'Oh a baby! How lovely!' she exclaimed.

Lucy smiled and stroked her bump with her free hand. 'How are you feeling, Rosa?'

'Much better. I am happy to be out of the hospital, it's not a nice place to be.'

'Well, you were in a coma,' Ava reminded her. 'And I hope you are going to take it easy.'

'I will, but I also realise that time is not on my side. So while I'm awake and fit, I will tell you the rest of the story.'

Ava put a hand on Rosa's arm. 'Only if you're sure.'

Rosa nodded. 'It's 1938. María arrived in London where she met the Browns and waited at their house for Henry. She started working as a nurse again and was taught English by Andrew. Henry embarked on one of the last ships out from Barcelona after the disbandment of the International Brigades.

***

London, England
1938

The wedding was a small affair with only Elisabeth and Andrew present, who acted as their witnesses at the registry office in Caledonian Road. Henry's mother was already very sick and couldn't make the journey to London for her only son's wedding. María wore a beautiful plain white dress. It didn't come as a surprise when, just two weeks later, Henry's mother passed away, having never met María. She left Henry with a substantial inheritance. He spent it on a nice apartment with two bedrooms, a living room and a bathroom close to the Browns in a quiet street in Holland Park. Henry joined the British war effort working for the government, which María was pleased about as the war in Spain had changed him, and she knew another stint on the front line would not be good for him. The years passed by and María began to miss the Spanish way of life – the sun, the traditions she used to get excited about as a child, and especially the food. With rationing still going on in London until 1952, it was hard for her to source enough produce to cook something resembling Spanish food without resorting to the black market. It broke her heart that she knew nothing about the whereabouts of her family. Since arriving in London she had written several letters to her family in Asturias and Isabel in Barcelona, but she hadn't received a reply. She didn't give up hope, though, that one day a letter would arrive. María opened the door to their apartment, finding a letter with her name on it propped up against the empty fruit bowl and a note from Henry: I received this in the office addressed to me to hand over to you. x.

Her hands trembled as she ripped it open, stumbling to the nearest chair. It was a letter from Isabel, at last. She was ill and in hospital. Once the country had fallen to the fascists, Antonio was sent to a labour camp, where he died. Isabel never quite recovered after that, which is why she has been in and out of the hospital for the last few years. María was shaking. Antonio had lost his life after the horror of the war was supposed to have been over. She felt despondent for the man who took her in and taught her so much, and who she was forever grateful to. She read on.

While in the hospital last time, I ran into the midwife who delivered your baby. I remembered her so vividly - her joy when she held your boy in her hands, her black curls trying to escape her hair net and the mole just below her right eye. I couldn't resist approaching her, the thought of that day still brings so much sadness to me. All I wanted to know was why you weren't allowed to hold him and why we weren't allowed to have his body for a proper funeral. She wouldn't look at me, María, and I knew something was wrong. You see, she remembered that day too because it was the first time a baby was stolen! Yes, my dear, a man who claimed to be his father while holding a gun to her head took your baby boy.

María let out a scream – her baby was alive! She hid the letter in her undergarments – Henry could never read it. The day she read that letter would forever be etched into her brain. In spite of her having no proof, María knew exactly who had taken her baby; she had seen him in the hospital, and he could not fool her despite his wearing a white doctor's cloak. He had been following her. All she could think of was finding her baby. She knew she couldn't travel to Spain, though, as the whole world was at war. Isabel had informed her that Franco had reinstated the monarchy and the Spanish royal family had returned to their homeland. So María took pen to paper and asked her aunt to help her find her boy.

The change in his wife didn't go unnoticed, and Henry tried his best to make her happy. During Christmas in 1951, Henry suggested that they open a restaurant that served Spanish cuisine in order that María could bring a part of her home to London.

María jumped at the idea, having lost hope of ever finding her child. They started looking for suitable premises and soon found an empty ground-level unit not far from where they lived. Although it was small, María knew with a bit of colour she could make it look like a restaurant from home. She spent every minute at the restaurant when she wasn't working at the hospital, preparing for the grand opening. Even when she found out she was pregnant, she was working hard, painting, choosing décor and sourcing the best Spanish wine she could get her hands on. Henry was ecstatic about María's pregnancy, hoping it would lift his wife from her melancholy. He made her promise she would rest more and he had already put an advert in the newspaper to find help for when the restaurant opened. One evening, just as María closed the restaurant doors for the day, she felt a sharp pain in her belly and a warm trickle down her leg. She flagged down a taxi to take her home, where she picked up her bag and left a note for Henry before setting off for the hospital. He arrived at the hospital in a hot flush, alternating between excitement and fear.

'How are you feeling, darling?'

'I'm fine, Henry. But please sit down, you're making me nervous.'

'Well, I'm nervous. How can you be so calm?' María averted her eyes, thinking of the last time she was lying in a hospital bed, ready to bring new life into the world. She shrugged. Henry didn't need to know the truth.

Their little daughter was the eye of her father. He cuddled her whenever she was awake and was happy to jump out of bed in the middle of the night to calm her. She was his world, and while he positively embraced fatherhood, María became increasingly withdrawn. Every time she looked at the baby, she was reminded of what she had lost. She struggled to feed her and bond with her. Elizabeth, by contrast, seemed to be a natural with her and was smitten; María assumed it was because she and Andrew couldn't have a child of their own. Elizabeth and Andrew showered their goddaughter with presents and cuddles. María on the other hand escaped whenever she could to send more urgent letters to any royal residences Isabel had written about. María reasoned that if she at least knew her son was safe, her motherly instincts might return, and she could move forward and be the mother her daughter deserved. One thing was for certain, though – if it was indeed Xulián's bodyguard who had taken her baby, he had to be with Xulián's family somewhere, probably with his mother, and they would do anything to keep an illegitimate child secret. María understood then and there that she would never receive a reply.

The day of the restaurant's grand opening was fast approaching, but María had lost interest, the thought of Spain causing her nothing but pain. More often than not, she excused herself from the preparations, leaving them to Henry and their newly employed waitress. She called at the Brown's place and handed over her 2-week-old daughter to Elizabeth, who was delighted to look after her while María went for a walk. After an hour of ambling around Holland Park, pondering how she would ever be able to build a bond with the child she had given birth to, she left the green space behind her and walked back towards the restaurant. As she did so, the earth started shaking beneath her feet. María recognised the sound of an explosion and instinctively ran towards it to help the injured. She turned into the street where their restaurant stood, arriving at a scene of utter devastation, smoke rising high into the clear blue London sky. María stood rooted to the spot. The humdrum around her perished as she stared at the crumbled remains of her future, memories of explosions in Madrid flooding her mind when out of the corner of her eye she noticed a man standing further away, observing the scene unfold in front of him. María took a few steps back so as to remain out of sight. She studied the long overcoat he wore, which was incongruous in this heat, his hat almost pulled down to his eyes, an impassive expression, and a cigarette dangling from the corner of his mouth. A shriek tore her eyes away as she watched a woman climb over the debris. A fireman held her back as a small body was pulled out from underneath the rubble. The woman pushed to get past the tall man to get her child. Barely able to stand on her feet, she broke down in his arms. María couldn't remember how long she had stood there for by the time the fire brigade had managed to put out the fire two big white bags were carried out on stretchers. María's heart plummeted as she watched the bags being loaded into a van. Onlookers bowed their heads, caps in hand, apart from one man with a smirk on his face who crushed his cigarette under his foot and turned to leave.

Rosa sighed and muttered, 'It's all my fault,' more to herself than anyone else in the room.

'What is your fault?' Ava prompted. A distant look in Rosa's eyes and she didn't respond for a very long time. She had dozed off.

Ava glanced at Lucy, who shrugged back. They left for some fresh air, giving Rosa time to recuperate. When they returned, she had woken up and was speaking to a man. The room went quiet around Ava. All she could hear was her heartbeat. Her hands went cold and clammy, thinking Diego had returned. The man got up and turned to look at them, a smile spreading across his face. Ava's jaw dropped. Her knees buckled underneath her. Lucy caught Ava's arm and led her to a seat, both of them not taking her eyes off the stranger.

'Hi Ava,' he choked, tears filling his eyes. Since finding out about him, Ava wondered what he would look like and how she would feel if they ever met again. Her heart was telling her to say something, to hold out her hand, while her head voiced suspicion about his sudden arrival after more than two decades. She had so many questions she needed answers to, but right now she needed to be held by her father. As she moved towards him, he opened his arms. Ava fell into them and she squeezed the father she thought she had lost so many years ago.

'I missed you, my darling girl. I am so sorry for everything.' Brian gave his daughter a kiss on the head as they sat down. He held out his hand to Lucy in greeting. Ava looked at her father and recognised where she had seen him before.

'You were at mum's funeral at the back and left before the service was over.'

'Yes, I was.'

'And you were also in the park, you hit Diego and Luke with a bottle! Were you following me?'

'Guilty, that was also me,' he answered, holding his hands up as if to surrender. 'I kept an eye on you after the funeral and noticed the two male friends you entertained. I didn't trust them.'

'Rightly so,' interjected Lucy.

'Why didn't you talk to me?' Ava asked, almost angry. He was there, and yet he let her suffer alone. Brian sighed, shaking his head.

'I was afraid it would've been too much for you, having just lost mum. But maybe I should tell you the whole story from the beginning.' He looked up as two nurses joined them. Shock registered on their faces. 'Maggie, Patty,' he said, nodding in their direction. He asked them to take a seat. Shaken, Maggie and Patty sat holding each other's hands.

'I expect you found the safe and the folder?' Ava nodded. 'When you were about two years old, I was at my parents' house, going through my father's possessions in the loft that he always said he would sort. That's when I first came across the manila folder.' He looked around the gathered group, unaware of how much they knew. It didn't matter, he decided, this story was for his daughter. 'My father had gathered witness statements from people saying they had seen someone suspicious a few days before the explosion he was investigating. Some mentioned having seen him at the scene, unmoved by the tragedy and unwilling to help. They didn't believe it was an accident, they thought he had something to do with it. You see, it wasn't that long ago that World War Two had ended. There were still many spies hiding in the streets of London, and many inhabitants didn't trust their next-door neighbours, so a man no one knew would always arouse suspicion.' Patty produced a teapot and cups out of nowhere, as well as some biscuits which she purposely put in front of Ava. Brian continued, seemingly starting to relax as he finally told the story he had kept secret for so long. 'My father also obtained access to a statement from the installer of the gas pipes, claiming he had connected everything properly and tested it. He had installed many gas pipes all over London and knew what he was doing as well as the consequences if he made even a tiny mistake. Knowing he would be imprisoned should they find him guilty of incorrect installation, he swore on his mother's life that he was not at fault.'

'Did he go to prison?'

'No, he didn't. My father took all the information to the police, but they dismissed him as a hobby detective and told him he should let them do their job. No one was ever prosecuted. It was always classed as an accident. But my father was persistent, adamant that the police were covering up for someone. He was certain that if the pipes were connected properly someone must have tampered with them afterwards. And if that wasn't the case, the pipes were never connected properly and the gas company should be liable.'

'Why did your father care so much?'

'He wanted justice. Several of the witnesses he spoke to lost friends and family in the blast. He was doing it for them mainly. And he was a good journalist, he had a nose for uncovering corruption.'

'Do we know who this man that people saw at the scene was?'

'No, he never found out,' Rosa chimed in, as if from nowhere, giving a wince as she did so. Everyone looked at the tiny figure in the big armchair, she waved her hand, indicating for Brian to continue.

He turned back to Ava. 'As I said, my dad didn't give up. He called the gas company, the fire brigade, the witnesses – he tried to speak to anyone who was there on the day. One day, a police officer turned up at his house, handing him an envelope with a picture of my mum and I walking in the park. By the time dad looked up from the picture the officer had disappeared.'

'Was it the same man?' Lucy asked.

'We don't know. But dad knew what it meant – that there were powers involved in this case who had the means to follow his family and threaten them. He called an old acquaintance at a local newspaper and packed our belongings the same evening.

'Sounds familiar,' Maggie snorted. 'Your family has a knack for running away.' Brian looked pained at the anger in her words and their truth.

'Yeah, why give up everything when all he had to do was burn the statements and focus on a different story?' asked Lucy.

'She's right. Seems a bit dramatic,' Maggie agreed.

'Maybe,' Brian continued. 'Those were different times, though. He had to provide for us and he couldn't risk anything. What if the police had concluded it was murder? Whoever was threatening him would have known of his involvement. We were in danger as long as they knew where we were.'

'But they never did conclude it was murder,' Rosa said, matter-of-factly, repeating Brian's own words, looking at him with raised eyebrows. Brian shook his head. 'Continue, please,' Rosa said sternly.

'Well, when I came across the folder and looked at the photo in the newspaper, I thought I was looking at your mother, the resemblance was uncanny. I showed it to Andrew, your grandfather, and although he didn't say anything, his reaction told me I was on to something. But Andrew wouldn't talk to me. After Elizabeth had also shut down when I asked her, my curiosity got the better of me, and I started investigating. Looking through birth, marriage and death records, I found Henry's and

María's. I also looked into Andrew and Elizabeth and found your mother's birth certificate, which named them as her parents. But I knew I had to keep digging and, through the census, found information on María, including where and when she was born, so I went there.

'Mieres.' It was almost a whisper. Rosa closed her eyes, a sad smile appearing as she remembered bygone days. 'What did you find there?'

'I found her brother, Juan Luis.'

Rosa's eyes shot open. 'He's alive?' Hope in her voice.

'Well, he was in his seventies when I visited him, fit as a fiddle though. He showed me the house where María grew up and told me about what had happened and how she was on her way to Madrid the last time he saw her. I had to break the news to him about his sister's passing in the explosion, but he had already come to terms with her being dead as he hadn't seen her again.'

'Do you have his address? I would like to write to him!' Rosa asked animatedly. This information seemed to shake years off Rosa, and she was more alive than Ava had seen her previously.

'Yes, I will write it down for you. He's still in the same house.' Brian answered.

'Then I know it.' Rosa smiled.

'Didn't you ever want to write to him?' Ava asked.

'A thousand times, but I was scared of not hearing back. I didn't know who survived the war.' There was a general sympathetic murmur; no one understood what it was like to have lived through the horrors of war.

'What happened then?' Lucy wanted to know. Brian looked across at Rosa to check if she was okay for him to delve further into the past or if it was becoming too overwhelming for her.

Having received Rosa's approval, Brian continued explaining how Juan Luis had given him the name and former address of Isabel and Antonio, who had taken care of María in Madrid, and Josefa and Ana. Juan Luis had been almost certain Isabel and Antonio weren't alive anymore. Brian had travelled to Madrid and visited the address, but no one seemed to be home whenever he called, so he started scouring the archives and registries. But, without knowing exactly when and where they might have died, he had reached a dead end. Ready to return to the UK, he had tried the house one last time, and this time, an elderly lady had opened the door. She had eyed him suspiciously, but when Brian explained to the lady that he had obtained her address from her cousin Juan Luis she let him into the house.

'It was the most beautiful house I had ever seen,' Rosa said.

'Indeed, it was stunning – marble floors, dark wood, it must have looked the same as María would have known it,' Brian confirmed.

Ava looked across at Rosa, processing what she had just said. Thinking back to the letters to Andrés, Ava suddenly wondered how Rosa knew so many details about María's life. And then it hit her like a slap in the face as she remembered that María had met her brother Pablo in that very same house her father visited a few years ago. Didn't Rosa shoot Pablo? Was this old lady sitting across her a murderer? Ava started to feel uneasy and shifty, but looking at the old lady she realised the story had to be told fully before she could pass judgment.

'Are you okay, my dear?' Maggie asked Ava, who was sitting beside her. Maggie handed Ava a glass of water. 'You look like you've seen a ghost.'

'I'm okay, just thinking about those letters and remembering things. Please continue.' Ava looked across at Rosa and saw her smiling. Immediately, Ava knew the old lady wasn't who she said she was.

'Okay, where was I?' Brian continued. 'Ah yes, I spoke to María's cousin Josefa, who explained that María's baby was stolen from her in the hospital and who the baby's father was. But suddenly María's letters had stopped arriving. For the second time, I had to explain what had happened in London.'

'Let me get this right,' Maggie cut in, 'you found out that Rose's mother was actually María, you met her uncle and discovered that somewhere she had a half-brother who was or is part of the extended Spanish royal family?'

'Yes, exactly, Maggie.' Brian confirmed.

'Did you find him?' Maggie asked. Brian shook his head. He had tried and sent several letters to the royal household unsuccessfully.

'I got so consumed by it that I didn't realise for a long time that I was being followed, until one day, just as I was leaving the house, I noticed an envelope had been pushed through the letterbox with my name on it. I grabbed it and opened it in the car park at work, and out fell photographs of Ava and Rose, their faces crossed out with a red felt tip pen and a note with just one word Stop. History was repeating itself.'

Ava had sat there silently, just staring at her father, but now she had to ask, 'Why didn't you just stop sending the letters? Why did you leave and never come back?' Tears flooded Ava's eyes. Was this really why she grew up without a father? Brian reached out to her, but Ava pulled her hand away, and instead, Lucy grabbed it to comfort her friend. Brian's sorrow was written all over his face. Ava noticed the lines around his eyes and how old he looked. She felt sympathy towards him, recognising that for the last twenty years he had had to live with the regret of what he had done. Could she forgive him? She wasn't sure. It had been his choice to leave. For her mum, it was a shock, and she was the one who had to deal with the aftermath. It hurt Ava more for her mum than herself. In fact Ava felt a degree of guilt that she was the one who got to meet Brian again.

'I was scared. I had become so consumed with finding Rose's brother that I sent more and more letters to Spain. Every royal residence I could find was on my list and many more letters were still on their way to Spain when I got the photos. Everything about it, the lengths they had gone to, I knew it wasn't an empty threat. After Tim, I couldn't risk it again. You were all I cared about, and if I disappeared you and Rose would be safe and could be happy.'

'Were we happy, though? Mum lost her husband. Suddenly she was a single mum, your parents were also gone, and I grew up without my father. Mum thought something terrible must have happened and that's why you left, but she never knew. She never read the letter you left in the safe. She died not knowing!' Ava was shouting now, and some of the other care home residents in the room were turning to look at her, but Ava didn't care.

'Where have you been all these years?' Lucy asked Brian, while Ava tried to calm down.

'I stayed close in the beginning, and I saw the pain on Rose's face. I intended to come back once it was safe to do so. But after a few weeks, she seemed back to her usual self, as if I had never existed, so I moved to Swanage and waited.'

'Your special place.' Ava mumbled.

'Yes, we spent many holidays there, and it's where I proposed.'

'You relied on mum finding a letter in a safe to end this whole shit-show.'

'Young lady! That's not how we talk.'

'Oh yeah, how would you know? You weren't there. You have no idea what my favourite colour is, when my first kiss was, where I went to university, nothing. I'm a stranger to you, and you to me!' Ava's finger was poking her father in the chest, harder with every thought she voiced, every feeling she expressed. Consumed by anger, she knew she had to get out of the common room. She stormed out, tears running down her cheeks. Brian pushed himself out of his seat, but Lucy was faster and already halfway out of the room.

'Give her some space. She's had a lot to deal with lately,' Maggie said as she placed her hand on Brian's shoulder, his head hanging with sorrow. Maggie and Patty realised they were still on shift and left the common room too.

The sun was starting to set when Rosa coughed, shaking Brian out of his thoughts. He looked across at her, a haunted expression in his eyes. 'Why didn't I come back?' he asked 'Were they really that dangerous?' Rosa nodded in response.

'Who are you?' Ava asked, storming back in to the room, Lucy, Maggie and Patty following closely behind, not wanting to miss anything.

'I think you know already,' Rosa replied, smiling back at her while pointing at the empty chairs to encourage Ava to sit down again.

'I have a theory: In the house in Madrid, you shot Pablo, who protected María, then came to London and caused the explosion to finish what you started. But that still wouldn't explain how you know so much about María's life. Or…' A startled expression crossed Ava's face. She slapped her hand against her mouth. It suddenly all made sense. Lucy and Brian looked expectantly at Ava, waiting for her to reveal her thoughts. 'You're not Rosa, Pablo shot her. All those letters in mum's possession, the original photo in front of the restaurant, everything you know about her life – you're María!' All heads turned towards the old lady.

'Yes, I am.' You could cut the atmosphere with a knife as the penny dropped that sitting in front of them was the closest link to their friend, mother, and wife.

'What is wrong with all of you keeping all these secrets? You could've told me from the beginning that you were my grandmother, and we could've saved a lot of time trying to solve the mystery.'

'That is correct, but like your father, sometimes we do things to protect the ones we love. I didn't know how much you knew, the shock of meeting me might have pushed you away.'

'But that note, *Always watch your back and trust no one*, freaked me out.'

'Ah, yes, that might have been a bit dramatic.' María agreed.

'If you didn't die in the explosion, then who did?' Lucy asked.

She sighed. 'Henry and our new waitress. They met to finalise the paperwork but…' María paused and looked away before turning back and continuing, 'once the fire brigade had put out the fire that followed the explosion, they went inside to search for bodies, but the bodies were too charred to be identified. For Henry, his dental records were used to identify him, but the woman was never identified – no records of any sort were found for her, I'm not even sure she had given us her real name. Consequently, everyone assumed it was me, the woman from Spain.'

Ava opened her mouth to ask another question, but Brian raised his hand to silence her. 'Let's give her a rest. I'm sure it was traumatic and is bringing back all manner of sad memories.'

'I'm sure you're right. And even if I sound like a petulant child right now, I really couldn't care less what you think, I am owed the truth. For the last few weeks I have been sent on a wild goose chase. Since the moment mum died I have been given clues,' she lamented, waving the piece of scrap paper with the warning, 'found old letters, a safe, the baby clothes of a boy who turned out to be a brother I never knew about, and learnt that my father is still alive. I feel my whole life has been a lie.' Without taking a breath, she continued, 'Then I met two men who both deceived me, one of them responsible for mum's death, and then you turn up out of the blue and think you have a right to lecture me? No, I want to know once and for all what was in those bloody letters that got my mum killed!' Hearing the words from Ava's mouth felt like a stab in Brian's heart, he had imagined his daughter would welcome him with open arms. Instead, everything he said was setting her off on another rant.

'Headstrong like her mother, that one is,' Maggie said, smirking. 'And also very right. Yes, we all lost our dear Rose, but none of us knows what Ava has gone through. I think we should put an end to this and get the truth out into the open, only then will we be able to move on.' Ava wanted to hug Maggie for saying this and thanked her with a smile.

'You remind me of a young girl who was sent to Madrid.' María's raw emotions instantly calmed everyone down, and silence descended on the group as the old lady delved into the past one more time. 'When I saw the two white body bags being carried out, I knew the life I had was over, but it also gave me a chance to disappear. As I said, I knew who was in those bags, but no one else did, especially the mysterious man witnesses saw, and that provided the perfect opportunity for me to escape. I recognised him in his disguise and understood he was there for me. As long as he believed my body was in that bag, they couldn't hurt me anymore. Like your father, Ava, I too, had to make a choice. Stay and risk him hurting my daughter or leave to save her life? I chose her safety over my feelings. Even though I struggled with her and couldn't seem to bond – I think they call it post-natal depression nowadays – she was still my daughter, and I loved her. But Xulián's family would do anything to keep the true heritage of my son secret, so they sent his bodyguard to London to get rid of me. I will never forgive myself that Henry had to die instead of me – if only I had been in the restaurant by myself, he would have stayed with your mother. But in the end, I only had one chance. I vanished from the scene, taking nothing with me and travelling as far away as I could, knowing our daughter would be safe with Elizabeth and Andrew and they would love her like their own.'

'Where were you all these years, and how did you end up here?' Ava needed to know.

'I like to think it was destiny to come to this place where I met my daughter again. As for the years in between, I lived in Manchester and worked for a wealthy family who became close friends. When the master's wife died, I became his companion and stayed with him after I got too old to work. It was only when he died, leaving me quite a bit of money, that I came here and met Rose.'

'Under a false name.' Maggie remarked.

'I had to, María had died all those years ago.'

'Why did you choose the name Rosa? She killed your brother and caused you misery almost your whole life,' Ava probed, feeling calmer now she was able to connect the dots.

'Yes, but I also knew everything about her. Keeping the lie that way was easier. And without a passport or any other official documents, no one could question it. I arrived in Manchester and simply said I had lost everything in a fire.' Ava puffed her cheeks out, this lady was her grandmother, and yet all she knew about her was how she had lied and deceived others. It sounded very much like someone else she knew.

'María,' Lucy interjected, 'why did Diego kill Rose? Which letter did he want?'

'If I'm not mistaken, Diego is part of Xulián's family. I got our dear Walter over there,' she pointed at a group of men playing Scrabble in the far corner of the room who were blissfully unaware of the drama unfolding on the other side, 'to help me with the computer. It didn't take long to find him in an official photo, standing tall next to his father and his uncle, my son. When I saw him at your mother's funeral, I knew he was there for a reason. If only I hadn't fallen and ended up in hospital, I could've warned you, but by the time I woke up, I had forgotten about him.'

'And the letter?' Lucy prompted.

'He will want the letter that can cause a scandal in Spain if exposed. A royal having an illegitimate child with a miner's daughter from the countryside having fought for the Republicans would be catastrophic. You'd think we have moved on so many decades later, but some families are very proud of who they are, and something like this can question their integrity. Not to mention that my son will inherit everything from his father despite not being his real firstborn son.' Ava sighed, it started to make sense why so many generations threatened her family. 'And the letter he wants is the one that proves it all. When I disappeared, I didn't write any more letters, I just accepted fate. Until one day, almost twenty years later, I had the urge to send one more. This time, though, I addressed it to Xulián's former bodyguard, explaining I was a friend who had found María's old letters and all I wanted to know was whether her son was still alive. He replied from his deathbed and confessed Xulián's mother had paid him to steal my boy and that he was going to be brought up by Xulián's brother. He also confessed that he was responsible for the explosion on orders from his employer and had threatened a journalist. He had nothing to lose and wanted to rid himself of his sins. It was all I needed to know that he was safe. Unfortunately, he had also mentioned that he told his old friend, Xulián's brother, that he had confessed to María's friend and asked for my forgiveness. That's why they knew about the letter, but they would've never found me. They only had a lead when Brian started investigating again.' Ava looked at her father, wondering again how different her life could have been had his father destroyed the manila folder. No matter how much anger she still had inside her, Ava knew that, now he was back, she was not prepared to let him go again, so somewhere inside her, she had to find the strength to forgive him for her own and her mum's sake.

Epilogue

The plane landed safely at Asturias airport, where a taxi was already waiting to take them on the 45-minute journey up into the mountains. María's heart was beating fast. After more than sixty years, she was finally back home in the lush green hills of her beloved home country. Oh, how it has changed, she thought as the car sped along the A8 towards Gijón before taking a right turn further into the heart of Asturias, circumventing Oviedo before climbing into the mountains towards home. Ava was sitting next to her with her mouth hanging open, gazing at the changing landscape, excitedly pointing at the wind farms on the hills. María squeezed her granddaughter's hand, happy to have her by her side and seeing the wonder in her eyes as she got to know her heritage. 'I always thought Spain was either arid or beach. I didn't realise it was so green!'

María laughed. 'Oh yes, because of where we are, we get a lot of rain, that's why it's so green, but be prepared for the weather to change rapidly.'

Stepping out of the taxi in the Plaza de Requexu brought back memories for María that were hard to describe. Looking around the square at the colourful houses and across to the San Juan church, it felt like time had stood still. 'Are you okay?' Catching herself, María nodded and smiled. They were there for a happy reason, the past would not ruin that. 'What's that statue over there?' Looking to where Ava was pointing, María admired a bronze statue she knew hadn't been there the last time she ran across the square.

'That, my dear, is an *escanciador de sidra*. It's the traditional way here in Asturias to pour cider from above the head into the glass as low as you can hold it. It adds lots of bubbles to the drink and is probably the best in the world. You will have to try it!' María tore her eyes away from the statue to watch an elderly man stroll across the square, helped by a beautiful young woman with a beaming smile. She waved at María, who just as slowly made her way towards the two. Her heart almost exploded.

'María *mi hermanita*.' The elderly man visibly shook, opening his arms to his long-lost sister.

'Juan Luis,' she muffled into his shoulder. They held each other for a long time, the seventy years they hadn't seen each other disappearing to nothing.

'Hi, I'm Ana.'

'Oh, you speak English! Perfect, because my Spanish is terrible,' Ava said, laughing. 'It's lovely to meet you. I'm Ava. Thank you so much for inviting us to your wedding!'

'It's my pleasure. When we received your letter, it was the best day of my grandfather's life,' Ana beamed. María immediately knew Ava would fit in with her Spanish family; her red hair and infectious smile made her instantly lovable. Ava still had much to cope with, even after the story was finally told. Despite her age, María felt it was her duty to her granddaughter to be there for her and support her while she rekindled her relationship with her father. After months of investigations and court appointments, Luke and Diego were brought to justice. They were sentenced to jail – for causing death by dangerous driving in the case of Luke and breaking and entering, theft, threatening behaviour, assisting an offender and conspiracy to murder in the case of Diego. So when the invitation to Ana's wedding arrived, María would not listen to anyone's advice of not flying to Spain. Even the doctor could not dissuade her. María knew she had to grab the chance to show Ava where she came from for her to understand her true heritage and give her the big family she was deprived of because of other people's choices.

Acknowledgements

I extend my deepest gratitude to the incredible individuals whose unwavering support and dedication brought my story from a mere spark in my mind to the pages of this published book.

A heartfelt thank you to my husband for his boundless patience and understanding during the countless hours spent immersed in the writing process in my cubbyhole and for offering both emotional and practical support throughout this literary odyssey.

I am indebted to my life coach Chris Araga whose encouragement fuelled my creative journey. Your belief in me provided the foundation for this endeavour.

Gratitude is also extended to my test readers, whose invaluable feedback and constructive criticism helped refine and enhance the narrative. Your insights were crucial in shaping the final version of this book. Special thanks to Mum, Anni, Andrew, Belén, Mar, Nancy and Rob.

Thank you to Matthew Baylis for his editorial input that played an instrumental role in bringing this story to life.

Last but certainly not least, I express my sincere appreciation to the readers who will embark on this journey with my characters.

About the Author

Meet Daniela, a debut novelist and seasoned marketer hailing from the picturesque landscapes of Switzerland. When she's not navigating the world of spreadsheets and market trends, she's weaving tales of romance, history, and intrigue like in her first novel, The Lost Manila Folder — a riveting journey that might just be more unpredictable than her morning commute on the tube. When not crafting compelling narratives, Daniela is a globe-trotter who draws inspiration from her travels, sharing life's adventures with her husband in the vibrant city of London.